3 1 3 8 1

W9-BNF-187

10-25

Winter

Rain

Terry C. Johnston

Winter Rain

Bantam Books   New York / Toronto / London / Sydney / Auckland

*for Jim Bourne
who helped point the way years ago,
with more gratitude than you
will ever know*

WINTER RAIN
A Bantam Book/October 1993

Library of Congress Cataloging-in-Publication Data

Johnston, Terry C., 1947–
     Winter rain / Terry C. Johnston.
     p.   cm.
     ISBN 0-553-09508-0
     I. Title.
     PS3560.0392W56   1993
     813'.54—dc20   93-15242
                                                                  CIP

Published simultaneously in the United States and Canada

Bantam Books are published by Bantam Books, a division of Bantam
Doubleday Dell Publishing Group, Inc. Its trademark, consisting of the
words "Bantam Books" and the portrayal of a rooster, is Registered in U.S.
Patent and Trademark Office and in other countries. Marca Registrada.
Bantam Books, 1540 Broadway, New York, New York 10036.

PRINTED IN THE UNITED STATES OF AMERICA
RRH   0 9 8 7 6 5 4 3 2 1

How solemn and beautiful is the thought that the earliest pioneer of civilization, the van-leader of civilization, is never the steamboat, never the railroad, never the newspaper, never the Sabbath-school, never the missionary—but always whiskey! . . . Westward the Jug of Empire takes its way!

—Mark Twain

The Texas Rangers . . . had an off and on existence ever since 1823, when Stephen F. Austin formed a band of ten Rangers to protect the first American settlements from Indians. . . . From that time on—throughout all their ups and downs, disappearances and reappearances—the Rangers were irregulars. They were irregular as hell, in everything except getting the job done.

—Oliver Knight

The more Indians we can kill this year, the less will have to be killed the next war.

—General William Tecumseh Sherman

Destiny is nothing more than the unforeseen coincidence of events, the emergence into action of hidden forces which, in a complex and disordered society . . . no contemporary can be expected to discern.

—Guglielmo Ferrero

CAST OF CHARACTERS

*Jonah Hook
*Hattie Hook
*Ezekiel Hook (Antelope)
*Prairie Night (Antelope's
  Comanche wife)

*Gritta Hook
*Jeremiah Hook (Tall One)

*Shadrach Sweete
*Pipe Woman

*Toote Sweete / Shell Woman
*High-Backed Bull

Danites

*Colonel Jubilee Usher
*Heber Welch
*Frank Bolls
*Charlie Smythe
*Joseph Simes
*Oran Strickler

*George
*Orem Slade
*George Hines
*Harry Hampton

Cheyenne

Roman Nose
*Hair Rope
Little Hawk
Tall Bull
*Wolf Friend
*Plenty of Bull Meat
*Tall Sioux
*Bullet Proof
*Red Cherries
*Four Bulls Moon

Porcupine
*Wrinkled Wolf
Starving Elk
White Horse
*Bad Heart
*Yellow Nose
*White Man's Ladder
*Feathered Bear
*Heavy Furred Wolf

Lakota

Pawnee Killer
*Bad Tongue

Kwahadi Comanche

Quanah Parker
*Wolf Walking Alone
*Snake Brother
*Coal Bear
*Burns Red
*Standing
*Rain Woman

*Bridge
*Big Mule
*Dives Backward
*Old Owl Man
*Tortoise Shell
*Four Spirits Woman

Shoshone / Snake

*Two Sleep

Military

Col. Ranald S. Mackenzie—commanding, Fourth Cavalry
Major Eugene A. Carr—commanding, Fifth Cavalry
Major William B. Royall—Fifth Cavalry

Texas Rangers

Major John B. Jones—Commander, Frontier Battalion
*Captain Lamar Lockhart—commanding Company C
*Deacon Elijah Johns—Lieutenant, Company C
*Niles Coffee—Sergeant, Company C
*Clyde Yoakam—Second Sergeant, Company C
*June Callicott
*John Corn
*Harley Pettis
*Wig Danville
*Enoch Harmony
*Slade Rule
*Billy Benton

Civilians

*Nate Deidecker
*Heber Usher
Major Frank North
Captain Luther North
Lieutenant Gustavus W. Becher

Lieutenant Billy Harvey
William Schmalsle
*Ezra Dickinson
William F. Cody

* fictional characters

Winter Rain

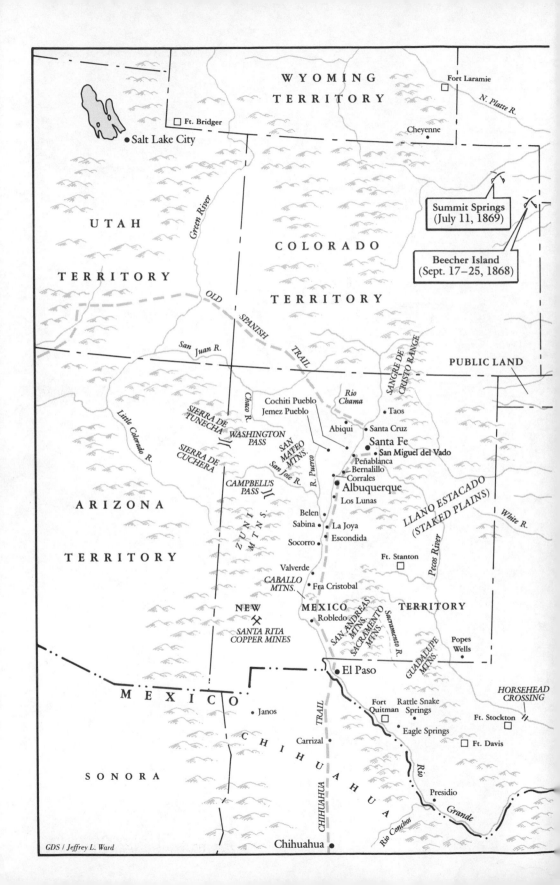

WYOMING
TERRITORY

Fort Laramie

N. Platte R.

☐ Ft. Bridger

● Salt Lake City

Cheyenne

UTAH

TERRITORY

COLORADO

Green River

Summit Springs
(July 11, 1869)

TERRITORY

Beecher Island
(Sept. 17–25, 1868)

OLD SPANISH TRAIL

San Juan R.

PUBLIC LAND

SANGRE DE CRISTO RANGE

Rio Chama

Chaco R.

SIERRA DE TUNECHA

WASHINGTON PASS

Cochiti Pueblo
Jemez Pueblo

● Taos

Little Colorado R.

SIERRA DE CUCHERA

SAN MATEO MTNS.

Abiqui

San Jose R.

● Santa Cruz

R. Puerco

Santa Fe
● San Miguel del Vado

Peñablanca

CAMPBELL'S PASS

Bernalillo
Corrales

ARIZONA

ZUNI MTNS.

● Albuquerque

Los Lunas

LLANO ESTACADO
(STAKED PLAINS)

White R.

TERRITORY

Belen

Sabina ● La Joya

Socorro ● Escondida

Pecos River

Ft. Stanton ☐

Valverde

CABALLO MTNS.

● Fra Cristobal

NEW

MEXICO

TERRITORY

SANTA RITA COPPER MINES

Robledo

SAN ANDREAS MTNS.

SACRAMENTO MTNS.

Sacramento R.

Popes Wells ●

GUADALUPE MTNS.

M E X I C O

● El Paso

HORSEHEAD CROSSING

● Janos

TRAIL

Fort Quitman ☐

Rattle Snake Springs

Ft. Stockton ☐

C H I H U A H U A

Carrizal ●

Eagle Springs

☐ Ft. Davis

S O N O R A

Rio

CHIHUAHUA

Presidio ●

Grande

Rio Conchos

Chihuahua ●

GDS / Jeffrey L. Ward

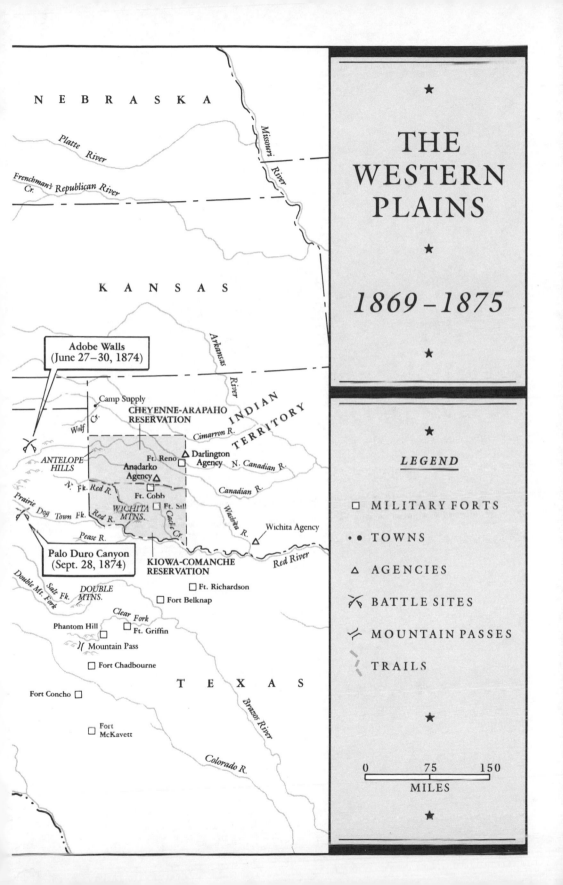

N E B R A S K A

Platte River

Frenchman's Cr. Republican River

Missouri River

K A N S A S

Arkansas River

Adobe Walls
(June 27–30, 1874)

Camp Supply

CHEYENNE-ARAPAHO
RESERVATION

INDIAN

Wolf Cr.

Cimarron R.

TERRITORY

ANTELOPE
HILLS

Ft. Reno △ Darlington
Agency

N. Canadian R.

Anadarko
Agency △

N. Fk. Red R.

Ft. Cobb

Canadian R.

Prairie Dog Town Fk.

WICHITA
MTNS.

Ft. Sill

Cache Cr.

Wichita R.

Red R.

Wichita Agency

Pease R.

Red River △

Palo Duro Canyon
(Sept. 28, 1874)

KIOWA-COMANCHE
RESERVATION

Double Mt. Fork

Salt Fk.

DOUBLE
MTNS.

□ Ft. Richardson

□ Fort Belknap

Clear Fork

Phantom Hill

□ Ft. Griffin

)|(Mountain Pass

□ Fort Chadbourne

T E X A S

Fort Concho □

Brazos River

□ Fort
McKavett

Colorado R.

★

THE
WESTERN
PLAINS

★

1869–1875

★

★

LEGEND

□ MILITARY FORTS

•• TOWNS

△ AGENCIES

⤫ BATTLE SITES

)|(MOUNTAIN PASSES

⋰ TRAILS

★

0   75   150
MILES

★

Prologue

H E CAME AWAKE with a struggle.

The overwhelming enemies were musky in their sweat-slicked red skins. Their heaving breath stank like rancid meat in his nostrils. The muzzles of their guns exploded in his face like the roar of riven earth on Judgment Day.

Still, his was not the sort of thrashing, physical convulsion someone suddenly awakened from a sound sleep might fight.

No, his struggle was all within the dream.

And that frightened him even more.

Of a sudden he smelled the air.

Its sharp tang reminded him. With a start he knew where he was.

Breath catching in his pounding chest, his hands grasped the edges of the grass-filled, tick-covered mattress beneath him in something close to relief.

As his head slowly plopped back against the pallet, Nathan Deidecker sighed and closed his eyes in emotional exhaustion, then drank in another breath of the cool, pungent air. Hungrily drank of the summer darkness outside.

Then realized why he had awakened.

Another low blat of thunder rumbled in off Cloud Peak rising thirteen thousand feet above the level of the sea out there in the blackness—not far off, its bellow slapped that high land in the deepest dark of postmidnight, the light of the heavens tracing down in tongues of fire just to the west of this small two-room cabin raised on a small promontory of ground by the back and shoulders and sheer will of the sinewy old scout.

Nate listened to another distant rumble, heard it coming almost serpentine across the heaving upvaulted land from a long way off, like it was some rock slide, a frightening avalanche careening down off the Big Horns toward him.

With the thunderous bellow fading onto the prairies below, the night stilled, and Deidecker marveled at just how clear and distinct and ominous sounds could seem out here in this country. Back east—hell, even back on the central plains of eastern Nebraska that he now called home—Nate could not recall ever really hearing any sound so distinct before.

As distinct as he now heard the whispers of this summer night.

Clear as rinsed crystal, he remembered the expression used by the old man just the day before when describing the property of light and sound and even how far a man might himself see in this immense, mind-numbing country.

"Damn right, Mr. Hook," Nate mumbled to himself now. Some things were starting to come clear as rinsed crystal.

A creak of old rope crept past the thick wool blanket that hung as a crude door across the single opening between the cabin's two small rooms.

Nate conjured a mental picture of the prairie bed: rough pine slats interlaced with hemp rope woven crosshatch to support its own grass-stuffed tick mattress.

Just someone stirring in their sleep, Nate thought. *One of 'em awakened by the thunder like I was. Maybe that godforsaken green lightning—*

As another distant, eerie flash backlit the Big Horns, there came another creak of the old rope, but louder this time. More stretch. And below that arose the muffle of voices. Whispered entreaties: low, husky, in need.

The green light's eventual clap washed over the valley, and in its dying, Nate realized what was happening in the next room. Not without a little wonder.

"He's . . . that old man's making . . . making love to—" And he stopped whispering a moment, self-conscious at even the tiny sound his night voice made in that great silence of the thunder's retreat. ". . . love to his woman."

Deidecker sensed something rise in his throat, not sour nor choking like disgust at overhearing a bestial act. Not even fear of being discovered as an unwilling voyeur. Nothing closely resembling strong sentiment aroused by his own need of a woman to come into his life. No, what the newspaperman felt, lying there on that fragrant, land-heady tick mattress dropped on Jonah Hook's whipsawn wood floor, was something that filled Deidecker not only with immense happiness for the old scout, but with a profound sense of awe as well.

"That man's too old to be climbing atop a woman," he contented himself to say, rolling onto his side, away from the insistent, rhythmic creak of that rope-bed in the far room. "Especially that one . . . that . . . woman."

Deidecker recalled just how dead she had been yesterday as he and the old scout talked of his early years come west to the prairies and mountains. She had been next to lifeless. *Dead* was the most apt word he could use to describe her, even wrote it down on some of the pages of his notes as Jonah Hook talked and Nate stole furtive glances at the old woman. He remembered now the way her pale blue eyes had gazed out at him without any light or the slightest fire behind them. As if Hook's woman were a shattered hulk of some weakened building, those blue eyes like gaping, paneless windows, staring out at him with nothing but bleak, hollow emptiness inside.

Abruptly Nate shuddered, remembering how Jonah described his return to his homestead in Missouri after the war and his service on the high plains fighting Indians—coming home to find the cabin windows broken, the fields gone to weed. His whole family ripped from his life. The daughter. His two sons. And that woman.

To rid himself of the frightening specter of that doomed homestead, Nate shook his head like the old scout's rangy yard hound shook its hide free of water as it clambered up the bank from the Little Piney River and forced himself to think on other things.

The newsman wondered, How's a man like Hook ever able to get it up? Not that the frontiersman was so old he physically couldn't. Not that at all. Just, how can a man desire a woman who clearly isn't involved in what he's doing with her at the moment? Her body might be in that room. But, Deidecker figured, her mind surely wasn't.

What with the way she rocked and rocked, and rocked on all that previous day out on that porch in the shadow of Cloud Peak.

The grassy yard lit up with a sudden green flare of phosphorescent lightning tonguing down from the peaks in splintered streaks. Landing so close to the cabin, it raised the hair on his arms, at the back of his neck. Its looming brightness surprised him, and for a heartbeat the eerie, unearthly glow illuminated the large room as if by the purest, unsullied daylight. As it did, the old chromotype gleamed again with a life of its own, once more drawing him as the slap of thunder gurgled off the high granite, rumbling down the slope toward the cabin.

It was in the silence of last night's first flush of darkness that Nate had looked at the browning tintype—awakened, then drawn by the reflection of the figures he studied with the moon shining in through the window right above his mattress.

Must be close to dawn, he thought without real calculation as the first huge, sopping wads of rain struck the porch roof like mud clods, so loud it startled Deidecker bolt upright from the tick. He shook like he was under fire from disembodied spirits out there among the ghostly green light and wind-tortured pines soughing in the sodden, thunder-riven darkness.

Then in a crack of that great, gaping silence Nate heard the old man's voice whispering, his pleas just barely audible.

By God, he's romancing her, Deidecker thought as he listened more to the tone and the inflection of the words—not really able to hear all that Hook was saying to his wife. But the newsman, here to get the story of a lifetime on one of the frontier's most famous scouts, did not have to hear every word to know that, as the old man rocked his body back and forth atop the woman, Jonah Hook was also murmuring to her as if she might truly be intent, really hanging on all that her husband had to profess to her.

And for the first time since Nate had come awake and begun listening to the old couple groaning and grappling in that near room, Deidecker of a sudden felt like he was no better than the man who knelt at a keyhole and peered in on the private, shabby lives of others, spying on their most intimate moments.

He rolled over again, stretching a hand into the dark, its fingers spidering across the rough floor until they captured his pipe and tobacco pouch. Deidecker rolled and found his feet, rose unsteadily, and padded barefoot to the door. Noiselessly he drew back into the room just as another flare of lightning, white-hot as brimstone, ripped into the yard, sundering the black night in two as he flung an arm over his face. Nate stood there, temporarily blinded until the light's sting faded from his eyes.

He was left with only the reassuring slap of the familiar thunder come to caress both him and this wilderness in remembrance of that streak of fire quickly swallowed by the dark void of this short summer night here in the lap of this great, silent land.

It was only then that he realized he had been robbed of breath, shocked by the closeness of the lightning's strike now. In awe at the very raw, killing power of it. Something so primal, so savage. Like arrows of fire stalking out of the great black dome of the heavens, flung down onto this wilderness.

As he stood there in the doorway, the sudden blast of the riven air assaulted his nostrils with the rank odor of the storm, not only permeating his heightened sense of smell, but seeming to penetrate every pore of his body. Bare-chested and shivering slightly, Deidecker stepped onto the porch, then stopped, warily cocking an ear back into the cabin as the thunder rumbled away, once more creating that eternal void of silence in its wake.

"I love you, Gritta," the old scout vowed in a whisper like rawhide dragged over rough ground. "More now—than ever. And one day, I know you'll come back from . . ."

As much as the newspaperman strained, he didn't hear the rest of Hook's plaintive words. Instead, the only sound from that blanket-doored room some twenty feet away was more of the fevered grappling in the dark.

Deidecker turned away to load his pipe, then struck a match, shielding it against the incessant breeze washing down from the peaks and the glaciers and that never-summer snow far above him in the darkness, where for that moment he wasn't sure just what was sky and cloud, and what might truly be hulking mountain ready to tumble down upon this high land of awesome silence intertwined with the brooding black of wilderness night.

Then with his next sharp tanged breath, the rain came hard upon that place.

And when it did, the breeze freshened like a cold slap against his bare cheek. He gasped in the sudden explosion of the summer-tanged ozone as the huge, wad-sized drops hurled themselves onto that crude porch, wetting his bare feet and soaking the bottoms of the canvas dungarees he had wisely purchased back in Omaha before journeying west to northern Wyoming.

Deidecker did not mind summer's reeking, prairie cold, really. Nor the chilling, bone-numbing wet of the storm's fury driven at him. Rather than fleeing, he instead settled there in the woman's chair, puffing bowl after bowl of his favorite pipe, brooding on all the old man had spoken of just the day before, thinking on all that he wanted to ask Hook with the thunderous coming of this second day among the memories and the ghosts of years and lives gone the way of summer snows. His bare skin warmed with the closeness of those strikes of green, phosphorescent lightning, and his mind electrified with all the old man had already told him. Then he began to dwell on all the old man had kept from telling him.

So Deidecker sat a long time, riding out summer's late storm there in the old woman's rocker, sensing for himself the chair's singular place worn down in those two ruts she had scoured into the rough boards of the porch over her years of roosting here below Cloud Peak. He could almost feel some of the woman's warmth remnant in the worn cotton pad, sense the touch of her flesh against his as he laid his bare forearms along the tops of the yellow-pine armrests worn white from those endless hours gone in staring up into the hulking immensity of these mountains.

Only when Nate realized the storm was passing onto the plains below, its fury headed east for South Dakota, did he become aware of the subtle change in the quality of light in the yard beyond, the texture of skylight drenched over the nearby hills and flung up against the tall peaks, uplifted like a young woman's breasts yearning for her lover's touch. So close. So damned seductively close.

Of a frightening sudden he became aware of the old man.

Hook was standing in the open doorjamb, as frozen as a winter-gaunt wolf caught in the action of hunting snowshoe hare, one paw in the air and the other three ready to spring, his eyes intent on Deidecker.

As much as Nate was startled to find the old scout staring at him in the murky, ashen light of predawn, he quickly reassured himself it was as natural a thing as could be: To find an old plainsman like Hook sneaking up on a man unawares, studying him as that hungry wolf would his quarry. Nate swallowed down his surprise like the most bitter, metallic taste of cold fear. And tried to smile.

"G'morning, Mr. Hook," he whispered as cheerfully as he could muster.

Hook tore his eyes from the newsman's, staring off into the darkness that reeked with the scent of the storm's passing. "I'll allow you didn't know," began the old man without budging from the open doorway. "But that there's Gritta's chair, Mr. Deidecker. No one ever sits in Gritta's chair. So I'll allow you didn't know any better, and pass it off this time."

Deidecker sprang up like he'd been bit, wheeling to stare at the chair, its flattened, faded seat pillow seeming to glare back at him accusingly.

"No . . . I didn't know," he stammered. "But . . . I'll . . . next time I won't—"

"Care for something to eat, Mr. Deidecker?" Hook asked, abruptly changing the subject. He turned slowly in the doorway, inching back into the cabin that filled ever so slowly with the seep of predawn's gray light. "Course you do. What man in his right mind don't want something to eat come morning get-up time?"

"I'll be fine till later. Usually don't get up this . . . really no sense in your making something to eat right now on my account. I'll wait till you and Mrs. Hook are ready to eat."

Hook stopped at the wood stove, turned, and gazed at the newspaperman strangely. "You best eat now, son. Lots of ground for us to cover this day—and you'll be needing your strength."

Deidecker smiled at that. "Don't take much for me to push my pencils over my paper, Mr. Hook. But thank you just the same—"

"Wasn't talking about us covering ground on your paper there," he interrupted, flinging a veined gesture at the corner of a small table, where Deidecker had stacked his writing tablets and a bundle of lead pencils. Hook gazed at the younger man with those cold gray eyes of his, wrinkled and chiseled at their corners with deep clefts, and turkey-tracked like a piece of barren earth gone too long without the blessing of rain. "We're riding today, Nate. Out there."

Deidecker sensed the rising chill of goose bumps as he watched Hook point an arm out the open door at the tall peaks slow a'coming purple, their snow touched with the dusty rose color of the east as he watched, without a thought on what to say. Struck dumb he was: choking on his own fear of where Hook was vowing to take him—that great, gaping void of wilderness that few men had ever wandered, a land most men of the last generation had wisely skirted in their business of bringing civilization to the West.

Hook turned away and dragged a huge cast-iron skillet off the stove, opened the griddle, and dropped in some wands of dried kindling before striking a lucifer to some char he then pitched into the inky netherworld of the squat black frog of a stove.

"Riding?" Deidecker asked when he found his voice. "You've got a saddle horse I can use instead of that buggy animal?"

Hook turned with a smile gone warm, something around his mouth that also brightened his eyes in that murky, gray gloom. "Of course, son. You'll need a more proper animal where we're going. One of mine. That buggy horse ain't fit for what we got to do today. Rustle together what you feel you need. We won't be back in here till late tomorrow. Maybe next day."

Something cold seized in Deidecker's chest. "We'll . . . spend the night . . . o-out?"

" 'Less you figure on some other way to get the whole story you're hankering for from me."

"N-no, I want the whole story, Mr. Hook. Just that, I'm not used to sleeping out. L-like you probably are."

"It's all right, son," Hook said quietly as he turned back to the stove stuffed back in its dark corner, said it in that fatherly way of his that reassured. All the edge and abrasiveness that had been in his voice at the doorway was gone now. "You best get over there and roll up your shuckings. We'll be riding out right after I rustle us up breakfast."

"Before sunup?"

Hook only nodded, snatching up the bail on the battered coffeepot and starting past Deidecker for the doorway.

"I'll just take some coffee, Jonah. Usually don't eat any breakfast."

Hook stopped. "You'll eat breakfast today, Mr. Deidecker." The old frontiersman said it in that most particular way that left no room for discussion. Then he turned back to the newspaperman. "Out here in this country, a man eats when he can—not when he necessarily wants to. So when the opportunity presents itself, a man eats."

"I understand."

Hook wagged his head. "Not so sure you really do understand, Nate," he replied quietly. "Not just yet, anyways."

Deidecker felt himself bristle with that challenge from this old man. True enough, Hook was thin and sinewy still with all his miles and all his rings. But Nate felt certain he could answer the call of anything physical the old scout could hand out. "I figure I can travel well enough as the next man on an empty stomach, Mr. Hook."

But with the way the old man gazed at him from the doorway, backlit with gray light seeping like alluvial mud off the high places in the Big Horns, Deidecker suddenly felt a little unsure of himself, with this man, in this place. Getting ready to push off into that immense unknown.

Of that moment a little bragging on his own manly qualities seemed antidote enough to help allay some of Deidecker's apprehension. "And besides, Lord knows, Mr. Hook—I've done my share of drinking on an empty stomach as well."

The old scout snorted with a single wag of his iron-flecked head. "Only two things I've found a man can do on an empty stomach, Mr. Deidecker. And drinking's sure as hell not one of 'em."

Deidecker sensed the seizure of even more uncertainty in that next long and painful moment as his thoughts whirled. "What, then?"

Hook came two steps back toward the newspaperman, with his free hand dragging off the top of the lard container beside the seasoned cast-iron skillet. "Only two things a man can do on a empty stomach?"

He plunged one of Gritta's wooden spoons into the lard and plopped a gray curl down into the gut of the skillet. Only then did his eyes narrow on Deidecker.

"Make love to a woman . . . and kill a man."

—————Book I

Into the Land of

Bondage

1

H E ROLLED AWAY from his attackers and vaulted onto his feet, crouching warily as he brushed the talclike powdery dirt from his eyes and mouth. He did not like the taste of it. But even more, he hated the taste of his own blood.

"Your lip, it is bleeding," sneered one of the older boys.

Another one of his attackers nodded as the group inched toward him, saying, "Would you like to give up now and see to the cut for yourself?"

With a shake of his head, the youngster prepared for these older boys to lunge for him again.

Long ago Jeremiah Hook had learned not to take any of what the other boys dished out. They took pleasure in tormenting him because he was white. Both Jeremiah and his younger brother Zeke.

As the biggest brown-skinned youth suddenly rushed him, lowering his head like a bull on the charge, Jeremiah slid aside, whirling to snag the boy's head under an arm. As much as the older youth tried to free himself, Jeremiah had that big boy secured in a headlock and began pummeling the sweaty, screwged face with blows from his small fist.

"Arrrghghg!" Coal Bear growled until Jeremiah clamped all the tighter, cutting off the youth's protest.

Unable to catch his breath, much less speak, Coal Bear hammered Jeremiah with a fist, connecting again and again above the back of the white youth's hip, right over the kidney.

Jeremiah crumpled, spinning to his knees in pain, dazed, as the big youth and his friend, Snake Brother, drove the white boy to the ground.

"Brother!"

Through the stirring dust and sweat stinging his eyes, Jeremiah watched his younger brother come flying in a leap, sailing out of nowhere beyond the edge of the lodge circle. Zeke hurled himself on the back of the biggest of Jeremiah's tormentors. There he clung like a blood-swollen tick to an old bull, his arms clamped in front of the boy's throat.

"Get this little gnat off me!" Coal Bear hollered raspily, as loudly as he could, the words strangling in his throat. Around and around he lumbered into a spin, trying to throw off his troublesome attacker.

"Get up, brother!" Zeke yelled as the whirling drew closer to Jeremiah.

"What goes on here?"

At the sound of that particular voice, both Coal Bear and Snake Brother came to a dead stop. Both started to talk at once, but the tall war chief raised his hand and shook it at them, signaling for their silence.

"Does this little tick want to cling to his enemy's back all day?" asked the warrior.

Jeremiah watched Zeke glance his way for approval. He nodded. Only then did Zeke slide from Coal Bear's back.

The gray-eyed war chief smiled. "Now, will someone tell me what is going on here?"

"We were playing only," the youth said.

"From where I stood," the gray-eyed one replied, gesturing back to a shady spot among the buffalo-hide lodges raised among the leafy cottonwoods along the creek bank, "the two of you were making sport of our young friend here."

Jeremiah swiped more troublesome sweat from his eyes, where it stung and muddied the dirt thrown at his face by his two opponents.

"If he is to be one of us, uncle," said Snake Brother, using a term of respect for the warrior, "then he must learn. It has been said by the elders' council."

The handsome war chief scratched his chin. "So let us see if he can hold himself against only one of you."

That instantly wounded Jeremiah's pride. "I can take them both!" he shouted back in that tongue still unfamiliar. Yet he struggled to learn the language. Just as he would learn to fight like these Indian boys.

The warrior smiled knowingly. "It is good that you do not shy away from what trouble comes calling on you."

"We will never turn our faces away from trouble," hissed little Zeke in his near-perfect Comanche.

Jeremiah glanced at his younger brother, sensing a swell of sentiment for Zeke. He was all Jeremiah had now, with his father gone off to war many winters before. And the band of looters who came to lay waste his father's farm but ended up instead carrying off those his father had left behind. Early on Jeremiah had determined that if he could not escape his circumstances with those bloodthirsty thugs, fleeing back to southwestern Missouri and home . . . if nothing else, he would then forge a family of the two of them. Little Zeke and Jeremiah Hook.

That little family was all either of them had had for so long.

Riding bareback tandem on a stolen horse into the Creek Nation over in Indian Territory with the band of white freebooters who had kidnapped them from the family home, Jeremiah rarely saw his sister or mother in those first few weeks. Then months had crept by.

It was only time, a lot of it. So much time that Jeremiah could not be sure how many months had slipped past. Perhaps even years. He was certain only that there had been several long summers broken by the cold of winter. And once more they were in the days the Comanche called the Moon of Drying Leaves.

Summer had come, and was retreating, burning the land quickly. Jeremiah had been but eight years old that last birthday before he was taken. He had counted three more summers since. He could celebrate no birthdays. There was no one to remind him of such a special event as one day flowed into the next, one week slipped into the next moon, each season cycled into the next winter until he began to sense just how much time had passed beneath his moccasins.

"You there," declared the tall warrior as he stepped over to the wary Jeremiah. "Seems you and your brother are such good fighters that we should put your white names away for all time now and give you the names of famous warriors of The People."

"Yes!" Jeremiah's head bobbed. Zeke's eyes grew as big as milk saucers.

"In four days, then," the warrior said, patting a hand on Jeremiah's shoulder. His other hand patted Zeke's too. "We will have our naming ceremony for you both." The warrior turned to the pair of older boys. "Coal Bear, teach them well for four days—the bow and knife. How to ride on the side of your pony."

The two bigger youths nodded, their dark eyes flicking quickly to the two white boys grown so dark-skinned, their long and wavy hair bleached by the light from the summer's sun.

"As you ask, uncle," replied the taller youth.

"I already ride well," Jeremiah said, catching up the warrior's hand.

He stopped. "You ride well for a white boy. But you have much to learn. Now you must learn to ride like a Comanche."

As he watched the young warrior stride away through the tall grass, Jeremiah swore he would learn to ride, just like a Comanche warrior. To mount and dismount from either side, to ride bareback, to ride even without a bridle—becoming one with a particular animal. This was a dream come true to a young boy of eleven summers. To become one of The People. To become a Kwahadi Comanche.

For so long Jeremiah had wanted only to be dead.

He and Zeke had been hauled up behind two of the looters come to their Missouri valley. Their mother and sister were thrown on other horses, behind other riders. After his warning barks, old Seth already lay dying in the yard, a bullet hole in his head, tongue lolling out like a swollen piece of pink meat dropped in the rich black dirt.

That night the unspeakable horror had begun as some of the laughing, hard-handed men had taken their turns holding the two boys down, while others assaulted Jeremiah and Zeke, sodomizing their two young prisoners as the men cursed what they called "godless Missouri Gentiles."

That was but the first night of many more to come, each day a living hell, making it painful to ride the bony spine of the horses as the boys were plopped behind the saddles of the looters during the day, assaulted by the smelly men each night. At first Jeremiah grew frightened when he began to bleed. Then he became ashamed when he passed more and more blood, oozing and sticky, drying in his britches like the tears he and little Zeke cried almost constantly, calling for help as the men clamped their wrists and ankles, dragged their dirt-crusted fingers through the boys' hair, and held their young faces against the stinking crotches. Laughing.

Always the laughter rang in Jeremiah's ears. The more he fought the men who held him down while others assaulted him, and the more he screamed, the more their wild laughter seemed to echo through the nightly camps where the two boys were beaten with the short rawhide whips the men used on their horses. It seemed so long ago now, like nothing more than another short lifetime, as Jeremiah remembered the shame of his tormented wounds weeping and oozing with a foul stench, his back aflame as flies laid their eggs where he could not reach to scratch.

Jeremiah rarely saw his mother those first days out of Missouri, at least not the woman he thought was her. She had been limp, carried from horseback to a tent at night, then back to her horse, where she was tied every morning for the day's travel. Later he saw the woman herded out of an ambulance the freebooters had stolen, looking as if she were half-asleep.

It was the same with Hattie. He had wondered if those men were doing cruel, unspeakable things to her privates as well.

But long as those days and weeks had seemed, the boys' imprisonment with the white looters was over before the following summer. They were bartered off to some brown-skinned men when a camp of Mexican traders rendezvoused with the white renegades. When a high enough price was settled upon for the two boys, Jeremiah and Zeke were sold into slavery.

"You're going to Chihuahua!" roared one of the white looters as he dragged Jeremiah over to the Mexican carts. "Their kind is gonna like having a young, tender gringo like you to play with way down there!"

"Where?"

"Mexico!"

"M-mexico?" Jeremiah had gasped.

"Them greasers allays pays good money for slaves bound for the Mexican trade down there, boy!"

While the Mexicans did once beat the two boys when Jeremiah and Ezekiel failed to do as they were told in that foreign tongue, at least the comancheros did not sodomize their terrified treasure as the procession of carts and horsemen began their trip south by west across the land haunted by the Comanche. The sores on Jeremiah's back and buttocks began to heal. The long, oozing welts started to shrink, becoming long, ugly red scars that laddered up the boy's body from shoulder to thigh. Those were hypnotic days spent beneath the hot sun in those carts rumbling across the shimmering heat of the frying-pan plains, bound for a place where Jeremiah somehow sensed no decent white man had ever set foot.

Then one chill night on that trackless prairie, a handful of the comancheros had argued over little Zeke. Jeremiah understood what it was they wanted, so he offered himself to them, hoping they would leave his little brother be. But they took Zeke, anyway. Took both of them.

He remembered the fury of his anger as they lashed his hands and ankles to the side of a cart, then ripped down his torn and bloody britches as he cried out to his mother's God for help.

But her God never came to take away the pain, the suffering, little Zeke's pitiful sobs. They were beaten savagely every time they cried out that night and for many nights to come.

Along about that time Jeremiah began wishing, even praying, that they could be killed and through with this torment. Or that they would be taken prisoner by the savage Indians that had so filled his childhood dreams for years.

Indians, yes—instead of white men who beat and sodomized them.

Blood-loving savages who would just outright kill the boys and be over with it. Hideous, painted, smelly warriors come to take away this torment.

It was of a cold, forbidding morning, the cloudy undergut overhead threatening to burst, that the two dozen comancheros suddenly jabbered excitedly, their voices raised stridently, some pointing to the southeast, where Jeremiah saw the sun was rising as red as the blood pouring from the neck of one of the hogs his papa would butcher back to home.

"Pa," he had whispered to the miles and the years in that noisy confusion, "why you never come for us sooner?"

That was the moment Jeremiah knew he would wait a long time for his answer, the same moment he learned the cause of the comancheros' anxiety.

Never before had the boy seen real live Indians. Oh, there had been those red-skinned men, women, and children he had gaped at from the back of a horse as the white looters journeyed into Indian Territory. But those Indians had dressed like white men, their faces charred with whipped expressions surrounding hound-dog eyes, the eyes of a people beaten and not liable to push themselves back up again.

But these Jeremiah looked at in wonder this morning—these were real warriors, by God! Just like the boyhood stories said Indians should be: long hair flowing, the color of a satiny blackbird's wing. Silver trinkets and round conchos were braided into those lustrous locks. Each man of them was naked to the waist where a thong held the breechclout in place. Most of the fifty or so riders had painted their bare legs with magic symbols, stars and hailstones and lightning bolts streaking all the way down to their moccasins.

None of them rode on saddles, no feet stuffed into stirrups. Jeremiah had marveled at that, wide-eyed, as the fifty rode up, slowed, and spread out around the comanchero camp before coming to a halt.

As much as he yearned to understand what was said between the Indian leaders and the leaders of the comancheros, as much as he sensed it had something to do with Zeke and him, Jeremiah knew only that the voices on both sides grew angry all too quickly for this to be anything close to barter. He sensed the charge to the air as the comancheros eased behind their carts, their hands seeking out their guns; as the horsemen on their hammerheaded cayuses grew increasingly restless, shifting their fourteen-foot lances from one hand into the other and pulling forth their short, sturdy bows.

Then a shot thundered from one of the comanchero pistols, breaking the impasse. In answer ten arrows hissed among the Mexicans before the rattle of gunfire grew too deafening, swallowing up the sounds of the Indian war cries and the *thung-thung-thung* of their short bowstrings. He remembered clutching little Zeke in his arms as they collapsed to the ground, rolling, pulling, dragging his brother beneath one of the wagons while the ground around them swirled with men's legs and ponies' hooves in clouds of stinging dust.

When it was over, the air became quiet, deathly still for a few moments before Jeremiah dared open his eyes.

"They gone?" Zeke had asked in his seven-year-old voice.

"Don't know," Jeremiah had answered, blinking his eyes into the gray gloom beyond their little haven beneath that wagon.

There then erupted a blood-chilling cry from one throat, answered by half-a-hundred more as the Indians came among the comanchero dead. They stripped the Mexicans of all clothing and danced about in their newly won coats resplendent with shiny buttons and braidwork, most still wet, stained dark with the past owner's blood. From beneath the cart, Jeremiah watched as the warriors began to butcher and mutilate the bodies of his former owners. And his fear rose high in his throat to think that now he was no longer among civilized human beings.

"Indians are heathens who don't believe in God," his mother had taught him at her knee back on the homestead in southwestern Missouri. So close to Indian country were they that she thought such an education worthwhile.

"What do they believe in?" Jeremiah had asked, though for years he remained without an answer that made sense in his limited view of the way of things in the universe.

He was thinking back on those lessons from his mother's Bible—how she told him what these savage, half-naked people would do to helpless white men—when Jeremiah turned about with a jerk, finding a painted, dust-furred face bending down into the shade to peer at his little brother and him. Jeremiah's heart seized in his throat to think that so much evil had happened to Zeke and him at the hands of evil white men—what horrors must surely await them if they were taken prisoner by these naked savages?

He cried and fought the Indians, struggling to get away from the first warrior, slamming into the legs of a second as he tried to scoot away from his clutches. Then a third face appeared before him, the face of a man who looked into his eyes, then held out his hand to Jeremiah. Another he held down for little Zeke, motioning for them to come out from their hiding place. One of the others gave the warrior a Mexican canteen. He pulled loose the cork with his teeth, drank and swallowed, then handed the canteen to Jeremiah.

For weeks now, maybe many months, he hadn't had a drink when he wanted it. He was never offered water except in the morning and again at each night's camp. Now this simple gift of water. Now these hideously painted savages were offering him a drink, from a canteen held in the same bloodstained hands that had hacked the manhood parts from the co-mancheros and stuffed those appendages into the Mexicans' mouths so that they draped from the brown chins like so many limp tongues.

Jeremiah gave Zeke the first drink, then took a long one for himself. Soon they took the warrior's hand and emerged into the stormy light of that bloody place, staring down at the oak-pale, brown-skinned co-mancheros who had brought down so much pain and fear upon the two boys. Now the Mexicans were gone and the Indians were done going through the carts, stealing all that the warriors could carry on their horses or pack on the animals once hitched to the traders' *carretas*.

At long last Jeremiah had his wish: that the Indians would come. For so long he had prayed for Indians to come kill them.

Instead the warriors hoisted little Zeke behind one of the older horsemen. He felt himself lifted from the ground, set on a pony behind a warrior whose skin smelled of camp fires and grease, slick with sweat. He smiled at Jeremiah and patted the white boy's leg as if to give voice to something unspoken between two different peoples.

As if to assure Jeremiah that he was now among civilized people.

And as those riders suddenly pounded moccasins into their ponies' ribs and shot off with a shout from half-a-hundred throats, Jeremiah thanked God that his prayers had not been answered.

Tears welled in his eyes as he hugged that nameless warrior, gripping the man as the pony raced away from that bloody place. Jeremiah looked back but once, barely able to make out the naked bodies sprawled on the ground. It was easier to see the black spires rising, adrift on the breeze above the burning carts.

For all that his young eyes had seen in that year gone from the Missouri homestead, for all that he had been forced to learn about the ways of white men and their evildoing in that same endless year, Jeremiah felt an overwhelming relief to be at last among a frightening, savage people.

These who killed and hacked and slashed off hair and manhood parts. These who nonetheless looked at the two boys with kind eyes and offered them water, then carried Jeremiah and Zeke off across the unmapped rolling plains, riding north toward the rocky escarpment coming purple beneath the gray light of that rainy morning.

So once more on this day, just as he had on every day since that morning the warriors had butchered the comancheros, Jeremiah understood he had been saved.

And came to believe that maybe his mother's white God was not the only divine power out here in all this wilderness.

2

H<small>ER BODY GLISTENED</small> beneath his.

Hungrily Jonah licked salty droplets from the crevice at the base of her throat, savoring their musky bitterness on his tongue like a man thirsty too long for the earthy taste of her, the strong womanness that rose to him now, filling not only his nostrils, permeating everything in him to bursting.

Still, somehow he held back, savoring the exquisite pain of waiting. Hook had promised himself that he would not be too anxious this first time back in the shelter of Gritta's arms. Lying with her at long last, just as he had dreamed so deliciously, for so many lonely nights.

Those nights swam before him the way smarter folks claimed a man's life swam before his eyes when he was dying. All those nights of bitter reverie—from the first cold morning he had marched out of their valley, taking off to fight for General Sterling Price gone to drive the Yankees out of Missouri. After Confederate blood had flowed freely on the slopes of Pea Ridge down to Arkansas, Jonah had been one of the few who stuck with the barefooted brigades to march behind Price, tramping east to Mississippi where he was wounded and left for dead, left behind in a pell-mell retreat, left for capture by the blue-bellies after the Confederate debacle at Corinth.

All that came bubbling up from his memory, seeping through re- membrances of long winter nights suffering with the predead stench of the human sties the Yankees called prison cells at Rock Island in Illinois. Nothing would ever drive from his nostrils the stench of that repugnant offal of human waste: not just the decaying feces, but as well the slowly rotting dead, the moldering flesh, the puffy, gassy, bloating corpses the Yankee guards came to collect of every morning.

Yet this sweet, fleshy, earthy fragrance of Gritta moving beneath him drove that stench of remembrance far, far from his mind now.

How musky was this perfume about her taut, smooth body. Smells of a fresh-scrubbing of lye soap and dashes of lilac water were quickly gone the way of her own heated fragrance as Gritta's hunger readied her to receive him. That heady smell near drove him crazy with anticipation of just how she would feel around him when at last he sank his own flesh deep inside her.

As if she sensed his very need, Gritta took his rigid weapon in both her hands. It proved more than enough to make him gasp in surprise, shock, wonder at that singular, profound sensation dreamed of timeless nights of the past. He had wondered all those years apart from her on just how it would feel when finally back within the circle of her legs and arms, lying against her with nothing but the cool night air between their naked bodies.

Gently, so very gently, she kneaded his swollen flesh between her two hands, sensing it throb and leap in his growing anticipation. Those woman's hands coarse and hardened to daily toil, the lot of a settler's wife, mother to children and the land itself. Yet at this moment Gritta's hands wrapped him with a touch like the finest of silk gloves, grasping him gently—so gently urging him with a furious insistence of her own.

"You do any more of that," he rasped at her ear, licking a droplet of sweat from the earlobe, "I can't save myself for you."

Gritta immediately guided him toward her waiting moistness. With him started within, she urgently clawed at the small of his back, fervently pulling him to her— burying him firmly.

Jonah groaned at the sweet ecstasy of that first full thrust, at long last feeling the heated liquid fire of her engulfing all of him as her legs drew up, encircling his hips, allowing Jonah to sink within her as far as a man dared go. It seemed as if he filled her like never before.

Gritta's head sank back, her eyes rolling in her own private, savage fury. And from somewhere down deep in her throat, a rumbling growl freed itself—a low, primitive coursing of bestial release like nothing he could remember hearing from her before.

Perhaps it was as he had feared. His wife was now a changed woman. Those years with the Mormon zealot had scarred her soul, taken their toll. This animal hunger in her now confirmed it: what the time apart from Jonah had done to her . . . what Jubilee Usher had wrought to change Gritta.

For a moment Jonah slowed his own fury, in a way wanting his old Gritta back now. Then as quickly he realized he did have her, telling himself there was nothing changed about her as he put his mind to think on it. This was the same woman, the same passion, the same furious swallowing of him that she had thrown herself into that second time their wedding night, not long after their first painful, hurried coupling. And then a third—and every time since.

How she murmured now in his ear—those secret, provocative things that drove him crazy atop her. Gritta clearly sensed what effect she had on him. And she brazenly used that power to her advantage. Seeking her own private brand of pleasure from the man who drove himself in and out of her now with an increasingly fevered pace.

He not only felt her tightening her legs around him, but he actually sensed her tensing that heated moistness around the rigid flesh he rammed into her with a heated intensity. Losing contact with everything else around him—Jonah became like a man possessed.

Then he forced himself to open his eyes and gazed down into the inky indigo-blue of hers. And slowed his hammering as he noticed that peculiar mix of passion and helplessness and total abandon he saw welling in Gritta's eyes, swimming there with the tears that began at last to spill down her cheeks.

Jonah stopped, his flesh no less hard, yet at rest inside her moist insistence. Gritta's legs locked around him, her fingernails still brushing at the small of his back. Like that, they gazed at one another for a long moment, unmoving.

"It . . . it has been so long, Jonah," she whispered past the sob threatening to choke off her words.

Gently swiping the hot tears from both of her cheeks, he felt his own eyes smarting, moistening suddenly.

"It won't happen again, Gritta. Us being apart. I promise you."

Fighting back his tears, Jonah looked up, finding the room familiar: this place that brought him contentment. "Just look around you, woman. This is our home. I finally brung you home."

She nodded, biting her lip. Of a sudden unable to speak, she clenched her eyes shut, tears seeping forth beneath the lashes. It moved something within him, something that had too long remained untouched.

"We're back home, Gritta. Believe it. You must believe it—as surely as you are here. As surely as I can take my hand and place it here . . . on your soft, sweet breast."

Jonah encircled her small, perfect breast with one hand, cupping it so that the nipple stood rigid at its center when he bent over it, kissing, licking, sucking on it while Gritta moaned, freeing that animal sound from the far back of her throat, a sound that emanated from the deeper recesses of what she was as a woman in need.

"This breast that has given life to our children, Gritta," he went on, whispering, his hot breath on the breast, his lips still near the swollen nipple that seemed to quiver as he spoke, yearning for more of his gentle, insistent touch. "Your body, sustaining the life of our babies."

She sobbed. "Only my dream of you, Jonah . . . my memory of you— only that sustained me for those years waiting for you to come for me. To find me. To bring me back home."

"We are home. I never gave up. Lord knows it was your hope and your prayers led me to you."

"I never gave up waiting for you, Jonah."

He stroked her wet cheek with his roughened fingers. "Now I brung you home, woman. Here beneath Big Cobbler Mountain. To our Shenandoah Valley. Where we first fell in love and married and began our family. Here is where I had to bring you again before lying with you like this."

Jonah had built up the fire in the stone fireplace to scare the chill from the place before he had gone to sit beside her on their rope-bed, that old tick emptied and stuffed anew with fresh cut Virginia grass. Like the young lover she had been their wedding night, Gritta had taken his hand in hers, then slowly laid it over her breast.

"This is what I've been waiting for, Jonah," she had told him there at the side of their wedding bed.

He had said nothing, but had instead covered her mouth with his, his tongue parting her lips fiercely, seeking out hers the way his swelling flesh strained to be free of his britches, yearned to sink inside her. Jonah had pushed her gently down atop the old comforter fattened with down, so fragrant with this sanctuary of their memories. Here in the valley of the Shenandoah, where he had first laid eyes on young Gritta Moser. And been instantly smitten the way only his mother could describe it.

According to Mother Hook, a man was a carnal animal, desirous of but one thing from a woman. So to control that man, to keep him in line and force him to practice his Christian industry, a woman had to portion out her sexual favors a little at a time—never could she truly enjoy that shameful travail she had to undergo in the name of God's high command to be fruitful and replenish the earth.

Yet right from first jump Gritta had been different. After that first painful, and blessedly short-lived, episode on their wedding night, Gritta had thrown herself into lovemaking with such an abandon that it surprised Jonah, a young man fully expecting no more from a woman than for her to lie there while he did his business and finished, when at last she would pull her nightshirt back down over herself and roll away to fall asleep like her husband.

That's what he had expected from the tales told him by a stone-faced Mother Hook.

But Gritta had been different from that first jump. She had come to him eagerly that second time, awakening him, every bit as hungry as he was for her, if not more so. It had startled him, perhaps even frightened him a little, to find such eagerness in this woman he had vowed to spend out his years with. He was worried too at first with what monster he had unleashed in his new wife. Yet he quickly came to enjoy and savor, to love, ultimately, that most secret person Gritta proved herself in bed with him. So quiet and strong before the rest of the world—it was like he alone knew her true self: a woman who became a ravenous temptress once they were alone beneath the covers. He loved her for it—if for no other reason than she wanted love, wanted to be loved as much as he wanted her to love him, answering his needs and hungers with the unquenchable fires of her own.

So it was they found themselves in this bed below Big Cobbler Mountain in the Shenandoah of Virginia once again. Countless miles and endless years it had taken in bringing her back here where they both began a life together standing to make their vows before the circuit rider, their families, and God Himself.

That was before they had pulled up deep family roots and resettled to

Missouri with young Hattie. Before the two boys come along. Before the Yankees and Sterling Price and Pea Ridge and bloody Corinth, where he had to lie in the damp, rain-soaked forest waiting for the Yankees to find him—afraid the tremble-fingered blue-bellies would shoot him on the spot, simply because Jonah had dragged himself on his belly across a few yards of wet grass on that forest floor, crawled toward a dead Yankee to steal the young soldier's rations. Some crumbs of hardtack and a handful of moldy salt beef. As bad as it was, Jonah had mused as he gulped it down greedily, at least the Yankees had something to eat in this god-blamed war.

Yankees had boots and shoes too, while most of the boys Jonah marched with come along to fight the blue-bellies with an empty belly and bare, bleeding feet.

The nights had been cooling off so suddenly in those days before the battle at Corinth that Jonah had coveted the dead soldier's boots like nothing he had ever coveted before. He took them, not without a struggle from the stiffening carcass, along with rank, torn stockings too. Not that it was hard getting those socks off the dead soldier. Just that everything was a struggle to Jonah what with the welling pain in his leg wound and the lost blood that made him faint, ready to puke with most any ounce of exertion he made.

But now it was over. His hunt for Gritta complete, and Jonah had brought her back to the Shenandoah Valley.

"Make love to me like you never have before," she whispered to him as his left hand cupped, stroked the other breast.

"Like never before?"

"Now, Jonah—now," she growled the words, insistent as she tightened herself around him, thrust herself up toward him, arching her back as he planted himself more firmly into her heatedness.

It drove him near crazy when she did that, never ashamed was Gritta of asking for what it was she wanted. She was so unlike what his mother had told him he was to expect of a woman on that morning before the preacher joined the young couple. So unlike what even his father had already confessed a man had right to expect of a wife and her duties to her sworn husband.

So this felt like that second time their wedding night, all over again: her crying out in pleasure as he hurled himself against her, frantically gripping her, holding her for fear their damp, sweaty bodies would slip loose and fly asunder when what he hungered for most right now was to melt together with her as one and never be apart. He was fearful with the savageness of their lovemaking that he would fling himself free of her: lose her again, if only for a moment.

That fear was something he could almost taste. Like the salty sting of the sweat he bent to lick from the crevice between her breasts.

Yet Gritta stayed with him, rocking with a fury that drove him ever higher.

"Let me feel you explode inside me, Jonah—please," she begged at his ear, biting it tenderly, her fingers raking the back of his neck. "I want to feel your heat," she moaned.

There was no more holding back once she did that to him. It was one command he had never been able to deny. Whereas he had spent a life of choosing what orders to obey, Jonah Hook was helpless when his woman demanded his immediate compliance.

The release came like a long-awaited volcanic shock quaking the entire Shenandoah Valley. Tingling from his belly down through his thighs, Jonah exploded in a growing crescendo of thrusts as he sought to plant himself deeper and deeper into her body—wanting never to free himself of this moistness, this heat, this joy of ultimate togetherness with her.

Then as he lay there atop Gritta, his breath slowing raggedly, for the first time sensing the sweat pouring from his own body and hearing at his temples his own heart hammering like it wanted free of its cage, Jonah marveled at what he had found with this woman—marveled that they had seen their special bond through the long years of his search to reclaim her.

The breeze of that evening felt good on his cheek as he snuggled closer to her, listening for the beat of her own heart, the slowing of her own breathing, the last of the whimpers in the back of her throat as the crescendo washed from her in eddying waves.

Gritta trembled beneath him like a frightened animal again, like she always did as he pulled his softened flesh from her. He drew the woman into his arms and brought her against him as he rolled onto his back. The breeze felt good and clean and cool and dry.

A sky above their bed hung dusted with more stars than he had ever recalled seeing over the Shenandoah before.

Jonah blinked, and blinked again. Drinking deep of the air as the Big Dipper whirled silently overhead.

The sky. The air.

Different somehow.

The coarse wool blanket beneath his hand startled him. Not the soft, years-worn goose-down comforter whereon he had made love to her.

As he sat upright, he trembled like a wet dog with distemper, the sweat on his brow and face and chest gone quickly cold and stale now in the breeze. Jonah drank deep of the night air. Only one place smelled like this—the high plains. Sage. But more than sage.

Wildness. Unfettered wildness.

He swallowed hard, near choking on disappointment.

"Goddamn," Jonah muttered, his head sinking backward in an arc atop his shoulders as he clamped his eyes shut angrily, cursing the dream that had come to haunt him again.

That haunting vision returned less and less with every year now, yet still it remained a torture he practiced on himself—forcing himself to believe again each time the dream returned that he was actually making love to his wife back home in Virginia.

How real it had been. The touch and smells and tastes of her. The utter warmth of her wrapped around him.

So cold now in the aftermath that he began to tremble uncontrollably, drawing his shirt to him across the dry grass. Dolefully Jonah dragged it over his head as the tears began to well in his eyes. So alone.

So damned alone, after all. Halfway gone to hell and back all these years. Having finally found his girl. Hattie.

The boys were gone—sold off somewhere into the Southwest. At least that was what he had learned from one of those who ripped his family from their homestead during the bloody days of the war.

And his woman—said to be the property of some maniacal bastard who laid claim to her in the name of his own God.

Jonah flung an arm at the night sky, shaking his fist at God, at everything that God wasn't for Jonah. God wasn't there to answer a lonely man's prayers, his pleas to put back together the shattered pieces of his family, his life, the circle of those he loved.

Instead, on that trackless high prairie sat a bitter, angry, lonely man filled with unrequited rage as he wavered to his feet and stood shaking beneath the great night sky—but more from the fury unspent within him than from the cold of this desert night in southern Wyoming Territory.

"Damn you for this!" he roared

Damn you for hurling your anger down at my family the way you done—when you should have taken out your wrath only on me!

Yanking his pistol from its holster, Jonah fired and fired and fired again until the hammer clacked repeatedly on empty cylinders. Each bullet sped into the black face of the heavens—perhaps into the face of God Himself—in futile hope of getting the Almighty's attention to his private pain, this hell only God Himself could be putting this lonely man through.

Jonah whirled and flung the pistol down onto his rumpled bedroll. He collapsed onto his knees, crumpling forward as he began to sob in earnest, not understanding why he had been cursed this way, not knowing just what he had done to merit having his family wrenched from him.

After all, he had grown to be a man who had never knowingly hurt a soul, never so much as harmed another until the Yankees had come to Missouri. Any man worthy of his backbone had to stand and be counted to turn back the blue tide.

Here he sat crumpled, knowing nothing more than that it hurt him beyond all endurance, this being without her. Not knowing if she was still alive, or dead by now.

For years now his clumsy prayers had remained unanswered. He knew that much. Still, he had been told a man called Jubilee Usher waited for Jonah somewhere out there with his army of Mormon gunmen—cutthroats protecting the Mormon zealot and his woman captive as they marched back toward the City of the Saints.

With a dirty hand Jonah swiped at his nose, slowly gaining control once more. He swallowed the sting of the salty tears, promising himself that one day soon he would stand in the streets of that Mormon stronghold and cry out the name of Jubilee Usher—calling the godless bastard forth to atone for his crimes against the family of Jonah Hook.

Drenched in starlight, he reloaded his pistol quickly, ramming home powder and wad and ball, capping all six cylinders in the indigo loneliness, the sweat encasing his flesh grown cold and stiff, gone stale and rank in the freshening breeze of postmidnight.

Where once his body had tingled with her touch, he now felt the cold seep of anger swollen into a furnace of rage.

It was like nothing Jonah had ever compelled himself to do in all his life.

This having to find her.

3

HE STOOD TALLER than most. Every bit as tall as the biggest men he had known in his forty-one years. Still, it remained the oxlike frame that made near every man give him wide berth.

In his corduroy cutaway and pegged trousers stuffed into the tops of his boots that sported an instep as high as a lady's, his fingers interlaced across his weskit of corded silk, and with that smile caressing his sensuous, Cupid's-bow lips full beneath the curl of his waxed black mustache, Jubilee Usher cut a most imposing figure.

Born in the hill country of western New York State, not far from Lake Ontario in Mendon Township, young Jubilee had grown up the eldest son of one of the closest friends to Mormon Prophet Joseph Smith, founder of the Church of Jesus Christ of Latter-day Saints. Smith himself lived but eighteen miles away in Palmyra. However, while it was the Church's founder who had the elder Usher's religious loyalty, it would prove to be another who earned young Jubilee's fierce and undivided obedience.

Brigham Young.

With the faithful the Usher family migrated, farther and still farther west to escape the persecution of the hated and blasphemous Gentiles.

With his own eyes witnessing the terror those heathen nonbelievers wreaked among the Mormon flocks, Jubilee came first to hate all those who were not Saints, then quickly grew to nurse an unquenchable rage for the nonbelievers who he saw as solely responsible for the hardships suffered by his people.

The faithful had followed Prophet Smith from New York to Kirtland, Ohio, in 1833. But over the next five years a rival Mormon sect grew in power and ultimately joined forces with the Gentiles in the surrounding countryside to again drive Smith's loyal followers west. It was during that five years of terror and uncertainty that Jubilee's father, Heber Usher, became himself a Pentecostal Mormon—a Saint who believed in the reality of spiritual manifestation.

That limb on the tree of Mormon faith proved itself to be the rock of belief where Jubilee clung for the next thirty years. With unshakable conviction he claimed he had been visited by the angel Moroni himself, commanded by the Lord to take up the sword of the one true Church against all heathens. And it had not been merely one visitation. No, Moroni came often to speak to Usher through those three decades, guiding the man—girding him with strength for the struggle against the devil and the Gentiles.

Preparing Jubilee Usher for greatness among the land of Zion.

"Cleave the Gentile from the land!" Moroni had commanded Usher years before. "Take thy sword and cleave the head from the body of these Gentiles!"

By 1840 at their new settlement of Nauvoo, Illinois, Joseph Smith had announced his own divine revelation regarding the doctrine of plural wives.

It made Jubilee smile now as his huge frame settled into the huge oak chair he had his Negro manservant tote around for his comfort. Here Usher sat of every morning and evening. Big as it was the day they discovered it among the possessions of a settler's farm they plundered, with its crowning back and leonine arms ornately carved, his Danites came to call the heavy chair Colonel Usher's throne.

This morning they would move out, continuing their march down the slope of South Pass, into the Pacific watersheds. And his old nigger George would once more struggle to make a place for the chair in the army ambulance they had captured back in Missouri, home of the Gentiles who had killed Joseph Smith. Where Brigham Young had been anointed as the Saints' new Prophet.

So again Jubilee smiled to think on how Young himself had only sporadic visitations from the angels, much less from God Himself, while Jubilee had almost daily contact with the grand and martial angel Moroni.

"Cause the fields of the Gentiles to winnow in the sun and their rivers to run red with their blood!" the archangel had commanded Usher.

At fifteen, looking much older than those tender years due to his early physical development, he had joined Porter Rockwell, Joseph Smith's personal bodyguard, with a handful of others in plotting the assassination of the anti-Mormon governor of Missouri, Lilburn W. Boggs. The Prophet himself had given approval to Rockwell's plot to murder Boggs during a secret temple ceremony for the Saint-elect. While many of the faithful came to know of the plans, few among the plotters proved as brazen and fearless as the young Jubilee Usher. Rockwell's avenging angels struck before scattering to disappear into the darkness of the middle frontier.

Through 1843 and 1844 the nearby Gentile communities of Carthage and Warsaw became increasingly afraid of the growing strength of Smith's theocratic community at Nauvoo. When a rival group of Mormons splintered off from the Prophet, printing their own newspaper as a protest over Smith's polygamist doctrine, paranoia came to rule around the throne, and again the mighty hand of the Church elders reached out to smite the unfaithful.

One of the fingers on that mighty, wrathful fist, brought forth to torch the upstart newspaper offices and destroy the evil printing press, was none other than a young Jubilee Usher, his face gleaming in the flickering light of those flames that brought to an end the threat to Joseph Smith's hold on the one true Church.

An unfaithful Mormon was as evil an enemy to God's Empire as was a blasphemous Gentile.

Fearing that civil unrest had come to that heated portion of his state, Illinois governor Ford declared himself in charge of the situation in June of 1844 and ordered the arrest of Joseph Smith, along with Smith's brother Hyrum. Days later, on the twenty-seventh, a mob of citizens from nearby Carthage and Warsaw townships blackened their faces and marched on the town jail, dragged the Smith brothers from their cell, and lynched the Mormon leaders to a chorus of cheers and hallelujahs.

Into that yawning vacuum of divine power now stepped the Prophet's chief lieutenant—Brigham Young.

And it wasn't long before Young and his Quorum of Twelve decided that they must once and for all escape the land of the unclean, to flee forever the murderous Gentiles. They were commanded by God to seek out their own haven, a pure sanctuary in the West, where God Himself directed Young to take his faithful. By late in the winter of 1846, the first expedition bound for the valley of the Great Salt Lake embarked from the Saints' nomadic Camp of Israel, bound for the unknown of that immense wilderness of the plains.

Across the next five years the Saints persevered just as the Hebrews fleeing the bondage of Pharaoh had done: building their dreams of Zion—raising their glorious City of the Saints from the valley floor in the heart of the Rocky Mountains. All the while Brigham Young grew more jealous of the one man who seemed to possess more power than did the Prophet here in the mountain West: Jim Bridger. Young dispatched 150 of his Danites, his "Avenging Angels," to burn Bridger's post and ferry, steal Bridger's stock, and kill Bridger if they could.

The Angels, among them twenty-six-year-old Jubilee Usher, failed to find Bridger at home—but they did quench their blood lust by murdering every last one of the old mountain man's employees at Bridger's ferry on the Green River before turning around and marching back to the land of Deseret, mantled in glory.

Still, the fact that he had not yet secured the scalp of Jim Bridger continued to nettle Brigham Young more and more with each passing month across those next two years, until in 1853 Jubilee Usher himself convinced the Prophet of the need to occupy Bridger's fort, and to inter-marry with the daughters of the Shoshone tribes as had Bridger, so that the Saints could wrest control and dominion of the various bands in that country from a handful of decrepit old mountain men.

Jubilee had begun to position himself closer and closer to the throne, speaking to the Prophet's own fears, and offering a solution that would certainly assure young Usher of a place at the right hand of Brigham Young himself.

Now of a morning as he waited for his Negro manservant to bring him sweetened coffee in the white china cup he so favored with breakfast, Jubilee remembered the end of that long ride to Bridger's fort. He sat here beneath the awning at the front flaps of his tent, hearing no sound from the woman. She had been his for . . . something like four years now, since he took her off that farm in southern Missouri, along with the chattel of a daughter and two sons.

The boys he had sold into slavery to the comancheros. Bound for Chihuahua, likely they were already somewhere in northern Sonora, Mexico, where they would be worked hard to repay the handsome price paid Usher for them. And the girl, ready any day for womanhood, was herself traveling with another company of Danites, commanded by his chief lieutenant, Major Lemuel Boothog Wiser. Tidy now, things were. Which left only the woman for Usher to concern himself over. He had a passion for her—that blond hair and those pale eyes a blue he had never before seen. Those eyes seemed to grow all the more pale with each passing day, as if the light behind them were flickering out, ever so slowly—as one would roll a lamp wick down until the lamp's glow grew ever so faint. And finally snuffed itself out.

Still, he did not underestimate the woman. Jubilee allowed nothing sharp to be brought around her. Nothing that could be used as a weapon. Not that he feared she would use it on him. Far from it. He was, instead, afraid the woman would use most anything to kill herself. Clumsily she had tried it twice before and had to be constantly watched when he was not with her.

"Thank you, George," Jubilee said to the Negro who poured him his coffee. Around them the camp buzzed to life with men loading wagons, finishing breakfast, saddling horses.

Sweeping some of the long black curls from his shoulder, Usher sipped at the thick, steamy brew and gazed off through the trees to the south. It would not be that many more days before they would march into the streets of Deseret—a homecoming after lo, these many, many years of self-enforced exile in the border states. Doing God's bidding.

So it was with bitterness that Jubilee again recalled how a dozen of Jim Bridger's old fur-trapping companions had held off Brigham's well-armed band of Danites back in fifty-three, until a blizzard had settled on the land. In their hasty retreat back to Salt Lake City, Usher had vowed he would never allow himself to be that cold again, nor allow his pride to suffer such a stinging wound as he had suffered at the hands of those smelly old trappers.

"Damn them," he now said quietly over the lip of his white china cup. "Damn their heathen souls to hell."

He heard the rustle of blankets and cloth inside the tent. A moment later Jubilee recognized the sound of the woman at her chamber pot. At least she was taking care of herself again. For a time there after Major Wiser had been ordered to take the girl off with his company, the woman simply gave up all moving on her own and was constantly wetting the bedding. Making for a smelly mess Negro George had to tend to every day.

But for the past few weeks now, the woman seemed to be pulling herself back together. There was an admirable strength to be found in her, this beautiful woman wasting her life away on a farm, married to a man who sweated over the soil, grunted over the animals, dirt and worse forever caked beneath his fingernails.

Strange that Jubilee always thought of the farmer's woman in that impersonal sense, even after these past four years. She had a name. Wiser had discovered it in a family Bible found in the cabin they ransacked at the homestead there in Missouri. Her folks had come from Germany, settling in the Shenandoah Valley of Virginia. Her name was Gritta Moser. Married to a man named Jonah Hook. Mother of three live births. All three children gone now the way of these blasted prairie winds.

He had cleaved the wheat from the chaff, much to his own liking. He smiled for it again.

"Rider coming in, Colonel!" announced one of the camp guards as the sentry loped up to Usher's awning. He flung an arm east.

"He alone?"

The picket nodded. "Appears to be."

"Bring him on in when he arrives."

The horseman proved to be one of Lemuel Wiser's men—sinking wearily from his mount, winded and windburned, gaunt from the miles and weeks.

"You've been on the trail for some time, my good man," Usher cheered as he rose, dusting both hands off on his flowered silk weskit, tugging on the points of the embroidered vest. "What news do you have from the major? I trust he's not lollygagging far behind you?"

The man swallowed, his tongue flicking at his cracked, bleeding lips, greedily accepting a canteen of water from one of the pickets, with a half-done nod of appreciation. "Boot— . . . Major Wiser's dead, Colonel."

Jubilee sensed something seize him cold and low. "You joke with me, man—I'll feed your heart to my hound!" Usher growled, instantly alarmed by the news. He took a moment to turn away from the rider to let this unfortunate disclosure wash over him.

Then Usher wheeled on the courier suddenly. "How did this happen? A card game? Perhaps a jealous husband? Such a dandy that Wiser thought himself to be."

Indeed, Boothog Wiser was—or had been—a devilishly handsome man who loved his women and his gambling with unerring and equal passion. Both were vices Usher frowned upon. Perhaps one or the other had caught up to Jubilee's young lieutenant at last. Perhaps a man faster with his gun discovered Wiser cheating at cards. More likely a jealous husband caught Wiser alone and dallying with his strumpet of a wife.

Although it came as a shock that Wiser could actually be dead, still it came as no surprise.

"Tell me all of it—or I'll slice your tongue in ribbons!" Usher roared.

"It was a man," the rider began, water droplets tracking dark veins from his sun-swollen lips, streaking down the fuzzy, dust-coated chin. "A man what'd been follering the major for some time."

"Explain it!"

The courier's eyes went small, like a ferret's, as he flicked them toward the colonel's tent. "The girl's papa," he answered in a small, trapped, feral voice.

That stung Usher to the quick. He straightened, still glaring at the rider. "The girl's . . . father?"

The courier only nodded, greedily swiping another drink from the canteen.

Jubilee Usher slowly turned himself to gaze at the closed tent flaps— behind which the woman, Gritta Hook, kept herself hidden. He could only wonder if she was listening at this moment.

He turned back on the messenger. This, like any fear, always filled him with all the more rage.

"Then . . . I take it we're being tracked by the woman's husband."

A week out of Fort Laramie and this was the last of his meat.

Jonah Hook speared the long sliver of flank steak on the end of the peeled willow and held it suspended over the low flames of the fire he had built at the bottom of a deep pit scooped from the sandy soil. There were no bright flames to be spotted by wandering eyes scouring the black of prairie night. When he finished his meal, Jonah planned to move on another three or four miles west, away from this creek bottom, there to make another cold camp for the night, far from fire and the odor of food that would hang about a place, far from any chance of some owl-hoot rider sneaking up on him out of the darkness.

He liked this moment of the day best, Jonah admitted. The long ride behind him, the warmth and cheer of the little fire close at hand, the fragrance of the sizzling meat rising to his nostrils, accompanied by the crackle of spitting grease as the antelope loin seared over the glowing embers. And with it a drink of the cold, clear waters taken from these streams that rushed down from the high country, eventually to join the North Platte and the Missouri and ultimately the Mississippi in its head-long rush to the sea.

That order of things really didn't matter to Jonah. He had never seen an ocean, and doubted he ever would for that matter. All he knew was that right here in this high country, the water was found cold and sweet, unsullied by alkali salts and untouched by the sun's heat.

Around his face swam a vapor of mosquitoes. As long as he stayed put, right where he was in the midst of what little smoke his fire put off, he held the troublesome winged tormentors at bay. True, they buzzed past his ears from time to time, but never seemed to land.

Out there in the beyond a lone coyote set up the first yammer of the night, calling for hunting partners to join in on the evening's stalk.

Their kind hunted almost silently, Jonah thought to himself, pulling down their quarry without much of a sound. Not like he had to with one of the big-bore guns he carried along on the pack animal. He glanced over at the two horses now, both hobbled and content to browse on the good grass he had found for them near the stream bank.

Jonah dared not shoot, as hungry as he might be for the next two or three days in crossing South Pass. He remembered this country. Three years it had been since last the southerner set foot along the Sweetwater River. His uniform was cut of Yankee blue then—galvanized out of that Rock Island Prison with the rest come west to fight Injuns. He had grown smaller and smaller every black night in that prison, afraid he was dying more and more every day like the others the guards dragged out by their heels most every morning. Desperate to do anything to escape that half-living, slow death, Jonah had joined with hundreds of others who vowed allegiance to the Union as long as they did not have to turn guns on their Confederate brethren.

Far from the Yankees' plans to ship us south to fight, he thought now, then snorted humorlessly. The Union had no desire to make their "galvanized Yankees" engage the southern secesh. Instead, Jonah and the rest were freighted west to the high plains, there to fight Indians and keep the freight roads open, fight Indians and keep the great transcontinental telegraph wire up, and just plain fight Indians.

This was, after all, the land that the Sioux and Cheyenne would hold on to so jealously.

Jonah had seen a lot of good men die, all of them ordered to wrench this godforsaken ground from the red men.

He clenched his eyes shut for a moment, pushing away the hoary vision of those pale bodies left behind when the warriors withdrew after every skirmish. Butchered, mutilated, limbs hacked free, desecrated in every way inhumanly possible. He doubted he would ever forget the sight of a soldier's manhood chopped off and stuffed in his gaping mouth, death-frozen eyes staring in mute wonder at the sky.

"Damn," he muttered, then shuddered as the light grew purple with hints of night's fall.

He brought the willow and his steak close, testing the flesh first by rolling the braised meat between thumb and forefinger. Then he gingerly ground a bite off between his teeth. Not quite done—but getting there.

He liked it rare.

As he hung the loin back over the flames and the grease began to fall once more among the rosy embers, Jonah thought of young Hattie. Surely there had been enough days for his daughter to make it to St. Louis from Kansas, where he had last hugged and kissed her good-bye.

He wanted to trust Riley Fordham, wanted to trust the Danite turncoat in the worst way—although Jonah had come to trust few men.

Still, Fordham was the type who had taken to Hattie in a brotherly way, offering to escort the girl east for her safety while Jonah continued on his quest to reunite his scattered family. Fordham vowed to enroll the young woman in a boarding school where she would be safe until Jonah came to fetch her once more.

Hook had killed more than a handful of gunmen to free Hattie from that handsome, fast-handed Boothog Wiser. And in the end it looked as if what he had ultimately accomplished was to warn the one called Jubilee

Usher that Jonah was indeed somewhere on the Mormon's backtrail, following, his nose to the ground like old Seth on the scent of possum or coon.

Across these last three summers, Jonah had learned a piece of tracking from one of the best—an old trapper named Shadrach Sweete. Hook was no longer a novice: he was becoming one with the land, just like any good Injun.

There was a bittersweet quality to that thought as he tried the meat again. Done enough for a man gone all day without proper victuals. He would eat his antelope now and think on the dark, black-cherry eyes of Shad Sweete's half-breed Cheyenne daughter, Pipe Woman. Her dusky face swam before him among the wisps of firesmoke drifting up into the branches of the cottonwood, branches that would quickly dispel much sign of Hook's camp fire here at twilight.

At times Jonah found himself ashamed that his thoughts of her got all tangled up with his remembrance of Gritta. It was like he would take a stick and swirl it back and forth at the edge of a stream. Stirring up mud and sand and pebbles until everything grew murky. Until nothing was clear anymore. Resentment for himself boiled up in Jonah like sour whiskey a day late to do a drunk man any good.

All he knew as he sat there over the fire, one hand holding that antelope steak while the other dragged in dirt and sand to snuff out the glowing embers, was that he had to see this thing through.

Had to find out if Gritta and the boys were alive, or dead.

Only then could he put them out of his mind and heart—and open himself to Pipe Woman.

4

*T*ILL DEATH DO *us part....*
    Gritta Hook tried desperately to remember more of the words,
her mind clawing at the marriage vows like her fingers once scraped at the
damp earth clodding up on the blade of her hoe as she weeded the long
rows of crops she and Jonah had planted together that last season before he
went off to war.

    She could remember only faintly how it had been left up to her and
the three children to plant the crops the spring after Jonah marched off on
foot behind Sterling Price to fight the Yankees plunging down from northern Missouri.

    "Till death do us part," she whispered, touching her lips with her
fingertips afterward, not so much to test their swollen flesh for the oozing
cracks as much as to remind herself of Jonah's kiss after he had looked into
her eyes with those deep gray ones of his—holding her hand on that day
when they stood before the preacher, before all their family and friends
come from up and down the length of the Shenandoah.

    A cold splash of fear shot down her back as that word came back to
haunt her.

"Death," she murmured as the old army ambulance lurched, then swayed side to side gently, rocking among the ruts worn deep in this trail south by west toward Mormon country.

She was good as dead now, Gritta decided. And if she wasn't by the time Jonah somehow found her by the grace of the Lord . . . well, she wasn't really sure just how she felt about that—him coming to get her now. Not after all this time with Usher.

She knew the man's name. More so, she knew the smell of him, how he kept himself scrupulously clean. By now she had learned there seemed to be a particular smell to each man.

Perhaps it was nothing more than the cinnamon oil he worked into his long black curls. So dandified. She thought about that long hair of his falling to his shoulders, what with Usher almost totally bald on top of his head.

But when she smelled that musk of his mingled with the cinnamon scent to his hair, and saw the look Usher got to his eye, she knew he had come to take her. It had been such a long time since last she had resisted. Gritta couldn't remember when she had tried to fight off the huge man. Slow she had been to learn that her struggles only drove Usher all the more mad with desire.

So she had given up resisting, retreating inside herself instead. Even there, far and away from everything painful, she still hated herself for conspiring with Usher to abuse her—a married woman vowed to give her years and love to her husband only. Tortured with guilt, unable to find any other direction to turn to for salvation, Gritta sank lower and lower into despair, never sure from moment to moment if she should go on living. What was the purpose in living when hope was gone?

God knows she had tried to end the pain for herself: snatching up a knife Usher had carelessly left lying about, dragging it across her wrists until the man wrenched it from her grasp. The next time it was a pair of scissors the Negro had forgotten in the tent after trimming the colonel's hair. But as those first days rolled into weeks and the weeks stretched into months, Usher had eventually learned enough not to provide her with anything that could remotely be used to take her own life.

He even left his brace of ivory-handled pistols with George when he came through the tent flaps with that evil in his eye.

One of these days, she promised herself, when he's lifting me into the ambulance, perhaps helping me down from it as his men begin to make camp for the night—I'll grab for one of those pistols and shoot Usher . . . no, I'll turn the gun on myself.

Then he can stand there watching me bleed to death, seeing the smile on my face as my life drains away at last. Long, long last.

"Till death do us part," she whispered the words again within the rattle and clunk of the squeaky, swaying ambulance.

What life there is left in me. The way Usher has drained me of everything already. The boys . . .

And for a moment Gritta went cold, more lost than ever.

. . . what—oh, God—what were their names?

She strained for their faces, yanking at her memory like fingernails scratching at damask curtains.

"Little Zeke," she finally said with a faint smile as she remembered.

Surprising herself that she had.

He watched the distant rider. Two Sleep knew it was a white man—the way he sat his horse, the way he pulled a second horse with its burdens behind.

But the man was not like so many who knew little of travel in country so open as this. He clung to the bluffs and rock outcrops. He rode hugging the timber when possible. And at last night's camp the white man had cooked his meal in a pit, eaten, and remounted. Then he rode another of the white man's two, perhaps three, miles before the rider dismounted in a copse of trees and made his cheerless camp among the willow and alder, hidden from any roving eye.

That is, hidden from any but the eyes of Two Sleep.

From the man's still-warm fire, the Shoshone warrior knew the white man had eaten antelope. From the bones left, the way they had been stripped clean and gnawed, Two Sleep guessed it might be the last meat the white man had along.

"He will be hungry before the day is out," said the aging warrior as he had climbed from his blankets in the gray light of early dawn that next morning. There came more and more tight complaints along his muscles with the waning of every moon. They felt much like the knots he would crimp in a new buffalo-hair lariat or green rawhide to make hobbles for his war pony.

"There isn't much game from here for the next day's ride."

And for that moment Two Sleep sensed some sorrow for the lone rider. But instead of going down the slope to share his dried meat with the white man, the Shoshone had instead quickly lashed his blanket over his saddle pad and made ready to leave—but only when the other one left his cold camp among the willow below.

"He sleeps long," the Shoshone had murmured to himself at dawn.

To the east the red sun came up beneath purple rain clouds, to be swallowed in the time it took the sun to travel from one lodgepole to the next. Far to the west above the uplifted land, the worrisome clouds were already unloading their long streamers of rain upon the parched, high land.

Small wonder the white man had decided to sleep late. There was little sunlight to awaken him, and all that he had to look forward to was a day of rain. The late days of summer in this country could be like that, Two Sleep had mused as he watched some stirrings of movement in the camp below, the plains grown hot as the bottom of a cast-iron skillet, the air cooling in the high, snow-covered places rising all around this land. Clouds created above those high places were ultimately sent scrambling over the hot valleys to spill open their rain-swollen bellies accompanied by noise and torment.

It had come and gone—that storm battering the distant rider for more than two hours along the westward trail before he gave up and sought some shelter among the cottonwoods beside the narrow river. At those first drops Two Sleep had slid from the back of his pony and stripped himself naked—everything but his moccasins—then rolled his dry clothing up within the blanket covered by a small piece of oiled hide.

Soon he grew used to the cold of the rain, the hammer of the cold drops pelting his unprotected body. Soon it began to feel good, cleansing.

He wondered if the lone white man knew about bathing. So many didn't. Two Sleep thought on all the white men he had known, most of them encountered along the Holy Road that took the whites to the western sun, or those men met at Big Throat's fort near the Shaded River. It was the one called the Green by the white men. Among them Big Throat was known as Brid-ger. He was called Big Throat among most of the tribes because of the swollen flesh of the goiter at the old scout's neck.

It had not been all that long since Two Sleep had heard rumor that Big Throat had abandoned the mountain West, had gone to Fort Laramie and beyond, even beyond the string of forts along the Platte River Road.

East, it was said, to a home Brid-ger had not visited for many, many winters.

"I call you Two Sleep," Jim Bridger had said many winters before to the young Shoshone warrior distantly related to the mountain fur trapper through marriage. Big Throat was the husband to Two Sleep's cousin, cementing a bond with the Snake Indians many, many summers back in time, when both Brid-ger and Two Sleep had been younger and full of the rising sap of youth.

"Why you give me this new name?" the Shoshone had asked as he passed the pipe on around the circle of warriors come to visit Brid-ger where the white man had erected his log fort.

Brid-ger had smiled, his eyes merry. "Because I have never known you to sleep, my friend. On our hunts, when I go to sleep, you are still awake. When I wake up, you are already awake. So I think when you finally go to sleep, you will sleep for two men, eh?"

The old men had liked Big Throat's reasoning, giving their approval to the name. So it was sanctioned, this new name: Two Sleep.

From that wedding day Chief Washakie had added his blessing not only to Brid-ger's marriage, but to Two Sleep's new name as well. The two men became even closer friends. Hunting together, making war on the enemies of the Shoshone together, loving their women and the Snake people and this land the tribe fiercely called its own.

"I will fight alongside you, Big Throat," Two Sleep had told the trapper when word came that white men were riding out of the south against Brid-ger.

The old trapper had gathered a double handful of his old friends, all men who had spent years among the mountain snows and valley streams with Brid-ger, men who moved a little slower these days but still aimed true and shot center. Those few punished the other white men come cocky and bold on their big American horses, giving the attackers a solid drubbing, these old warrior friends of Brid-ger's did. It was these that Two Sleep came to know as friends when the Shoshone warrior came to live among the whites, instead of living among his own.

But in the end some of those old friends abandoned the country. Some went west, some back to the east, where it was rumored the white man numbered like the stars above Shoshone country. Still, Big Throat and Sweete had stayed on, guiding for the pony soldiers who marched against the Lakota and Shahiyena warrior bands. It was good work for the friends of the Shoshone to do—this tracking and guiding, leading the soldiers against the camps of the Snake's most hated enemies.

Only Big Throat and Sweete had stayed on in this country spread high and wide beneath the setting sun that now dipped out of the clouds like a raindrop slowly loosening itself from a cottonwood leaf. For a moment the land flared red-orange as the sun appeared, then lost itself almost as quickly behind the far foothills and vaulted peaks.

Gone was the day.

Like the rumor said of Big Throat. He was gone east, back among his original people, the ones he belonged to before he had been adopted by the Shoshone.

It could not be true: that Brid-ger would give up on this land and go back to the places where the white man clustered together in great groupings that reeked of his offal and the air hung gray in the sky. Out here the wind blew free enough that the land cleansed itself when a Shoshone village packed up and moved on.

But stories had Brid-ger gone from the high plains and snowy mountains for good. A grand era had come to an end.

This, Two Sleep had decided, he must see for himself.

So he took this journey to Brid-ger's fort where the soldiers came to roost from time to time. That way Two Sleep would find out if the rumor was true.

For many days Two Sleep traveled without seeing another human being. Only the sweep of the red-tailed hawks circumscribing lazy loops against the sky. Only white-rumped antelope bounding off from the path Two Sleep had chosen, then stopping to look back at the solitary rider. No others ventured into this shimmering heat rising off the parched land—until the Shoshone spotted the two horses weaving like black water striders a'dance among the rising waves of heat along the far horizon.

It had proved to be this white man traveling alone along this road. A brave thing, Two Sleep decided. If he met the wrong Indians . . .

But at this time of the year, this far west—why, the Lakota and the Shahiyena were far to the north, hunting. Still, the Arapaho were a different matter. They were a fickle, funny people.

They were almost as amusing as the white men Two Sleep had learned to gamble with, learned to drink with. Whiskey and cards—the white man's two most potent gifts to the Shoshone. He thoughtfully considered those gifts as he watched the solitary white man drag his saddles from the weary, rain-soaked horses down in the willow.

Two Sleep was compelled to draw closer to the stranger than he had wanted, mostly because of the thick, sluicing rain that seriously hampered his visibility. But as well, the Shoshone knew the rain cut down a man's ability to smell danger, as well as softening the ground and everything on it so that the warrior would not betray himself in this stalk.

Yes, he loved the card games: monte and euchre. And with much practice at them in the shadow of Brid-ger's fort, Two Sleep had become better than most of the white men he played. Better than them all, except that sour-faced Sweete. Never could read the man's cards in that face. Sweete kept his hand too much a secret behind that impassive face.

Two Sleep wanted to get close enough to read this stranger's face, to see if the white man packed along any whiskey in his spare packs. Two Sleep would show himself if there was a chance to drink some of the man's whiskey. He would walk boldly in and announce his presence without fear, use some of his white-man words learned at the game table in Brid-ger's fort.

Words like *goddamn:* the wagon the cursing white teamsters pulled behind his lagging oxen and mules as he yelled out, "Goddamn!"

Two Sleep guessed it meant something else too, for the white man used the word a lot at the card table.

Sumbitch, too. What the white man called himself, or some of his bad cards, or a balky mule. Or one another.

Two Sleep liked the way that Brid-ger and Sweete eloquently strung those flavorful words together when they talked among themselves, especially when excited or under the spell of whiskey. How Sweete especially put a lot of them together as he signed and spoke what little Shoshone he had learned from Two Sleep. Sweete knew Shahiyena; the white man's wife was born to that tribe. Nonetheless, he tried to learn Shoshone at the card table.

Among white men there were a confusing number of words for one thing, Two Sleep thought as he saw the white man stop at the edge of the willow, unbutton his fly, and water the rain-soaked ground.

Especially that—all the words the white man had for his manhood. The warrior had learned from the best to call it many things: his cock, his dick, his peeder, his prick, and the funniest to his tongue, his love-stinger.

Why the white man did that, Two Sleep had decided he would never find out. Maybeso it was only to make his language seem all the harder to learn.

By now the lone white man was getting smarter, looking for dry wood beneath a tree thick with foliage. He started a small fire as Two Sleep watched, then stood long enough to take off all his clothing and drape his garments over low branches. The leaves of the tree suspended over his fire, and the heavy, wet air of the passing storm, muted the rising smoke.

With water on to boil, the white man rummaged through his packs until he found what he was looking for. He settled back against his saddle to drink, naked.

From the looks of the way the man drank, Two Sleep guessed the white man had some whiskey along. A bottle of it, perhaps more than one bottle—but at least the one the white man was sucking at with no small degree of satisfaction.

Frowning, Two Sleep brooded on how he would approach the camp—certain of only one thing. He would have to show himself before the white man got too much in the drinking way, or he might shoot a strange Indian—out of fear, or devilment.

Best to show himself and soon. Or, Two Sleep figured, he would simply have to do without any of that stranger's whiskey.

Still, perhaps the white man would be willing to gamble away even more of his whiskey.

The Shoshone smiled.

Besides whiskey, maybe the white man had some cards too.

No reason either one of them had to be lonely ever again.

Not with a deck of cards, and enough whiskey.

5

September 1868

JONAH HOOK SENSED it, felt it to his marrow. Someone was watching him. But who, and why, his hunger-numbed mind refused to sort out.

For the better part of a day now he had known. There were subtle signs that only time in the wilderness can teach a man. Something nagging made him more than a little concerned that it might be one of Jubilee Usher's men who had doubled back, coming wide around to see about rubbing out the man stalking the Danite trail.

Then the rain had come, sooner than expected, the storm racing faster than even Jonah could have figured it would. Caught out in the open when its first explosive dance started over the sun-baked plains, he shuddered beneath the thunderous cacophony of raindrops hammering the hardened ground like the echo of a thousand lead balls rattling inside a steel drum. It seemed as if the sky itself reverberated with the chorus of that driving rain, mirroring its pounding of the thirsty land and that single man struggling along beneath the onslaught of the skies.

Forcing himself to push on until he finally gave up, Jonah pulled his two horses into the willows beside the Sweetwater. He remembered the

Sweetwater, with thoughts cured three winters over, time served in the Yankee army, protecting that telegraph wire from the Sioux and Cheyenne. This season of the year those warrior bands were all far to the north, hunting most like. Nary a sign of anything for the last three days now on his ride coming west out of Laramie.

Quickly he had tied off the animals, then dragged saddle and packs from their backs, letting them graze on the sun-stunted grasses back in a copse of alder where they would be less likely seen. He hurriedly made it look as if he were going to spend the night right there, then slipped off among the willow as if he were going to relieve himself, with one hand tugging his britches down over his hip as he went.

But once behind the thick growth of alder, Jonah rebuckled his belt and stuffed his shirttail back in his pants, squatting beneath some over-hanging branches, where he gently parted the drying leaves with the barrel of his Winchester repeater. He waited, watching across the stream. To his right lay his campsite and the plunder he hoped would be bait enough to draw in the sneaky bastard dogging his backtrail.

He fought the sleep struggling to overtake him as the rain hammered the ground at his side, battering the leaves above, soaking his old hat that served as little protection. Jonah shuddered, growing chilled to the bone, and tried desperately to keep his eyes open.

"Keep 'em moving," he told himself, remembering the words of Sweete and Bridger about sentries who had tired and fallen asleep because they had not kept their eyes moving. Staring at one thing too long proved deadly when a man was weary. Such a fool woke up too late—finding himself out of the frying pan and into the fire—if he woke up at all.

There came a rustle of movement to his left, along the creek bank, on the far side. Then a half-dozen birds took to the wing noisily, startling Jonah as he whirled the repeater about.

In the deepening silence that followed their frightened departure, Hook reasoned that no white man was going to make a successful sneak on him. All he had to do was wait and watch his campsite. That was the place the backtracker was surely headed. Likely the man had come across the river where the birds had taken wing and was moving downstream on the near bank, making for Jonah Hook's camp.

The wet ground made it hard to hear a thing, and the sodden air didn't carry a sound well at all. Two marks against him, Jonah brooded.

"Damn," he muttered as more of the cold rain spilled from the hat brim down his collar.

He was sitting in a cold puddle of it now, yet he dared not move. His stalker was likely drawing close. He held his breath a moment, listening, straining against the rain for sound. His eyes must be deceiving him. He'd be damned, but it sounded as if someone were already in his camp, rummaging through his packs.

Try as he might, Jonah could not see a soul. As well as he had chosen this spot, for some reason he still could not see anyone rustling the oiled canvas. But, plain as sun, Hook could hear the sound.

Slowly rising on one knee, Jonah inched forward, parting more of the leaves and branches with the rifle muzzle. Then he saw the top of a man's head.

"A Injun," he said under his breath, swiping a damp forearm across his lips.

Brushing his thumb across the Winchester's hammer to make sure it was cocked, he rose to a crouch and prepared to make his play—just as the Indian pulled free one of the glass bottles Jonah had purchased back at Laramie.

A loafer, by God. Nothing more'n a good-for-nothing, whiskey-bellied loafer!

Hook burst from the willow and alder, Winchester at his hip and leveled at its target.

"Goddamn you! Leave my whiskey alone, you drunken redskin!"

At the white man's growl exploding from the rain-soaked under-growth, Two Sleep scrambled awkwardly for his feet, moccasins slipping on the wet ground, and flew backward, tumbling headlong over more of Jonah's packs. Yet he slowly raised one arm in the air, grinning sheepishly at the white man, almost apologetic, for certain triumphant. Somehow in his fall he had miraculously kept the whiskey bottle aloft, safe, and un-broken.

"Drop it, I say!" Jonah roared, half-ready to laugh at the Indian sprawled in the mud, intent on that bottle of whiskey.

But as he said it, the Indian's empty hand came up filled with a pistol. That hammer cocked loud enough to be the clattering of an iron wagon tire rolling over granite.

Little did Hook like staring down the bore of any weapon, much less a pistol he figured was gripped in the shaky hand of a whiskey sodden

Indian. Unpredictable, that's what their kind was. And this one might up and pull that trigger as soon as look at Jonah, just for the whiskey. Just another dead white man, more or less—

"Two Sleep," the stranger blurted plain as paint.

Hook wagged his head, not sure he had heard what he thought he had. Plain-spoke English.

"What was that you said, you drunk devil?"

"Two Sleep. My name—Two Sleep. But not drunk."

He looked sideways at the intruder, suspicious. "Speak English, do you?"

With a nod of his head, the Indian used the hand holding the bottle to scratch the side of his face where some brown mud clung, dripping onto his shoulder from his fall.

"You're a sight to boot," Jonah went on. "Put that belt gun away before one of us gets hurt."

"You shoot Two Sleep?" the Indian asked.

"Sure. Always shoot whiskey thieves, I do," Hook replied, the beginnings of a grin crawling across his lips.

He didn't want to like the Indian, didn't want to trust him. But Jonah couldn't deny that he was already beginning to do both. "Still, I ain't yet shot a man I was drinking whiskey with."

The pony beneath him answered every urging he gave it with the elk-handled rawhide quirt, whipped across the mustang's rear flank to keep him first among the riders returning to the camps with such great, momentous news: white men were stalking their trail, coming on fast, greedily eating up the ground between them and the great gathering of lodge circles.

Already it had proved to be a memorable summer for High-Backed Bull, having sworn his allegiance to Porcupine, who in turn took his faithful warriors north to join with the great Shahiyena war chief, Sauts: the one known as the Bat. Among the white men, however, the muscular one was called Roman Nose.

This summer the Northern Cheyenne of Roman Nose and Tall Bull and Two Moon were joined by the great Brule Lakota village of Pawnee Killer. Their alliance had proved fruitful in recent moons: ever since the shortgrass time in late spring, the young warriors had been striking out, raiding into the land of the white settlers as far south as the Solomon, the Saline, even south to the river the white man called the Smoky Hill, where the pony soldiers built their string of forts and the iron road for their smoking horse.

As he reached the smooth, grass-covered brow of the last hill, High-Backed Bull saw the camp circles laid out in rings below him in the river valley, the River of Plums. The fighting bands had been following its course for the last three suns, slowly ambling to the north and west, in no hurry. It seemed they had come to dare the small party of white men to catch up with them.

Behind the young Shahiyena warrior now, he heard the yips and cries of the others, mostly Brule, a few Dog Soldiers like himself. They raced over the ridge and sprinted this last slope at a full gallop, urging their ponies ever faster, calling out to the camps below, feeling across every inch of their bare flesh the excitement of the news they brought.

Women at the river turned from bathing young children, washing clothing or cradleboards, or filling skin pouches with water. Still others rose from morning fires or scraping the skins pegged out across the prairie, hides surrounding the three great camp circles. Children began crying out in the contagious excitement, darting here and there with the news of approaching riders, while camp dogs set to the howl and yip. So much clamor was it all that the old men who sat in the shade of the lodges rose finally with wonder, shading their eyes from the late-morning sun.

Then High-Backed Bull saw him—the tall, muscular one, emerging at last from his lodge near one horn of the camp crescent farthest to the east—the direction where the white man marched, coming on at a hurry.

As High-Backed Bull yanked back on the single horsehair rein, bringing with it his pony's jaw, the animal skidded to a lock-kneed stop, prancing in a wild circle around Roman Nose. The war chief grabbed for the rein and held on as he peered into the light of the high sun, and the face of the young scout.

"You bring me good news?"

Catching his breath, finding his tongue so dry from the race that it stuck to the roof of his mouth, Bull asked, "I am first?"

Roman Nose nodded, impatient. "You are, High-Backed Bull. What do you, the first to ride in, have to tell me?"

The pony hurled flecks of foam as it threw its head from side to side—

at a full gallop seconds before, then suddenly commanded to halt and stand obediently still by both rider and the man on the ground.

Bull gazed into the war chief's dark eyes, wishing his own were as dark and truly Cheyenne as were those of Roman Nose. "The white men—"

"Yes, the half-a-hundred?"

Swallowing hard, Bull went on, "They are less than half a day behind now."

"Do you think you know where they will camp tonight?"

Sensing pride that the war chief should ask such an important question of him, High-Backed Bull straightened on the pony's back. "I cannot be sure, but I believe there is a place where they might find firewood along the shallow river, camp on the sandy bank."

"How far?"

He thought a moment, rerunning the miles of race back through his mind. "Not far. I believe it would take us no longer than it would for a man to eat his supper."

Roman Nose smiled, gazing off to the southeast, into the distance, as the Brule riders brought their ponies to a halt around him, kicking up dust in rooster tails, bringing the barking dogs and yammering, excited children as magnets would draw a scattering of iron filings.

"We must go tell Pawnee Killer!" shouted the war chief over the growing clamor. "Tell Tall Bull and Two Moon—get their ponies! We have a war council to attend." He began to turn away into the crowd.

This time it was High-Backed Bull who reached down and snagged the war chief's upper arm. "A war council?"

"Yes, my friend. We will plan our attack on the half-a-hundred who have followed us for many days, stalking our backtrail."

"Then . . . at last we will fight these white men?"

For a considered moment Roman Nose stared back into the young warrior's eyes, perhaps seeing there what few others might. "You hunger deeply to fight these white men, yes?"

"Any white man."

Roman Nose nodded. "Perhaps for now any white man's scalp will do, young one. Yet come a day, we both know you covet but one man's scalp."

"Come a day very, very soon, Roman Nose."

"We will make quick work of these who follow us, like the meadowlarks follow the hawk . . . until the hawk finally tires of the game and turns—to strike!"

Around them the entire camp became pandemonium with the news on every lip. Young boys brought up ponies for the Northern Cheyenne chiefs, who mounted amid the wild cries for revenge, cries to punish the white stalkers. The Shahiyena sent their leaders off to hold a war council with Pawnee Killer and the headmen of the Brule camped upstream no farther than ten arrow-flights.

"May I come with you, Roman Nose?" Bull shouted above the commotion.

Turning his pony about, the war chief smiled. "You will not be allowed to attend the council, but—yes. Come. You will hold my pony while I sit with the others."

"It will be an honor to care for your pony while you decide how the white men are to die."

The emissaries from the Shahiyena camp reined their animals from the camp circle and loped upstream where moments before the excited Brule scouts had arrived carrying the news. Already the Killer's headmen were hurrying to the chief's lodge, where the buffalo-hide cover was being rolled up on one side to allow the breeze to cool the shady interior.

Just beyond the lodge stood a hide awning stretched across a framework of lodgepoles, providing shade for a half-dozen Lakota women scurrying about to start a fire to boil meat and fry bread for those attending the war council. First the men would fill their bellies, then smoke with prayers that the truth be spoken—and only then would there be talk of making a fight of it against the white men.

High-Backed Bull ground his teeth at that—impatient to whirl about and confront the half-a-hundred by himself if he had to—just to fight them was everything now. To take a scalp or two for his own honor. To see the fear well up in the eyes of the enemy, to know the white man's heart had turned to water and he had likely soiled his pants at the mere sight of the Hotamitanyo—the mighty Dog Soldiers of the Shahiyena.

Roman Nose dismounted and handed the rein over to Bull. "Paint yourself, my friend. Make your medicine and that for your pony here. We ride as soon as this council is over!"

"To kill the white men? Kill all of them?"

"Does not the badger kill the field mouse when it tires of the chase?"

"*Keee-aiyeee!*" Bull yipped. "None left standing! None left to tell the tale."

As Roman Nose disappeared into the council lodge, High-Backed Bull dropped from the back of his pony, taking it and the war chief's toward the shade of the awning where the women chattered and brought their kettles to a boil. From a fringed pouch he carried over a shoulder, he took out three small skin bags, along with a fragment of mirror he had taken from a looking glass broken during a recent raid on a white settlement. Propping the shard of mirror in the fork of a nearby plum brush, Bull mixed the first of his dried pigments, earth colors all, with grease from the nearby Lakota kitchen.

Black. The color of victory.

From his hairline down to the middle of his nose, the young Shahiyena painted the entire top half of his face with black, from ear to ear. Next came yellow, color of the Life-giver in the sky above. He applied the yellow in long vertical stripes, each a fingertip wide, that ran down the lower half of his face until they reached his jawline.

Last to be applied was the brick-red ocher earth-paint, its crimson smeared between the yellow lines until the lower half of his face was striped with both the power of the sun and the provocative color of war. The color of blood.

For a moment more he admired his reflection there in the midday sun, the bright, greasy patterns smeared against his earth-colored skin there in that fragment of a mirror stolen from a smoking sod house a white family had raised along the Saline River, where for many generations the Shahiyena had hunted their buffalo.

Yes, Bull thought, smiling, approving of the work he had done on his paint. He strode over to paint potent, powerful symbols on his pony.

This face of mine will be the last sight many of those white men see this day! he told himself as he painted red circles around his pony's nostrils, to give it the power of breathing wind this day.

Then I will open their bellies, rip out their hearts, and smear myself with their warm blood. I will revel, dancing on their steaming entrails, then smash their heads to jelly after I have torn their hair from their heads! How I will celebrate in the spilling of their white blood!

Of a sudden Bull's hand stopped above its painting of the hailstones on the pony's rear flanks, coldly remembering his own white blood. Half of his heart was white. Half of his blood. It made the sheer exultant happiness of this moment instantly turn to gall in his mouth, a taste so sour that he choked on it.

Bull spat on every last thought of his white father.

"Until I can dance in your blood," he vowed with a growl under his breath, madly smearing the crimson paint in lightning bolts on the rear of the pony to give it speed in the coming fight. A look of cunning played summer shadows across his face.

"Until I can dance in my own father's blood!"

6

"IT'S TIME YOU went dry," Jonah told the warrior.

"Dry?" the Shoshone asked, anxiously raking the back of a hand across his cracked lips.

"You gone and emptied me of what whiskey I rode out of Laramie with. Ain't no more."

Two Sleep blinked into the bright light, wishing he wore a white man's hat to protect him from this torturous sun, then straightened stoically. "Better now, we are. Got no whiskey for me."

Hook nodded, a wry smile scratched in his features, merriment signaled in the deep crow's feet clawing at the corners of his eyes. "Yes, better now. Neither one of us needs whiskey for what we got to do."

"Tracking mens took your family."

Without a reply Hook heeled his horse a bit, urging it to a slightly faster pace. They could afford to cover ground a little less carefully for the next few miles, the broken country ahead making for less chance of being seen. Wasn't much to tracking his prey now, what with the wide, scarred trail they had to follow. While not quite cold, the Danite trail was still a matter of a week old—about as long as he had been riding west with Two Sleep.

They were drawing close to the Green, beyond it Black's Fork. Farther still lay Bridger's old fort. From what he sorted out of the Shoshone's talk, they might make the old post by tomorrow night. If not, the day after. Likely they'd run onto word of the Danites there. Those soldiers would know something. A band of white men passing by with an ambulance and a half-dozen high-walled Studebaker wagons wasn't the sort of thing a few lazy-eyed soldiers would miss out in this lonely, desolate country.

"Never did get this far west myself," Hook later admitted for lack of conversation as they made camp.

"Connor?"

"Naw. Protecting the wire from the Injuns. Was later we tracked Injuns for General Connor."

"Connor jumped the wrong village, said many."

Jonah screwed that around in his head for some time. "Seems I remember a few of the scouts saying something about that. Wasn't Sioux or Cheyenne."

"Indian tell you right. Connor wrong."

A shudder passed through him, like old Seth shaking water off his back. "Not my affair no more. That's three years gone now."

Two Sleep seemed to regard him a moment, then took his eyes off the white man. They did not speak for some time until Hook offered the Shoshone a dark sliver of chaw. The warrior took the offering of tobacco, stuffed it inside his cheek, and nodded his thanks.

"Can't for the life of me figure out why a man like Jim Bridger would want to build a fort here in the middle of all this nothing," Jonah murmured. "Not when he traveled a whole lot of prettier country in his days— trapping beaver, hunting buffalo. Don't make much sense to me, him deciding to set down roots here when there's a lot other country more pleasing to the eye."

"Brid-ger see trail here. Brid-ger come here," Two Sleep replied after some thought. "Trail here where the white man goes west to the sun's bed."

"California," Hook added. "It's called California . . . and Oregon too."

"Two name for same place?"

Hook snorted. "Naw, two places."

"Why all want to go there? So many wagon, so many people—that place fill up quick."

"Naw, not fast. Lots of land, I heard. Good sun and some rain. Grow some crops." Jonah could see that Two Sleep had himself grown bewildered. "Crops: like corn and wheat. Folks grow crops to sell."

"Hard work, this grow?"

He nodded, pursing his lips a bit. "Hard, but good work."

"Man work the ground alone?"

"Not if he can help it, he don't."

"Your boys, maybe you help them work the ground, you get back home."

His belly went cold as winter ice. "They . . . they're not back there. Not home no more."

"Oh," and the Shoshone fell quiet a moment. "They in front, ahead, out there with your woman, eh?"

With a shrug Jonah answered, "No. Last I got wind of 'em was in Indian Territory. Got sold off to some Mexicans."

Two Sleep wagged his head sadly. "Comancheros take boys far away. Go to slaves."

"Likely."

"You work the land hard again some day. Grow crop?"

Hook gazed at the far hills, studying the sky tinted with the strange mineral hues of sunset. "Maybe. Lot of doing between now and that time. Never really thought about farming again till you brought it up. Don't really seem like something I wanna do without the boys, without my family around."

"You work the ground, grow crops. Like a man grows his children, Hook. You work hard, grow your children. See them grow. Man always must say good-bye to them."

"Don't you understand? I didn't see 'em grow. That's the damned shame of it."

Both of them went silent for a long time, Two Sleep broiling skewered venison over their greasewood fire, Hook jabbing at the burning limbs with a wand of green willow. Each deep in his own thoughts.

"Man grows crops, sell what he don't eat. Money he gets?"

Jonah looked up, seeing the warrior's old eyes bright. "Yes, money. Money to gamble at cards, you red heathen."

The Shoshone wagged his head. "No, money to buy whiskey—what else for, you white heathen!"

A couple days back, Hook had owned up to liking the Shoshone more and more as the old Indian talked of a bygone time shared with Bridger and Sweete. Talked of those halcyon days at the end of the beaver trade and before the start of the white man's war against himself back east. Those years were gone the way of dust now: a time when Two Sleep had learned the rudiments of the white man's confusing language, learned better still the power of whiskey. Best yet, he learned the potent numbers and symbols emblazoned on the pasteboard cards the white man used to gamble. No carved pieces of bone, no painted sticks for this Shoshone. Those numbered, painted, powerful cards and their manifold combinations had fascinated him right from the start. They had been good days.

"I see why Shad liked you," Hook said, right out of the blue that evening camped among the cottonwood on the west bank of the Green.

"Sweete a bad gambler."

"He was, was he?"

"Worse I ever see."

"Damn good teacher, though, don't you reckon?"

Two Sleep smiled at that, dragging a hand beneath his runny nose aggravated by the smoke from their cooking fire. "Damn good teacher, Hook. But not every man a good learner, like you."

"Why—I figure that's about the first compliment you've give me, you red heathen."

Two Sleep grinned. "Better you know tracking and fighting and Indians, Hook. You no good learner at cards and whiskey."

"How the hell you know? Way I figure it, you learned just what you needed to get along in the white man's world, sure enough."

"And you, Hook? You learn all you need to get along in the world out here?" The Shoshone swept one arm around in a wide arc.

"Likely I have. So there's only two things left for me to learn."

"Two Sleep know one thing you want to find: where your family go."

Hook nodded in agreement. "That, and why they was ever took from me in the first place."

The white men had come riding into this river valley late in the raiding season, this Drying Grass Moon, following the Shahiyena trail. The white men hungered to find this string of villages clustered beside the Arikaree, hundreds of their skin lodges breasting against the summer-pale sky, their great pony herds cropping grass for miles around on the surrounding

prairie, dropping their fragrant offal among that left in the timeless pass-
ings of the shaggy buffalo.

Upstream from the camps of Tall Bull and White Horse stood two
large villages of Brule Sioux who rode under the bellicose Pawnee Killer—
where High-Backed Bull now waited impatiently with the other young
warriors for the council to conclude. Only then could they be about this
business of killing the half-a-hundred.

It was Pawnee Killer himself who had brushed up against none other
than George Armstrong Custer's gallant Seventh Cavalry one summer
gone now, when the shortgrass time filled the bellies of the Lakota war
ponies grown sleek and fast. And for this summer's hunt, the Brule had
joined the Shahiyena camps composed mostly of Dog Soldiers under
fighting chiefs. Close by stood a much smaller camp circle, a few Northern
Arapaho who traveled in the formidable shadow of the mighty Roman
Nose.

For the sake of mutual strength following their independent raids on
the settlements in Kansas, these warrior bands had come together with the
rest to hunt buffalo here where the immeasurable herds still gathered in
the great valley of the Plum River, what the white man called his Republican. Last moon, while celebrating their annual sun dance on a tributary of
the Plum called Beaver Creek, roaming scouts from the villages had first
reported spotting the half-a-hundred. From their dress, the fifty did not
appear to be soldiers. Still, this was a season for some precaution. The news
of the white men caused the bands to begin migrating to the northwest.
Surely, the tribal leaders reasoned, if we see these white scouts on our trail,
close behind will come the long columns of soldiers.

It was aggravating, yes, having such an annoyance on their backtrail.
Still, the half-a-hundred were hardly worth the effort of putting on one's
paint and taking the cover from one's shield, thought High-Backed Bull as
he paced back and forth in the bright sun of that waning afternoon.

"These are fighting men, warriors—this half-a-hundred," declared
Porcupine when he had finished tying up the tail of his pony in preparation
of battle.

"They are not soldiers!" High-Backed Bull snapped, the unrequited
tension pinching his face like the coil of a rattlesnake. "They are nothing
more than ground-scratchers . . . the same sort of white men we have killed
all summer long."

Porcupine shook his head. "No. I think you are wrong, my young friend. I am afraid we will find this band of ground-scratchers is something very different from those who fought us beside their dirt houses."

"How are they different?" Bull demanded. "Because this half-a-hundred comes looking for us? Like foolish old hens?"

"No. They are different because they are not soldiers, who are paid to fight. This half-a-hundred comes with some quarrel in their hearts for us."

"Why would you fear some white men who might have a quarrel with us? We have left many to grieve after our raids across the white man's settlements."

"I fear any man who comes into a fight with the strength of his heart to make him strong," Porcupine said. "Much better for me to fight a man who has only the power of his muscles, perhaps his cunning and wiles. But—the one I fear the most in battle is the man who comes to make his heart right. On and on that small band of white men has followed our trail, like a persistent wolverine intent on clawing its prey from their hole. Following . . . forever following."

Try as he might, Bull struggled to put the warnings of Porcupine, his mentor, out of his mind. For a moment or two at a time he watched the Dog Soldier and Brule camps alive with the steady throb of war drums.

"This half-a-hundred poses no threat to us, Porcupine," he declared a short time later when he squatted in the shade of a lodge, watching the chiefs gathered in Pawnee Killer's council a few yards away. "You confuse me. Those white men are so outnumbered that this time not one man among us will have to worry himself with protecting our villages while women, children, and old ones escape onto the prairie—just as Pawnee Killer's band had to do when Long Hair attacked last summer."

"*Aiyeee!*" cried Hair Rope nearby. "This time we will work to even the score for Pawnee Killer. This time we will attack and wipe these half-a-hundred off the face of The Mother of All Things!"

"Hear this, for what I say are the words of a warrior of the Sha-hiyena!" Bull shouted in reply, his blood running warm. "Those white men. Those half-a-hundred. Some are wearing scalps that soon will hang from my own belt!"

By this time the Lakota and Shahiyena delegations had finished their proscribed meal and passed around the pipe. As well, the young warriors in all camps were now stripped of their hunting clothes, having donned their finest war regalia. In this warm season that meant most wore nothing more than moccasins and breechclout. Still, what marked each individual's battle costume was not his clothing or lack of it—rather it proved to be his headdress, perhaps a simple hair covering fashioned of a stuffed bird or small animal totem, setting off his peculiar face and body paint, all of which added to those decorations each man had lavished on a favored war pony.

Bull stroked the muzzle of his animal after he had tied small eagle wing-tip feathers down the length of its mane. Small, fleet, wide-chested little cayuses we will ride this day, he thought to himself as he watched the imposing figure of Roman Nose from afar. These grass-fed ponies would now carry their owners into battle as the Lakota and Shahiyena butchered that small band of white men foolish enough to march squarely into the steamy gut of this ancient Indian hunting ground.

The white men had now become the quarry.

The afternoon dragged on so that by the time a young, flat-nosed warrior announced the council's conclusion from the doorway of Pawnee Killer's lodge, the sun had fallen well past midsky.

"We ride them down before the sun sets in the west!" the Brule chief exclaimed as he emerged from his lodge.

The immense Lakota village shrieked with renewed fever as the other war chiefs emerged into the afternoon light. Young boys scurried through camp, bringing extra war ponies in from the herds. Women chattered loudly, no one in particular listening, as they brought forth the weapons their men would use. Out into the sunshine of this battle day came the short-horn or Osage-orange bows, skin quivers filled with long iron-tipped arrows fletched with owl and hawk feathers. Out came axes, knives, and war clubs—some of river stone, others carved wood, a few nail studded like archaic maces. Long buffalo lances shadowed the ground, many more than ten feet long with tiny grooves radiating from the huge iron spear points, the better to drain a victim's blood. Here and there the afternoon light glinted from a firearm, either pistol or rifle. These were white-man weapons bought with blood beyond the Lodge Trail Ridge two winters gone: a glorious fight when many of these same warriors had joined in butchering Fetterman's soldiers, the hundred-in-the-hand.

Last into the light of a battle day came the potent, protective shields, pulled ceremonially from their hide wrappings by the women. Gently each wife smoothed the fluttering feathers and straightened tiny, tinkling brass cones, perhaps brushed a finger over the magic symbols painted across the bull-hide surface or stroked the teeth on a small weasel skull or a badger jaw, perhaps elk milk teeth or a buffalo scrotum filled with private power. These were powerful totems: the strongest of war medicine evoked come this moment of battle. Come now this time to slaughter the half-a-hundred.

"Porcupine!" Roman Nose called out as his face emerged into afternoon light. "Bring the young Bull with you!"

"We are going to kill these white men at long last?" asked High-Backed Bull as they hurried over to the tall war chief.

Roman Nose nodded, bending his head and whispering, "Long ago I vowed never to become a chief—like these old men. Too much like women, I think: much talk, and not enough fighting!"

As some Brule herders brought up the council's ponies, Roman Nose turned slightly, lifting his nose into the air as he was greeted with the fragrance of stewing meat and fry-bread pungent on that warm afternoon breeze. As was the custom at this season of year, the Lakota women had prepared the council's meal outside beneath the hide awning so that the interior of Pawnee Killer's lodge would not be unduly heated beyond the chiefs' endurance. Roman Nose began to rub his stomach, signifying his satisfaction with that ceremonial meal just completed.

"Your belly is as full with meat and bread as are your ears with the words of the old chiefs?" Porcupine asked the Nose.

When the war chief failed to answer, High-Backed Bull turned to look at Roman Nose, finding the war chief's hand frozen where it lay on his belly, a grimace of horror crossing his features, as if he suddenly had trouble swallowing something, as if his throat had constricted.

Three Brule women huddled over two steaming kettles where they had boiled the hump meat Pawnee Killer had served his guests. A third, and smaller, kettle crackled with spitting grease, where the women fried their bread made with flour stolen in those recent raids along the white man's roads and in the white man's settlements.

Bull watched the big chief's eyes narrow as he was handed the reins to his war pony by a Brule pony boy. Still Roman Nose refused to take his gaze from the old Sioux woman who repeatedly speared the fry-bread from her kettle . . . each piece impaled on the tines of an iron fork.

Iron!

In terror Bull instantly realized the seriousness of this transgression, knowing that Roman Nose's personal medicine had been destroyed. The young warrior looked back to his war chief.

His eyes misting in realization, Roman Nose quietly began to keen the soaring notes of his death song. His gaze fell to the ground. Only then did Roman Nose turn away to climb slowly aboard his pony like a man touched-by-the-moon—weakened by grief, crazed with terror.

"What is this?" Tall Bull demanded of Roman Nose, brusquely pushing his way past Bull with his own pony. "We should be celebrating the deaths of the half-a-hundred! Why do I see you crying as if a relative of yours has been killed?"

"Yes, Roman Nose!" chided Chief White Horse as he brought his pony to a halt nearby. "Why this look of mourning, when it will be the white man who will be slaughtered!"

"Long ago," Porcupine began as his war chief continued the wail of death song, "Roman Nose's medicine-helper forbade him from eating any food that had been touched with the white man's iron."

Tall Bull looked from the young warrior again to the face of Roman Nose, confusion on his face. "Yes . . . all Shahiyena know of his powerful medicine calling. But I do not see what that has to—"

"I can use the white man's weapons," Roman Nose interrupted suddenly, his words drenched with overwhelming grief. "I can touch anything with my hands. But I am not to take any food into my body that has been touched by the white man's own medicine!"

"What are you telling us?" White Horse demanded, his own eyes flaring with the first hint of fear.

"Behold!" Roman Nose roared with the fury of a man who had received his death sentence. He pointed to the shadows beneath the awning where the old Lakota woman dipped her fry-bread from the spitting kettle with a crude iron fork. "Behold my death!"

As quickly as he had shown them the cause of his grief, the tall war chief turned away without uttering another word, leading Porcupine and High-Backed Bull, along with many of his faithful Hotamitanyo, veterans all of so much bloodletting over the length and breadth of Kansas.

For the first time that momentous day, a day when all should be celebration, when all should have been total victory in wiping out the half-a-hundred, Bull sensed a tremor in his own medicine, a shaking to the root of his own power, knowing that the potency of Roman Nose's medicine—magic that had seen the Hotamitanyo through countless skirmishes and battles—that medicine was now gone the way of summer snow.

7

B LOOD FROTHED AT the man's lips, his red-flecked orbs gone wall-eyed in pain, as much as in fear of staring into the face of death.

The face of Jubilee Usher.

How Usher always relished this power, momentarily cradling a man's life in his hands—in this case, feeling the slow, unmistakable crackle of cartilage in his victim's windpipe as the trachea collapsed under the ever-tightening vise of the Danite leader's clawlike grip.

"G-g-ghg-ghg . . . ," gurgled the victim, his fingers frantically, desperately raking at Usher's hands as the colonel continued to squeeze all hope of breath reaching the lungs below the crushed windpipe.

Jubilee tore his eyes away from the pasty gray of his victim's swollen face, the man held at arm's length, legs dangling, boots barely skiffing the grassy sand of their camp on the west bank of Muddy Creek, putting Usher's army west of the Green River and Fort Bridger, closing in on Zion.

"Look, ye of little faith—and remember!" Usher roared, finding again a fascination with his own voice at this decibel. "Mark it well on your memories and fail me not. For just such a fate awaits the next of you who would entertain even the faintest thought of trifling with the woman!"

"He didn't . . . didn't mean nothing by it—"

Usher whirled on the speaker, his present victim still dangling at the end of his huge arm, legs dragging behind like a clumsy, ill-stringed marionette out of control. The man had already wet himself, a dark stain down one leg.

"You dare tell me he meant nothing by his sordid transgression?" Usher spat into the speaker's face as the man backed a hurried two steps, suddenly stopped by the solid cordon of his cohorts.

"I found him with her," Jubilee continued, sensing his victim's grip loosen at his wrist. The man was dying, if not already dead. "He had the woman's dress up . . . well, let's just say he had shamefully embarrassed the woman by near disrobing her when I discovered him . . . *surprised him,* those filthy britches of his opened. Ready to commit his nameless sin against this helpless woman. And you say he couldn't help himself!"

"J-just that, Colonel . . . ," the man stammered, dragging his own hand across his throat as his eyes bounced between Usher's and the bloated, ashen face of his friend, "none of us, we ain't had no . . . no women since't—"

"This is not the first time I've demanded chastity from you, men!"

He swallowed and nodded eagerly as a pup who wanted to please a master. "And the woman likely was looking . . . she was—"

"Looking?" Usher bent over to scream in the man's face, spittle flung across the henchman's unwashed, sunburned cheeks. "You mean to tell me you've been casting your eyes at her too?"

"N-no!"

With an audible crunch of the last of the trachea's cartilage, Usher hurled his arm around, flinging the dead man at the end of it into the brash speaker. Screeching in sudden fear as he fell over backward, sprawling on the ground beneath the body, the Danite pushed and struggled to get out from under the corpse of his dead friend as it voided its bowels in a noisy, gaseous explosion. Jubilee stood over him as the man finally clambered to his knees, almost whimpering, staring up into the bright afternoon light until the sun's own rays were eclipsed by the huge form.

"Just whose side are you on in this battle of God versus evil?" Usher inquired, this time so quietly that it caught every man of them by surprise. "This final battle at the end of the world, a battle between the faithful and the heathen? Between the clean"—then he pointed down at the dead man crumpled beneath his feet—"and the unclean. Where stand you?"

"Colonel Usher!"

Jubilee wheeled about at the call, the rest turning with him. A rider came skidding to a halt in a spray of dust that sent golden spires through the slanting afternoon sunlight. The dust settled in a cascading cock's comb that Usher strode through to reach the horseman. Two more riders came to a halt on the heels of the first.

"Heber—what changes have the years wrought in our City of the Saints?"

As Heber Welch slid from the saddle, wind galled and dry as a high-plains buffalo wallow in late summer, Usher caught him up and gave the man an immense, intimate embrace. It was meant only for this sort of trusted friend—the one Jubilee had chosen weeks before to ride ahead without delay, reaching Salt Lake City to determine the condition of affairs for Usher's return after these many years away from the real seat of Mormon power.

Welch's eyes flicked over the rest quickly, then hung on Usher's as Jubilee pulled back to arm's length. "Your father, Colonel . . . he—"

"You saw my father? He was your namesake."

"I am his godson. His namesake."

"So you have been like a brother to me," Jubilee said, studying the man's face for the portent of the news brought him at a gallop.

"He is ill."

Jubilee sensed the very real stab of remorse as the news pierced him through. "I have done my best over the years to correspond with him. To apprise him of my good works . . ." Then his eyes went half-lidded of a sudden, suspicious. "He is still a member of the Council of Twelve?"

"The others have . . . they've removed him, Colonel."

Swallowing that news like something foul, fetid, and raw, Usher gazed into the distance, a bit south of due west. "The rest—they cower before Brigham Young, yes?"

"Your father . . . ," Welch started to say, paused, then finished, "it seems he doesn't want you to come back to the City."

Usher turned back to Welch slowly, his face gone almost expression-less below the smooth skin of his bald head, its long fringe of coal-black, curly hair hung from ear level to drape far past his shoulders like a silken shawl. He pushed a perfumed ringlet behind an ear. "Not back to the City. Why in God's name would my father tell me not to come back?"

Welch gulped slightly. "Your father . . ."

"What does this have to do with my father any longer?"

"Only that your father says the Prophet has . . . has—"

"Has what?"

"Declared you without the grace of the Church."

That seized Usher cold, low in the pit of him. "He has cast me out?"

"Your father told me—"

Jubilee clamped his hands on Welch's shoulders as a man would seize a brother in crisis. "Is he bedridden?"

Welch nodded, his thin lips pursed in resignation. "There is little fight left in him now, Colonel."

Releasing Welch, Usher turned away, staring into the west once more. "Brigham Young waits only for me to return—so that he can excommunicate me. Is that it, friend Heber?"

"Yes," he sighed, as if admitting something reluctantly. "Yes, Colonel."

Usher was a long time in replying. Behind him the men stood quietly for the most part, taking this sudden turn of their communal affairs in stunned silence.

When Jubilee finally did utter a sound, it came behind a long sigh. "The Prophet has become concerned for his own private power, men. Any fool could see that. Brigham Young is casting out all those who pose any threat to his godless usurpation of the Church's power. My father knows this—that's why Young saw him removed from the ruling Council." He whirled on Welch. "Isn't this what my father told you, friend Heber?"

"Y-yes, Colonel."

Usher turned on the rest, some three dozen of his most faithful. "The time will come to test the Prophet's power against my own." Jubilee liked the effect those words had on that band of brigands he had nourished over the years. The eyes of a handful showed some recognition of that power held by Brigham Young. Usher vowed to remember those who showed such outright fear of the man who was of a time the best friend Jubilee had in this world.

But the rest of the faces showed instead the intense glee he himself felt at the thought of pitting his power against the dynasty of Brigham Young. These he would remember as well, and reward them once he had ripped the mantle of the Church from the hands of the false Prophet.

"Young's hands are tired, men. We have no choice but to remove the Church from his control one day soon. Not now—but soon."

"Colonel," Welch reminded. "Your father."

He gazed at Welch. "We will make sure my father, my family, is safe before moving against Young. You can return with word from me that he will be safe."

Heber shook his head. "No. Not that he is in danger. Just that—he worries for you, Colonel. Wants you to stay away, ride far around the City. He wants me to remind you of Brigham Young's power to send gunmen."

"Gunmen? Heber—I was always one of those gunmen. The blood I shed in those early days for the sanctity of the Church. The lives I took in the name of Brigham Young!"

"Your father wants you to stay far from the City."

Usher's stomach leapt with bitter shock. "Ride far around? Just where should we be bound now, if not back to the seat of Zion itself?"

Welch pointed. "South. To the far lands. Where your father suggests you stay and recruit yourself. Until he can regain his health and send word for you to return at last. In triumph."

"South," Jubilee said the word almost reverently. "What in God's name is south of the City of Zion, except . . . desolate waste?"

"Your father told me your family has an old friend there. A man you will remember. A friend who will remember you."

"Yes?"

"You are to stay with his people. Your father said them folks don't get along with Brigham Young neither. Not much anymore."

"Who is this my father suggests we stay with until our appointed hour, friend Heber?"

"Name of Lee."

Usher nodded, a grin forming that lighted his face. His dark eyes crawled across some of his faithful. "Do any of you remember brother Lee?"

He saw a few heads nod in recognition. "Yes. Then you will remember the Mountain Meadows. And how brother Lee led an army of our faithful against a wagon train of vagabond Gentiles come out of Missouri to invade our sacred State of Zion."

"The righteous killed 'em all!" a voice called out.

"Lee took up the sword and killed them all!"

There came a sudden explosion of cheering, a roaring of blood lust remembered.

"Men, women, and children! Yes all!" Jubilee shouted above the melee. Then as suddenly he shushed the crowd into silence. With a long, mighty arm he dragged Welch beneath his shoulder, clutching him there fraternally.

"Yes, my faithful. For the time being we must wait, forcing us to ride south . . . and there we will stay within the bosom of our own kind. At dawn we ride for the land of John Doyle Lee."

By the time Tall Bull, White Horse, and Pawnee Killer had led their blood-hot warriors south to the Dog Soldier camp beside the shallow flow of the Plum River, the sun was nestling into its western sleep. High-Backed Bull sensed they would not be marching down on the white men this day.

As quickly he decided to ask a few others to join him on a black-night raid on the white man's horses. If no others would join him, he had decided he would ride alone. No matter what, the young Shahiyena warrior was not about to wait out the night before spilling white blood.

As the war chiefs gazed over the combined forces of Shahiyena, Lakota, and Arapaho warriors, numbering more than ten-times-ten, and ten times over again, a thousand horsemen in all, they reluctantly gave in to the failing, red-earth light of that summer day. No man in fear of his own soul would consider fighting at night. If a warrior were killed during a battle after the sun had disappeared from the sky, his spirit would forever roam this earth, unable to walk the Seamon, the sacred road of the dead. He would not spend his forever days beyond the stars in Seyan. No man dared tempt such a fate.

That is, no man but High-Backed Bull.

"The rest won't ride until the sun climbs out of its bed," Bull told the first friend he felt he could trust with the horse raid.

Wrinkled Wolf's eyes grew big. "You aren't waiting?"

"We will go as soon as it grows dark enough," the Bull answered. "There won't be but a fragment of moon tonight—"

"We will get caught!"

"I won't!" Bull whispered harshly, slapping his chest. "There are white men wearing scalps this night, scalps that I want to carry on my belt. I want to take that hair before the others have the chance. Are you with me?"

Wrinkled Wolf nodded reluctantly. "Yes. You said I would get the American horses we take."

"You, and your brother, Four Bulls Moon. Get him to come along with us too. You will share the white man's horses. I don't want any—only the scalps. Only to cut out tongues and eyes. To hack off hands and feet, to slash off the manhood parts and stuff them in the lying mouths. That is all I want this night. Go. Get your brother. See if he has friends who still have courage to ride against the white man in darkness."

As High-Backed Bull waited in a plum thicket at the edge of the Dog Soldier camp, his pony picketed nearby in readiness, tearing noisily at the summer-cured grass, the warrior listened as the great Shahiyena village assumed a festive atmosphere. With news of the white riders drawing close behind them, every man sixteen summers and older had prepared for battle, readying his medicine, caring for his weapons. Most of the firearms now possessed by these warriors had been spoils of the Fetterman Massacre two winters before: single-shot muzzle-loading Springfield muskets. Only a handful owned repeaters captured in recent raids on the white man's roads.

In this merry village of Dog Soldiers the Shahiyena hosted Pawnee Killer's Brule as everyone—men and women, children as well—reveled the coming night before they would resume their march to wipe out the half-a-hundred. Word spread from fire to fire this evening that the fighting force stalking the villages had camped no more than ten miles downriver, within easy reach before the sun rose to heat the ground where the mighty horsemen would spill white blood in one swift charge come morning.

The thunderous horde of horsemen would surround and attack the half-a-hundred, the camps cheered. No more to it than squashing a tick grown plump and lazy between your fingers, watching the blood trickle and ooze over your hand. A momentary distraction only, thought High-Backed Bull—then the warrior bands would continue as planned on their sweep of their ancient buffalo country.

Along with Roman Nose, chiefs Tall Bull and White Horse had sworn to stop the smoke-belching medicine horse that rode on the iron tracks. The Shahiyena bands had joined Pawnee Killer's Lakota for the greatest of all raids against the white man's settlements as summer began to abandon this high land. With the coming of autumn on that full moon following the first frosts licking the prairie ponds with ice, there would come the planned sweep through the white man's villages. Enough of them now to drive the white man back from the buffalo ground for a long, long time to come.

Porcupine had told his young friend what the war chiefs had decided on for the coming time of war. No more hit-and-miss raids along the roads nor striking an outlying settlement. Instead, the Lakota and Shahiyena had decided to ride toward the east in bands of fifty to a hundred warriors at most, scattering out to do their killing, leaving no white man alive, carrying his women and children away into captivity. Leaving the white man's lodges in smoking ruin. Driving off all his horses and slow-buffalo for their own.

For but a short time would they raid and kill and burn, while that full moon shrank to half its size. Then all warrior bands were to turn from their destruction and point the noses of their ponies north, to journey toward the land where Red Cloud himself defended the ancient hunting grounds west of the sacred Bear Butte. No more could the soldiers bother them there, for word had it on the moccasin telegraph that the white man was abandoning that country, leaving his forts behind, from the dirt fort on the Powder River, to the one high on the Sheep River.* The red man had won!

But High-Backed Bull had sternly refused to ride with them when the time came. He had decided his destiny could not lie in a land where the white man would not be found. Instead, with narrow, hate-slitted eyes, the young warrior had vowed to stay close to the land of the whites—there the better to kill them, one at a time . . . spilling their blood until he once more ran across the one white man he wanted more than all the others.

Until at last Bull could gaze into the fear-glazed eyes of the one who had fathered him.

* Bighorn River

8

"IT IS COLD, High-Backed Bull," whimpered the young warrior to his friend walking beside him.

He was shivering too with the retreat of the sun, but still his blood ran hot, his heart burning in his ears as they drew farther and farther from the Shahiyena camp. "Soon enough, Little Hawk—you and Starving Elk won't have time to think about the cold of this night."

The two Cheyenne brothers walking their horses downstream from the village circles with the Bull had been on many raids against the white man's wagon roads and his outflung settlements of dirt-scratchers. But not one of them had ever attacked a camp of white men who had so boldly stalked them. Of a sudden, the Bull held his hand up and stopped in the darkness, listening.

"I hear it too," said Starving Elk.

"The white men aren't coming to attack at night?" asked the young Little Hawk.

He was certain they would not. Yet the white man was known for often doing the unexpected. As the quiet plodding of hooves drew closer, he held his breath, following the sound around the brow of the nearby hill, knowing the horsemen would not dare expose themselves along the rolling skyline.

When he squinted into the starlit darkness, the Bull was certain he could not see a thing. Yet when he did not try so hard, in fact did not look directly at what he wanted most to see, then he saw them: movement at first, then the shadowy forms of horses, the smoky men atop moving slowly, yet steadily downstream.

And just as his own mind was attempting to sort out why the enemy probing at the warrior camps would not be marching upstream, the half-dozen horsemen halted, and the buzzing of their talk carried through the still summer night's air.

He thought he saw the fluttering of feathers atop the head of one. Then the rustling fan of unbraided hair washing out from the shoulders of another. It all made him bold enough to call out.

"Who is there, in the darkness?"

"Shahiyena?"

"Yes."

"Burnt Thigh, we are. We thought you to be enemies."

The Brule Lakota urged their ponies back along the curve of the hill toward the three who remained on foot beside their animals.

"I thought you might be some of the white men, come to see how strong we are," the Bull told the others as they halted before him. "My name is High-Backed Bull."

The leader nodded. He was young too: that much the Bull could tell of the cheeks and nose under the dim starlight.

"Our camp, like yours, is celebrating the victory to come tomorrow when the sun arises from its bed," the Lakota said quietly. "I am Bad Tongue."

"The fight will be over all too soon," the Bull replied sourly, perhaps a little too sharply. "And there are too few scalps to go around."

"You wanted to take some scalps tonight?" asked the Brule.

"We came for the white man's big horses," Starving Elk replied quickly.

"I came to take a few scalps for myself before they are gone in the morning," the Bull boasted. "Brought down like the buffalo cows that they are, hamstrung by the quick-footed wolf pack."

"Ponies and scalps," said another of the Lakota. "You come with us and we'll find enough for all of us."

The Bull turned to the two brothers.

When Little Hawk had nodded to his older brother, Starving Elk said, "Yes. Let's join the Burnt Thigh." He gazed out at the night sky, shivering, perhaps with more than the cold.

The Bull turned back to the Lakota leader. "One must be very brave to fight both the white man and the night spirits. It is good to have friends along, Bad Tongue."

"Yes," the Brule replied. "Good to have friends along. Come, ride with us."

The three Shahiyena mounted their ponies, the two brothers on animals they had crept into the herd to catch without a sound—for had either of them been discovered, the punishment would be severe. The old ones and war chiefs wanted no foolish coup-hunters alerting the white men prior to the massed attack at dawn.

They inched over hill after hill, searching for the camp, looking for the faint glow of the white man's fires, stopping from time to time to listen for the snuffling of his horses and mules, to put ears to the ground while others held their ponies quiet, to sniff the air for the distinct smell of fresh offal dropped by those weary animals driven in the chase up the Plum River. No sight of the white man here. No sound to hint they were drawing close. No smell to betray the big animals.

Sandy, grass-shrouded hill after bare knob they climbed until—

"High-Backed Bull!" Bad Tongue hissed sharply in his crude, un-practiced Cheyenne. When the oldest of the Shahiyena drew alongside at the crest of the hill and knelt with the others, Bad Tongue began his hands-dancing, talking in sign.

"Yes, I can see!" High-Backed Bull answered with his hands, his heart leaping, his blood throbbing at his temples. Quickly he glanced at Starving Elk and Little Hawk, their young heads bobbing eagerly in anticipation.

Still far off across the starlit prairie twinkled the faintest glimmers of light: enough to see that they were a handful of fires, their dim, bloodlike glowing beneath the star-dark skies. White-man fires gone low with neglect. He knew that the white horsemen would likely be asleep.

"They will have guards on their herd," the Bull said softly.

Bad Tongue agreed with a nod. "We will not have to worry about their guards."

"Into their horses and drive them out again before the guards know what bad wind blew through camp," the second Brule added.

"Let's go close enough to see these soldiers?" Little Hawk asked.

Bad Tongue turned on the youngest of that group. "Yes, my little friend. We will go close enough for you to see all the white men."

"When we have driven off these horses, then we can ride back to wait for the others to attack at dawn?" Starving Elk added. On his face was written that look of apprehension, as plain as his earth-paint.

The Sioux warriors stood with Bad Tongue, all five as one.

"We Lakota did not come to *see* the white man, my Shahiyena friends. We came to take his horses."

"You may come to take the horses and mules," sneered High-Backed Bull. "The Shahiyena came to take scalps this night. Do you ride with me, Starving Elk?"

Starving Elk took a deep breath, looking at his younger brother. "I . . . I go to steal the horses. My brother, Little Hawk, can choose if he wishes to return to camp now—before the attack."

"No! I will ride with Starving Elk. He is my brother and I will follow him."

Without another word Bad Tongue led the half-dozen Sioux atop their barebacked ponies, unfurling blankets, some unrolling stiff pieces of rawhide brought with them. One even pulled a large hand drum from a coyote-skin cover he had slung over his shoulder.

"What is this you are doing with these things, Bad Tongue?" asked High-Backed Bull as he pulled his old Walker Colt's revolver from the belt around his waist.

The Sioux warrior glared at his Cheyenne companion. "Make ready, Shahiyena. For the Burnt Thigh are making ready to put the white man afoot!"

"*Aiyeeee!*" shouted the Bull as he nudged his pony past the Lakota horsemen, heels pounding his animal into a lumbering gallop. "The Shahiyena are not content to take horses. I have come to make the white man's knees turn to water—to let him hear the sound of my war music!"

In the darkest time of that night, Usher found the one he was looking for among the recumbent, formless mounds beneath the blankets, their feet to the fires in that camp on the west bank of the Muddy River. He stood a moment more above him, listening to the tone of the snoring, only to be sure. Then he knelt and shook the man awake.

The sleeper came up startled, lunging for the pistol at his side as he blinked his eyes at the huge man hulking over him.

"Strickler, it's your colonel." He put a finger to his lips and motioned the man to follow.

Jubilee arose and moved off, knowing Oran Strickler would not fail to follow. Satisfied when he heard the sound of blankets coming off and the creak of cold leather boots scrunching across the sandy soil behind him.

When he had stopped among the cottonwood and turned, Usher hissed, "I have come to trust you as much as any of these."

The man hawked up some night-gather in his throat, flung it into the darkness, then replied, "I been with you from the very start, Colonel. I was riding along with the same wagon train when we was took."

"You got as much stake in all of this as I, don't you, brother Strickler." Usher could tell just what effect that endearing term had on the man. It had quickly softened the harsh night edges of the Danite's face.

"Perhaps—like you say—it is time for a change in Deseret. The American government, its army sent out to aim its guns down on us—something should've been done long ago."

Usher placed a hand on the tall, thin man's shoulder. "We need only to show the many others in Zion the error of Brigham's ways. Was a time I would have followed Brigham through the fires of hell."

"We done that, Colonel. And we're on our way back again, by damned!"

He snorted, then threw a thumb over his shoulder. "Back there, on our backtrail—we all know we've got that sodbuster following us."

"The woman's husband."

"He's not her husband!" Usher snapped, then composed himself a bit. "She's mine by rights of all divine law now. By rights of time, by rights of angelic purpose, by right of might."

"But don't it bother you that this sonofabitch just keeps coming on when he ought'n to know better, Colonel?"

Usher chuckled softly, the breath before his face steamy in the cold. "It will bother me much less when that man is taken care of—for good and all time."

He nodded. "That where I come in, is it, sir?"

"That's right, my brother." He reached overhead and snapped a narrow twig from a branch. This he waved in an arc across their Muddy

Creek camp. "Take three with you. No—make it five more. And ride back the way we came. Likely he is this side of the pass by now."

"Somewhere between South Pass and the Green, I'd lay a wager on."

"No money required. Only the man's blood."

"We'll go in the morning."

Jubilee shook his head. "No. I want you to find your five and go now. Saddle up, draw your rations for how long you calculate you'll be gone—and leave now."

Oran Strickler swallowed hard. Then scratched at the thick, un-shaved growth across his dirty cheek. "You want me bring you something back?"

"If you can do it."

He waited for Usher to elaborate. When the colonel did not, Strickler asked, "What you want? His scalp? His balls? Maybeso his whole head, eh?"

Usher draped a big arm over Strickler's shoulder. "No. If you can, I want you to help me reunite the sodbuster with the woman. For just a few minutes, I want to be able to look into both their faces and see the looks they will give one another, how they will regard me—before I kill him. Slowly. Slowly."

"You . . . you figure on killing him right in front of his . . . uh, the woman?" Strickler corrected himself.

"Yes. As simple as that," Usher replied. "Now. You have your orders. Bring him to me alive. Do not—on pain of death—do not return to me without this sodbuster alive."

Strickler swallowed again, turned, and disappeared back into the dim glow of the dying fires. Usher listened to the snoring, the footsteps halting here, then there, listened to the unintelligible, whispered voices, heard the faintest betrayal of the rolling of blankets and the shuffling of bodies out of camp toward the horses. Into the darkness. And it grew quiet once more around Jubilee Usher.

Deathly quiet.

He had chosen the right man. And Oran Strickler would choose his men just as wisely, Jubilee felt certain.

Just as certain that one day he would sit in the Prophet's chair at the center of Zion, leader of God's chosen people.

His only doubt lay with her. By watching with her own eyes the killing of her husband by Jubilee's hand—would she give up all hope of rescue, all hope of returning to that sodbuster and their former life together?

Only then would she relent and give herself totally, irrevocably, irretrievably over to Jubilee Usher.

9

FAR, FAR AWAY on the distant edge of the awakening land a thin smear of gray bubbled along the horizon like marrow scum risen to the top of blood soup brought to the boil.

High-Backed Bull and Bad Tongue had led the others around the base of the bluffs and ridges in this rugged, naked country heaved up with dark monoliths and black blottings against the paling, starlit sky that wheeled nonstop overhead in the land's incessant crawl toward the coming day of blood on the sand by the Plum River. Once they had stopped to water the ponies, watchful not to let the animals have too much, only enough to slake their thirst. Then the horsemen crossed to the north bank of the river on foot, remounted, and set out again to the east.

The big bear among the stars lay but a hand's width from the horizon when Bull touched Bad Tongue's arm and signaled the rest to halt behind them. He sniffed at the air.

"Smell," Bull whispered.

The rest drew the cold, high desert air into their noses noiselessly. The Brule said, "Fire."

He nodded to Bad Tongue. "The breeze has come around out of the south." Bull pointed. "Beyond those ridges, we will find them."

"The big American horses," Bad Tongue growled in his poor Cheyenne.

"The half-a-hundred who have dared follow our camps," Bull corrected. "The half-a-hundred who will lose their scalps for it."

"Do not spill your own blood on this ground," Bad Tongue admonished. "So anxious to spill the white man's are you."

Bull snorted derisively. "The rest of you can go get what you want now. And I will ride in for what I came for."

Bad Tongue clamped a hand on the Shahiyena's arm to stay the Dog Soldier. "Porcupine and Roman Nose—any war chief would say for one or two of us to spy on the white man's camp first before riding in blind."

Bull gazed at the starlit face of the Brule and could find no reason to dispute the Lakota's fighting wisdom. "All right. You and me."

"On foot."

Bull nodded and slid from his pony, handing the rawhide rein to Starving Elk. He strode off without waiting for Bad Tongue, nor did he look back. He only heard the warrior off to his left.

At the crest of the second ridge, the odor of burning embers, of fried meat, the wind-carried fragrance of fresh horse droppings, all became so strong that they bellied to the side of the slope rather than crawl directly at the top. There below, a matter of a few flights of an arrow, lay the eerie reddish glow of the white man's camp. From time to time dark shadows blotted the crimson into the black of the prairie momentarily until the glowing embers of their old fires reappeared. Perhaps they were the enemy's pickets moving back and forth between the warriors and the distant fire pits. Perhaps some of the bigger shadows were animals.

A snuffle, then another, was heard in the middle distance. Most of the animals were actually grazing closer to them than High-Backed Bull had expected: off to his right hand and just below the base of the high bluff that overlooked the white man's camp. He smiled, tapping Bad Tongue in their mutual silence—then pointed down to the main body of the herd as one of the mules released a caustic, metallic bray. There came an uneasy shuffling of hooves before all fell silent again.

"There is one guard I can see," Bad Tongue whispered. "That means there will be at least two."

Bull agreed. "At least one you cannot see." He pushed himself backward until he was behind the edge of the slope and got to his feet. "Now the rest of you can go steal your big American horses."

Bad Tongue raised himself before the Shahiyena. "And you—you can take advantage of our noise, High-Backed Bull. Looking for scalps to take."

In silence they hurried back to the rest, coming out of the darkness as the gray boiling back in the east broadened, stretching into a more definitive line that strung itself from north to south. Full darkness would not last much longer. It was time to strike.

He mounted while Bad Tongue explained the position of the horse herd to the rest. Bull looked at the two brothers. While they listened to the Brule, their eyes were nonetheless on High-Backed Bull. He waited until Bad Tongue finished his clipped instructions, then nodded at Starving Elk.

"You and Little Hawk—go with the Burnt Thigh. Help them run off the horses."

"Where are you going?" Starving Elk asked, his voice a pitch higher in the starlit darkness.

"I will meet you across the river. On the south side when you have started the horses and mules, driving them back to our camp."

He would wait for no more questions. Bull reined away abruptly, moving east along the base of the sharp-sloped ridge. Without any thought other than instinct, he decided to race into the white man's camp, charging among the half-a-hundred from the east, as the rest raced into the herd. That way, he considered, the white men would have their attention on the west when he came lunging up their backs. No doubt he would be backlit by the sun's coming—but High-Backed Bull calculated that the surprise he would create would be more than enough to outweigh that danger to himself.

At the first break in the bony ridges that reeked of alkali, the Shahiyena brought himself up short, finding that he had not come east far enough to begin his attack. Instead, Bull found himself still to the west of the crimson fire pits and those few shadows moving against the pale, red lights. Still, he was closer to the enemy camp now than before—able for the first time to make out clearly the black mounds of sleeping men curled in their blanket cocoons across the gray ground.

He reined about and urged the pony on east.

It was then that his ears brought him the sound of muted voices from the camp, brought him the first hint of pony hooves hammering the cold night wind that tortured this high desert land.

Bull smiled and hurried his pony toward the graying east just as the night split with the bellow of a white man, a warning from the far side of camp where Bad Tongue and the others would be making their attack.

"There's one of the sonsabitches!"

Unprepared that the rest should be discovered, Bull was forced to bring his pony around sharply, sawing the rawhide rein so savagely, he nearly spilled the pony. On the far side of the crimson fire pits and the dark mounds erupting from the ground, a white man had bolted to his feet, throwing a rifle to his shoulder.

"Don't shoot!" another hollered, up and sprinting for the first shadow.

Bull sensed his heart rise to his throat, the blood's fiery cadence hammering in his ears as he sat there atop his pawing animal, the wind grown strong in his face, the light coming up on his left shoulder, and the camp below him exploding into life. More of the mounds stirred. Harsh, whispered voices exchanged words among those who had been gathered feet to the fires only moments before, abruptly brought to life as the hammer of hooves on the sunbaked prairie brought its sunrise song to the unsuspecting white men.

Then the riders broke over the last rise. In the space of a moment, all was a furious blur, like a reflection on the surface of a wind-chapped pond. Bull saw them against the horizon in the graying light, more like wisps of shadow, like curls of greasy smoke from some creosote-soaked sagewood fire—black and mobile, stark and streaking between the carbonite earth they moved across and the starry sky that served as their only backdrop.

One after another each shadowy form raced fluid as spring water off a midstream boulder, sliding down the high ground on horseback, feathers in a breeze-whipped spray clustered at each warrior's head as the eight emerged from the top of that far knoll. The sky oozed red of a sudden, smothering the gray of night, coming the dusty crimson of sunrise. Below the riders as those horsemen drove their animals down the long slope, beginning to screech at the top of their lungs, the valley of the Plum River lay drenched in bloody gray light.

"Here come the rest of 'em!" came a shout from among those at the far side of the white man's camp.

Bull watched two more of the enemy bolt into motion as if they had been shot out of a gun. The curses of those coming awake of a sudden were now lost among the pounding of footsteps and the hammering of unshod pony hooves distinct on the cold morning wind.

The war cries cracked the air like fragmented shards of thunder, distant but drawing closer with every beat of a man's heart.

"They're after the horses, men!" a high-pitched voice cried out from among those on the west.

For Bull it was time to ride.

That same voice again hurled itself over the throbbing camp, men and animals startled into motion, curses and orders and shouts and cries of confusion creating pure bedlam.

"Turn out! The bastards are after our horses. Turn out! Get hold of the—"

For Bull the white war chief's last few words were drowned under the onrush of the pony thieves. Bad Tongue and his Brule, along with Starving Elk and Little Hawk, all tore into the west side of the white man's camp, every last throat of theirs shouting and shrieking. They flapped blankets and rattled dried buffalo hides, one of the Lakota beating on that small drum, the rest blowing on eagle wing-bone whistles they carried about their necks—making noise enough for twice their number.

A new voice bawled as Bull tore into the camp unheard for the deafening racket. "Get your asses up and moving, boys! Indians!"

"Turn out, men!" someone else ordered, a tall, thin one suddenly in the midst of the camp a heartbeat later.

It was he that Bull chose for his first ride-down on that sandy ground, as the figures ahead of him dropped to their knees, throwing rifles to their shoulders, spitting bright, blinding orange flame from the muzzles, a noise no louder than the pounding of his own heart in his ears.

White men—and he had his pick of them as he leapt the pony over a mound of baggage.

"I dropped that bastard!" someone yelled far ahead across the camp.

Then of a sudden the first of the white men turned, finding the lone warrior among them, the stone club at the end of his arm swinging in a red-orange, dizzying blur out of the coming sunlight.

"Jesus-God! The Injuns behind us too!"

Ahead of him the white men dived this way and that, some struggling to control their rearing horses as he rode them down. Again and again he swung the iron-studded war club, driving it at any target: white enemy, his horses and mules.

Across camp, on the west, one of the red horsemen trembled, then toppled from his pony onto the gray, unforgiving plain, where he was lost in the darkness of the grassy sage.

"Less'n a dozen of the bastards!"

"Hold those horses! Hold those—"

Bull's throat hurt with the cry he bellowed at the white men—unable to remember when he had started to holler, knowing he had never stopped once he had begun that charge into their camp.

"Goddammit—shoot when you got something to shoot at!"

Bad Tongue and the rest of the warriors were rushing toward Bull, having reached the far western edge of the fire dotted camp itself, having spooked the big horses and the braying mules.

Screeching horsemen rattled their rawhide and blew their shrieking, frightening death whistles, joining the whinnying horses and brass-lunged pack animals, along with the sporadic gunshots from the pickets—that entire camp thundered into instant pandemonium. Every white man had come to his feet and gone among the animals, furiously pulling at hobbles and reins. Likely some of the white enemy had lashed their horses to their belts through the night rather than trust to picket pins. As Bull charged among them screeching his war song, some of the white men waved pistols at him, seeming unsure of their shots as others stomped at the coals of their fires to kill the bloody backlight.

His pony collided against a big American horse, almost going down, High-Backed Bull nearly unhorsed as the pony careened sideways, then regained its legs. He whirled about, sawing the single rein.

"Get the sonofabitch!"

A bullet whistled past, close enough to call out his name with its high-pitched whisper. He sensed the heat of its passing flight. Surrounded for the moment by the animals yanked and prodded, rearing and snorting, High-Backed Bull pounded his heels against the pony's flanks as more of the blurred shadows closed in on him.

Horses yanked their handlers about like grass-filled antelope-skin dolls, legs and arms flung akimbo. A white man scampered by, vainly clinging to the reins of his horse that succeeded in dragging its owner through a glowing fire pit. The ground around the yelping white man erupted into a shower of red-orange pricks of light.

In the sudden swirl of blinding motion as the cursing men closed in on Bull, one of their big horses bucked, knocking aside a white man holding another two of the animals . . . and into that sudden aperture the warrior shot as quickly as the owl snatches up a den mouse in its claw.

His leap through the breach blinded him momentarily. Gunfire roared in his ears, the bright, flaming blasts of the enemy's guns both blinding him, then lighting his way through the camp as he raced to join the others. Rattling hides and crying out their yipping, brave war songs, the eight swept off the western horizon between the river and those low, inky bluffs north of that camp—come ablaze in sunrise's crimson-tinged whirl of noise and the clatter of hooves.

He pulled among the horsemen with his next ragged breath—his throat hurting from the strain of his cries. Bad Tongue had turned them all at the bank of the shallow river, leaping their ponies into the water, sand erupting in billowing cascades, droplet diamonds splaying from every flying hoof like scarlet mica chips in their crossing at the west end of a narrow sandbar. At its far end stood a lone cottonwood, perhaps no taller than a man.

Yet the eight young warriors urged no herd ahead of them as they clambered up the south bank of the river and plunged through the plum brush and swamp willow, where the shouts of the white men and the crackle of their guns faded on the far shore behind them.

Two only could they claim: a pair of the enemy's ribby mules noisily dragged their picket lines through the brush, frightened and braying, with the warriors close on their tail roots.

Two only. Bad Tongue's stampede had proved a failure.

Angrily Bull reined up, bringing his pony around. He watched the backs of the other young warriors disappear to the west, heading upstream with their two hard-won prizes. They had really won nothing at all—save for alerting the enemy.

"What'd they get?" a voice bellowed across the river.

"Two of the damn mules!"

"Ammunition?"

"No, sir."

A new voice warned, "They'll come now that it's light, Major!"

"Saddle up, men!" the high-pitched voice shouted above the clamor of cursing men, their frightened animals still being quieted. "Sergeant, have these men stand to horse!"

As the white men sorted themselves out on the far side of the river, Bull turned slowly, letting his ears guide the position and pitch of his head, sensing something coming. Then, there it was. He listened to the distant coming of thunder: a sound to stir a warrior's heart.

On the far bank it appeared very few of the enemy heard it too—its faint presage given birth out of the western horizon. Now his young heart leapt, soaring with its day-coming song of death.

"Lookee here, Major!" a ragged baritone voice rang out across the shallow river.

"Damn you, Trudeau!" sang the high-pitched white war chief. "No one gave you the right to scalp that—"

"No one tell Pierre not to take scalp! Sioux, it is—"

"Get that damned thing out of my face!"

"At least it means I kil't one of the red bastards!"

"Stand to horse!"

"Listen! You hear that?" someone asked at last. "Listen, goddammit!"

"I do. Goddamn!"

"Major! Best be moving your boys now!" one of them bawled loudly, already yanking his horse behind him.

Then Bull felt the hair rise on his arms as the rumble grew closer, like distant thunder rolling toward them out of the west. As he took his eyes off the far bank to gaze quickly to the east, the far end of the sandbar grew pale in the coming light, where the lone cottonwood stood.

"They're coming!"

"To the island!"

"Cross to the island!" arose the chorus from more of the white throats.

Its urgent call was immediately echoed by the rest of the half-a-hundred in tatters of voices and the hammering of white men clambering to their saddles.

"Make the island!"

The heart-stopping thunder of more than a thousand hooves hammered the sun-cured prairie.

Bull thought he could see them now, at long last after the breath-robbing seconds of waiting, able only to hear their coming. The pulsing horde emerged from the dark like some swelling, ghostly apparition Bull couldn't quite see yet—not really. More so did he sense its coming.

As the white men bolted from their camp beside the river, plunging their horses into the shallow water, fighting their way toward the narrow sandbar, others stood hollering orders, waving the rest into the river as the first phalanx of mounted warriors erupted with star-flung muzzle flashes, diamond light pricking the horizon of that crimson dawn.

Bullets whistled overhead, splattering in the water. The nearby river bluffs echoed the war cries from hundreds of throats.

"There they are! They're on us now!"

"God—will you look at 'em!"

Then there arose yelps right across the river from Bull. Some of Roman Nose's or Pawnee Killer's warriors had chosen not to join in the general charge on the island, but instead had swarmed down across the flat near the river where the white men had been camped around their fire pits only moments before. These daring, willing-to-die warriors plopped to their bellies among the willow and plum brush only yards from that sandbar, there to begin their sniping at the white men milling about the narrow sandbar, confused and leaderless for the moment, their horses stumbling on the uneven, river-washed sand.

"Shoot the goddamned horses!" one of the enemy yelled.

"Bring 'em down!" came the echo again and again.

"Shoot the horses!"

As bullets whined over the willow where he hid, Bull watched the white men put their pistols to work, dropping their big American horses.

"This will turn Bad Tongue's heart to fire," he whispered to himself as he led his pony upstream quickly. "These white men kill what Bad Tongue wanted so badly."

Behind him the hundreds of brown horsemen reached the upstream end of the sandbar, where they dropped to the far side of their ponies in a spray of grit and watery jewels, firing beneath the animals' necks at the enemy trapped on the island. Here and there the white men began to return some fire poorly, but most started to dig in behind the heaving bodies of their dying horses, clawing frantically at the sand with their hands to form rifle pits.

In the red light's dance across the valley that dawn, the full coming day reverberating off the ridges to the west, echoing with the curses and pain-filled yammer of the white men, the war cries and high-pitched victory calls of the eagle wing-bone whistles, the angry bellow of the horses and mules going down in a bloody spray of gore and bowel-ruptured, urine-soaked sand—Bull decided this had to be the most beautiful dance he had ever witnessed.

Now he had only to take his scalps from the dead when this day's crimson dance was done.

10

H E GNAWED ON the bone, the same bone the big staghound clamped its jaws around, growling, hissing at him menacingly. Jealously wanting the bone for itself.

Jubilee Usher laughed, stroking the crown of the animal's head. That only provoked an even angrier growl for its keeper, a growl drenched with all the more threat.

Glaring into the yellowed eyes of the vise-jawed staghound from his end of the bone, Usher met the dog's gaze unflinchingly, knowing as he did that there were others gathering at the periphery of his vision to watch the standoff. They were interrupting their breakfast this morning as the colonel's army went about striking camp, loading the four wagons and ambulance for the next leg of their journey back into the land of Zion. Those who had been with him from the start already knew they weren't bound for family and friends among the Saints in the City of Deseret. At last night's firelit meeting—half church service for the faithful, half an occasion to study his flock for the weaker of his avenging angels—Jubilee had begged understanding and obedience.

Without fail, without stop did Usher complete this chore of leadership: studying his ranks for those who might buckle at the knees this close to home, this close to all that they might remember.

Now more than ever Jubilee needed to be sure of those closest to him. Now that word from the center of the faith said that Brigham Young drew his own faithful to him—as if the Prophet himself sensed the coming danger in those who flocked to the Usher clan.

So it was that Jubilee had moved this band of gun-toting, iron-hardened men last night beneath the stars, made this rough lot of scarred, unsentimental men get down on their knees as he strode among them, lightly touching their heads with his anointed hand, dipping that hand empowered by God Himself in water he told them had come from the river Jordan in far-off Palestine. From the land of Christ, he instructed, the land where the Gentiles of old had crucified the one and only Lord—hung him upon a cross to die in sweet, redeeming agony—before that Christ arose three days later so that he might appear to the ancients in America, their very own ancestors: the chosen Saints of this Latter Day.

"When a man moves his hand with the will of God—then he of rights will be called the Prophet of our beloved Church!" Jubilee had told them. "But . . . when that man fails time and time again to raise his hand against the Gentiles who caused to suffer the Christ our Lord—the very Gentiles who persecuted and hanged Joseph Smith and his brother Hyrum—then that man no longer carries the will of God mantled about his shoulders!"

"Brigham Young has failed, Colonel!"

He had smiled when that voice raised itself out of the firelit darkness, row upon row of the tight crescent of his faithful gathered at the flaps of his tent. He moved again among them, touching, anointing their heads from the carved clay bottle, blessing them every one, praising them for their good, godly works of terror and bloodletting among the Gentiles, telling each of the place carved out for him in the land of immortal spirits as reward for his defense of the Kingdom against the heathens in this wicked, temporal land of America.

To a man they had willingly pledged themselves to him anew. Impassioned, pledging their service, they would give their lives up for his, so that he might one day right the path of the one true Church for all time and the glory of God's plan on earth. Their flesh was all any one of them had to offer now that they vowed to abandon the circle of family and friends they would leave behind in the land of Deseret controlled by the crazed and jealous, power-hungry Brigham Young.

"Let Young's most dangerous fear now become his greatest undoing!" Jubilee had roared at them, his eyes finding those of George, the Negro manservant who dutifully stood nearby, outside the wall tent where the woman lay.

He knew George did not believe in the way of the Church, yet steadfastly believed nonetheless in Jubilee Usher. It did not matter, Usher had decided long ago. For, after all, for those of color—the black African, the red-skinned Indian, and the yellow-hued Oriental—the feet of none were yet taking the right path. None but the white man had been blessed by the Christ and his mighty angels come to visit ancient America. From time to time people of color were placed in Usher's path to serve him and the greater good Jubilee was to play in this life on earth.

Still grappling with the dog, with one hand now he reached behind him and found the plate of bones George had collected at last night's supper. Seizing the biggest his fingers could blindly determine, Usher presented his favorite hound a dilemma. Slowly he brought the big bone up before the animal's eyes, where it could plainly see the temptation. All the while the dog never loosened its tension on the bone held perilously between it and its master's jaws. Jubilee watched the eyes, glorying in that instantaneous indecision he caused the animal. He saw the first flicker of bestial desire flame into jealousy, then the moment of action as the hound opened its great, salivating jaws and lunged for the bone Usher held in his hand.

As quickly Usher flicked away the temptation.

Rather than chase down the new treat, the hound immediately lunged back for the bone it had been tussling with its master for—yet it too was gone. Usher had risen. All of it in smooth, seemingly orchestrated movements, calculated precisely. Knowing animals the way he did, perhaps Usher was able to read eyes the way he did better than any man he knew—to act before others had time to react.

The menacing growl rumbled from the animal's throat as it rocked farther back on its legs, as if ready to spring with its teeth exposed, staring up at its master now in anger, robbed of not just one, but both the bones.

"You'd love to gnaw on my flesh, wouldn't you, Alexander?" he said, reaching out to pat the top of the great head.

The hound snapped at the hand. And as quickly that huge, manicured hand batted the dog's head aside with a ringing snap. It lay whimpering a moment, sprawled in the grass, then picked itself up, a totally different being from what it had been a moment before: now contrite and pleading for its master's beneficence. Usher stroked its neck, presenting the hound the bone.

"Go on now, Alexander. There are more where that came from."

Jubilee straightened and held his hands out before him. George hurried up, a china bowl cradled between his ebony paws like a pale offering of a full moon in the blackness of the firmament, a crisp hand towel draped over one forearm. Usher washed hands and face, dabbed them dry, then dropped the towel over the Negro's shoulder.

"Time I should awake the woman," he told no one in particular, as those who had gathered began to move off of their own accord, back to the breaking of camp, the loading of the wagons, and the saddling of horses brought in from the good grass down by the river where they had been hobbled of last night.

Yes, he thought. How he loved gazing upon her skin in the morning, slowly disrobing her, taking her hands and placing them around his own flesh to arouse himself, bring himself to readiness. At long last across these years, he had finally brought her flesh back to a pristine, milky purity by keeping her out of the sun—and the horrendous toll that it took on a woman's beauty, aging her before her time. Usher had instead stopped the clock, allowing the woman only the shade of a tree, the depths of the shadowy ambulance, or the protection of their oiled tent. With such vigilant protection, she would stay every bit as beautiful as this, for many a year to come.

Her eyes found his as he came in and closed the flaps behind him. Then those same blue eyes crawled to and held the top of the tent. And did not move as he unbuttoned his britches, took her hands, and wrapped the unwilling fingers about his swelling flesh.

Jubilee eagerly set about slowly pulling apart the folds of her sleeping gown, aroused at the pure, unsullied beauty of her.

Truly, this was one woman worthy of him—worthy enough to be the wife of the new Prophet of Zion.

Bull drove the pony relentlessly down into the shallow riverbed, sandy spray glittering like a thousand gold-starred nights in this red-tinged coming of day, galloping to join the rest as they surged down the north bank of the Plum River, completely filling the riverbed, screaming and screeching, their guns barking, iron-tipped arrows snarling in the cool dawn air at the half-a-hundred. Scarlet light played off the ten-foot buffalo lances bedecked with colorful streamers and scalp locks of many hues, every man resplendent in feathers fluttering from rifle barrels brandished overhead as they came on.

Bull was now among them, deep in their throbbing midst, a part of that massive flow like a red tide, a crimson coursing of a heartbeat destined to pound all life right out of the half-a-hundred. The leaders swept close to the sandbar, forcing their wild-eyed cayuses into the river itself, circling north of the island as they dropped to the off side of their ponies, there to hang by nothing more than a heel and wrist clutched in the matted, beribboned manes, from first to last of them firing, yelling, lobbing hissing arrows among what frightened, milling horses the white men had not already killed themselves.

The scene had almost a surreal effect on the young Shahiyena: this great flood of warriors washing over the river valley. Never before had he been part of something so overwhelming, so savage, so undeniable. It not only gave his heart strength for the coming fight, but gave his spirit rebirth for the days to come when he would hunt the one he sought more than any other.

The hundreds had appeared out of the west as if out of nowhere, as if the ground itself sprouted the naked horsemen. Suddenly blooming out of the thickets, up from the streambed itself, they magically appeared at the top of every hill, in every direction as they swarmed toward the helpless whites, every mouth screeching its own irreverent death songs.

There had been no sound when first he had drawn off and stopped to look back on the white men reaching the island—then nothing more than the echo of hammering hooves. But with his next heartbeat, the riverbed flooded with screeching, painted horsemen sweeping past the island. High-Backed Bull had actually felt the breast of the earth tremble beneath his pony's legs before he urged the animal into that great cavalcade two thousand hooves strong.

Yipping like coyotes out on a bloody spree, waving blankets, firing their bows and rifles, the whole heavy procession became a blurred parade of colors running out in water-strewn streamers of new light seeping into the valley of the Plum River.

As Bull brought his pony about and in a wide sweep to the west once more, to make a second pass along the north end of the island, he caught a glimpse of three of the whites who had not joined the rest among the thrashing carcasses of their horses on the sandbar. While most hurled themselves down in the tall grass and swamp willow, hiding behind the plum brush and the first of the dying horses, there were three who hung back, hugging those murky shadows beneath the low, overhanging river-bank. From there the trio could not be seen by the onrushing warriors until it was too late and the horsemen were directly in the teeth of the white man's guns.

In the first charge the three had done their greatest damage. As the great red wave split at the western end of the sandbar, the horsemen were forced to veer sharply to drop off the low bank into the dry part of the riverbed. Now a handful of the Shahiyena and Brule already lay in the sand. More fell in their second charge as the three rifles exploded in the face of the red man's attack, forcing its way down the bank into the very gut of the river itself.

Bull reined up and watched a moment, horrified, three more heart-beats. Brown-skinned warriors crawled, wounded and bleeding, dragging themselves up the dry wash into the willow and plum brush, into hiding. Those that were spotted by the white men were shot where they crawled.

He had to let others know. Roman Nose . . . Pawnee Killer, anyone. Yet Bull reined up, knowing he alone was called upon to drive the three from their burrow.

His medicine alone had shown him where the trio hid, firing their rifles into the face of each renewed charge. His medicine alone had chosen him to wrench the badger from its hole.

As he grappled with what his plan would be, the mounted chargers pulled off, followed by a half-dozen riderless ponies still heaving at a gallop in the chase. High-Backed Bull cursed: the white men had broken their concerted charge. And for that failure dead and wounded warriors lay less than the length of two arms from the sandbar. The half-a-hundred now forced the horsemen back to their old way of fighting: the circle. The spinning, whirling wheel that pitted each warrior, solitary and alone with his own medicine, against those hated white men hunkered down on the grassy island behind the bloody carcasses of their big American horses and mules.

Behind the leg-flung carcasses the enemy scraped at the sand, clawing up chunks of grass and knotted roots, beginning to scrape their way down.

While a new charge formed itself.

"Stop!" Bull warned, knowing as he did how senseless was his warning.

Instead he could only watch helplessly the blur that wound itself up like the spinning of a dust devil whipping mindlessly across the sun-blistered prairie. Down the horsemen tore into the glittering riverbed, beating their way past the north shore of the island, across the riverbed to leap their ponies onto the south bank, back up the bank in a grand sweep, and into the riverbed once again in a whirl of color and numbing noise. From beneath their snorting ponies' necks they fired arrows, but it was mostly rifle and pistol fire, each horseman dropping from the far side of his little pony at the critical moment approaching the end of the sandbar.

While the white man's repeaters kept up a steady racket, unshod hooves reverberated against the dry riverbed in a thunder of terror and noise, the screeching of the horsemen matched only by the cries of their wounded ponies as the animals reared, fought, and pitched sideways as each successive bullet struck.

And on the island, those mad curses muddled with grunts of angry, scared men, scrambling and scratching at the sand—with every precious second digging lower and lower still, like frightened burrow mice as the hawk swoops overhead, claws outstretched.

Still he recognized the squeal of the last of the frightened animals as it struggled, reared, and lunged back to fall on its handler—flinging up cascades of golden, gritty, blinding sand as it went down. Here and there the island cracked with the sharp blasts of the white man's Colt's pistols.

Eerie, the young Shahiyena warrior thought as he watched, that humanlike screaming of the horse as its rider shot a bullet into its head, bringing that last of the big animals down in a resplendent spray of sand and blood. It fought to the last: biting, hurling phlegm and piss as it thrashed headlong into the grass, legs still fighting as a second bullet crashed into its brain.

The white man lunged behind his huge brown barricade, safe from the oncoming charge. Another rush came from the north bank, the white men frightened by the quirts slashing, slapping pony rumps as the horsemen tore past. There was more deafening sound now, thunderous and numbing to the young warrior as he grappled with how to reach the trio of white men huddled beneath the bank. To ride until he drew near . . . or do it all on foot.

Frightened voices filled the steamy air above the island. Though he could not understand it all, Bull did know some of the white man's tongue: what he had learned from his mother—even more, what he had learned from the white man who had fathered him. Those words he believed he knew best: the profane, desperate prayers. The cries of men hit and bleeding, calling out for help.

It took no special talent to know the warriors had severely hurt and crippled the half-a-hundred in their first few charges, in less time than it took a man to light and smoke a small pipe bowl of tobacco. But they had failed to squash the enemy the way they had planned. It had not been the quick work they had whipped themselves into believing it would be.

For now it became nothing more than hot, gritty labor—the white men having plopped down behind the heaving carcasses of their dying horses, laying their hot barreled many-shoots rifles over the still-quivering bodies of their dust-slaked, bloody, arrow-pocked barricades. Gray-black powder smoke drifted like a smudge against the blue sky above the sand-bar. Below erupted clouds of spurting yellow dust as warrior bullets struck here and there, yet to find a target.

And in the midst of the sandy riverbed lay the naked bodies, most not moving any longer, picked off by the white men on the island, perhaps finished by the three under the bank in their burrow.

The hair on his arms tingled at the faint bugle call from upstream, brassy and clear on the cool air of that dawn. Likely it was one of the renegade turncoats who proudly carried his shiny medicine at all times— soldiers once themselves.

That one who called himself Kan-sas. Cly-bor was his white name. But the Dog Soldiers who had taken him in when he had deserted the pony soldiers called him Kan-sas. He carried his shiny gold horn on a leather cord over his shoulder. It was likely he who called with his horn for another charge now because many of the horsemen were milling upstream, as if waiting for someone to take control of them.

"Where is Roman Nose?" Bull wondered aloud, reining about and moving out upstream to see for himself. Porcupine would be with him, he knew. No matter what the other war chiefs might try, it remained for the Nose to bring order out of the chaos of those first few charges.

And now near the upstream end of the island, the bullets from Sha-hiyena snipers began to fall among the hastily dug rifle pits behind the carcasses. Some of the brown-skinned horsemen had abandoned their ponies, diving among the reeds and willow along both sides of the sandy riverbed. There they parted the brush and fired at anything that moved on the sandbar. Still, Bull considered as he gazed along the shallow, sandy riverbed, the white man had exacted his terrible damage on the horsemen. Across the sand and in the lapping river itself lay not only the wounded and dead warriors, but the dying, squealing war ponies as well.

The gall rising in his throat, his decision was made, and with a savage yank on his rein, Bull brought his own animal around abruptly.

"Maiyun!" he called to the mysterious ones. "Help me!"

Instead of forcing it down into the riverbed as the others had, he chose to race along the edge of the north bank. Then, surprising the trio who hid in their burrow, he cut sharply to the right, pushing his reluctant animal directly for the badger's hole where the three white men waited.

One of them turned and broke as soon as the warrior was but twenty feet from the overhanging bank. The other two attempted to bring their rifles up to fire, but Bull was into and over them before they drew sight on him. Swinging his war club, screaming his death song, he knocked a rifle from the hands of one of the whites, hurling the man aside like white water sliding past a midstream boulder as his pony raced by.

Then Bull found himself in the shallow river again, alone this time. And on the shore he watched the many warriors rise from the willows and plum brush, holding aloft their rifles and weapons, cheering his brave, heroic ride as his pony sidestepped, fighting the grit and water, frightened of the bullets that hissed all about him now that he forced the animal into the teeth of the enemy guns.

"Wimaca yelo!" Bull cried back at those who cheered him. "I am a man!"

Pounding his heels into its flanks, Bull abruptly nosed the pony straight for the sandbar, its small hooves clawing at the side of the island, vaulting over the breastworks of two horse carcasses and down into the midst of the improvised rifle pits where the enemy dived and lunged out of the path of the lone, crazed horseman.

He astonished himself as well as his cheering brothers as he reached that lone cottonwood at the far end of the island without a bullet having touched him. He had taunted *naevhan,* sneered at death. His heart pounding like never before, High-Backed Bull urged his snorting, sidestepping pony into the stream, crossing to the north bank, where he reined it for a low hill. It was there he halted at last, stopping to survey the white men imprisoned on the sandy island.

Then he heard the raucous cheers of the women and children and old men gathered on the next ridge. They had watched his daring ride and celebrated that small victory with High-Backed Bull.

"Hotoma! Hotoma!" they cried, showering him in their celebration of the mysterious medicine bravery of the Shahiyena warrior.

As his wind-stung eyes cleared of the tears and dust, he scanned the slopes of the surrounding hills. On the crests of most had appeared spectators from the villages. Besides women and the little ones come to watch, came the old ones and the boys eager but too young to fight. The chiefs proved themselves wise once again—bringing their people here to watch the battle.

With an audience of his family and friends, not to mention the young women a young warrior hoped to court—all of them there to cheer him on from the nearby bluffs—what man would not redouble his efforts to make a grand show of rubbing out the half-a-hundred?

Then as Bull watched, the cheers and war cries came of a single purpose. Most of the spectators on top of those ridges were turning, as if watching the approach of something. Or someone.

And in his heart High-Backed Bull realized it could be but one whose arrival caused such a thunderous reception: Roman Nose.

In his heart Bull cried for his war chief. Knowing the end had come for this the greatest ever to lead the Dog Soldiers.

Though he knew his medicine was gone now the way of the shortgrass in spring, his power gone the way of puffball dust on a summer wind, the great Shahiyena war chief had come at last to lead his faithful, trusting warriors, lead them down on that sandbar and the half-a-hundred.

While his heart leapt with joy at the arrival of Roman Nose, High-Backed Bull's heart also sank. The white man's iron fork had sealed the terrible, unstoppable fate of this bloody morning.

Clearly Bull knew there remained no way to alter the course of the war chief's destiny. With his charge into the teeth of the white man's guns on that sandy island, Roman Nose was fated to die.

11

THERE HAD TO be at least a thousand warriors in the valley, counting the Dog Soldiers of Tall Bull and White Horse. Why, Roman Nose led at least half that number himself.

The fight should have been over sooner than it would take a man to eat his breakfast.

How was it that they hadn't rubbed that sandbar clear of those half-a-hundred?

Why was it taking so long?

He glanced at the sun, found it halfway on its climb to zenith. A half day's time lost and no scalps for any of them to brandish. That lay in his belly like the cold pig-meat the white man gave the reservation Indians imprisoned far to the south and east.

The taunting grew louder from the warriors sniping back in the cover of creekbank undergrowth, and for the next hour or more things quieted over the island while the Lakota and Shahiyena marksmen did their best to keep up a steady rattle of rifle fire from their brushy shelters. On the steamy sandbar, High-Backed Bull could watch the figures burrowing down like den mice as the white men silently scratched at the sandy earth with their hands, knives, tin cups . . . anything they could use to claw holes in the ground and scoop up walls of the damp sand against the snipers' bullets. From time to time the half-breed son of trader Bent taunted the enemy in their own tongue. Charlie Bent cursed them, lured them, told the white men what awaited them when at long last Roman Nose's charge came to ride them down.

Intrigued, Bull watched how those fragments of English spoken at them caused the white men such confusion, such enjoyable consternation. And for a few moments he wished he had paid better attention to his mother and sister, learning the white man's tongue from them, if not from the man who had fathered him. To know more of it just might serve some real use one day soon, he decided: to be able to speak the language of the man who had fathered him, the language of the man he would seek among the whites.

Tying the long war club behind to the latigo on his pad saddle, he brought his Springfield carbine over his head and shoulder, where it hung from the rawhide sling. He never carried that many of the heavy lead balls, nor much of the powder the weapon took. Still, he itched to get a clear crack at one, just one, of those white men. Any of them. Like the snipers, waiting, waiting for the chance to blow a man's head off.

He dismounted and tied his pony to some brush, where it could browse as he moved along the north bank at a crouch, slowly parting the willow with the rifle barrel to peer at the island. It struck him then just what a feat he had accomplished—riding onto the sandbar, over the carcass barricades and rifle pits, all the way to the end of the island—

Of a sudden, unshod hooves hammered the sandy riverbed. More than ten horsemen broke from the nearby trees shading the creekbank, darting into range of the sandbar, racing past the north side of the island. As they galloped closer to the enemy, one of the group swooped toward the near side of the island.

One of the whites, a man with a black beard hung to midchest, suddenly bolted up from his rifle pit, aimed, and fired. As the puff of dirty smoke spat over the rifleman's head, the daring warrior pitched sideways into the shallow creek.

On instinct Bull aimed down the barrel at the cloud of gray smoke, at the bearded one, and snapped off his shot.

The smoke wreathed his own head as he angrily swiped it away, just as a man would swat at a troublesome buffalo gnat. Bull saw the bearded man slowly collapsing in his pit, a hand clamped at the side of his head while others lunged to help him. Bright crimson seeped across the man's shoulder, shiny and mirroring the brightness of midday light.

The rest of the daring horsemen completed their rush past the sandbar before circling back to regather upstream. But without stopping, they made another sweep beneath the jaws of the white man's guns. No warrior fell in this daring ride into the maw of death.

As the last rider turned and urged his little pony onto the north bank, another bugle's blare resounded up the valley. Obeying the call, the milling horsemen turned and slowly made their way beyond the first bend of the shallow river. Other warriors appeared on both banks, hundreds upon hundreds of them, emerging from the cottonwood and plum brush where they had been waiting, every one of them now nosing his pony toward the mouth of a gorge hidden beyond the trees, just past that first bend upstream.

Bull's eyes stung with salty sweat as he glanced once more at the sun's position, then continued reloading the single-shot Springfield carbine taken at the base of Lodge Trail Ridge two long winters before when the warrior bands had wiped out the hundred-in-the-hand.

Already the day was hot. And they weren't in the heat of it yet.

For the longest time that morning, bullets had kicked up the sand and slammed into the still, bloating horse carcasses the white men huddled behind as the temperature rose. But after that insistent bugle had called the horsemen to disappear beyond the river bend, the snipers slowed their racket.

Ramming the lead ball home, Bull gazed at the umber ridges that hemmed in this valley, studied the sunburned bluffs and grass-cured hills where the women, children, and old men gathered to watch the coming slaughter. Then he peered at the tall grass and scrubby brush on the sandbar, at the bodies of those horsemen who had not made it out of the riverbed. Less than five yards from the island itself lay a half-dozen painted naked warriors, some of them still crumpled just as they had struck the sand. One was crushed beneath a dead war pony. The rider who had gotten closest to the white men in their burrows Bull recognized as a Shahiyena, from the magpie the warrior tied to his greased hair. He was not a young man, for the iron of many snows had begun to fleck the man's hair, and from where Bull stood, he could plainly see the deep crow's-feet scoring the corners of the warrior's eyes that stared blankly at the pale sky.

"*Nohetto!*" Bull prayed. "There is no more." The man had lived many seasons and died as a warrior must—killing whites.

Just as Bull now renewed his vow.

The hot, still air fell all so quiet now that the horsemen had ceased circling and disappeared upstream, now that the snipers on both banks had silenced their withering fire. In the summer crackle and the rising heat, flies droned and other winged tormentors hovered over all.

He stared again at the island, hoping for another chance at one of the white men. Then his eyes were pulled magnetically to the dead warrior once more. The body lay in the shallow flow of yellowish water that this late of the season seeped slowly down the middle of a wider channel it had cut between rows of cottonwoods and scarred cutbanks of grassy sand at spring's flood stage. Except for that narrow flow of water itself, the riverbed lay as dry as uncured rawhide here late in the Moon of Black Calves.

Bull's head pounded with the heat, and the droning, buzzing silence, and the waiting—for it seemed the broad, corn-silk-yellow sky overhead and the shimmering sand of the river bottom conspired with the undulating, heat-shimmered hills to form a bowl reflecting like a mirror down on this narrow valley. As he lay watching the mice busy in their island burrows, the hot, suffocating breezes nudged the dry, brittle grasses where he remained hidden, waiting. The stalks irritated one another, the way the cricket talked mating with its legs. And from time to time he listened to the murmurs of pain and fear and frustration from the enemy on the sandbar.

Tiny voices whispering in Bull's head told him to stay put. To watch.

That his time was coming.

Another brassy bray from that deserter's army bugle raised the hair on the back of Bull's neck.

Its echo floated downstream toward the island. Looking now at the trees near the mouth of that ravine at the great bend in the riverbed, he found he could not see anything to give him the faintest clue what Roman Nose and the other chiefs were doing with the hundreds of horsemen who had disappeared from view what seemed like a long, long time ago.

From the corner of his eye, Bull caught the movement against the pale sky and turned to see a handful of feathered war chiefs crowning a nearby hill, all of them gazing at the sandbar, as if studying the defenders on the island. Then, as suddenly as they had appeared, they too slipped out of sight.

"I think they want to see how many of these white men can still hold a rifle," he told no one but himself.

Something would spring loose soon, he prayed, now that Roman Nose had come. Then his heart sank. Of all the emotions Bull felt at that moment in the brush beside the island—anger, desperation, hate, even some fear—it was sadness that most filled his heart as his thoughts hung on Roman Nose, the way his legging fringe would catch on brambles, or snag on cockleburs. Sadness that Roman Nose had finally come to lead these warriors—when it meant his own death.

A part of him grappled with that—not wanting to believe, as Roman Nose believed, in the power of an old Lakota woman's iron fork. Surely the might of Roman Nose would prove stronger!

Yet if the war chief's water spirits had told him—it must be.

Bull's heart sank again as his eyes peered across the riverbed to the far side. On both sides the banks rose slightly higher than the sandy island itself, giving the Lakota and Shahiyena snipers an ideal field of fire. All morning long they had forced the white men to stay hidden for the most part, down in their pits and low behind the bodies of their dead animals.

"That place where the white men burrow like mice will soon reek of rotting horses," he said to himself in what little shade he had found in the brush as the sun rose directly overhead. And in saying it, he hoped the white men would all be killed long before the big carcasses began to bloat and stink.

He saw a few of the whites momentarily poke their heads from their rifle pits, staring upstream beneath shading hands flat against their brows. At almost the same moment, Bull felt it beneath him—sensed it in his legs: the electrifying pulsations trembling up from the ground into his own body. He felt them coming before he had even heard them.

The thunder of more than two thousand hooves.

He heard them scant heartbeats before he saw them.

Slowly rising to his feet there in the brush, Bull found the sight hard to believe, felt more joy than he sensed his heart could hold. Of all the pony raids, and scalp hunts, and revenge raids they had made on the frontier settlements . . . still nothing had prepared the young warrior for what it was that galloped around the far bend in the wide riverbed.

From bank to bank the front row of horsemen stretched some sixty warriors strong. Directly behind them came row upon galloping row of riders. Eagle feathers fluttered on the hot breeze. Scalp locks of many hues, tied to rifle muzzles, caught the morning's wind. Their loose and braided and roached hair was plastered with grease, some standing as a provocative challenge to any would-be scalp-taker, all danced with the rhythm of the charge.

Even at this great distance Bull could see every pony had been painted with potent symbols. Still more many-colored scalp locks hung pendant from lower jaws, every tail was snubbed—tied up for war in red ribbon or trade cloth. Their bows, along with old Springfield muzzle loaders and a scattering of repeaters, were all brandished aloft as the horsemen came on in a splashy cavalcade, held in check by the only man on the northern plains who could hold these warriors in such an orderly, massed charge.

"Roman Nose!" Bull whispered in awe as his eyes found the tall war chief at the center of that front row.

He knew him instantly, not only by the horned headdress and the brilliant scarlet silk sash tied at the waist, but by the great gobs of red paint the war chief had used to encircle that summer's pale pucker-scars fresh from the sun dance held on the banks of the Beaver River. On his face he had painted the patterns prescribed by the spirit helpers in the war chief's visions: great streaks of ox blood across his eyes, yellow-ocher brushed across his cheeks, a black smear painted down his chin. Bright, unmistakable colors he had worn into so many battles. And this was to be his last.

"*Aiyeee-yi-yi-yi!*" Bull cried at the advancing front of copper-skinned bodies, choking on the sentiment he felt for the valiant war chief.

More so he raised his voice in salute to the one who rode to his death. Proudly. Bravely. A leader of his people to the last. A man who had refused to take a wife, to have his own family—believing instead that the entire tribe was his own to watch over and protect.

A sworn enemy of the white man.

And in that moment Bull felt the certainty of it reach the very marrow of him: come the death of Roman Nose, that powerful spirit, that all-consuming hatred of the whiteskins would come to seize control of High-Backed Bull.

Rifle fire suddenly crackled from the creekbanks, increasing to a fiery intensity. It was plain to Bull as he ducked back into the plum brush that the snipers intended to force the white men to keep their heads down under a deadly barrage of lead hail. Still, that roar of the guns could not drown out the growing crescendo of pounding hooves bearing down on that narrow, unprotected mound of river sand and summer-washed gravel in a riverbed the white man called the Arikaree.

Then as suddenly as the rattle of rifle fire from the banks had resumed, it withered away into a frightening, stone-cold silence. No more than a breath later arose the first of the wild cries bursting from the women and old ones gathered on the surrounding hilltops. Another breath and their eerie, keening blood-songs rose in volume, rose to become a swelling death chorus enough to chill the blood of any white man still alive on that island.

Swallowing hard, his mouth gone dry at the mere sight of the oncoming charge, Bull looked back to the oncoming horsemen. Lazy, oily smoke drifting from the silenced Indian rifles wisped in dark clots across the steamy riverbed as row upon row of horsemen followed Roman Nose downstream toward his appointed moment with destiny.

Something told Bull as he watched that advancing phalanx of brown-skinned cavalry that he was seeing history made. Not just the fact that Roman Nose would ride directly into the teeth of those white-man guns . . . but that no man, white nor red, had ever before seen Dog Soldiers execute an orderly, massed charge. Like the white man's own yellow-leg cavalry!

They would talk of this day, speak of this moment for generations to come among the Shahiyena.

Then a flicker of movement at the end of the island caught his attention. One of the white men dressed in soldier-blue rose slightly, as if in pain, his pistol in his hand. Turning, he gazed over those huddled in the rifle pits dug in a rough oval along the length of the narrow sandbar.

The white war chief, this one, Bull decided.

He stood above his half-a-hundred and bellowed his order above the thundering approach of the two thousand hooves.

"Now!"

With that command, some forty guns exploded on the island, their muzzles spewing brilliant tongues of yellow and orange-tinted fire.

Their first volley unhorsed but two riders.

On came the rest with even more resolve, racing into the face of those forty guns. Kicking their ponies into a full gallop without slowing for the two who had fallen.

Roman Nose spat back at the white man's rifle fire with an unearthly war cry, popping his hand against his mouth as he arched his head back, flinging his death curse at the heavens.

In no more than a pounding heartbeat that blood-crazed cry was taken up by the five hundred who rode with him. Above the riverbed charge the hilltops reverberated as the renewed chant thundered from the throats of the women and old ones.

"*Again!*" the white chief screamed.

A second volley roared from the sandbar. The smoke from all those weapons hung in tatters in the still, breathless air above the white riflemen, staining the pale sky an oily, murky, smutty gray.

"*Fire,* by damned!" And another white man in soldier-blue had risen to holler his order to the others.

More horsemen spilled this second volley, their riderless ponies coming on with the mass flanks of the rest. The whole of them charged without slowing, heeding not the rifles nor their own fallen. Those throaty cries for blood redoubled now as gaps were ripped open in their ranks—yet every bit as quickly those holes filled anew with warriors surging up from behind. The copper phalanx quickly made solid once more.

Bull's heart swelled at the sight, burned with pride at the fearless oncoming despite the wavering of their snorting ponies. A few animals stumbled on the uneven river bottom and tumbled into others. But ever onward the slashing hooves pounded, new horsemen and mounts come to take the place of those who went the wayside. Glittering diamondlike river spray and mica-fine rooster tails of gold dust cascaded heavenward in the high sunlight of this momentous day.

"*Now!*"

The first soldier chief's command had barely escaped his lips before the sandbar ignited for the third volley into the face of the five hundred.

The phalanx surged even closer now. Bull judged it to be something less than two arrow-shots from the end of the island. Certainly killing range for the white man's big guns. With every one of the white man's bullets, surely the horsemen had to fall.

In what little Bull could see through that thickening, murky haze of yellow sunlight slanting through the musty powder smoke, the naked, painted warriors began to spill over one another with that third volley. Ponies pitched into the riverbed too, collapsing as if their cords had been cut in bloody, tumbling, spinning heaps.

Piles of blood and sand and bodies and carcasses built up, a sight that brought shrieks from the hillsides as the women and old ones watched the slaughter of their chosen. Yet, with as much damage as the white man was doing to the horsemen, still Bull saw the horde coming, felt the unmistakable thunder vibrating up through the hard surface of the ground beneath his moccasins, heard the reassuring reverberation of their charge still ringing from the hills. And the closer they came, it seemed the more furious they drove their ponies, the louder rose their war cries.

"*Fire!*"

With that fourth volley the warriors ceased their mighty screeching, having drawn deathly close beneath the guns' fire-spewing muzzles. Most not already hollering in pain and frustration now rode on grim-lipped toward death's call on the sandbar. Bravely, without question, they came on, as if possessed—following their chosen leader still a'horse at the center of that front line. Every rider of them weaving back and forth, making it hard for the white man to take a bead on a copper-skinned target.

Brazenly racing on into the face of his own death, Roman Nose raised his arm, exhorting the hundreds come behind him across the sandy riverbed, splattering water and grit and gravel in a huge, stinging curtain as they charged down on the half-a-hundred.

"*Now!*"

A fifth volley cleaved the air like summer thunder.

Smoke of a dirty gauze obscured the island as Bull plopped down at the edge of the plum brush, bringing the Springfield carbine to his shoulder. If he had a chance at this range, he would pick off one of the white men.

If only to do what one mortal could to turn the day, what he could to change the fate of Roman Nose.

12

THREE HEARTBEATS FROM the sandbar, Roman Nose ceased weaving.

His eyes locked on the great war chief from the riverbank willows where he crouched, High-Backed Bull watched Roman Nose clamp his legs tightly round his faltering pony. Dark splatters dotted the animal's chest, each hole streaked with crimson.

With one breath Bull prayed the pony would not stumble and fall, pitching its rider into the sand, directly into the path of the row upon row, the hundreds rushing on the heels of Roman Nose.

And then he knew the hand of the Great Everywhere guided the war chief's animal in this fateful charge—there was no faltering in the dying pony's gait. Perhaps it was driven on by the sheer will of its rider, into the gaping jaws of the white man's guns that continued to spew great tongues of fire at the onrushing ranks.

A flurry of movement at the far end of the island caught Bull's eye. Turning, he saw a handful of the white men crabbing about in their rifle pits while the rest ducked back into their rabbit holes like tortoises. One of the brave chose to rise, emerging slowly from the dense, yellow-gray powder smoke, to stand and meet the charge every bit as bravely as those courageous Shahiyena warriors called "wanting to die."

Roman Nose had seen the white man too.

Bull wanted to yell—scream—shriek—anything to distract the white man.

But before he could utter a sound, both men fired—their guns exploding at the same moment, the blast of their weapons swallowed by the roar of other gunfire, the cries of horses, and the screams of men going down in a spray of blood and sand and river water, all swallowed by the smack of lead against bone and sinew and flesh.

Roman Nose had not fallen. Like a war club he swung his own rifle from the muzzle as his wounded pony clawed its way up from the riverbed onto the edge of the sandbar. It faltered, pitching forward onto its front knees, then struggled back up unevenly, back into a ragged gallop right into the teeth of those first white guns. Sand coated its bloody chest where uncountable wounds stained its coat.

The solitary white man still waited, rifle at his shoulder, firing at the war chief as he leapt past.

When one of those bullets finally struck Roman Nose, it was as if Bull himself felt the course of its hot lead into his own body.

Could it be that this terrible event had occurred right before his eyes?

The sudden change in the pitch of those wailing cries from the nearby hilltops told Bull he had not been the only one to see it happen. The women, old men and children too . . . they had watched the fall of Roman Nose.

Through tears Bull saw the war chief grip his pony's mane as the animal careened sideways off the sandbar, losing the last of its strength now as it crossed the shallow riverbed and plunged into the willow on the far side. Roman Nose wavered unsteadily, his head wagging as if connected to his shoulders by nothing more than loose strings.

Bull whirled from the plum brush, sprinting downstream along the north bank, refusing to believe what he had seen. The hot breeze stung his face, making him unaware of the tears that spilled across the furred earth-paint on his cheeks as he reached the sharp cutbank opposite the far end of the island. There he hurled himself off, lunging into the shallow water, and splashed across while the terror of that fateful charge played itself out. By the time Bull clawed his way up the south bank and into the willow, the white men had broken Roman Nose's greatest charge. Wounded ponies and bloodied men parted like water flowing past a great boulder, clearing both sides of the island, cleft before a sure and sudden death in the face of the white man's weapons.

Seven terrible volleys had torn into their brown ranks: spilling warriors, turning row upon row of the naked horsemen to the side, like waves crashing against a rocky coast. Sweating, gleaming, crimson-smeared bodies tumbled onto the pale sand, bobbed in the shallow, churned waters beaten to a red froth by two thousand thundering hooves.

Bull cried in utter despair as the white man's pistols began to bark, firing into the backs of the retreating warriors. As his heart came into his throat, he watched the half-a-hundred finish off those wounded horsemen who had fallen close enough to the sandbar's rifle pits.

In anger, fury, and rage, Bull turned away, eyes smarting

And heard the snuffle of the pony.

He found the animal, found Roman Nose nearby—his strong legs now useless. Pushing back the gall rising in his throat, the young warrior knelt to find the great war chief unable to move. Only his arms could he move. Eyes stinging in anger, vowing revenge for the murder of Roman Nose, Bull pulled his war chief from the willows where Roman Nose had dragged himself with one agonizing pull of his arms after another. There were many bloody pucker-holes in his back, more wounds than Bull took time to count.

Away from the bank, where he rolled Roman Nose to face the sky, Bull saw by the throbbing of the huge, muscular neck cords that the war chief experienced wracking spasms of great pain.

"I . . . have lost my legs," Roman Nose whispered, his eyes half-lidded in pain.

"I will go for help."

"No—do not go," he began. Then attempted a smile. "Yes. Go for help, High-Backed Bull. You see, I cannot ride." He coughed. "No more will I ever ride."

Turning away for a moment to hide his own grief, Bull felt overcome. This tragic end for a man whose very name had struck such fear into white hearts, turning them to water across many raiding seasons. He nodded, unable to speak around the sour lump in his throat, then hurried away. Bull cried as he caught up his horse and rode upriver for help.

Now as the sun began to sink in the west with a rose-brown crack of light, after a long afternoon wherein he never left the war chief's side while the gentle hands of women turned Roman Nose and bathed him, cooling the war chief in the shade of a leafy arbor, Roman Nose smiled up at Bull.

"How I have missed never taking a woman now," Roman Nose said quietly, looking at the young warrior as a cool rag was brushed across his chest. "I miss never coupling. I never married. You must, my young friend." Then the chief's eyes fluttered to Porcupine. "See that High-Backed Bull finds a woman—one to enjoy his life with."

"Roman Nose denied himself for his people," Porcupine replied. "Roman Nose will remain the greatest warrior of the Shahiyena."

The dying man turned his head slightly, gazing now at the young woman closest to him. At first it seemed he struggled to say something, but could not force the words out. After a moment Roman Nose appeared to grow content with his own painful silence, content in listening to the chants of the medicine men gathered nearby, their hand drums thrumming, buffalo scrotum and bladder rattles filled with stream pebbles. Beyond the whispered sacred prayers of the shamans, bigger and louder drums hammered to accompany angrier singing and women wailing in grief. The many dead and dying lay nearby on the bloody grass, scattered among the plum brush, those lost in the fateful charges now keened and prayed over by those who had watched the failure of one attack after another.

"Yours was a charge the Shahiyena will speak of for winters to come," Porcupine told Roman Nose.

"For generations to come: as the old ones pass down their winter counts and battle stories," Bull added. "A charge when the great Roman Nose knew he was destined to die. Still, he led his warriors into the face of those hot-mouthed white-man guns spitting fire into our ranks. It was a day to be proud of my Shahiyena blood—to watch a great man lead the rest, riding to your certain death."

Roman Nose's eyes found those of High-Backed Bull. "To be a man—this was enough in my life."

"You die having carried our struggle with the white man onto the island itself when so many others turned away," Bull said. "Watching you this day has given me the courage to take a vow on the blood of my war chief: to ride now into the white man's world and face my own destiny."

Roman Nose almost slipped away then, his lids fluttering, but he opened them slightly, his eyes glazing as he asked, "Your father?"

Bull nodded. "I vow to kill him."

"This is dangerous medicine," Porcupine warned. "Your blood is his blood."

Weakly reaching out with his trembling fingers, Roman Nose sought Bull's hand, took it, and squeezed as tightly as he could. "I faced the guns on that island because my medicine told me that it was here my end would come."

"Our chief is right, Bull," Porcupine agreed. "You have had no vision telling you to seek out and kill this white man."

Like a duck shaking water from its back, he shrugged off any fear of offending his personal spirits. Bull's eyes clearly showed he wanted no fraternal touch. "I need no vision to tell me," he said softly, a distinct edge to his words. Then he tapped his heart with a finger. "What vision I need to complete my vow comes from here. Where I am told what I need to do."

"If your heart is strong, then you must go," Roman Nose said, his eyelids flickering with a spasm of pain.

"It is a fool's errand," Porcupine protested. "To go alone . . . why, he is only one man—when you can ride with us against many more—"

"Would Porcupine call my ride into the face of those guns a fool's errand?" the war chief asked, his eyes gazing directly overhead into the deepening twilight.

Bull could see the eyes were nearly glazed in death-seeing. "Your spirit will ride with me, Roman Nose," he said. "As I go to kill white men wherever I can find them—you will be by my side."

"If you remain true to your heart, High-Backed Bull," Roman Nose said with a noisy rasp as he struggled with a wave of great pain crossing his gray face, "then my spirit will forever ride with you."

Bull watched the great war chief's eyelids open widely, then slowly fall with his last, painful breath. The hand that held his own loosened, sagging. He rose from the body.

Going quickly to his pony Bull galloped off—unshod hooves spitting spirals of golden dust into the purple twilight—riding toward the deepening gloom of night.

Into the night he raced, north by east. Where High-Backed Bull knew he would one day find the man who had fathered him.

"*I seen two* of them horses before," Jonah said quietly to the Shoshone lying against his shoulder in the steamy midmorning air after the passing of summer's late thunderstorm. Slattish cloud banks hurried on east toward South Pass and that great divide of the continent.

"The riders—these have your family?" Two Sleep asked, his words hushed among the rocks where they lay studying the overland trail that skirted this Red Desert Basin country east of the pass.

Together they had traveled west from Independence Rock, that great turtle's hump rising solitary and magnificent from the tableland of the central plains, from Devil's Gate, where the Sweetwater tumbled off the continent's spine toward the North Platte, rushing ever onward to feed the great Missouri. Climbing through the treeless, sage-pocked arid desolation that would take them to the high pass through this unpeopled country, they had decided to pull off the trail, hunker back in the high rocks and have themselves a look in both directions. Less than two hours' ride from where they now lay, every melting snowflake, every drop of rain that fell to kiss this high, dry land, would either flow east or to the Pacific. From here on out to the top of the pass it was country where a man had little choice but to expose himself against all that sky, against all that naked ground.

But here they lay in the shadows of the outcrop overhead, their stock tied below and behind the jagged bluff, grazing on summer's last dry offering of grass. They had watched the half-dozen horsemen riding stirrup to stirrup, fanned out and coming on at an easy lope as if they were about their mission with a deadly zeal.

Not long after sunup and a cold breakfast of some hard-bread and what leavings of meat they'd fried the night before, the Shoshone warrior had spotted the first wisps of dust faintly smearing the horizon to the southwest. In this clear-aired country, that was too much sign to be just one man, even two. Even enough dust was raised to be a small war party.

"Ute," he had told Jonah as they both had begun to scan the bare flesh of this high country for some kind of hole in all that nothingness where they could make themselves scarce.

"You get along?"

"When we . . ." Then Two Sleep shook his head and shrugged. "Sometimes."

But Jonah did not like the look in the Indian's eyes. Something there like a farmer watching the approach of a spring thunderstorm rumbling headlong for his fields—wondering if that storm meant needed moisture for his newly planted seed, or if those clouds foretold wind, hail—disaster.

It had been so long since he had thought of things like a farmer. Was he anymore, that? Was farming any longer in his blood? People of the soil stood ankle-deep in the land. Did a man ever forget those roots gone back generations? German stock like Gritta's, or the Irish poured in on his mother's side back a ways. Some Scotch too—Jonah figured it was that blood which made him taciturn and not given to a lot of talk like the old man Sweete.

For so long now he had been a man-hunter, someone ready to kill for the sake of cause, or heart. And now as he lay watching the half dozen approach across the dusty plain below, two of them on familiar animals, Jonah wondered if he ever would be anything else—wondered if he ever would be blessed enough to work again in the soil with his hands and the sweat of his brow, the strength of his back, driven by sheer will alone at times . . . or if the rest of the days in his life were of a set pattern already.

To follow the faint spoor of his family.

Forced to kill those who were sent back to drive him from the trail—perhaps to be killed by them once and for all.

No longer did he nurture and grow the plants of the field and their farm animals.

Now he knew he had become a destroyer. Like the dark side of nature's own hand.

His mother had taught him better. And Gritta too was of the same mold as his mother's family. At her knee he had oft learned that man was made to wage peace in God's kingdom.

What was a simple man like Jonah to do? So often had he grappled with that dilemma—knowing Gritta would disapprove of his tracking after her, killing for her—all the bloodletting in her name. He knew she would shame him for all the sins he had committed in coming after her and the children. He should have turned his cheek, she would say the Bible admonished them.

"An eye for an eye, tooth for a tooth," he said almost under his breath after a long time.

"What?"

He shook his head at the Shoshone and fell silent again, thinking hard on that biblical command he continued to follow all these lonely days on the wind. He thought back to the last time he saw her, standing in the yard with the children around her long skirts like autumn-dried leaves wind-heaved against the base of a corral gatepost. One last time he had turned and waved, then forced himself to walk off down the lane to the road where others were waiting. His war was just beginning.

For some weeks already a few zealots on both sides of the states'-rights question had been tramping back and forth across the forests and fields of southern Missouri, gaining converts and picking up what money they could when they passed the hat. Fires of smoldering southern passion burned anew in Jonah's breast when Confederate General Sterling Price showed up down in Cassville. The farmer, father, and husband told his family he had to go, to fight for all that he held dear.

Price had kept his swelling legions on the move: destroying bridges, removing rail ties, setting fires beneath the iron rails until they could be bent shapeless, firing into passing trains until most rail traffic slowed and eventually halted. Yet within a matter of weeks Brigadier General Samuel R. Curtis, that West Point man out of Iowa, marched in with his Yankee army to destroy the Missouri State Guard. A week later the Union soldiers met Price's ragtag band of volunteers at Springfield, down near Jonah's home where Gritta and the children had stayed behind to work the fields.

In their bloody clash Curtis turned Price around and drove the ill-equipped rebel army farther south still, beating the Confederate's rear flank like a man would flog a tired, bony plow mule.

It turned out to be so bad a beating that Price could count less than twelve thousand left in his army by the time they reached Pea Ridge in northern Arkansas that cold, sleety March of 1862. There Price finally rejoined General McCulloch and turned like a whipped dog ready to stand and fight. As much passion as those farmers put into that battle, General Earl Van Dorn and Iowan Curtis still made quick work of the southern plowboys on that bloodstained ridge strewn with bodies torn asunder by grapeshot and canister.

Price barely escaped with some remnants of his command: those who could still fight; those who had not already headed home, shoeless and demoralized, their spirits broken.

Jonah stayed on, determined to see the war through, walking barefoot as he followed Price's legion east into Mississippi where the great Corinth campaign was shaping up.

It was after the sound of the cannon and muskets, the screams of the dying, all fell silent, after the Confederates withdrew that the Yankees discovered Jonah at the bottom of a scooped-out depression left behind by a canister explosion—a raw scar of a hole in the rich, black soil where the Missouri farmer had crawled when he could not retreat with the others, unable to move any farther with that bleeding leg that seeped his juices in a greasy track across the forest floor.

The Yankee surgeons had wanted to take his leg off, saying it was the only way to save his life. Jonah had stared at the nearby pile of bloody limbs the hospital stewards were slow in burning, and swallowed down his pain, refusing their offer of knife and saw. If he was to die, he told the Yankee surgeons, then let it be here in the South. So be it.

"Better to die quick with two legs on southern soil than to die the slow death of a cripple prisoner of the Yankees, with no hope of ever making a run for it," he had snarled at them, his words sounding braver than he felt as he gritted his teeth on the rising pain that tasted like sucking on a rusty iron nail.

Instead of amputation, Jonah had asked for whiskey—been given brandy instead, which, along with sulfur, he poured into the open, ghastly wound. Two days later he dug the Union minié ball out while the surgeons themselves watched, unashamedly in awe at the rebel's grit. Pinching that smear of lead bullet up between his fingers, and slowly opening the pink-purple muscle with slow, steady strokes of a surgeon's straight-razor, Hook finally poured more of the brandy into the empty bullet hole, then promptly passed out.

After his capture in Mississippi, Jonah had been marched and wagon hauled, then put on rails mile after mile northward to a squalid prison that swelled with new prisoners arriving every week: Rock Island, Illinois.

For the longest time Jonah had feared Rock Island would be the last place he would close his eyes, never again to sleep in Gritta's warm, sheltering arms.

But after weeks and months that became years of waiting, forced to watch others die the slow death of starvation and typhus, diphtheria and scurvy, Jonah was offered the chance to wear Yankee blue, to go west to fight Indians while the Union finished cleaning up the southern rebellion.

To wear Yankee blue meant to survive, to live out enough days until he could get back to that valley in Missouri where Gritta and the children waited. As long as he did not have to turn a gun on a southern patriot, Jonah agreed to come west with the eighteen hundred who were herded onto railroad cars for Fort Leavenworth, Kansas, from there to march farther still to the Great Platte River Road where the telegraph wire required protection from the Sioux and Cheyenne.

It was here in this very country where he and Two Sleep watched the half dozen approach that Jonah Hook had first battled the red lords of the central plains.

He smiled grimly. For now in this very same country, things had once more come down to the simple matter of blood choices, the simple matter of him or the Danites likely sent back to eliminate him.

Kill, or be killed.

The longer he spent out here in the West, Jonah brooded now as he filled the long barrel tube on the sixty-six Winchester—the easier the choices were for him to make.

13

AUTUMN NIGHTS IN this high desert were enough to make a man's blood run cold all of its own. You didn't have to be waiting out the fall of the moon before you went about killing to feel the cold all the way to your marrow.

Beneath a cloudy glitter of stars Jonah shivered slightly within the single blanket as he sat with his back propped against the rock wall. Beside him squatted the Shoshone. The sky was still too light for what they had planned and polished together throughout that day of watching the approach of the six gunmen. Watching them ride on past.

When the hoof dust from the half dozen had reached the limits of the horizon, Two Sleep agreed that they could take up the backtrail of the Danites.

For the longest time there in the shrinking shadows of that rock shelf as they had waited to ride out, the Shoshone had argued against going after the six.

"Better to go on. Ride where you finish this," he had told the white plainsman.

Jonah figured he had studied on the situation just about every way a man could, and come out with only one solution: he had to rid his backtrail of the six.

"Can't go on west," he had told the warrior. "Having them at my backside. Not knowing really where those six are. When they'll show up on me." He shook his head. "No. There's only one way—and that's to take care of 'em."

"Want to follow them? Kill one, by one?"

Jonah shook his head again. Then stared into the Shoshone's eyes. "No. I don't have that much time to burn now. I got the scent of that bastard strong in my nose right now. After all these years—at long last I can smell him. Nawww, I ain't bound to lose him—to lose my woman again just 'cause I messed up watching things over my shoulder."

The warrior had pushed up from the rock shelf, stood brushing his hide leggings before they went to their horses. "I don't go now—you still ride?"

"I will." Jonah had nodded, confirmed. "A man must. You don't go—it's all right. I'll go on alone."

"Yes. You alone before I come. You go do what is right anyway. That is why I go with you now."

There had been no more words, nothing more between them but the clasp of hands in that practice of solidarity between men.

And now it had been hours since the Shoshone had declared his allegiance to Hook's plan to go after the six, to take them off his backtrail in one fell swoop. Hours since they had really talked. Having seen where the Danites had camped, found what side of camp the horses were grazed, seeing the size of their fire as autumn's twilight squeezed down early on this land—the two sat propped against a handful of man-sized boulders less than a mile from the Danites' fire, waiting for moondown, waiting to move in and put an end to Hook's backtrail problem.

Jonah finally said what he had been thinking ever since they emerged into the bright fall sunlight in the Red Desert Basin earlier that day and reined their horses into the tracks left by the six.

"Thank you, Two Sleep."

"You say so when we are done, Hook," the Shoshone replied. "When we go back to go on get your family."

He sighed, gazing up at the spinning sky overhead, stars clear as dewdrops on corn silk of an early summer morning, the whole shiny glitter of them seeming almost close enough for him to reach out and knock those droplets off with a flick of his fingers. Not knowing why he couldn't reach that far.

"You don't have to do this, you know."

"I know," Two Sleep replied. "I do it with you."

"That's just it. Can't figure out why you'd want to walk in there with me—when the odds are agin us."

The Shoshone looked over at the white man riding beside him. "Odds better when I come, no?"

"This bunch is likely good at killing, Two Sleep. They didn't get into Usher's group—they didn't stay alive in that bastard's outfit less'n they were awful good with guns."

"This Usher you tell me—he send the best back for you, yes?"

Jonah nodded. "I suppose he would. His best. Do it clean and quick."

It was the warrior's time to sigh and contemplate. "Then—you . . . me. We do much more to be better."

After he had patted the Shoshone's arm reassuringly, Jonah gazed a moment at the aging warrior in the pale starlight. "It still doesn't tell me why you come along. This ain't your fight. Not riding on with me to the land of the Mormons neither. Can't make sense of why you just don't ride off down that road where you was heading when you bumped into me."

"Told you. Like your whiskey. Like your company."

"Don't have any more whiskey, goddammit. You seen to that."

Two Sleep nodded, pursed his lips. "So all I got is a friend to ride with, yes?"

"No. It's gotta be more than that. More reason for you to pick this same bloody road as I picked for myself. Some good goddamned reason to put your life down for me. Why? Why you doing this for me?"

"Not for you," he answered abruptly. "This trail is for me."

"You? How—"

"Last chance for me, Hook."

Jonah wagged his head, failing to make sense of any of it. Yet. "What the hell for—"

"I lost my woman. Lost children too," the Shoshone admitted.

"White men? Like these bastards?"

"No," he answered. "Got my own devils, Hook. You got yours."

"Who then? Who took 'em? You know 'em?"

"I know. Lakota."

"The Sioux?"

"Brule. Burnt Thigh. Bunch under Pawnee Killer."

"Happened not long ago, I'd suppose."

"No. Long time. Fourteen winters now. They gone a long time."

"They? The Lakota come in and took your family?"

"Them didn't die. Woman. She tall and pretty. My daughter too. Twelve summers old then. Both taken."

"Other children?"

"Three boys. All fighting age." He bent his head, staring at his lap.

Studying the way the Shoshone held his impassive face surrounding those liquid eyes, Hook realized the man was still mourning. Even after all this time. Fourteen years, going on fifteen.

"What happened to them? Your boys? The three of 'em."

Still bent over in prayerful repose, Two Sleep drew a single index finger nearly the circumference of his neck, then used that finger to draw a circle around his head, ending his wordless description by yanking on his own greasy topknot.

"Goddle-mighty," Jonah exclaimed quietly. "Them Brule killed 'em all—all three of 'em?"

Two Sleep held up both his hands, palms up in a plaintive gesture. "All gone. Sons gone on Star Road now. I put them in the trees. Above the ground. Where the wind talk to them for all time."

Hook found himself instinctively gazing up at the night sky paling as the moon fell far in the west. He swallowed hard, brooding on the loss of his own sons. Lord—the two of them took at once. From what Shad Sweete had told him, they was as good as gone now: in the hands of comancheros, spirited all the way south to Mex country. Death'd likely be a better fate than that, he figured. And what of Gritta? Her fate no better than that of . . .

Jonah forced himself to squeeze that off, like stopping the stream of warm, creamy milk from the cow's udder back home, and looked over at the Shoshone instead.

"The Brule, they'd be cruel to your . . . your woman. And your daughter?"

"Yes," he answered immediately. "No," he replied a moment later. "After all time gone from land of the Shoshone—the two now Lakota. My woman, she get old." Then he made a cradling motion down at his belly. "Maybe she carry many Brule baby. Make many Lakota warrior."

Jonah watched as the Shoshone was seized with a spasm of grief, something sour in his throat that was as quickly swallowed down.

"My girl," Two Sleep continued, his words with a rocky edge to them as he spoke, "she have Brule babies too now."

"You don't know . . . can't be sure."

He nodded his head so emphatically, it shocked Hook.

"I know. The Lakota take women—make them Brule. Make Lakota warriors in their bellies. Marry and have many babies. Or . . . or the women they kill quick."

"Your . . . the women—would they fight the Brule? Or would they have the Lakota babies?"

Two Sleep rubbed his eyes with his gnarled knuckles, as if some sandy grit were troubling them. "They gone," he said finally, brushing one palm quickly across the other.

"Dead?"

"Dead," the warrior answered.

"You mean: they're good as dead."

"They have babies for Lakota fathers," Two Sleep agreed, "a bad thing for Shoshone woman."

As good as dead, Jonah thought to himself. A woman of one tribe forced to give birth to sons of an enemy tribe—she was as good as dead to her own people.

"She wait. They wait for me," Two Sleep continued after a moment. "Wait for first winter. A second and a third winter. They see no one riding to come for them. Maybe they dead now. Maybe after all winters they say Two Sleep not come for them—they carry Lakota babies. They come to be Lakota mothers. They not Shoshone no more. They be Lakota now. They forget Two Sleep."

"But you never forgot them."

Two Sleep dragged a hand beneath his nose hurriedly. "I never go find them. Afraid. No man go with me. I was young, strong in seasons ago. Not now. Too many winters gone. Other warriors give up on Two Sleep. So now I afraid to go."

Hook watched the Shoshone slowly drop his head on his forearms that lay cradled across his knees, hiding his face. There arose no sound from the warrior. Nothing to betray him but the slight, silent tremble as Two Sleep shuddered with the wracking sobs.

It grew clear to Jonah as he reached out, knowing nothing else to do but to touch the man's quaking shoulder.

"After I told you my story . . . you up and decided you're coming with me—'cause you want to help me get my family back. That it, Two Sleep?"

He raised his face, eyes glistening, but cheeks still dry as the flaky soil in this high land. "I come to help you. Too late to help me. Too late to help my woman. Help my daughter. Too late now help my sons gone far on the Star Road fourteen winters. But . . . still time for you, Hook."

"Yes, Two Sleep. There is time for me." He barely got the words out, choking on the unfamiliar taste of sentiment. It was something he had not often savored in his brooding past. But here, with this old Indian, in the cold of this autumn night somewhere near the windswept continental divide as they waited to pit themselves against six gunmen, Jonah Hook felt again that unaccustomed warmth of human kindness.

By riding along with the white man, Two Sleep was trying to find a way of forgiving himself after all this time. After living so long as a failure— with the fear, the terror, the utter shame of never trying. Happened that a man crawled far enough, long enough around the whiskey cup, he just might find himself reaching the handle.

Two Sleep got to his feet, clutching his thin blanket about his shoulders. "I brave enough now, brave for all the days I not brave enough to go find them. I ride with you—so it make things right for me."

With the Shoshone finally expressing it, Jonah knew the warrior was right. By riding along to help Hook, Two Sleep was somehow righting his medicine, his spiritual power long gone stale and rancid—long gone the coward's way of hiding down in the white man's whiskey and gambling and the emptiness of a coward's sanctuary. But for some reason Jonah Hook had come along to offer a way, the only way, the warrior could make his medicine strong once more. By helping another man put his family back together.

"I'm not sure I know how to pray much anymore, Two Sleep—but I figure the Lord is somehow listening," Jonah said. "I figure you're here to help make things right for both of us."

Waiting out here in the dark among the clumps of sage, stretched prone on the cold ground as a gust of cold wind slapped his face, Jonah sensed what a brown-skinned warrior must feel as he lay beyond the welcome, warm ring of a white man's firelight. It seemed evil was always executed beyond the pale of darkness.

The Danites' fire had gone to red coals untended and writhing in the pit they had dug to conceal the flames and thereby prevent discovery by a chance and wandering war party.

Jonah found little amusement in that. The Mormons had no reason to worry themselves over wandering Indians tonight. It was instead the darkness and the cold autumn wind snarling across this high land that would cloak the danger.

The six had picketed their hobbled horses downwind from camp. He had learned always to graze his animals upwind, as a source of early warning. Especially in darkness: the time for evil.

How he wanted to feel the warm blood of these Mormon zealots on his hands again. Just as he had at Fort Laramie when he killed Laughing Jack. Before he stuffed the body beneath the river ice. A long, long time ago it seemed now—so many miles gone under his heels since.

Then he remembered the taste of his rage as he knelt over the bleeding Boothog Wiser back in Nebraska, in the end killing Jubilee Usher's lieutenant before he could allow himself to flee with his daughter. Hattie.

Here in the cold he keenly sensed the loss of her, wanting again the soft, warm touch of her as he embraced the skinny girl teetering on the verge of womanhood there on the Kansas railroad platform, sending her east to St. Louis—far from harm, far from this wild, cruel land that had become his prison.

Four, maybe even more of them, had Jonah tallied for himself already as he drew closer and closer on the trail of Jubilee Usher, closer to reclaiming his wife from those who had ripped his family apart. He lay there now in the dark of that moondown, brooding on how much easier the killing got when he thought of these men as nothing more than animals: beasts who were meant to die. Easier it was for him to pull the trigger or use the knife, to do what he had to do when he thought of the Mormons as—

The scrape of boot soles on the sandy soil leapt out at him from the darkness.

Muffling the sound against his body, Jonah lightly brushed his thumb back across the hammer of one of the big .44-caliber pistols, then the other hammer, to assure himself they were cocked. His eyes strained beneath the

dim starshine now that the moon had fallen. The sky was quickly whirling
to the coldest time of the day—the moments before the first faint strands
of gray would emerge out of the east. And with this wind blowing the way
it was, torturing the sage . . . he was thankful none of the Danites could
smell him bellied down in the darkness.

Ten feet away the man stopped and turned slowly, as if himself trying
to make something out of the night. From the hole he punched out of the
starry skyline, the gunman carried a rifle across the fold of his left arm.

"Bolls!" the man whispered harshly.

There came no answer.

Jonah knew he wouldn't have much time to act if the Mormon grew
nervous. He might just up and turn, shouting a warning back at the other
four who lay sleeping like black humps of coal on the prairie, their feet to
that shallow fire pit.

"You asleep, Bolls?"

And when no answer came, the man there to relieve the watch started
to turn again. Jonah slowly raised his pistol—wishing he could do this
another way: use his knife as Two Sleep had on Bolls, the first guard, lying
somewhere out there in the darkness. It would be quieter, and every bit as
efficient.

"Where you, Bolls?"

He wouldn't have much more time, a heartbeat or two only—

As the guard turned his back on Hook, Jonah rose from the sage,
pistol flung back at the end of his arm. He could knock him in the head if
he could cross the ten feet before the man heard him.

The guard whirled back, rifle coming up to block the barrel of Jonah's
pistol as it fell to graze the side of the Mormon's head, slashing downward
against flesh and bone. The fury of his attack caused the guard to stumble
backward a step as Jonah clumsily lashed out with the pistol in his left hand.
Swearing, the guard brought the rifle down. It spat bright, blinding fire,
the bullet keening wildly into the black of desert night.

It had passed close enough to make Hook fling himself onto his belly
and pull a trigger himself, aiming by feel—like that night with Major
North's Pawnee scouts, clustered among the baggage of Chief Turkey
Leg's Cheyenne camp when the young Cheyenne warriors came charging
out of the blackness. Now he saw behind the muzzle flash a second bright
blast from the guard's gun as the Mormon was flung backward.

Only one thing would have made the man arch backward like that. Jonah knew he had hit him.

Behind the roar of those three shots came the frightened cries of the nearby horses and the rustle and grunt of men clearing their blankets and canvas bedrolls, hollering out questions and orders, chambering cartridges in their weapons, one of them kicking dirt onto the red embers.

When a gunshot rang out, the muzzle flash caught the corner of Jonah's eye. The fire tender pitched headlong across the remnants of the uncovered embers. He wasn't moving.

"Out there!" one of them shouted, pointing into the darkness.

Three of them fired a succession of shots.

"Careful! Hines—go see if we got 'im."

"Me? In the dark?"

"There's five of us—"

"Four, Cap'n."

"Four then, by God! And there's likely less of them out there or they'd rushed us. Goddamn Injuns!"

Another shot rang out on the far side of the camp, causing the horses to cry out, hammering the ground in their hobbles, tearing against their pickets. Jonah knew Two Sleep had moved like mercury spilled on a table after his first shot had killed the fire tender.

"They're after the horses!"

A pair of shots rang out as the gunmen whirled in a crouch to the west—all but one of them. The one that Jonah had failed to see. Hook rose from the blackness of the sage again, intending to take them in the back. And to his left as he did, Jonah heard the *click-chunk* of the hammer an instant before the night whited in muzzle flame.

The bullet stung his left wrist, snarling past his belly.

Like something hot he lost the pistol in that hand, felt it spinning to the ground, still intent that he would not lose the one in his right despite the pain that came to his belly as the wind whined past, kicking dust into his eyes. Another shot collided with the flaky sand at his side, the flash bright and searing in the deep of desert blackness. The gunman moved slowly toward him. Then a third shot as Jonah rolled, hearing the whispering hiss before it too screamed into the ground where his head had been a heartbeat before.

Behind him arose the rattle of more shots shattering the twenty-five feet to the fire, dying as the cries of men and protests of their horses split the dark. Finishing his roll, Jonah raised his gun hand—hearing the unearthly war cry of the warrior.

"It's Injuns, Slade!"

"Kill 'em, Charlie! Kill 'em all!" the man coming for Hook cried out.

Hook fired as the steps loomed closer. He heard the bullet hit, that unmistakable sound of a wet hand slapping putty. Then the grunt of the gunman.

Still, the Mormon came on after only a moment's hesitation.

"Sonofabitch—I'll have your balls!" the man grumbled, and fired into the blackness, then fired again.

A third time the hammer fell on an empty cylinder as Jonah steadied his pistol and aimed it at the black hole punched out of the starshine in the high desert night sky.

He fired. Heard the bullet smack soddenly into its target—the wind socked out of the man. Jonah heard him take one more step, then another, grumbling liquidly as he came.

"Slade?" a voice called from the far side of the fire. "Slade?"

Then the voice was cut off, gone garbled and wet—choking. Like a man drowning in his own juices.

He heard the one called Slade pull a second pistol, cocking it in the growing silence of that blackest of time when night was prepared to give itself to the first seduction of day.

"Get you . . . you red sonofabitch!"

Where had he hit the man? Jonah wondered. The way the bastard cursed, that thickness to his words spoke of fighting down the pain. But— that he was still moving.

Hook fired his last shot into the darkness, then rolled back in the direction he had come, struggling to drag a second, loaded cylinder for the pistol from his coat pocket.

Without time to move the man was atop of him, collapsing to his knees soddenly, snatching Hook by the collar of his coat and yanking his face up close. He weaved a bit, putting the muzzle of his pistol into Hook's face, wobbly.

"You . . . you ain't no Injun," Slade spat, his tongue thick with blood. "Who the hell are—"

With the plunge of the wide blade, Hook watched the Mormon's night eyes grow big as Sunday saucers.

Jonah grunted as he fought to drag the big skinning knife the full width of the gunman's belly, feeling at last the warm, syrupy blood gushing over his hands as he disemboweled the Danite crouched over him.

Dark fluid gushed from the man's mouth as he struggled to find the words, sputtering. Until finally . . .

"The . . . the goddamned farmer."

14

Moon of Leaves on Fire 1868

THE PALE-EYED WAR chief had made sure the two boys had homes and families when first they were brought to live with the Kwahadi. They were not only cared for and fed, but taught the way of the Antelope Comanche as well. They learned about weapons and riding, how to hunt the dwindling herds of buffalo, to stalk deer and antelope and turkey. They grew better with every season in the rough-and-tumble wrestling that was nothing less than preparation for the killing arts of making war on the white man.

Jeremiah longed for the day he would be allowed to go on his first war party.

Eleven summers old he told his adopted father he was now, and learning more of the language from Bridge every day, forgetting more and more of his own as the seasons turned. Like his brother Zeke, Jeremiah hungered to ride out on the raids, to come back bearing the red-hued scalps, draping themselves in glory with the rest of the young warriors.

"But first," the pale-eyed war chief explained, "first you must learn patience. Learn all you can while you wait. When it is time, you will ride with me."

"And bring back scalps?" Jeremiah had asked.

"Yes. Many scalps, Tall One."

Jeremiah had liked his name from the start, when it was given him by Bridge, his adopted father, many seasons ago. Only rarely did he have reason to recall his Christian name. Fainter still in the recesses of that old life was his family name. He could not remember the last time he had said it with his own tongue, or heard his brother use it. They no longer spoke much English to one another. Having grown so accustomed to using the Comanche, they used the tongue even when by themselves. It had been a long, long time now since anyone was wary and watched them. No longer was anyone concerned that the two boys would run off, try to escape.

How silly that would have been, Tall One thought. The People had rescued the two boys from pain worse than any death a youngster could imagine. While the white marauders and the Mexican comancheros had toyed with and tortured the two brothers, the wandering Kwahadi had given the white children shelter, food, a purpose to learn—had given them family once again.

Their new family replaced that which the freebooters had destroyed more than three years before. It grew harder each day for Tall One to remember the faces of his mother, his sister, harder still to recall the face of his father. Seven years gone now. Tall One had been only four when his father walked away from that tree-ringed valley, marching out of Jeremiah's life.

"Do you remember Papa?" he had asked of Zeke in those early days among the marauders, the comancheros, and finally here among the Antelope People.

Young Antelope could only shake his head. It made sense that there remained no memories: he was something on the order of two years old when their father marched off to fight the war.

It all seemed so far away, and utterly meaningless now—something that made Tall One ultimately angry at his father. If anyone was to blame for what had happened to the farm and their family, to their life together, if anyone was to blame, Tall One figured, it was their father. Had he been there when the freebooters rode in, things likely would have been different. No one would have gone through the pain they had.

But for the past two winters now, he and Antelope had a new home. Zeke was a runner. At nine summers he was faster than many of the older boys. So it was when the names were chosen, Antelope fit Zeke best. Tall

One seemed to grow more and more overnight now, his toes repeatedly punching holes out the end of his moccasins, his leggings shrinking with the coming of each new moon, so it seemed. They had taken to their new life with unsated appetite. And with all they learned about the Kwahadi, the more they forgot of what life they had lived before.

That remained like another lifetime for Tall One. Like it belonged to another person. It was, after all, a story he but dimly remembered: that story about . . . yes, his name was Jeremiah. Again, his other name came harder. And the face of his father, hardest yet to recall.

For the longest time Tall One was unable to figure out exactly who these people were. He recalled what the Mexicans called the band of warriors on the morning the brothers were captured by the horsemen far out on the Llano Estacado, the Staked Plain of the Texas panhandle country.

The Mexicans called the horsemen Comanche.

Yet the warriors and their women never used that term. Instead, they referred to themselves as The People, and seemed to have some fuzzy and descending hierarchy for all the rest of the tribes and other-skinned people. Over the seasons Tall One came to discover that there were other bands of The People: Honey-Eaters, the Waterhole or River Pony, and Hill Falls Down, while the Buffalo Followers and Root-Eaters were among the most populous of the bands. But these Antelope, these Kwahadi, seemed to wander wider and farther than all the rest put together. Even so, never did they journey within sight of the white man's forts nor the territory the white man had established for the Indian nations.

The Antelope People stayed free, hunting buffalo, ranging long distances to kill the infringing white settler and steal his spotted buffalo, his horses and wagon mules. Then they returned to the nomadic villages to dance over the scalps, make love and more babies, sing their songs, and cast new lead bullets before riding out for more attacks on the white man.

"It is a glorious life," the pale-eyed war chief explained to a large circle of young boys, each of them naked but for his breechclout, painted according to his youthful imagination, and gripping his juvenile spears and bow, war club and crude iron knife. Each one hungrier than the next to be a full-fledged Kwahadi warrior.

"There are only our people out here," he taught them. "The rest are enemies we must be rid of. Grow strong, my young friends," the war chief instructed them, striding over to Tall One. "There will come a time when each of you is called to make war on our enemies."

"Especially the white man!" young Antelope interrupted eagerly.

Tall One glanced at his younger brother. "How can we prove we are ready to go with a war party?"

The pale-eyed one laughed easily, joyfully, not in a way that made fun of the young, eager boys. "You will know—just as the rest of us will know. There will be no doubt in our minds, no doubt in your heart—when you are ready to ride and defend our land."

"Who of us will be ready first?" asked Coal Bear, Tall One's best friend.

A full-blood Kwahadi, he was more than a winter older than Tall One, yet stood nearly a head shorter. Most of the older boys seemed squat compared to the white boy, built squarely and closer to the earth than either of the two brothers. Their Comanche legs seemed to bow naturally at a young age as well—a trait that made them ready to ride the wild-eyed cayuse ponies early in life.

"I will be ready first," Tall One said, though he was not sure he really believed it. Although Coal Bear was shorter, he was older and native to this land, and because of it, wiser in living among these rocks and sand buttes, the watercourses far-flung like the shallow tracks of the gobblers he dimly recalled roosting in the trees back . . . somewhere . . . somewhere in his memory.

Coal Bear laughed. "One day you will be ready. And one day, I am sure, you will be a powerful warrior. Perhaps even as powerful as I will be. But for now, you are still a white-tongue—wanting to be a Kwahadi!"

Tall One dived for his friend, catching Coal Bear around the neck and driving him to the dirt where they grappled, punching and kicking, laughing all the while. It was the one thing that drove the white boy into a rage—this being called a white-tongue by the others, but especially by his best friend. And Coal Bear knew it. Soon they released one another and sat gasping for breath, smiling, choking for air as they laughed in spasms.

"One day he will beat you good, Coal Bear," said Antelope. "My brother will beat you good."

"He knows it, Antelope," Tall One said. "That is why he pokes his fun at me now, while he still can."

"Yes—one day you will take many scalps from the white-tongues,"

Coal Bear admitted. "One day when you are no longer a white-tongue yourself."

Tall One was finding it hard to wait for that day. His skin had become all the darker these last two years spent next to naked in the sun, year round, except the coldest days of winter. Now winter was approaching once again. They would soon be seeking out the deep canyons, as they had in autumns of old, there to sit out the onslaught of cold weather that would batter the Staked Plain. Tall One yearned almost as much for the coming winter—a time of sitting around the lodge fires, listening to the old men tell stories of the beginning of the earth, tales of the coming of the First Person, the very first Comanche and how he needed a woman to sleep with and have his babies and cook his meals. A woman was very important then, as now.

As well the old ones taught Tall One and Antelope about their religion. At first Tall One had been afraid, remembering what his mother and father told him about Indians and how savage they were—utterly, hopelessly godless. As time passed, he had grown confused as the old men began to speak of their spirits in a reverential way. The way they held and handled their pipe, cut their tobacco, and handled their medicine objects—all of it was just the way the dark-coated circuit preacher would hold his communion goblet or pass out the broken bread or say his long ranting prayers, eyes uplifted to the top of the tent that passed for a church back in . . . back where he had come from in that other lifetime.

While the Comanche had no pantheon of gods, no religious order to things, they nonetheless lived closest to the earth about them. Here, in this land, they revered the buttes and rocks, the summer breeze and the winter's wind, the springs and creeks and rivers, along with the sky overhead that filled with lazy clouds, or with nothing more than endless blue. Easily and without fuss, they saw themselves as only part of the greatness in a world where everything, from rock and leaf to animal, had a spirit.

"Man is born evil," his mother had taught him, drumming it into the minds and hearts of her three children. "He is evil and is saved only by the grace of God. Man will always be evil, and there is nothing we can do about it."

"But we try to be good," he had told her, sitting at her knee before the fireplace, the light flickering on the pages of the family Bible.

She always shook her head at him, smiling in that way of hers that softened her hard-bitten theology. "Try as we might, only the Lord Jesus Himself can make our way to heaven for us. For man was created to be evil—and evil he will stay until the day he dies and goes to dwell in heaven with the Almighty."

As much as he had feared these people when he had come here to become part of their life, frightened to his core when he was dropped from the back of a warrior pony, Tall One now feared all the more going back to what was before. It did not fit, like the clothes he had shed long ago, not only because he had outgrown them, but because he had quickly worn them out.

"Let's go down to the creek and watch the girls bathing," suggested Coal Bear.

The younger boys bobbed their heads eagerly, especially Antelope. It was a routine that Tall One enjoyed, almost every day in camp sneaking down to peek through the willows and rushes at the young girls bathing and washing their hair as they stood or sat in the creek. The boys stared goggle-eyed at those different bodies beginning to show the growth of pubic hair, beginning to soften with the curves of rounded rumps and widening hips, the swell of those budding breasts.

"And we will pick out a wife for you, Coal Bear," Tall One said.

Coal Bear swung an arm up on Tall One's shoulder, then draped his other arm around the neck of Antelope. "My two little white-tongues, when are you going to realize that soon enough there will come a time for marrying just one. But for right now— all these pretty girls belong to us!"

The lot of them laughed as they strode from the lodge circle, heading downstream, where they would cross and double back toward the pool where the girls bathed.

It had been a long, long time since Tall One had thought of his sister. She would be as old as many of the girls he spied on. If she had lived. If she hadn't been killed by the white men who came and stole them away from . . . from the land where his family once lived. He could not remember her face any longer. Her name came even harder.

Yet Tall One said a small prayer for her as he followed Coal Bear and the others. A prayer that the rest of his family would in the end find the peace and happiness, the contentment, he had with these people and this land, with a new family.

•   •   •

For the longest time Jonah lay there while the dead man's blood turned cold and sticky, the disemboweled body sprawled across Hook's legs.

He still had a grip on the knife, and somehow found the Mormon's pistol, wrenching it from the dead man's fingers. The gun was gummy with gore.

It did not take long for things to grow as quiet as a graveyard in the desert night around him—except for the irregular wind that would gust from time to time to remind him that his ears still worked, heaving first from that direction, then circling around to blow from another. Below the wind keening through the sagebrush Jonah heard the nearby snuffling of the horses as they returned to grazing on the scant grass. He had cocked the dead man's pistol some time back, though he constantly ran a thumb back and forth over the hammer pad to assure himself he was ready when the rest came out of what darkness the night had left it.

How many, he could not be sure of—but likely the rest had taken care of Two Sleep. After that war cry and the explosions of white-hot light that rocked the night, Jonah couldn't be sure who was still alive. Except for the pain here and there on his body. The pain reminded him he wasn't dead and gone to heaven, not yet. One thing for certain: it was still too damned dark here to figure he'd landed himself in hell.

Yet it was growing lighter, almost imperceptibly and as cheerless as a hangover slapping a drunk's face. But day was coming nonetheless in the relentless crawl of the earth beneath the skies. Gray had begun to seep sluglike out of the east when he realized the horses were no longer just grazing—they were moving. Then footsteps, unsure and advancing quietly, inched toward him out of the murky dawn light.

He tried to lie as quietly as possible, turning only his head slowly to follow the soft crunch of the footsteps. Jonah felt more than heard the movement on the earth as the feet circled around him many yards out. He tracked the sound with the barrel of the dead man's pistol, knowing he would have to pray for one more loaded cylinder when the Mormon he was hearing came out of the dark.

"Hook?"

Calling to him like this, he could not be sure they didn't know his name.

"Hook? Where you?"

Jonah thought he saw the movement of something dark off to his left and leveled the pistol in that direction.

"C'mere and get me!" he whispered harshly.

Ready to fire at the first shift in the dark shadow as it rose from the sagebrush, Jonah felt the breeze stiffen, and he suddenly recognized the long, loose hair.

"Think you was one of them," Two Sleep said as he strode up and crouched beside Hook.

"I almost killed you, you stupid Injun." He said it with relief.

Two Sleep gazed around a moment. "All them gone. Make quiet so quick. Two for you. Rest for me."

"You're bleeding."

Gazing down at the spot where his shoulder met the arm, the Shoshone replied, "Chew some root. Wrap up for two days. Something small. You hurt?"

"No, don't think so," Hook replied as the Indian grunted, heaving the heavy body from Jonah's legs. He sat up watching the ground turn gray in those moments while his head finished its wild, spinning dance. "They all dead?"

Two Sleep nodded, finally stuffing a pistol beneath the belt that wrapped his wool coat around his waist. "You want scalps?"

"No." He shook his head, hanging it between his shoulders. "Only one scalp I really want."

"He not here?"

With a struggle Jonah got to his feet, leaned on the Shoshone for a moment. "I got an idea where to find him."

"South." Two Sleep turned and strode back to the fire pit, using one foot to push a body off the pit where the clothes had smoldered and the flesh begun to burn with a sickening stench. "Coals in fire hole cook our meal. We eat. Wait the day till you ready to ride."

"I don't need no breakfast, you dumb Injun," Hook snarled sourly. "You remember we lost more'n a day already—riding back to take care of this bunch. I don't aim to lose no more time tracking Usher."

Two Sleep stared wistfully at the food and collapsed to one of the Mormon bedrolls. "Then we sleep. No sleep for me in night. Sit with you till ready to attack and fight. No sleep for me. I'm tired."

"Sleep if you want," Hook growled as he threw the first of the

Mormon's weapons down onto a rumpled blanket. "I'm taking all the guns, and what food they got. I'll leave you something to eat when you wake up from your nap. Figure to take any horses not lamed up to carry all of it."

"You go now?"

He dragged another gun belt from one of the bodies and pitched it onto the blanket with a clatter of polished steel. "Soon as I get our horses down here."

Two Sleep grumbled as he clambered to his feet. "You make me sleep on horse again today, Hook. You a hard friend to have."

"Don't have to go with me. Stay—take care of that shoulder."

The Shoshone stopped before the white plainsman. Staring Hook in the eye. "Yes. Yes I do have to go with you. Two of us. Not alone you go."

And Hook understood, staring into the dark pools of those eyes in the gray light of day-coming. "All right—I figure you do have to go with me after all is said and done. And I'll admit I'm glad you're along for the ride."

"I get the horses, Hook. Then we go," he said as he turned away from the white man, striding off across the sagebrush flats toward the boulders where they had hidden their animals, slowly rubbing his wounded shoulder.

Gazing for a moment to the east at the growing light, Jonah sensed more than ever the pinch of time, the way new boots pinched his feet. "Damn right we'll go, Injun. Lost enough bloody time already."

Book II

Forged in

Fire

15

S PRING HAD COME to the southern plains. Flowers bloomed and birds flocked in great heaving clouds over every new pond filled by the last thunderstorm. Chilled of a morning, the air nonetheless warmed long before the sun ever rose to its zenith. Shoots of young grass crowning the rolling hillsides nourished the winter-gaunt ponies with the promise of strength for renewed raiding.

An endless wind blew out here, this far west beyond any white settlement—wind that tormented Tall One's long hair, tied in braids now. It had been something on the order of four winters since last a pair of scissors had touched his hair. Filmy, milk-pale memories of a chair set on the narrow porch of a log building . . . a small boy seated there, a bed sheet swallowing him from the chin down . . . a dark, thin man busy above the boy with a comb and scissors. Cutting his hair.

Hair. The source of the Kwahadi warrior's greatest pride.

Tall One touched a braid wrapped in the fur of a buffalo calf as he peered east, wondering about that man from his memories.

Every day it seemed he grew more and more filled with doubt that he had ever lived another life, more than he was filled with yearning or remembrance of the past. Still, he could not deny that smoky wisps of ghostly trails troubled his mind when some smell, some sight, some texture, triggered recall. He always choked them down, afraid the memories would cause him doubt in what he was, who he had become with the Antelope People.

Most of all, Tall One was frightened to death that the Kwahadi would find out he was not what he wanted most to be—a young Comanche warrior waiting for his first pony raid—but that he was nothing more than a lying, thieving, murdering white-tongue after all. No different from all the rest of the lying, thieving, murdering white-tongues.

He shuddered in the dawn breeze as light ballooned around him, the sun rising reddish-yellow as a prairie hen's egg from the far eastern edge of the earth, a great blood-tinged benediction at the far edge of everything he had ever known.

It would not be a good thing to be found out, Tall One feared, for his people to think him no better than a lying, thieving, murdering white-tongue. Especially after yesterday when some far-roaming Kiowa warriors carried their news to the Kwahadi village of last winter's struggle with the enemy soldiers far to the east in what was called Indian Territory. That sort of thing always made the pale-eyed war chief laugh, his white teeth showing as he threw his head back, hands on hips, finding it very funny that the white man would call a section of all of this country "Indian Territory," when it all belonged to the Indians.

Long ago the Kwahadi themselves had roamed far to the north, where a few buffalo hunters were only beginning to shoot their way into the endless herds here and there beyond the banks of the Arkansas. Comanche war parties had wandered far to the east, where the *tai-bos* had driven the tribes from their native eastern lands, and clear to the south, where the pony soldiers and the Tehanno Rangers fought and struggled against the Mexicans. Just about everywhere now, *tai-bo* settlers wanted to grow their crops and raise their spotted buffalo.

On ground the Comanche had ruled for generations, making war and driving out the Caddo and Tonkawa. This was a land the speedy Kwahadi ponies ruled, they and their red-skinned war lords of the fourteen-foot buffalo lance.

Tall One had seen the older boys practice with those graceful, deadly lances, more a weapon for warfare than a tool for hunting nowadays. Riding in at a full gallop with the lance level with the undulating prairie, the young horsemen practiced spearing a burlap sack filled with grass and brush, rocks weighing down its bottom to give it the heft of a full-grown white man sitting saddle-high on a scaffold of mesquite branches. Each of them was taught to drive that grooved lance through the enemy's chest, to use it as a huge lever as they picked up their victim and unhorsed him, leaving the enemy to lie writhing on the plain.

Oh, how he wanted to go to war.

"You are unhappy the pony soldiers did not attack us last winter?"

Tall One whirled with a start, surprised to find the pale-eyed war chief behind him, his voice fracturing the dawn silence of this broken country east of their village, where he had gone to take refuge with his thoughts. Here the dogs did not bark, the ponies did not snuffle or whinny. Here he had believed he would be alone.

"Yes." Then he thought better of his answer. "No. I . . . just—"

"You want a chance at the *tai-bo*'s soldiers, just as any Kwahadi warrior does," the pale-eyed one replied. "Me too. Sometimes I want so badly that we ride them down and get this war finished once and for all time, Tall One. To wipe this land clean, return it to what it once was for ourselves and the buffalo. To drive the white-tongues out forever."

He recognized that distant fire burning behind the pale eyes. Tall One grumbled, "The Kiowa messengers say the soldiers slaughtered the camp of Black Kettle's Shahiyena camped on the Washita River."

The war chief nodded. "Then those soldiers turned around and fled when the Kiowa and Arapaho camped downstream rose up and hurried to meet the attack."

Tall One smiled at that. "How I would love to have been there to see the look on those soldier faces when they saw the warriors rushing to chew them up."

A smile crinkled the corners of those pale eyes. "Still, even though those soldiers fled, they came back the following moon, to harry the Kiowa of Lone Wolf and Satanta. Almost hanged both chiefs from a tree."

His throat constricted uncontrollably. "A terrible death, this hanging—for the soul cannot come out the mouth."

He put a hand on Tall One's shoulder. "You are learning well, my friend. And one day soon these will be more than mere words—they will be the feelings in your heart."

Tall One felt stung, challenging the war chief. "I feel it in my heart now!"

"Easy, Tall One. No one questions that you are Kwahadi already. All I mean is that the more you learn with every day, with every turn of the season, the more you become one of the Antelope People."

"You are my family now. The only . . . only family I can remember having."

"When we brought you here, you became part of a larger family still, Tall One," he said, gazing to the east as the red globe finally cleared the edge of the earth. "There are other bands of The People. Root-Eaters, Buffalo Followers, and Honey-Eaters. Others you belong to as well."

"More than anything, I want to belong to the same people you do," he said, yearning for the comfort of having his place.

The pale-eyed one looked down into the young man's face with a kind smile. "Perhaps you have touched more truth than you know. Perhaps, in a way, you and I do belong to the same people. Yes."

"Your mother?"

"You know of her?" He grinned. "Yes, of course you do. The others have told you, of course." Then he turned away as a cloud of something dark passed over his face, gazing up at the cloudless spring sky above them as he spoke sadly. "Winter before last, I learned that my mother was dead.

"We knew she had been captured by the Rangers, knew they returned her to the white-tongues, the Pah-kuhs, the ones she lived with before my father captured her to live with the Kwahadi.

"The *tai-bo* who told me at the Medicine Lodge council with the peace-talkers—he said she died of a broken heart."

Tall One's eyes wandered to that cloudless spring sky above them too. He could more than imagine how it must feel to be so lonely for your people, filled with so much yearning that your heart seemed as empty as that cloudless sky overhead. How the woman must have mourned, yearning to be returned to the people she loved. There were times when Tall One had imagined he knew just how great such grief was.

But that was before he had come to this life with the Antelope People.

The war chief gazed down at Tall One. "Tell me, my friend—if the white-tongues come for you, will your heart be glad to go back to what you had before?"

The words stabbed him with panic. "No—"

"Or will you find your heart truly broken when they take you back, find yourself missing the rain and wind in your face, the smell of many fires on your skin, the feel of a pony's muscles at the chase beneath your thighs? Will you long for the feel of this freedom no other man knows?"

"Yes. Yes!" he repeated eagerly. "I would remember. But—I am not going anywhere—"

He interrupted the boy by gently placing his fingertips on the youth's lips. "I wanted to know. For my own heart. For, you see, Tall One—the soldiers did roam across this country all winter long."

Tall One tugged the war chief's hand from his mouth. "I know that as well as any. Our skill in hiding kept us far from the wandering soldier columns all through the winter, even after the camp of Kiowa-Apache and Honey-Eaters was attacked and driven from their lodges, forced to abandon everything they owned."

"The soldiers are coming, Tall One. I want you to know that. Come a day soon, their Tonkawa eyes will find our village and the soldiers will attack. Come that day, what side will you be on?"

"The People!" Tall One answered strongly.

"Will you fight—and die alongside Antelope warriors—die to protect our women and children?"

"I will! I will!"

"There is nothing in your heart—no remembrance of your time among the white-tongues, nothing that will change what your heart feels now?"

"Nothing." And then Tall One gazed steadily up into the pale eyes. "If the white-tongues take me by force, then—like your mother—I too will die of a broken heart. Knowing that I have been ripped from my true people, Quanah Pah-kuh. Unlike you, *I* alone will know that great pain your mother knew. Like her, I too will die of a broken heart."

In these first days of summer, beneath the full Moon of Fat Horses, High-Backed Bull rode once more with the Dog Soldiers of Porcupine.

For much of last autumn and winter, he had journeyed far, hoping to discover word of the one who had fathered him, perhaps some whisper of where his mother had gone. But from the Little Dried River far to the south, to the Powder River country in the north, no one had heard of Shell Woman, or her daughter, Pipe Woman. More important, no one knew the whereabouts of the tall heads-above white man who had long ago hunted for beaver in the snowy mountains, the one who they said now scouted for the white man's army in these troublesome days.

This hunt for him would take time, for Bull knew the man he hunted could disappear among the whites like a big fish diving through endless clusters of minnows.

With the coming of spring and the rising of the shortgrass like a green blanket spread across the breast of the prairie, Bull had come across Porcupine and all his old friends. This season they rode with the Dog Soldier camps of Tall Bull and White Horse after last summer's death of Roman Nose and the infuriating standoff on the Plum River. The winter was spent preparing for their new raiding season. As the Kiowa of Satanta and the Brule of Pawnee Killer had raided last summer, as they themselves had raided across the length and breadth of Kan-sas, the Dog Soldiers vowed they would again make the buffalo ground run red with the blood of white men. This year they would push even farther north, push into the country the enemy called Ne-bras-kas, sweeping wider, ranging farther east, before they finally cut south as summer's long days waned and autumn made its coming known.

Only then would the Dog Soldiers retreat from the land stolen by the white settlers, leaving in their wake the dead and wounded, the slaughtered cattle and the charred ruins smudging the clean prairie sky. This would be a summer to drive the white man back to the east, where it was said he numbered like the blades of grass.

"I cannot believe this," Tall Bull had declared haughtily when confronted with that frightening but questionable news by messengers from tribes who lived farther to the east. "Your words are only the scared talk of those who would rather run than fight the white man."

"Neither do I believe it," Bull had said. "As a child I grew up around the white man's forts." The war council grunted their approval of his statement. "I have never seen so many white men that they would even number the blades of grass where Tall Bull raised this lodge of his."

He was proud of the smile those words had elicited from Tall Bull and White Horse both. And ever since, the Dog Soldier chiefs had seemed to desire the counsel of the young warrior of twenty-four summers, never failing to include Bull in those talks made to decide on which path the Hotamitanyo would take.

That recognition proved to be a pain-giving balm: soothing some of his self-loathing, taking his mind off his hatred of his own white blood. For too long had he wanted acceptance by his father's race. When Bull did not find it among the whites, he returned to his mother's people, only to discover that they too distrusted him, if not shunned him outright. Sired by a white man, born of a Shahiyena mother, and wanting nothing more than acceptance—for too long Bull found a home among neither people.

But now, it seemed, not only had the fierce and renegade Dog Soldiers made a place for him at their talks, they truly desired his counsel.

Quite by accident Bull had discovered that the only way he could find acceptance among the Shahiyena was to turn his back completely, irrevocably, on his white father and the white world. Although there were enough reminders of the mixed blood flowing through his veins, what Bull nonetheless hated himself for was the white taint to that blood. More than anything he feared that it would one day prove a stain to his medicine, his power, would ultimately undo his life.

Try as he might through that solitary journey of his last winter, Bull's time alone had done nothing more than allow him to brood on just how much he differed from the rest of these young warriors crowding the camp. Though he stood taller, though he might be bigger, of greater muscle, Bull wanted none of that. More than anything, he wanted to be dark-haired, black-eyed like them. He wanted most to have a father he could walk with through this camp of Hotamitanyo. A warrior father. A father he could be proud of. Not one of the enemy.

So he sat and cleaned his heavy pistol this last day before they would ride forth at dawn, drawing the cleaning cloth in and out of the barrel of the Walker Colt he had taken out of the dead, frozen hands of a soldier near the pine fort two winters before at the place where the Shahiyena and Lakota had slaughtered the hundred-in-the-hand. Others had claimed the muzzle-loading rifles. Bull had instead rushed in to claim one of the many-shoots pistols: a powerful, destructive weapon.

"You clean that gun so much, you will wear it out," chided Porcupine as he settled to his haunches in the shade beside his friend.

"Yours could stand some cleaning too," Bull said sourly, not looking up from his task.

Porcupine sighed as he leaned back against the buffalo-hide lodge. "This magic that sent you riding into the teeth of last winter, it did not help you find the father you seek. Why are you so sure you will find him now?"

He stayed his hands, the powder-streaked rag protruding from both ends of the pistol barrel. "Last winter I hoped to find word of him, or my mother. The time of cold is a season when the soldiers do not march, when the army does not need its scouts—its eyes and ears to guide the soldiers to the sleeping Indian camps."

"You believed you would find this father of yours in a lodge where you would also find your mother?"

He nodded, then said, "But I found neither one of them," as he dragged the oiled rag from the barrel. "So now I have greater faith in the journey we will make this summer. If we kill enough white men, capture enough women, steal enough of their spotted buffalo and burn enough of their dirt lodges—the pony soldiers will come after us."

Porcupine snorted. "That is one certainty no man will gamble against, Bull. The white man always swats back at that which troubles him."

Bull nodded. "Yes. But even more important—I know I will find my father this summer. If we kill and steal and rape and kidnap enough—then we will leave a wide and bloody trail for the army to follow."

"And you believe your father will lead the soldiers on that trail we will leave them to follow?"

With a smile Bull answered, "My father will not be able to deny the smell of Indians in his nostrils. He will lead the pony soldiers after us."

"Then you will find your father at last," Porcupine said.

"No," he replied. "I will kill him."

16

H IS OLD FRIENDS were going, one by one by one.
Compañeros and saddle-partners, trappers and frontiersmen,
trackers and guides and scouts for the army like Shadrach Sweete—they
were all dying off on Shad, one by one by one.

The end of the halcyon days of the fur trade had driven the first of
them from this land. Some fled back east to what they could muster to live
out their lives. Others like Meek and Newell pushed on to Oregon country.
Shad tried that, and in the end came back to what he and Shell Woman
knew best: living a nomadic life crossing the plains in the shadow of the
cloud-scraping Rocky Mountains. A man did what a man must to provide
for his Cheyenne wife and family. And for almost twenty years he had
found work here and there, at times guiding for those long, snaking trains
of emigrants bound for Oregon or California. Then too he had scouted for
the dragoons in those pre-war days and built a reputation so that when the
Army of the West came out here to stay, Shad Sweete had all the work a
man needed.

Like Jim Bridger had done, like Kit Carson.

Times like these, riding out ahead of an army column, searching for some sign of a hostile village on the move, made Sweete draw in and think on all that he had done in those glory days in the West, brood on all that had been taken from him.

Of late there had been more and more taken from the old man.

The first real blow was Ol' Gabe. Not until last winter did Shad hear that Bridger had give up and gone back east to Missouri, gone to live with a daughter back yonder, there somewhere. If it was so, that meant Jim had been gone from the plains almost a year now this summer. Going blind, some even claimed. Sawbones doctors didn't rightly know how, but some ventured that too much high, bright sun made that happen to a man.

Ol' Gabe going blind—after all the glory that them two eyes had seen?

"Wagh!" Shad had snorted the grappling roar of a grizzly boar. To think of the un-goddamned-fairness of it.

"Still, the army came to call on the legend," Major Eugene Carr, commanding officer of the Fifth U.S. Cavalry, had informed Sweete before the whole shebang set out from Fort Lyon, marching south to drive the hostiles toward Custer's Seventh Cavalry waiting east in the country of the Canadian River. "No less than General Philip H. Sheridan himself asked Bridger's advice on waging a winter campaign against the Cheyenne and Kiowa riding out of Indian Territory to commit their depredations on the settlers in Kansas, Shad."

"And what'd Ol' Gabe tell that little pissant of an Irishman?" Sweete had asked.

"Word has it Bridger wanted an audience with Sheridan his own self, personally—to tell the general what a damned fool idea the winter campaign was."

Shad had himself a good laugh at that, conjuring up that scene between the little banty-rooster of a general and that tall, rangy old trapper. "Had to come to Fort Hays his own self, did he? Just to tell Sheridan what the dad-blamed hell he was getting his soldiers into, I'll bet."

Later still that winter Shad had learned from army scout California Joe Milner that Joe had been at Hays to see it for himself when Bridger rode in from Missouri to have a palaver with Sheridan—been there to see the old eyes nearly gone a milky-white, to see how stooped Bridger had become with the crippling rheumatiz and joint aches, how all those years climbing cold mountains and wading through icy streams had made the man little more than a thinning caricature of the giant he used to be.

Joe said, "Gabe was most afraid of his claim to the fort."

"Fort Bridger?"

Milner had nodded, balling a fist up and laying it alongside his own neck. "He weren't the same man, Shad. Hardly could twist his head without causing hisself some pain from that knot of goiter eating away on his neck."

"What's this about the fort? Why, I helped him raise one of them buildings and a corral there myself. Ain't his claim with the army settled yet?"

"That ten-year lease he said he give the army is up now, but he ain't seen a dollar cross his hand in payment."

"Government ain't paid him for using that fort—all ten year worth?"

"No—and now even Sheridan hisself told Bridger the army's went and declared his land what they call a military reservation."

That bit of news had caused a cold knot to grow in Sweete's belly. "So they took it all from him—same as the army's gonna take anything else it wants." He waved a hand in a wide, western arc. "Take everything it wants from the Injuns, Joe."

"Blessed God, Shad. Should've seen how that old man longed for the olden days."

So it hurt now to think of Jim Bridger, gone blind, gone sad and melancholy tucked away there on his daughter's farm back to Missouri, tricked out of the deed to his fort by the army he said could use it. A sad, sad man who had made many fortunes over in his lifetime, forced now to spend his last days penniless, what with the money the government had stole from him.

Then Shad found out about Carson.

Already a year dead. Sweete didn't get word of it off the army grapevine until Kit was long gone. Buried a year last May.

Why, it seemed like only yesterday that Carson himself had lost his beloved Josefa, his Mexican wife.

Could it be true? So much time gone?

From the tales around Fort Lyon, Kit's last year was one that saw the old trapper's own ailments increase in number, especially the severity of the pains in his neck and chest.

"I come to be troubled with this great affliction because of that footrace I had with the Blackfoot, you know," Carson had explained to Shad many a winter ago—five, maybe six. "Staying alive back then just may be what's gonna kill me now."

"Always better to wear your hair and die a old man, Kit," Shad told him.

Carson had said he wasn't so sure.

An old man.

Damn, but Carson was no older than Shad himself was. And that realization shook Sweete to his roots now as he gazed down into the wide river valley covered with rolling swales of belly-high grass, the watercourse clearly marked by the leafy cottonwood and scrub plum brush.

Losing his Josefa likely had just about meant the end of Carson's string, Shad thought, staring west into the brilliant golden rays of crimson light as the sun sank out there on Colorado Territory where a year ago that old friend had taken his last breath.

"Damned shame too, Little Kit," he spoke to the hot summer breeze, squinting his eyes to make a vision of the short trapper swim before him in the shimmering waves of heat rising from the plains. "Damned shame any of us grow old afore our time."

More than anything Shad felt a sense of being lost, more that than he felt any sense of loss upon learning that Kit had gone ahead and crossed the great divide that one last time. Seemed he felt lost a little more every year, feeling as if he were being left with fewer and fewer of the fragments of his memories of those seasons spent with the old ones. What were Meek and Doc Newell and some of the rest doing out to Oregon now? How about Scratch—was he still lodged up with that Crow gal and their young'uns, high up on the Yellowstone? There were a few who hung on by their fingernails, refusing to give in to the women and the canting preachers and the whining barristers come to curse this great, open, free land.

But now even Jim Bridger had give up and gone east to die. And Christopher Carson more than a year buried in Taos.

Kit was no older than Shad.

Fact was, the army was hiring younger and younger scouts all the time. All Shad had to do was look around him every morning when the scouts rode out ahead of the column, every evening when they came in to report on the day's foray. This was a young man's business—this making war on the Indians of the high plains.

For the better part of the last year Carr's Fifth Cavalry had employed the services of two youngsters who knew their business—both William F. Cody and James Butler Hickok. At first a sullen Shad Sweete had no choice but to figure the army was intent on driving him out—what with the way it was bringing in all these young, snot-nosed kids.

Still, as time went on, two of those youngsters had proved themselves up to muster during Sheridan's grueling winter campaign. Cody and Hickok would do to ride the river with. Sweete figured he could trust them both to cover his backside in any tough scrape of it.

Shad gazed off to the right, finding the distant rider on the big buckskin horse he had traded from one of the Indian trackers. Bill Cody, chief of scouts for Major Carr and the Fifth. Between them rode a half-dozen trackers from Frank North's Pawnee battalion. Behind those Pawnee came Carr's cavalry and the rumbling wagons of their supply train. Cody was signaling to Sweete, waving his big slouch hat at the end of his arm, reining his horse around and heading back to the head of the column. Likely they'd make camp down on the good grass there in the valley beside the creek. The Driftwood.

More than two weeks ago they had marched out of Fort McPherson on the Platte in Nebraska. Carr's orders were to clear the country south as they searched for the bands of marauding Cheyenne wreaking havoc among the settlements of Kansas. It was easy to see even from this distance that Cody rode right past the Pawnee without giving sign of how-do or saying a thing one. Bill didn't care a lick for them—cared even less for Frank and Luther North. Shad had to agree with Cody's feeling for those North brothers earning their handsome reputation at the expense of the Pawnee. Ever since the Connor expedition back to sixty-five, Shad wasn't shy in admitting that those bald-headed Pawnee trackers worked hard at their job—this hunting for their old tribal enemies.

He talked with them in sign when he had to, and they gave the old mountain man their grudging respect. With their hands they called him "rawhide man," because, they explained, he was like an old piece of leather chewed on and spat out, and still none the worse for wear after all his years.

With a smile Shad had accepted the handle hung on him by the trackers, and with respect for their abilities his hand had gone up to crook a finger at his brow: plains sign talk for Pawnee—the Wolf People.

For those past two weeks the Pawnee were always the first to rise in the morning and the first to go to saddle. Under Luther North, the younger of the brothers, the Pawnee kept ahead of the Fifth Cavalry a distance of two to three miles throughout the day, as well as dispatching outriders to cover a wide piece of country on both flanks. Down from the Platte River, Carr had driven them. They saw no sign of hostiles as they pushed across Medicine Lake, then Red Willow and Stinking Water creeks, Black Wood and Frenchman's Fork, until the Fifth Cavalry struck the Republican River.

It was there on the fifteenth they had been hit by a small raiding party for the first time one evening. The seven Cheyenne warriors had disappeared over the nearby hills with more than half of the wagon master's mules, leaving behind one of the civilian herders on the slope of a hill, scalped and stripped. A second herder wore three arrows in his back for all his trouble, and clung to life tenaciously across the next few days.

Immediately pursued by the Pawnee, the Cheyenne quickly abandoned their mules, hopeful of making good their escape into the rolling hill country south of the Republican. In the end Captain Lute North's trackers dropped two of the horse thieves from their ponies, while five escaped. But Carr was fuming when North got back with his Pawnee. Angry at the trackers for charging out like an undisciplined mob without any orders, the major discharged Luther North from command until his older brother rejoined the column two days later when the entire outfit reached the Solomon River.

Where the Pawnee promptly found some recent sign of the hostile village.

After a fruitless search for the Cheyenne up and down the Solomon, Carr moved his column northwest to the Prairie Dog. From time to time across the next week, the trackers had come across sign of a small war party here and there. But, no travois trails scouring the earth.

Angrily growing desperate to find the enemy, Carr pressed on to the northwest, crossing the Little Beaver, then Beaver Creek itself, and back to the Driftwood. As summer matured, the sun hung higher, it seemed— hotter too. June grew old as they plodded across each small drainage, creek, and stream, climbing north by west, each new day stretching longer and longer still like a rawhide whang.

How Shad hungered for some of Toote's cooking. All too quick the army fare had grown tasteless: salt pork and hard-bread, beans and biscuits. Even the coffee tasted as if it had been boiled in the wagon master's axle grease and stirred with one of the engineer's rusty nails. The country hereabout lay alkaline, cursed with natural salt licks.

Hardly buffalo country.

Yet just yesterday the Pawnee had run across a small herd of buffalo and succeeded in dropping more than thirty in a surround. Then Cody did just what had earned him a reputation in supplying the army and the railroad with meat: on his new buckskin pony the young scout dashed off on a half-mile run, dropping thirty-six bulls and cows all by his lonesome. From that moment on, Cody was big medicine with North's trackers.

"Why you figure we haven't found any travois sign yet, Shad?" asked the young scout as he settled down beside the older plainsman at their evening fire.

Sweete stared into his cup of coffee and finished chewing the mouthful of buffalo loin contemplatively. "Could be there ain't no villages on the move. Only war parties."

"What's the chance of that?" Cody asked, sweeping some of his long blond hair back from his bare cheek. "Pretty damned slim, you ask me."

He nodded. "Damn slim, Bill. Or, you told me I had to put money on it—I'd say they got their village hid away someplace, far enough away from where they been raiding that we ain't run across sign of it."

"What happens if we keep up the pressure on the war parties?"

"They'll split up until there ain't much of a trail to follow."

"Long as we got one trail to follow, Shad—we got 'em. Right?"

"You know well as me, Cody: we only need one trail. We follow it—we'll find the rest eventual," Shad answered.

The young scout smiled as he leaned forward to cut a slice of the buffalo loin staked over the coals in Sweete's fire pit. "And when we find the rest of the war parties—we'll sure as hell find Carr's village of Dog Soldiers for him."

Here in the first days of the Moon of Cherries Blackening, High-Backed Bull found himself disgusted with Tall Bull and the way the man yearned after the white woman they had captured many suns ago.

Since then the Dog Soldier chief had lusted after the captive, keeping her to himself as his private concubine. Each night when he was done with her, Tall Bull threw the woman from the lodge, where the camp dogs were immediately drawn to her—likely drawn by the smell of the blood from her beatings, perhaps the earthy fragrance to her after Tall Bull's coupling.

Bull almost felt sorry for the woman as night after night he watched her crawl away naked from the chief's lodge, her small bundle of bloodied clothing clutched beneath an arm, doing her best to fend off the curious camp dogs.

So the disgust he first felt for Tall Bull had grown to revulsion. Not because the chief was a man who claimed his carnal rights to the white prisoner—but because Tall Bull was slowly losing interest in making war on the whites. Because of the woman, it seemed Tall Bull thought of little else but coupling. Not of attacking. Not of stealing horses and the spotted buffalo. Not of killing the whites. Every day he appeared to think of his loins a little more.

Though she was white, Bull could not bring himself to blame the woman. He cursed any man, especially a war chief, who thought of little else but coupling with a white person. That thought alone stoked Bull's inner rage. More and more it took increasing effort to keep from hating the white part of himself.

"You are always cleaning that gun," Porcupine said. "Come with us, Bull."

He looked up from cleaning the big Walker revolver to the handful of older warriors standing in a crescent around him. Bull gazed down the barrel, finding satisfaction in the gleam of metal in evening's fading light.

"Where do we go?" he asked almost absently.

"To talk to Tall Bull," said a war chief of great reputation. "You will want to hear what we have to say."

"Does White Horse grow weary of this waiting too?"

The war chief started to turn away, saying, "Come with us, High-Backed Bull. And you will hear me speak what burns in your own heart."

They found Tall Bull and took the chief to White Horse's lodge, where they quickly smoked a pipe without great ceremony.

"It is time we spoke of making more attacks," White Horse said directly.

Tall Bull's eyes flicked slowly from man to man around the circle. Yet he said nothing.

"This summer heat makes you grow restless, eh?" Wolf Friend asked his question of White Horse.

Bull watched for a sign from the face of Tall Bull, then that of his closest companion—Wolf Friend, one who would do his best to support the chief.

Bad Heart was hardly a friend to any man who did not want to make war on the white man. He and Bull were the two who stayed most loyal to Porcupine across the seasons. Bad Heart sneered as he asked, "Why does Wolf Friend ask this of White Horse? Does he think White Horse grows restless because he does not have a white woman to copulate with?"

The group laughed together, a little uneasily as they passed around a water gourd. Outside, the lodge skins were rolled up; beyond, a group of children hurried by in the deepening dark of twilight while the moon rose yellow as a brass rifle cartridge in the east.

"White Horse is right," agreed Plenty of Bull Meat. "We dare not let up on the white man now."

"*Aiyeee!* It is for us to keep attacking until the white man and his kind are driven out of this country for good," Yellow Nose said.

"What of the soldiers?" prodded Tall Sioux. "We go in search of the white man's settlements to attack . . . then the soldiers come after us. No—it is not the earth-scratchers we must attack now. I say we must go after the soldiers who come marching winter after winter to attack our villages."

"Tall Sioux speaks true," said White Man's Ladder with a cautious tone. "Soldiers search out our villages, butchering our women and children who cannot escape. Remember Black Kettle's people?"

"Black Kettle ate the scraps of food the white man didn't want to throw to his dogs," Porcupine muttered angrily.

"This is true! And now Black Kettle is dead!" Bull roared angrily. "Killed by the Yellow Hair on the Washita—because he believed in the word of the white man."

"Yes," Porcupine agreed. "Because Black Kettle thought he could have peace with the white man!"

"These old men who want peace . . . the ones who act like old women," White Horse growled, "their villages are filled with those who want to make peace with the white man. I say it is good that the soldiers catch and destroy them!"

Bull's voice rose. "We should not cry for any who die, for any who are caught by the soldiers—for they were stupid not to fight back with the last ounce of their strength!"

Tall Bull raised his hand for silence, ready to speak at last. "Perhaps High-Backed Bull's words are right. We cannot go on wandering this

prairie, trying to avoid the white man. Instead, as you say—we must attack
. . . and attack again. Track down every one of his outlying settlements. Kill
the white people squatting there on our buffalo ground."

"Still, what of the great smoking horses that move back and forth
across this land once grazed freely by the buffalo?" Bullet Proof asked.

"Because of the smoking horses, the herds have been cut in half,"
Feathered Bear moaned with a wag of his head. "No more will the buffalo
cross the iron tracks the white man has planted for his smoking horse."

"It is as if the white man has laid down two lines on the prairie," said
Red Cherries. He pointed an arm. "One north of us in the land of the
Lakota. One south toward the reservations. Now the herds can no longer
move freely."

"*We* no longer move freely across the land of our fathers!" White
Horse growled.

"This was the land of our fathers at one time," said Yellow Nose.
"Will we be known as the sons who gave away this land of our ancestors to
the white man?"

At that moment on the far side of camp, there arose a commotion.
Muffled shouts were heard coming from the east, along with the metallic
barking of dogs.

"Let our words rest now where our hearts lie," said White Horse.
"We must not be the last generation to ride free across this prairie. We
must fight, Tall Bull."

"Yes!" agreed Porcupine. "While other bands may run away, it remains for us to carry on the fight."

Energized, his blood running hot with talk of the coming struggle,
Bull said, "While other bands tuck their tails like scared rabbits, running
away to hide on their reservations—we Dog Soldiers must take the fight
into the lap of the white man!"

"When?" asked Heavy Furred Wolf. "When will we ride again!"

Tall Bull looked at the one who had asked the all-important question.
"From the mood of this council, I see no reason to delay."

"Tomorrow!" White Horse replied.

"Yes—let us ride tomorrow," Tall Sioux echoed.

The growing commotion outside the lodge drew their attention once
more.

As did most of the others in that circle, Tall Bull turned to the two young boys running up to the council lodge at full speed. He asked them, "What is this?"

"Our scouts!" huffed one of the two, out of breath. "They ride back on the run."

"On the run?" Tall Bull asked.

"They bring word of the white man."

"I think we will attack soon!" Wolf Friend cried in happiness.

Tall Bull grabbed one of the boys by his shoulders. "What is this news of the white man? Where?"

"Pile of Bones saw marching soldiers."

"Soldiers?" White Horse asked, crowding close upon the boy now.

His young head bobbed as he caught his breath from his run. "Pile of Bones saw them. Many. He says there are ten-times-ten for each finger on one hand."

White Horse looked around the circle of warriors. "Surely these are the same soldiers who have dogged our trail for more than a moon."

Bull grinned, spreading his arms wide as he roared joyously, "It is good, my friends! These swallows follow the hawk too closely. Now the hawk will turn and destroy the sparrows in one bite!"

"Attack!" shouted White Horse.

"*Aiyeee!* We kill them all!" Tall Bull roared.

Giddy with blood lust, Bull growled, "Swallow every last one of the sparrows and spit out their bones!"

17

GRITTA STARED AT the water crock, unsure that her prayers had really been answered. Not quite ready to believe the Negro had turned his back on the crock and left the tent without it.

Yet there it stood on the table, next to the tin bowl that he filled with warm water for her every morning. Beside the bowl lay the dingy scrap of coarse linen and a sliver of black soap she was expected to use in bathing herself. By itself the heat of this land was enough to make a person stink, not to mention the stench left on her skin by the grunting beast who had dressed and left only minutes ago. Almost immediately the Negro had come in with the steaming crock, poured some hot water in the tin bowl, set out the linen and soap, then hurried off without taking the crock.

Outside she could hear the big man's voice booming in laughter, hear the clatter of fork and knife on his plate as he went about his breakfast. This same ritual he practiced every morning, seated at his table in the shade of the tent awning after he had completed his foul business with her. Such a creature of habit, this one.

She stared at the crock.

Somewhere inside, a small voice echoed, dimly calling out to her in a voice Gritta did not recognize. Not at first. Yet it was the voice of a woman calling to her, a voice somehow familiar. Tantalizing her with the promise of release from woe: a means to leave behind this mortal, earthly veil.

"Don't wait. You can't afford to tarry a minute longer."

Whirling about, Gritta expected to find someone chiding her. But found no one there in the tent with her.

Loud noises swallowed up the small voice and invaded her small, private world. Horses whinnied and stamped out there, just beyond these tent walls. Something deep within her, something that clung on to the familiar routine of each day now reminded Gritta that the men would be breaking camp shortly.

"You must act now—if you are going to act at all," scolded the tiny voice inside her head.

She glanced over her shoulder again, found no one there, and shuddered to think it was her disembodied soul speaking to her. Ordering. Demanding.

"The crock. Go to the crock."

Glancing one last time at the gap in the tent flaps, Gritta willfully stepped over to them and straightened the canvas so that they overlapped, just as she did whenever she sponged herself of the mornings before leaving the tent and boarding the ambulance to ride out the day. She went back to the table where the bowl and crock sat, then stared down at her hands. They had gone soft, not feeling like her hands at all. Marveling at their smooth texture, she ran one over the other, then pushed up the loose sleeve on the left arm and gripped that wrist tightly in the vise of her right hand. The white skin slowly bulged as the blood trapped in the veins, gone bluish beneath her skin—so pale now after so, so long without the sun. They did not look as if they were her hands.

Perhaps it would not hurt her—since these were not her hands any longer.

"The crock. Take the crock."

"Yes," aloud she answered obediently, releasing her wrist and seizing the tall crock between her trembling hands.

"Break it!"

Bringing it over her head, she flung it down against the edge of the table, clenching her eyes at the explosion as shards and slivers rained across her, warm water splattered, steamy, drenching the front of her open dressing gown. The sudden flush of moist heat felt welcome, reassuring as she fell to her knees in the muddy puddle there beneath the tiny table and found what she was instructed to find.

"A big one. Do it right the first time!"

Savagely dragging the gleaming shard of crockery across her wrist once, she gazed down at the sundered flesh beading with the bright red blood.

"Again! Cut it—you must hurry! Cut it—again, again!"

Once more, twice, then three times more she raked the shard across her inner wrist. Shiny, gleaming, warm liquid made her swoon as she crouched there on her knees, drenched with crimson as the clamor suddenly ballooned around her.

Hands seized her, yanking Gritta's left arm away from her body, other hands grappling with her right hand, prying the sharp sliver of crockery locked in her fingers. Gritta felt far more pain in those fingers the others bent backward than she felt in that welcome, reassuring warmth in the wrist.

"Damn you! Damn you, George!"

"I'm sorry. So sorry, Colonel Usher!"

"Get her feet!" Usher ordered as Gritta began kicking to free herself: lashing out, flailing about at those rescuing her.

There were more than two of them on her now. The fog of faces, smells, cursing voices all tumbled together as they pinned her legs, lifted her.

"Get the wrist, dammit!" Usher growled. "Stop that bleeding."

"She's fighting too much, Colonel! Goddamn—it's just spraying all over me!"

"George—by God! Get something and wrap her wrist!"

"Yessir!"

As they threw her down on the mattress, yanking her arms out from her body and pinning her legs atop the rumpled blankets, Gritta began to sense the first rise of pain in the wrist. The warmth was seeping out of her— replaced by spidering slivers of a cold so icy, she knew she had done some damage.

In the struggle an arm crossed in front of her eyes, and she snapped for it, feeling the taut flesh give beneath her teeth.

"Eeeeiks! The bitch . . . she's got a holt of me! Get her off! Get the goddamned bitch off me!"

Someone pulled her hair, yanking her head back brutally. Gritta felt some of her hair come loose as she struggled against them, at the same time sensing some of the flesh tear loose from the man's arm still locked between her teeth. His blood felt warm and thick on her tongue as the pain grew across her scalp.

"Jesus damned Christ! Lookit this, Colonel! The bitch gone and took a hunk outta my arm."

"Damn you, woman!" Usher bellowed.

She saw his arm swinging toward her, his balled fist at the end of it like a blur, and unflinchingly met it with the side of her face, staring up at him with a smile on her lips. Her head lolled crazily to the side. Usher swung at her again, backhanding her across the other cheek. Still she looked up at him with real triumph lighting those cloudy blue eyes of hers.

Usher glared at her, his eyes wide with disgust, starting to pummel her again.

Gritta glanced over at the wounded man gripping his bloody arm, dark fluid oozing between his fingers where he held himself. Then she looked back at Usher and spat her tormentor's bloody flesh right into Usher's face.

His left hand swiped the bloody gore from one eye, some of it trickling down into the black mustache and beard, his face twisting into something of unmitigated terror. Usher struck her with an open palm, again and again and again until she sensed the bile burning the back of her throat.

Coughing it back, choking down on her own vomit, Gritta was powerless to move against the hold they had on her as she convulsed on the hot, stinging fluid trapping her lungs. She felt herself slipping away.

Blessed, blessed death—come take the one who is ready.

"You got that wrist now?"

"Yessir."

"Simes!"

"Colonel?"

"You and Hampton take George outside."

"Sir?"

"Take the nigger outside and tie him to that cottonwood by the fire."

"Tie him—"

"Yes, by damn! George will be punished for this."

"Colonel—I'm terrible sorry for—"

"Get the nigger out of here! *Now!*"

The commotion quieted somewhat after that, allowing Gritta to turn her head, to roll it slightly to the side and spit out the blood from the wounded man, spit out her own blood from the tongue she had cut on her teeth, spewing free the sour, stinging bile trapped at the back of her throat where it had gagged her.

Convulsing for a moment, Gritta knew she was going to die as Usher dragged her head back so she would have to stare directly into his face, her chin clamped painfully in the palm of his hand.

She winced as his other hand brushed some of her hair out of her eyes, his fingers then tracing down the side of her cheek, where she flinched with pain, sensing that her flesh was already puffing in hot protest to the beating. In the end his fingers stopped at her throat, where they slowly, agonizingly tightened.

She had no will to fight him. As her eyes rolled back in her head she thought she saw other faces behind his. But they only watched in fascination as Usher tightened his grip all the more. No one held her now. Her arms felt light and free: she could grab his hand, pull it away from her throat if she had wanted. But Gritta did not try to stop him. She wanted him to kill her.

Though she could not speak with her lips, her eyes told him what to do. In silent triumph they roared out at Usher.

"Kill me! Yes, go ahead and kill me!"

The warmth trickled from the corners of her eyes as he released his crushing grip on her windpipe. Gritta's body betrayed her, savagely drawing in that first hungry draught of air.

"Don't — you — ever — try — something — like — this — again," he said each word singly, menacingly, almost at a whisper so that she felt stung by the hot breath of each syllable flung against her face.

Usher leaned back from her, drawing out one of his long-barreled pistols, and placed the muzzle against her temple.

"This would be too damned easy, woman."

He drew the hammer back, his face working around those glowing eyes, contorting as it twisted one way, then another, before a sinister smile finally eased the contours of the face above hers. Usher slowly dragged the pistol's muzzle down her swollen cheek, down the bruised flesh of her neck, circling one breast, then tracing its way down to her groin. He jammed the muzzle hard against her pubic bone.

Again she betrayed herself, and tears flowed with the pain he caused her, working the pistol barrel inside her.

"Here. This is where you hate me most, isn't it?"

She only stared, silently weeping, beginning to hurt across every inch of her body. Shame hurt her most of all.

He slapped her again, hard enough that she felt the flesh of her cheek tear against her teeth. Still, she forced herself to stare up at the taunting, smiling face hovering in the heat above hers. Usher drove a fist into her cheek again, then pressed the pistol barrel deeper into the most private part of her—where he had defiled her time and again across the eternity she had suffered with him.

"You'd like me to kill you—wouldn't you, woman?"

He released the hammer slowly, then cocked it again, over and over as he rubbed his crotch luridly with a left hand, then suddenly turned to the others in the tent.

"Tie her to the bed. Tight. I don't want her getting loose while I'm outside seeing to the nigger."

Usher wheeled about, ramming the pistol back in its holster at the front of his hip, and tore through the tent flaps.

"Wagon master!"

"Colonel?"

"Bring me your whip!"

As two men began lashing her to the rough-hewn posts of the prairie bed, she heard George begin to whimper, begging Usher to stay his hand. In the utter stillness of that morning George begged for his master to grant him mercy—

Then came the first crack and the Negro's shrill cry. Almost inhuman. Like the soul-grating screams of the women Usher's men used up before they were killed.

Again and again the whip snarled against flesh, until George's cries softened into the blubbering whimpers of an infant, sobbing incoherently.

"Pull him down!" Usher ordered beyond the tent flaps. "Throw him in one of the wagons and let's be moving—I want to put forty miles behind us today—put this piece of country far behind me!"

Gritta listened as the men who had tied her stood at the flaps, holding them aside and staring out.

"He opened that nigger up like a gutted hog," one of them whispered.

"Never'd want him to take a whip to me, not that one."

Her sundered wrist was bound with a thick strip of her dressing gown, around which they had looped the rope. Her scalp burned where the hair had been torn loose, her eyes grown as puffy as her lips, the blood's ooze slowing.

Gritta cried bitter, slow tears, cursing herself as she listened to George's blubbering fading in the distance as they dragged him down, hauling him off to a wagon.

She cursed the voice that had driven her to this. Not that she regretted the pain she had brought upon herself. Instead, the woman cursed herself for the selfishness that had brought such evil down upon the Negro.

She vowed when she next tried to kill herself that she would not put another living soul in the path of Jubilee Usher's wrath.

18

Early July 1869

S HAD FELT SORRY for the young soldiers that Monday morning as the column was breaking camp. The day before had been the Fourth of July—and because of it Carr had kept a tight rein on his troops. He ordered all guns kept silent, with no wastage of ammunition. It hadn't been much of an Independence Day, most grumbled that morning as orders came down to saddle up: not much fun singing songs of flag and country, without firing off a round or two in celebration.

Flag and country—these sentiments seemed about as far away for these youngsters at this moment as the Oriental silk trade would seem to an old Rocky Mountain beaver trapper.

As he finished saddling and dropped the stirrup over the cinch, Shad Sweete heard his name called out and turned to find Cody reining his big buckskin to a halt.

"Where we riding off to today, Bill?" he asked, gazing up at the young scout.

"Ain't *we*, not this morning, Shad," Cody answered, crossing his wrists over the saddle horn. "You're riding out with Lieutenant Becher's Pawnee patrol."

"The German?"

Cody nodded.

"Sounds like Carr's got different work lined out for you."

"Wants me to keep this column's nose pointed north. Figures that's where the Cheyenne are." Cody gazed off into the distance. "They're out there somewhere."

Shad stuffed a moccasin in a stirrup and lifted his immense frame into the saddle. "We'll find them, Bill. That, or them Injuns find us first."

"Either way—Carr will get his fight."

"I see it through the same keyhole as you, Bill," Shad agreed. "Carr wants a fight of it—to show what this outfit's made of."

"Can't blame the man—especially after Custer's had him all the opportunity to write his own name in glory."

"Keep your eyes on the skyline today, Cody," Shad said, nudging heels into his mount and easing away. "I smell Injuns on the wind."

A Nebraska resident like the North brothers, Gustavus W. Becher had come to America from Germany less than nine years before. He had immediately joined the Union Army and proved himself a capable leader. In his late thirties, Becher was now one of Major Frank North's white officers, commissioned as a lieutenant and assigned immediate command over fifty of the Pawnee battalion. He and the gray-headed plainsman in greasy buckskins would be the only white men riding along with the Pawnee on this important probe into the country west of Carr's line of march.

"Goot mornin', Mr. Sweete," Becher called out in his thick accent. "Glad to have you along." He turned to the Pawnee sergeant nearby, telling him in his inimitable German-clipped Pawnee tongue to mount the troops.

Becher turned back to the plainsman. "You care to ride vit' me, Mr. Sweete?"

"Be a pleasure, Lieutenant."

The German's smile formed little more than a straight line at his lips. "Let's go find some Injians for General Carr, vat say?"

It wasn't long before the rising sun made its full and glorious presence known at the horizon. As it climbed higher into the heavens, the heat bubbled around them and the ground radiated like a glowing skillet beneath the riders feeling their way up Rock Creek from the Republican River, probing north by west through that morning as the distance shimmered in mirage.

"Man can boil in his own juices out here, Lieutenant," Shad said. "This country is like a frying pan, yes."

"Maybeso like a griddle."

"Fry you from the bottom und the top."

After a short rest at midmorning to water their horses and let the animals blow, Becher ordered the Pawnee back into the saddle until noon, when the lieutenant signaled another halt to rest both men and animals. Here they were still miles from the next creek to cross, so each man had to settle for jerky, washing it down with what he still had in his canteen.

As he settled to a squat beside Becher, Sweete could read the strain at the corners of the man's eyes, in the way the lieutenant held his mouth. That normally implacable German stoicism was beginning to crack under the weight of not finding the smallest hoofprint or camp fire that could belong to the enemy Major Carr wanted more than most anything.

"Vat do you make of it, Mr. Sweete?"

Shad just shrugged. "If they're out there, Lieutenant—we'll run across sign soon enough."

"Better sooner than later, eh?"

"You want to make a fight of it, I see."

Becher chewed on some of his dried meat before answering. "If there is to be the fight of it vit' these Cheyenne that every man says there vill be—then I vant it to come soon. Better that it come sooner than later . . . no goot v'en the soldiers grow veary of the chase."

"Did you chase the enemy much during the war?"

Staring at his dirty boots, the lieutenant nodded. "Yes. Chase and vait. Chase and vait some more. Then we finally fight. V'en we did—many . . . many men died. Then we chased some more."

Shad cleared his throat, sucked down some warm water from the canteen, and swiped a hand across his lips. "S'pose I agree with you then, Lieutenant. If there's bound to be a fight with Cheyenne Dog Soldiers— better that we go ahead and get it over with."

After some twenty minutes Shad had them back in the saddle, this time pointing the trackers due north toward Frenchman's Fork, feeling their way into that sandhill country that rolled in broken rumples west into Colorado Territory—an endless, vaulting monotony of tableland shimmering beneath the summer's highest, hottest sun, baking grass and sand, man and beast, in its unmerciful crucible.

To break some of the monotony, the old beaver man told Becher he would outride the left flank for a while, keeping the main column of Pawnee in sight. For the next two hours he kept his horse pointed north for Frenchman's Fork, enjoying the solitude. The hotter the humming air grew, the more Shad drifted into a hypnotic reverie, dreaming on the high, cool, beckoning places to the west. Off yonder would be North Park, Middle Park, and the Bayou Salade—where Ol' Bill Williams himself claimed he would reincarnate as an elk bull with one lopsided antler just so all of his *compañeros* would recognize their old trapping partner.

Shad thought it strange to hear gunfire—knowing that most every old hivernant of the mountains would know which bull was really Ol' Bill—

—then Sweete realized it wasn't his daydream. Real shots crackled off to his right. More than four hundred yards to the east Becher was instantly in the thick of it—the lead of his column caught by surprise in the rolling land that had hidden the enemy until the moment of attack.

Shad could make out Becher's German-laced Pawnee. Could hear the Pawnee's shrill war songs.

And behind it all arose the unmistakably deadly wail of eagle wing-bone whistles and the war cries of Cheyenne Dog Soldiers.

As Sweete pounded his heels against the horse's tired flanks, he watched the fifty Pawnee split themselves into three squads, sending horse holders to the rear more than fifty yards.

Dropping to their knees as the full brunt of the onrushing wave washed toward them across the sunburned grass belly-high on the rolling sandhills, North's trackers prepared to make their stand. Shad dismounted near them quickly, leaving his horse behind, and huffed the last of it on foot.

"How many you t'ink, Mr. Sweete?" Becher hollered as the racket of throats and gunfire grew in volume.

"Hundred. Maybe more, Lieutenant."

"Count them, by dam't! I vant to make an accurate report to General Carr." Becher ripped open the reloading door in the stock of his Spencer and drove home a full Blakeslee reloading tube. "Und v'en you're done counting, you can fire at vill, Mr. Sweete. Any time you like!"

"Give me something to hit—and I'll do just that!" Shad snapped back at the German.

He was waiting for the enemy to close on them, while the lieutenant and the Pawnee fired at the Cheyenne horsemen still more than three hundred yards off to the north, but coming rapidly. Bright, glittering sunlight bounced off their weapons and war paint and shields and greased scalp locks. Two bunches of them each made a sweeping arc back against the other just out of rifle range. ·

"This bunch knew ve vere here?" Becher asked.

Shad shook his head, still waiting, watching. Looking over the distant riders as best he could. Wondering . . .

"No—they likely didn't have an idea one of finding us here. Just bumped into us, I'd lay."

"Dam't well look ready to fight, they do—this bunch not looking for us, Mr. Sweete."

"You're right on that count, Lieutenant. This bunch does look all dressed up for a scrap, don't they?"

With each side-to-side sweep of the double arc, the near-naked horsemen drew a few yards closer, and closer, then closer still. Yet, for all the lead fired and as hot as things were growing, two, and two only, of the Cheyenne lay motionless on the slope of the grassy hillside. Again and again the horsemen probed the Pawnee squads, jabbing here and there, feinting a full frontal charge of it before pulling back. Yet, as daring as the Cheyenne were becoming, there was little the frustrated Pawnee could do but watch the enemy horsemen ride in close, then drop to the far side of their ponies as they swept magnificently along the Pawnee flanks.

If Dog Soldiers were good at anything, they were good at taunting their enemy before they came in for the kill. And in this case, the Cheyenne were old, old enemies of the Pawnee.

"Mr. Sweete!" Becher hollered, his voice near cracking in volume as he hurled his shrill call over the tumult of gunfire, death songs from the horsemen sweeping past, and deafening war cries from the Pawnee trackers themselves.

Shad crabbed over and did his best to shrink his big frame down in the dry, stunted grass. "Lot of noise to it. And damn if they don't put on a pretty show—their parade too." He watched the look of incredulous confusion cross the soldier's face.

"I vas getting ready to ask you v'at you t'ought the odds vere that ve vould be overv'helm't," Becher said sourly.

"They ain't working up much steam, Lieutenant," Shad said, tearing the grin off his face when he found the soldier in no mood to make light of their situation.

"Vat the hell that mean?"

"Means them horsemen likely break off soon."

Becher eyed him severely. "You expect me to believe that? After they already lost two of their number? Vat makes you so sure they von't do everyt'ing to run right over us?"

Shad chewed his tongue a moment to keep from snapping at the German. "Lookee here, Lieutenant. I wasn't told to come along to help you with the Pawnee—you got things well in hand there. I thought I come along to help tell you about the enemy. If you don't want my—"

"Just speak your piece, Mr. Sweete."

He drew himself up a bit, then gazed back at Becher. "To them Dog Soldiers—these odds ain't near good enough in their favor. Besides, Lieutenant—them warriors really are just as surprised as we are. Shit, I figure they already found out they can't run us over, like you figure they'll do to us. So my bet is them Cheyenne gonna pull on back, ride off to fight another day."

Becher's eyes quickly swept over his three squads, as if to assess some of the growing commotion among the trackers. "I just pray to Gott you're right, Mr. Sweete. From vat I see—ve're in trouble already as it stan'ts. These men don't ha'f enough ammunition vit' us to make a stan'ting fight of it."

Shad only nodded and fell silent, thinking a prayer might not be so bad a thing, after all. Yanking up the flap to his sizable leather possibles pouch he had hanging over his shoulder, he was reassured to find the three extra Blakeslee loading tubes for his Spencer rifle inside. Through his many years trapping the high streams of the Rocky Mountain west, Sweete had carried greased patches and huge molded balls of Galena lead along with vent picks and flints and repair tools for the three flintlock rifles he had packed up one side of the Shining Mountains and down the other across two decades of chasing castoreum. But no more were there the two powder horns hung from that pouch's wide strap.

None of that heavy truck did he carry these days, abandoning the bulky trappings of that bygone era—powder, ball, and patch. Still, he never quite shook the feeling of being naked without the pouch—its continued comfort beneath his right arm served to remind him of just how far man had advanced during the bloodletting of the Civil War in learning how better to kill his fellow man.

No more was it a matter of taking one shot—reloading—and shooting again, all within the space of a minute. Now a good marksman could efficiently empty a handful of saddles at a respectable range in the same time another man reloaded a muzzle loader for his second shot. Yet as Shad brought back the hammer on the Spencer and started to nestle the rifle into the crease of his shoulder, the old trapper stopped, squinted, then shielded the high light from his eyes with a hand.

He was studying the heaving, galloping ponies a little closer, the clay paint dabbed and smeared across their necks and flanks: crude hieroglyphics and potent symbols. Shad strained his old eyes across that shimmering distance to make out the face paint and hair fobs of the onrushing horsemen. For a moment he thought . . . then could not be sure with the glimmering cascade of sand and hoof.

From the start Bull had grown straight and strong as a lodgepole pine. Back in his youth the boy had already shown the ropy muscle of the deer in his powerful legs, the rippling muscle in his arms like that under the hide of a mountain lion. Maybe that was Bull atop that blaze-faced gelding dotted with crimson hailstones . . . maybe not. But—even at this distance, he told himself, wouldn't a father recognize—

In a swirl of sand the two files of horsemen racing down their flanks suddenly sprang themselves back atop their ponies like a child's string toy and performed a pretty arc back against one another as they swept noisily away from the Pawnee.

"What'd I tell you?" Shad roared at the lieutenant when the two swirling columns scattered over the far slopes to the north, leaving Becher's Pawnee behind to hurl their angry oaths at only the summer sky.

"By Gott, ve did it! Three of them dead by my count, Mr. Sweete."

"Them Pawnee of your'n did it, Lieutenant," Shad admitted. "Wouldn't believed it had I ain't seen it with my own eyes—them Injun trackers fighting like white men. By damned this bunch stood and took the best them Dog Soldiers had to dish out. Beehelzebub! But I was feared they would bolt and go to horse to mix it up when the Cheyenne rushed us."

"To horse?"

"Yep. Only natural for a Injun to want to fight from horseback. Brought up that way. And, after all—these Pawnee is first, last, and always will be Injuns, Lieutenant."

Becher rose from the grassy sand to signal in his three squads. Horse holders huffed up with their mule-eyed mounts as Shad once more grew aware of the heat beating at the back of his neck. Up and down his neck he dragged the greasy, smoke-stained folds of a huge black bandanna, resplendent with a splash of red Taos roses, pushing aside the shoulder-length waves of iron-flecked hair.

"V'ere you t'ink ve are now, Mr. Sweete?" Becher asked, dragging a sleeve down his nose where a drop of sweat clung like a translucent pendant. "Colorado Territory alrea'ty?"

Sweete peered off to the northwest. "If we ain't—we're damned close, Lieutenant. Don't really make a bit of difference to the general, does it? I figure all that's important to Carr now is that he has a trail to follow. And a hot one to boot."

Taking the reins to his mount from a Pawnee horse holder, Becher said, "Goot. Ve ride back now to bring up the main column."

"As hard and long as Carr's been pushing his soldiers, I'll wager the general's gonna be damned pleased to hear about us getting run at by these Dog Soldiers."

Becher nodded, smiling. "Very please't, I t'ink. So vat is special to these Dog Soldiers? Vat makes these bunch so important to us?"

With a knowing gaze on the hills where the horsemen had disappeared, Sweete replied, "Because when you get jumped by Dog Soldiers, you get hit by the best the Cheyenne nation can throw at you. The baddest, bloodiest red outlaws as ever forked a pony."

Swelling his chest with unabashed pride, the lieutenant grinned. "Vell, then, Mr. Sweete. No more do ve snoop our noses around on this gottforsaken groun't vit'out any sign. Goot size war party like this— painted and feat'ered—they vere out for no goot. And now Carr's got them!"

"Out for no good is right as rain. Them Cheyenne are letting the wolf loose, I'd say."

The German smiled even wider, smoke-stained teeth like varnished pine shavings. "Let's get these Pawnees back to Major North—so I can tell General Carr ve got Cheyenne wolves to track now!"

19

BULL SWORE HE saw him. Saw the man who had fathered him among the Shaved-Heads.

As he rode away with the rest, more than a hundred in all, High-Backed Bull twisted to look over his shoulder at the disappearing figures behind him among the sandy hills. The Shaved-Heads were standing now, still in their three bands. Others hurriedly led their big American horses to those who had held the Shahiyena at bay during the heat of the battle. And near the center were clearly two white men.

He could tell by the hair hiding their faces.

That bigger one—how many men of his size could there be on these plains? How many wore what appeared to be greasy buckskins? That low-crowned hat with its wide, floppy brim slightly upturned in the front . . .

"Leave them be," Porcupine said as he came alongside Bull, the whole of the raiding party urging their ponies into an easy lope upon seeing the Shaved-Heads were not going to pursue. Though he did not ask it, Porcupine's face registered some question. "We will fight them another day, my friend."

"When?" Bull asked, glancing one last time over his shoulder, hoping for another glimpse of the tall white man across the shimmering, mis-shapen distance.

"Three families will mourn tonight," Porcupine said. "Think first of the sadness that will visit our village. Only when the men have cut their braids, when the women have bloodied themselves and wailed can we take up the path of these soldiers and their Shaved-Head wolves come sniffing on our backtrail."

"When!" Bull snapped angrily, turning on Porcupine so suddenly, he flung sweat from his painted brow. "How long?"

Porcupine's eyes narrowed as he measured the young warrior riding beside him. "You are Shahiyena. And you ask me that question? Control the fire in your heart and think of your people. You are a Dog Soldier. Do not let me find you fighting this battle by yourself."

Sensing the sting of something heating its way through him with the war chief's words, Bull finally nodded. "Two days. Yes?"

He nodded at the younger warrior. "Two days, Bull."

"Then we can ride to attack again?"

"Two days and we will ride to avenge the death of three of our own. We are Hotamitanyo."

"We know the yellow-leg soldiers are coming—why won't Tall Bull or White Horse fight them in force?"

"If the day is right—we will attack the soldier column. Until then—we will be content to steal their horses, to harass the Shaved-Heads who guide the soldiers and watch for our chance to frighten the ones who drive their supply wagons."

"We can make the day right here and now, Porcupine. We can—"

"Wait two days, Bull. Those who have lost must have their grief, shed their blood."

"And what of us who carry a vow? What of us who have sworn to drench ourselves in another's blood?"

July was already eight days old.

For two marches following Becher's scrap with the war party, Major Carr kept his cavalry doggedly plodding north by west along the Republican River, without deviation. Then yesterday a platoon of North's Pawnee had come upon a scatter of footprints near the edge of an abandoned enemy encampment. They had called Major North and Shad Sweete over.

"We can't be sure, can we, Mr. Sweete?" Frank North asked.

Shad had shrugged. "S'pose not, Major."

"I'm for waiting."

"Waiting?"

"To tell the general. Wait till we have more proof. Till we got more of something solid to show him. Just from this"—and North's hand had pointed down to the windblown scatter of running tracks—"I don't think any of us can say for sure."

That was the indecision of yesterday. But this morning, they found their proof.

Telltale footprints that North showed to Carr.

Sweete had watched the effect those tiny impressions in the hardened sand had on the major. What he and the Pawnee had come across were not moccasin tracks—but instead the prints of a woman's slim boot. Carr had knelt over them, reaching out with a fingertip as if to measure the depth the tiny heel had made in the soil. Maybe even to measure the terror the woman must have experienced as the village hastily packed up to flee his oncoming troops.

"It raised the hair on the back of my neck too, Shad."

Sweete turned from staring hypnotically at the fire to find Bill Cody settling beside him. "What got your hackles up?"

"Thinking about them white women held captive by that bunch."

"Does Carr know there's two sets of them tracks?"

Cody nodded once. Staring into the fire, he answered, "I suppose he does know."

"I saw for myself the look on the man's face. He wants that village bad, Bill."

"How can you blame him, Shad? Them bloody Cheyenne. No telling what them bucks been doing to them Christian women—" Cody broke it off, realizing his mistake with the old plainsman. "I'm sorry, Shad. Just running off at the mouth like I do a'times. You and your family . . . didn't mean nothing by it—"

"No offense taken, Bill."

Cody stared contritely at the ground. "Just that when I looked at them boot prints—made me think on my own Lulu. Thank God she's safe back in St. Lou. Glad as hell she ain't out here to get caught up in this war."

Shad poked at the fire a moment before saying, "You know damned well who those women are, Bill. We all do. Know who their husbands are.

Ain't a man can move his white woman out here to this country that he don't know what chance he's taking with 'em. Go ahead and tell me that ain't why you keep your woman safe back to St. Louie."

Nodding, Cody replied, "I know it's gotta be Tom Alderdice's wife. And the other—Weichel—the German woman. Yes. Safer for Lulu back there."

Shad emptied his cup of lukewarm coffee. "Carr's not bound to stop this column for much of anything now that he's got a scent in his nose to follow. Damn well that he should too—'cause if we don't catch this bunch of outlaw renegades now, we likely never will."

"Naw. We can follow 'em wherever they go, Shad. Look: we come upon sign of 'em after all this time—we can do it again."

With an emphatic shake of his head. "You listen, Bill Cody—that bunch of red renegades gone and wheeled off to the north now!" He pointed into the deepening gloom of night. "Making for the Laramie Plains. From there, it's only a frog jump over to the Black Hills. That's sacred ground to them Cheyenne. For the Lakota too, for that matter. This bunch gets up there to say their prayers near the big medicine of their Bear Butte—why, we'll likely never see trace of them two women again."

Cody contemplated that for a moment before saying, "You figure we ought to tell the general he's gonna have to hump up and get his outfit high behind—or he ain't got a chance at catching that village?"

"If Carr don't push this bunch of worn-out men and broke-down horses even harder than he's been doing already . . . yes, we ain't got the chance of a horse fart in a winter wind to find them—"

Keening yips and howls abruptly resonated in the middistance of that summer night. Cheyenne war cries.

Shad's hand was filled with the Spencer, and he sprang to his feet with Cody, both of them sprinting toward the hammer of oncoming hoofbeats, that staccato drumbeat flooding off the hills beyond the dull, starlit splotches of tents in North's Pawnee camp.

They both had taken no more than a matter of steps when the Pawnee camp exploded with noise and the glare of gunfire in the night. Yellow flashes streaked the great indigo blackness as the muzzles of the trackers' pistols erupted. He could make out the voices of the North brothers shouting orders, hear the curses of other white officers, among them Becher's distinctive German—then it was all smothered under the racket of more gunfire and thundering hooves. Sleeping scouts and sleep-deprived pickets were suddenly jarred into a battle for their lives.

Frank North emerged from the shadowy flit of light and darkness as some of the trackers doused fires and pulled down tents. As a backdrop the tents and fires made a perfect target of a man. One of the Pawnee lumbered past, away from the fight and muttering angrily.

"Was that Mad Bear?" Cody asked the major.

North nodded, staring after the Pawnee.

Shad asked, "Where's he bound for?"

"The horses hobbled back there on the line. Likely he's going to mount up," North replied with a shrug.

"Better stop that one from going out there on his own, Major," Shad advised.

"I'd sooner try to stop a Cheyenne charge with a buffalo-tail flyswatter, Mr. Sweete!"

"Not that much firing from the Cheyenne," Cody said. "Can't be that many of 'em rushing camp."

"Shit—you know better'n that, Bill: could be a whole passel of 'em waiting out there in the dark for any of us to follow," Shad replied. "Draw a few of the cocky ones right out there and swallow them up like nighthawks."

Without needing any more advice, North flung his voice into the dark, shouting in Pawnee at Mad Bear, ordering the tracker back from his pursuit.

"Anyone hit in your camp, Major?" Cody asked.

North shook his head. "My tent got shot up. Looks to be all the damage right now. Those bastards came right past my tent, slinging lead into it. Lute's tent too. Then the sonsabitches were gone. Raced right out of camp and headed for the remuda to chivy our horses."

"Doesn't sound like they got a one of your animals—for all their trouble," Cody said.

"We had every one hobbled and cross-lined on my order," North said proudly.

Luther North suddenly took form out of the confusion, grumbling. "Frank—this shit is beginning to sour my milk."

"What's bothering you, little brother?"

"Twice now we been hit by these bastards—at night."

Cody nodded. "The army doesn't figure Injuns are supposed to attack at night."

Luther wagged his head, angry. "And now Mad Bear's gone after 'em."

"Sonofabitch," Frank growled. "I tried to stop him."

"Me too," Luther replied. "Didn't do no good, though. He just rode off shouting at me how he was worth a half-dozen flea-bitten Cheyenne on the worst day of his life—"

A trio of shots from the west side of camp interrupted the younger North. All four white men turned and dashed onto the prairie lit with no more than dim starshine here a matter of hours before moonrise. It was but a few yards before they bumped into ten of the trackers, who were talking excitedly.

"What they say?" Shad asked.

Luther North answered, "Mad Bear took off after one of the horsemen come running through camp. This bunch says they saw Mad Bear hit the bastard's pony, spilling the buck. So Mad Bear took off to claim him. Out there in the dark—and that's when they heard some more shots out there."

"Figure any more of them Cheyenne out there?" Cody inquired.

"Just shadows is all," the elder North said.

Moving into the darkness with the rest for about fifty yards, Shad watched a shadow loom against the starry sky. A smattering of the Pawnee tongue came out of the night at them. A moment more and they came upon one of the trackers hunched over a near-naked body sprawled on the ground.

As the tracker rolled the body over, Luther North asked, "We get one?"

"Dammit!" roared Frank North.

Shad recognized the dull sheen to the brass buttons on the blood-stained army issue the dead man wore.

"Shot in the back," Cody declared as the rest of the Pawnee began wailing, collapsing to their knees in grief around their fallen kinsman. "Went right through the heart."

"Then he weren't killed by the Cheyenne, Major," Shad explained to Frank North quietly.

"Ain't that a goddamned pity." The major wagged his head. "The others say they saw Mad Bear out there chasing them sonsabitches. But in all the confusion, they opened fire thinking he was one of them thieving murderers. Damn, if that don't fry my—"

"I want the Cheyenne too, Frank," Luther declared against the backdrop of the Pawnees' wailing death songs. "Want 'em bad as Carr does."

"They've got to be close, fellas," Cody said.

Shad agreed. "Damn straight they're close. Hitting us twice in three days. That village of theirs ain't far."

"We better go report in to Carr before he gets his belly in an uproar, Frank," Luther said.

"Won't he want to get his hands on this bunch soon now?" Cody said. "I'll suggest to him we lay in camp a day and send out some of your scouts to backtrack on this bunch, Major North."

"Sounds like a damned good idea to me, Cody. We'll be ready to ride out at first-light."

"Yeah," Shad agreed as he stared into the night-drenched distance. "Time we finally come up with something more than track soup to feed the general on."

Carr went along with Bill Cody's suggestion and ordered a day's layover for his troopers on the ninth of July while sending out several parties of Major North's Pawnee battalion to scour the area for sign of where the Cheyenne raiders had disappeared.

At the request of Captain Luther North, Shad Sweete had joined young Lieutenant Billy Harvey and five of the Pawnee to scout a sizable piece of country south and west of where Frenchman's Fork dumped itself into the Republican River. For more than fourteen hours beneath a mercilessly brutal sun they had punished themselves in the saddle, halting here and there only for brief watering of the animals, eating what they had in their saddlebags as they rode. In their wide sweep of the undulating plains of eastern Colorado Territory, early that evening the eight finally struck the Republican, still some twenty-five miles above the camp of Carr's Fifth Cavalry.

It was there that Lute North called for a brief rest to discuss their options with this much ground still to cover before nightfall. "If your asses are as sore as mine, I figure we could treat ourselves with some time out of the saddle. Ride in to meet up with the column come dawn."

"Just what this old man was thinking!" Shad replied as he climbed down and began rubbing his thighs in the way of a horseman long on the trail.

"Wait a minute, Mr. Sweete—don't you figure it best for us to ride to that hill yonder to the north? Just to take a look around before we settle down for the night?"

"You expecting company, Captain?" asked Billy Harvey.

"The Cap'n's right," Shad said, dragging himself back into the saddle and moving away with Luther North toward the top of the tallest hill in the area.

As the sun was settling in a fiery show of midsummer crimson, North called for a halt twenty yards from the crest and ordered one of the Pawnee to belly up to the skyline for a look around before the rest betrayed themselves.

The tracker began his walk upright, slowly crouching lower and lower until he was on all fours at the crest. Then suddenly he dropped to his belly amid the tall grass. Shad was dropping from the saddle by the time the Pawnee had pushed himself backward and was signaling in plains sign talk for the rest to dismount and join him. North ordered one of the trackers to stay behind with the horses.

When they arrived back of the crest, the sun was just then easing out of sight beyond the far mountains that from here appeared to be nothing more than a ragged hemline of horizon. Yet it was not the sight of those faraway and seductive high places, North Park and the rest of the central Rockies, that seized Sweete's attention.

It was what awaited his eyes down in the valley of Frenchman's Fork that made the blood pound at the old trapper's temples.

About a mile on west of where they lay, the creek flowed in gently from the north. Between that wide river bend and the bottom of the slope where the seven sprawled on their bellies was cut the gash of a deep ravine that every spring would fill with runoff to feed Frenchman's Fork. But this was summer, and the rainy season was long behind them. Instead of runoff, what filled the wide, sandy path of that ravine seemed to be the whole of the Cheyenne nation on the march between the willow and alder, plum brush and cottonwood. Ahead and on both sides of the column rode the painted, resplendent warriors atop their prancing ponies, old men and women trundling along on foot among the travois ponies, children and dogs darting here and there and everywhere noisily among the entire procession. On the nearby east bank of the fork, pony boys worked the huge herd.

Shad could see the lust for that herd in the Pawnee's eyes as he glanced at the others, could see the lust for all that finery of blankets and robes, kettles and clothing. Although they wore pieces of the army uniform and dressed by and large in the white man's clothing, riding army horses and carrying army weapons, the Pawnee were still Indians who coveted the spoils of war that could be wrenched from their ancient enemy.

"That Tall Bull's bunch?" whispered Lieutenant Harvey.

Luther North nodded, a finger to his lips for quiet. "Can't be no one else, can it, Mr. Sweete?"

"I figure the lieutenant here guessed right."

"What a stroke of good fortune, fellas," North continued. "For some time now the army's figured it was Tall Bull's band of Dog Soldiers that's been causing all the trouble after Sandy Forsyth's bunch made Roman Nose a good Indian at Beecher Island."

"That bunch is Cheyenne, all right," Shad replied. "Damn—but that's one big shitteree of 'em too, boys."

Less than two hundred yards away, the entire procession wound past the hilltop unawares, many of the ponies burdened with fresh, bloodied buffalo meat shot and butchered that very day. The seven observers fell quiet for long minutes as they peered down on the colorful, noisy caval-cade, until they saw the vanguard move out of sight among the brush as the village neared the mouth of the fork.

"Look at 'em, Mr. Sweete, and tell me if that bunch don't look about as done in as Carr's outfit is."

"You ain't far from the mark, Cap'n. Tall Bull's village ain't had it any easier than Carr's cavalry—not with women and young'uns to tote along, what with all their lodges and truck."

North turned with a grim smile crossing his crusted face. "I've swal-lowed enough dust to last a lifetime, but—we've got some news to carry to General Carr. Let's get."

"While the getting is good, fellas," Sweete agreed. "I got a bad feeling that some of those bucks down there might just want to ride on up here and take a look-see around the country . . . like we done."

North signed his Pawnee back from the top of the hill, and together the seven trotted downhill to the grazing horses. Taking up their reins, the outriders walked their animals downstream more than fifty yards before mounting.

"You care to lead out, Mr. Sweete?" The tension and excitement of the evening's momentous discovery was clearly etched on the soldier's face as his eyes burned into the old trapper's.

As much as he didn't care for Lute North, Shad had to admit the major's younger brother was acting downright civil about things. "Don't mind if I do," Sweete replied, turning to the five trackers and making some quick hand talk.

"What was that he told them, Cap'n?" asked Lieutenant Harvey.

North snorted as Sweete swung his horse around and put it into a quick lope that had worked itself into a hand gallop within ten yards. "That old scout just told them Pawnee they'd better lock themselves down on their ponies—because they were in for one fast ride!"

20

FOR THREE NIGHTS High-Backed Bull had cursed himself for not scraping together the courage to turn around and ride back among the Shaved-Heads, taking the scalp of the one he had shot in their raid on the soldier camp.

Not that any of the other Dog Soldiers found fault with him. Indeed, Porcupine and the handful of the others in on the horse raid all sang Bull's praises for charging alone among the enemy to count coup. Bull realized Porcupine knew the truth: that the young warrior had been less interested in counting coup on the Shaved-Heads than he was intent on assuring himself that the tall man he had seen during the fight among the sandhills was not his father.

Still, the truth is ofttimes an elusive thing, likely dressed in the clothing of an impersonator and often hiding behind the paint of a warrior's mask.

Perhaps if he had waited after the rest of Porcupine's raiding party fled the area near the soldier camp. Perhaps if he had stayed behind, not to take the scalp of the Shaved-Head he killed, but to lie just beyond the fringe of firelight. Watching. Patient. Then he might have caught a glimpse of the tall man his mother called Rising Fire, there among the soldiers and trackers. In the end Bull cursed himself, deciding he had missed the chance to kill the one who the white men called Sweete.

"There will come a time soon when we go after the soldier horses, to trouble them on our backtrail," Porcupine had said.

"No. They're getting too close for us to hit them and run any longer," Bull countered. "The distance has narrowed so that we can no longer take the chance of leaving our village behind. Instead, the warriors must remain close to protect the women and old ones."

Porcupine had looked at Bull strangely, then said, "Why do I have the feeling in my belly that those are only words to you—and not the guiding fire in your Dog Soldier's heart? Why can I no longer trust that you really believe what you are saying?"

Maybe the truth did indeed parade itself in any costume to fit the occasion.

But he was not the only one in that camp who toyed with the truth. Why had Tall Bull and White Horse said they would gladly turn over their white captives to the soldiers, if only the soldier column would stop dogging their village? Bull knew better. Neither of the war chiefs would willingly give up their white women. Not without a fight. And in these last days, that was what troubled him most: brooding on what it was about those white-skinned ones—about his own white blood.

Was it the evil of the white women that made the thinking of the two war chiefs run crooked? Was that why Tall Bull and White Horse thought more of themselves than they did of the rest of their people?

So was it his own white blood that caused Bull to test and push and strain at the truth? Was it the blood from the one the whites called Sweete that made it so easy for High-Backed Bull to lie?

No longer was Bull only angry. Now he was afraid. Feeling tainted and dirty, from the inside out—not sure if he could trust himself any longer.

As the sun came boiling up over the far edge of the world that dawn after Luther North's scout had watched Tall Bull's village going into camp, Major Eugene Carr issued his simple marching orders for the tenth day of July:

Upriver at all possible speed to catch those Cheyenne.

Even Lieutenant Becher's detail of ten Pawnee had themselves a running scrap of it with a small war party on the ninth.

The trail was about as hot as it could get, to Shad's way of thinking. And to look around at the grimy, dust-caked faces of those young troopers this morning, a man could see there wasn't a damned one of them who didn't know he was headed into a bloody fight of it.

It was only a matter of time now.

Through that morning Shad and the Pawnee scouts came across two of the Cheyenne campsites, in addition to the camp he had watched Tall Bull's people setting up the night before. In a matter of grueling, sand-slogging miles, Major Carr's Fifth Cavalry had eaten up the Dog Soldiers' lead by three days. It was there at the site of the enemy's last camp that the regimental commander halted, ordering the entire outfit prepared for any eventuality from here on out. As well, Carr sent back a half dozen of the Pawnee trackers and two soldiers to bring in with all possible speed the supply train due down from Fort McPherson.

As the sun grew all the hotter and the men sat sweating beside Frenchman's Fork, Shad watched a discussion on the command's readiness turn into a petty argument as tempers flared, embroiling both Carr and Major Frank North. While the civilian did all that he could to urge keeping the column on the move to catch the enemy before the Cheyenne reached the South Platte, Carr steadfastly clung to his need to resupply his command before coming in contact with that enemy.

"But if you're suggesting that I have no other choice, Major North—then I'll order a forced march with two battalions. The rest I'll leave behind to await the supply train."

"We've got to move now, General. That village finds out we're back here," the younger Luther North grumbled, "they'll bolt on us. And we'll be left with nothing but feathers—instead of capturing the whole goose."

After grappling with his dilemma, Carr finally decided. To the North brothers and his officers he explained, "This is simply a gamble I have to take. I can't push ahead recklessly, what with the certainty that I will scatter that village full of bloody-eyed warriors to the four winds . . . and have them bump into my supply train out there, somewhere, rolling in here with an inadequate escort."

"You fail to put this command on the march right now, you might be missing the greatest opportunity of your career," Frank North grumbled.

"Yeah," brother Luther agreed. "General, what do you think Custer would do if he had that village of red bastards within reach?"

Such transparent goading clearly angered the distinguished Civil War veteran. Carr was bristling as he finally squared his jaw and glared back at the two North brothers. Shad admired the soldier all the more as the soldier's words came out clipped and even, but with the ring of a hammer on a cold anvil.

"Major, and Captain—I'll note your exception for the record of this campaign. Know this now, so that you do not find yourselves attempting to bait me in the future. Eugene Carr will let others rush in for the glory: George Armstrong Custer and those like him. And while this regiment is under my command, our rear guard and all civilian teamsters in my employ will be protected. I'll not have their deaths on my conscience for the sake of personal glory. By Jupiter—there won't be a single Major Joel Elliott abandoned by the Fifth Cavalry!"

Shad watched Carr stomp away, his adjutant hurrying behind in the major's wake.

"He's still saddle-raw over last winter's campaign," Cody said quietly as he stopped beside Sweete.

"I heard your outfit came up empty-handed."

Cody nodded. "Busting snow, saving Penrose's brunettes, starving ourselves and killing our horses in a prairie blizzard—while all the glory for Sheridan's campaign went to Sheridan's favorite fair-haired boy."

"Custer?"

"He jumped a small village on the Washita, ran off the warriors, and captured some squaws. Then turned tail and skedaddled—as I hear the tale of it—leaving Major Elliott and eighteen men to get chewed up by the warriors from the villages camped farther upstream."

Sweete said, "If I found Carr was the kind of commander what left any of his own behind—then I'd be the first nigger to pull up my picket pin and leave this campaign to the rest of you."

Cody nodded. "Likely, I'd be pulling out with you. But Carr ain't a Custer."

After making camp and waiting for his supply train to come in from McPherson, Carr ordered the fires extinguished before dark, suggesting the men get what rest they could.

Two hours past midnight on the morning of 11 July, he had them up in the gray, waning light of moonset. No fires were lit. No coffee was brewed. Only the cold leavings of last night's supper and a daily ration of hard-bread were allowed as the men saddled and counted cartridges. By four A.M. the major had his column moving out in light marching order.

This was to be the day Major Eugene Carr's Fifth U.S. Cavalry hoped to chip away the last shreds of Tall Bull's lead.

Theirs had been a gallant, courageous effort already: more than 150 miles covered in the past four days of endless, torturous march—driven to the point of utter exhaustion by the man who had stared, and stared some more at those tiny boot prints in the sand days back.

Once again Shad stood amazed at the hardiness of these youngsters as they grumbled back and forth through the darkness, at least until they were ordered to horse. Once in the saddle and moving out beneath the last of that summer starshine, the column fell silent. No sound but the squeak of prairie-dried leather, the chink of bit and crupper, the slap of carbine on a sling against a McClellan saddle: horse soldiers about their deadly business of bringing war to the Dog Soldiers who had for too long cut a bloody swath through the far-flung settlements of white families staking out new lives for themselves on the ancient buffalo feeding grounds.

The red man was in his time of the yellow leaf. And the soldier was come to hurry the final day.

By the time the night weakened its grip on this high prairie, holding morning in temporary abeyance above this tableland in far-eastern Colorado Territory, the Pawnee rode back to the head of the column to report that they feared the Cheyenne were breaking up into three bands. North delivered the bitter news to Carr, gloating a bit as he did.

"Thank you, Major—but Bill Cody already surmised as much."

A gray cloud passed over Frank North's face. "With your permission, General: I'm suggesting you put out a reconnaissance in force, in three parties."

Carr turned to his young scout. "Mr. Cody here believes the Cheyenne will be regrouping before going into camp."

"They're breaking up—and you're going to let them slip right through your fingers, General!" North said, his voice cracking in anxiety.

Carr glanced at Cody, perhaps experiencing some self-doubt. "How can you . . . how can we be so sure the Cheyenne won't escape?"

Cody's eyes flicked at Sweete.

"Go 'head, Bill. Tell the general what you and me talked about early this morning."

Cody squared his shoulders. "General, Mr. Sweete and me figure Tall Bull is a cagey old bastard—just splitting up to throw you off his track. We'll bet the farm that village already knows your pony soldiers are hot on their trail."

A look of panic crossed the major's face. "Then you're agreeing that the village is splitting up."

The young scout shook his head emphatically. "Even if he is splitting up the village to throw you off, in the end Tall Bull's still in the same boat we are."

Carr's brow bunched in confusion. "Which is?"

"His people gotta have water."

"And that means something to us?"

With a nod Cody answered, "They'll have to regroup by the time they reach the Platte."

"The South Platte?" Carr inquired, gazing into the glimmering, sunburned distance. "That means we've penetrated Colorado Territory."

"That's right, General," Shad spoke up. "It's time you pushed this outfit, dragged the last these men and animals can give."

"Bound where, Mr. Sweete?"

But Cody piped up, "For the Platte, General."

"You get your outfit there first," Shad emphasized. "Have your men between the river and that village when it re-forms and comes up for water."

"And if we don't get there before Tall Bull does?" Carr asked.

Sweete shook his head. "Those Dog Soldiers will get their families across the Platte and you'll be eating their dust from here all the way to the Laramie Plains."

"We miss 'em at the river, General," Cody pleaded his case. "We'll never catch 'em."

"I take exception with these two, General Carr," Frank North broke in. "What's to guarantee that village is moving toward the Platte? No, General—I say if you don't follow all three of those trails, you'll lose everything this campaign was sent out here to do."

Carr contemplated his dilemma, looking from Sweete to Cody, then to North, and finally peered over his men and animals behind him, that long, dark ribbon stretched out across the fawn-colored terrain, sweltering beneath the same sun that he had hoped would bring him the destruction of Tall Bull's Dog Soldiers.

"All right—Cody's and Sweete's advice to the contrary, I've decided to divide the command into three wings here. Captain, you and your brother will take Captain Cushing along with most of your Pawnee to scout the middle trail heading due north. Major Royall?"

William B. Royall saluted smartly. "General?"

"Major—you will command half our unit. Companies E, G, and H. Take Cody along with some of North's Pawnee to scout the right-hand trail leading off to the northeast. There, onto that open land yonder."

Royall nodded, clearly showing his happiness at being freed for the chase with half the regiment. "I assume, General, that you're going to lead the third wing yourself?"

"I am. Direct command of companies A, C, and D. Mr. Sweete, you'll ride with me. Sergeant Wallace will follow with four of the companies. In addition, six of the Pawnee are to be assigned to Mr. Sweete here. If for nothing else, the trackers can now serve to communicate between our separate wings. I'll hold M Company in reserve, to remain some distance to the rear with the supply train."

By the time the sun rose blood-red on that day, portending even greater heat than in days already suffered, Major Eugene Carr had completed his division of nearly three hundred officers and soldiers, including civilian and Pawnee scouts.

Less than an hour later, after traveling at as fast a clip as the weary mounts could stand, Carr had to admit that the trail sign was irrefutable.

"I can see now that the Cheyenne are moving toward the river," Carr said quietly to the old plainsman beside him. "Just as you and Cody said they were."

"You can still flank 'em if you push now, General," Shad replied.

Carr nodded. Then stood for a few moments in the stirrups, squinting into the distance. "If my command can flank them from the northeast—getting the entire outfit between them and the river—then we will have them bottled up."

"Then it won't make no matter if you find Tall Bull in camp, or on the move already this morning."

"Which would you prefer, Mr. Sweete?"

"On the move, General."

"Why?"

"You surprise those Dog Soldiers in camp—the men gonna fight like hornets while the women and old ones skedaddle in retreat. Your men will get no quarter from that bunch if you catch 'em hunkered down in camp."

"But if we surprise them on the march?"

"The whole bunch will be at a gallop from the first shot—covered by the warriors just long enough to make an escape, scattering as they go."

"If choices are mine to make, Mr. Sweete—I choose to make a fight of it: like Custer had for himself on the Washita. For these men who have obeyed my orders and endured such hardship in the last few days—I want my chance to make a fight of it for the glory of the Fifth." Carr's eyes narrowed on the gray-headed scout. "By damn—we *must* catch Tall Bull in camp."

At the edge of the earth, the sun had gone from blood-red to orange, then bubbled to a pale yellow before it now hung ash-white against the immense pale-blue dome overhead. Already the air in Shad's face carried all the heat of a blacksmith's bellows.

"If you figure your boys are ready and got some fight left in 'em, General," Shad said, swiping his big black bandanna across his dripping face, "then let's go seize this day!"

21

"Your face is masked with the worry of an old man, my friend," Porcupine said.

"This camping place—I do not like it," High-Backed Bull grumbled. With a hand he swept a gesture across their village in the narrow valley beside the springs.

Their next march would take Tall Bull's camp of Dog Soldiers to the Buffalo Dropping River itself, that river which the white men called the Platte. From there they would cross and turn directly north for the high plains where the white man's Medicine Road had cut deep ruts in the flesh of the earth. Beyond those plains only a matter of but a few days' marches stood their sacred Bear Butte. There Tall Bull and White Horse and Porcupine would renew the flagging spirits of their warriors. They would refresh their vows and perhaps hold a sun dance. Once there, the fighting bands would have little worry of being followed by the soldier columns.

But until then Bull would worry. The soldiers were back there. Coming slowly, slowly. But coming all the same.

"Why here?" Bull asked Porcupine. "Why did Tall Bull have us stop here beside this spring?"

Porcupine shrugged. "This is the place our people have camped across many summers. At least once each year—so we know this country well. Besides, the water is good here."

"But why stop for so long?"

"The old ones gave their approval. They told Tall Bull it was safe to camp here, safe to rest the village."

"The rattle-talkers see no need of caution?" Bull asked, incredulous. "No need to keep on moving with the pony soldiers coming behind us?"

"No. They consulted their medicine and recommended some rest for the village. It is not so bad, Bull—not with the way we have had to drive the animals and people for far too many suns. They deserve a chance to rest, to make repairs, before we are pushed on again."

"We will be pushed, Porcupine—the pony soldiers will push us!"

The older warrior tried a halfhearted chuckle. "You worry so for a young man. Leave that to the old ones."

"Leave the worry to the old ones, who talk only to their stuffed owls and dried badger entrails?" Bull suddenly stood, staring down in the new sunlight at Porcupine. "It seems I can trust only to one thing anymore. To my weapons, to the sharpness of my scalping knife—to the quickness of my pony and the strength of my arms to continue making war on the white man."

"You must relax, young one," Porcupine answered soothingly. "I think you see the one who fathered you in the face of every white man. He—"

"I know he comes soon. *He* leads pony soldiers. For many winters he has betrayed my mother's people by leading soldiers to the camps of the innocent. I know he comes, soon."

"He is old now, Bull. Gone are his days of fighting—"

"We must move on!" Bull interrupted. Then a light crossed his face, his eyes growing wide in abrupt, exquisite excitement. "Or—we can lay a trap for the white men. To draw their soldiers in and destroy them." He lunged for Porcupine, gripping the bewildered war chief's shoulders. "Say yes—that we can lure the white men into a trap!"

Porcupine shook his head. "This is a place of rest, decided upon by the chiefs."

Bull yanked his hands from the older warrior, feeling sickened to his stomach, doubt rattling around inside his belly the way stream-washed pebbles clattered around inside a stiffened buffalo-scrotum rattle. "You have gone soft on me while I was not looking, Porcupine."

"The medicine men have said—"

"What they say does not change a thing. The soldiers are still behind us."

"We are far ahead of them—and they have been moving so slowly. You saw for yourself when we have attacked—"

"This bunch of pony soldiers—they will not stop. They will keep coming, and coming. They want Tall Bull's woman back. They want the other one too. These soldiers will not stop until they have destroyed us. Those women that Tall Bull and White Horse will not release, they will be our undoing."

Porcupine put an arm around Bull's shoulders, attempting to calm his young friend in some way. "The soldiers are too far behind us to attack. But if they do find us before we have crossed the river, Tall Bull has made a vow that will please your heart."

"What is this vow of his?"

"Tall Bull has sworn that if the soldiers come—he will see that his white concubine is the first to die."

"We must be damned close if you and your trackers have spotted Tall Bull's pony herd," Major Carr said evenly to the old plainsman, who had just brought him the momentous news, although the major's eyes had become animated as they peered into the distance. Then he dragged the steamy wool slouch hat from his brow and wiped a damp kerchief across his retreating hairline.

"I figure it's time we brought in them other two wings, Major," Shad Sweete advised.

He nodded. "Very good. Go ahead and get one of your trackers over to Major Royall's unit. Bring Cody back. I want him to take these six Pawnee and ride ahead to find out if that is the herd . . . if they can see the village—or some sign of just where I'll contact the enemy."

Cody rode in, received his orders, then immediately pointed his big buckskin northwest, leading six Pawnee off among the hills in the direction he believed he would find the camp.

Time dragged itself out in the steamy heat of the plains as the horses and mules grew restless, deprived of water, restive for grazing. For what seemed like hours in the growing heat beneath the rising sun, they waited. Then—

"There!" Carr called out, pointing.

Sweete twisted in the saddle to find Cody headed back in at an easy lope. He wore his characteristic irrepressible grin.

"By damn—you found something, didn't you, son?"

Cody nodded at Sweete, then turned to Carr. "It's just like I told you, General. So I left the trackers there to keep an eye on things till your men can come on up."

Carr smiled approvingly. "I take it they have no idea we're about to ride them down?"

"You caught 'em in camp—and they ain't running yet."

"No camp pickets out?" Carr asked anxiously. When Cody shook his head, the major responded enthusiastically, "By Jupiter—I'll have them this time!"

"If I can advise you on your approach to the village, General," Cody said. "I've spotted a way in—a small detour. Take your command around and through these low hills yonder . . . keeping off to the right. We'll keep wide of the village and come in from the north where the river lies. From there you can start your charge."

"Without detection?"

Cody nodded. "We stay hidden behind those hills, that bunch won't have a clue until you're riding down on top of them."

Carr issued his orders to have his command reunited, and in a matter of minutes the entire column was pushing forward once more, just about the time Sweete noticed the plodding wagon train pulling into sight at their rear. The wagon master's teamsters and mules had been having their time of it slogging the overburdened wagons through the spongy soil and the clinging sand of the Platte Bluffs.

By keeping to the ravines and following the scouts as they blazed their trail behind the low hills, no man allowed to break the skyline, Sweete and Cody led the soldiers within sight of the village, then turned and galloped back to the head of the column.

Cody held up his hand to signal the troops to halt. "You've got less than fifteen hundred yards to cross until you make contact with the outlying lodges, General."

"They haven't spotted you?" Carr asked nervously.

"You've caught them napping. Warm day like this—most of their war ponies are still out grazing in the herd. Men relaxed back in the shade of the lodges. Children playing at the springs."

"A total surprise?" asked the major as he squinted into the summer blue of the sky, finding the few lazy spirals of smoke caught on the hot summer breezes in the near distance.

"There's good, flat ground for your cavalry to cross getting into the village," Shad said.

Cody agreed. "Tailor-made for a cavalry charge, General."

"This is our day, boys!" Carr cheered before he returned to the head of his column to break out his attack squadrons.

As the major issued marching orders down through the cavalry command, North's Pawnee scouts were already at their toilet, preparing for the coming fight. After stripping saddles from their horses and stowing them in the freight wagons, the trackers bound up the tails of their ponies in anticipation of action. That done, the scouts then tied their own long hair back and mixed earth-paint with due ceremony. Weapons were polished while here and there small knots of the brownskins smoked a bowl of tobacco together before mounting up. Many of them now pulled from their bedrolls a blue army blouse, the better to be recognized in the dust, confusion, and fear of battle by the young, untried white soldiers of the Fifth Cavalry.

Carr assigned H Company under Captain Leicester Walker to charge in on the left flank while Lieutenant George Price and A Company would make the dash on the right.

"You are to turn the hostiles' flanks if they attempt escape," Carr instructed his battalion leaders. "Their backs will be to the river. That must be their only path of escape. Once you have secured the village from escaping on the flanks, ride to the rear of the village and seize the pony herd."

"General, I figure them Pawnee will jump that Cheyenne pony herd before any of your boys can get there," Sweete said.

Carr turned to Frank North. "Major—you'll be sure to have control of your trackers and see that they do not interfere with my attack."

North nodded once. "They'll run for the ponies, General. But you can be sure I'll keep 'em out of the way for you."

"All right. Captain Sumner with D Company, and Captain Maley leading C Company, you both will take the front of our charge. Major

Crittenden will ride in command of this center squadron. Major Royall, your squadron of companies E and G remain in reserve immediately in my rear. Ready your units for the attack, gentlemen."

As the company commanders passed orders down the line, Major Frank North boldly placed his Pawnee battalion on the far left flank, in plain sight of the village, awaiting the order to charge. When Lieutenant Price with A Company had moved off about five hundred yards to the right and signaled that he was ready, Major Carr finally rose in the stirrups. Since Lieutenant Price's company had the farthest distance to cover before reaching the village, the charge would be guided on it. Like the power of a passing thunderstorm to raise the hair on his neck and arms, Sweete sensed the electrifying tension crackle through the entire outfit as Carr issued the first order of the coming attack.

"Sergeant Major: move out at a trot!"

Joseph H. Maynard turned in the saddle to bellow his command. "Center-guide! Column of fours—at a trot. For-rad!"

Prancing away with the rest, Sweete noticed that the dry, hot wind had picked up suddenly, blowing out of the west, born out of the front range of the Rockies far, far away. With a glance toward the high mountains, how he wished he were there among its beckoning blue spruce and quaky. Then he found his thoughts yanked brutally back as the clatter of those hooves and the squeak of leather, the rattle of bit chains, went unheard in that unsuspecting village of Dog Soldiers. In a matter of heartbeats, the three flying lance points had closed to a thousand yards . . . and still no sign they had been discovered by the Cheyenne.

In the next moment there appeared ahead of Shad a young horseman atop a white pony, standing guard among the distant herd grazing lazily on the grassy bench. As if shot, the Indian reined about abruptly, racing headlong for the village, hair flying, down the long slope into the valley.

Sweete turned his head, trying to listen to the loud voices swirling around Carr and Cody at the point of the charge, hearing only shouts and curses—unable to understand anything for the noisy charge of the three hundred. One thing was certain as sun to the old plainsman: the soldiers intended to reach the village before that lone herder could warn those in camp.

Carr hollered out again, near standing in the stirrups, flinging his command behind him at his bugler.

John Uhlman jammed the scuffed and dented trumpet to his parched lips as the entire command loped onward toward the village. But no call came forth.

Up and down the front men began hollering, adding to the confusion, as bugler Uhlman tried again to blow his charge. Then Quartermaster Edward M. Hayes shot up beside Uhlman and yanked the horn from the bugler's hand as their mounts jostled.

Hayes brought the bugle to his mouth and blew the soul-stirring notes of Carr's charge.

Up and down the entire line throats burst enthusiastically, raising their raucous cheer as hundreds of Spencer carbines came up and the jaded horses were ordered to the gallop. Although they had been driven far beyond endurance and the call of duty across the last four days, those gallant animals answered the brass-mounted spurs for this one last dash.

Without thinking, Quartermaster Hayes flung the bugle to the ground and pulled his pistol free.

Shad watched a clearly dismayed John Uhlman glance behind him at that trampled tin horn lying discarded among the grass and cactus. Then he too was swept along by something now out of control.

Sweete felt no different: caught up in this, swept up and charging down on a camp of his wife's own people. Snared in something that was no longer in his control. Something he no longer understood. Perhaps, he thought, he was every bit as bewildered and as frightened as the young bugler.

Not knowing where this day would find him. And at what cost.

"People are coming!"

At the distant warning cry, High-Backed Bull shaded his eyes with one hand against the sun risen now to its zenith. Others in the camp stood or came to stop what they were doing, right where they were standing. Children still played, a few dogs barked. No one seemed particularly alarmed.

Two nights before, they had camped beside the upper reaches of a stream the Shahiyena called Cherry Creek. Yesterday afternoon Tall Bull and White Horse had led them to this place of the springs that gurgled forth from beneath the White Butte.

Five summers gone Big Wolf and his family had been killed by soldiers a stone's throw from this spot.

Bull turned and looked across White Butte Creek, which ran through camp in a southeasterly direction. He found Tall Bull and Two Crows standing beside the chief's lodge, peering into the distance without apparent alarm. They wanted the village to wait and rest here for two days before crossing the river and heading north to the rock formation where years before, at the foot of what the white man called Court House Rock, they had starved the Shaved-Heads they met there in battle.

This was no cause for excitement—perhaps. Nearby, others were saying there should be no alarm. After all, hunters were out in the countryside looking for buffalo. Others had gone in search of antelope. Surely no enemy could surprise this village of proven warriors.

"There! On the hills!"

Many were the ones now bursting from their lodges in curiosity. Even the children were pointing at the distant figures loping back and forth on far slopes: horsemen with long hair waving on the hot, dry wind, brandishing rifles aloft. A sign of greeting.

Visitors?

"Perhaps these are Pawnee Killer's Lakotas," someone suggested.

"Yes," another agreed loudly. "So much shooting—they must have been successful in their hunt!"

Bull squinted into the bright light once more, attempting to make sense out of the throbbing forms on horseback coming out of the north.

Then his mouth went dry and his heart went cold. The first bullets whined into camp, striking meat racks, splintering lodgepoles, crying overhead in warning.

The Shaved-Heads had come—returned to savor the sweet taste of victory in their mouths!

As two wide phalanxes of dust-shrouded pony soldiers broke over the top of the hills, Bull whirled.

Porcupine was running toward him shouting, "*Aiyeee!* Pony soldiers come behind the Pawnee!"

Some of the Shahiyena already lay bleeding underfoot of the others who scattered in panic, sweeping up children, gathering an armload of possessions before fleeing in the wake of the white soldiers. Hearing the smack of lead against flesh like the slap of his hand against wet rawhide, Bull saw one woman's lower jaw disappear in a blinding corona of crimson. She sank to the ground, gurgling for but a moment until her chest heaved no more.

Now they were surrounded on three sides, coming in from the east and west as well as the north, the hooves of their iron-shod horses hammering the baked, sere earth.

"There!" he shouted, pointing to the south, immediately joined by other young warriors who had also taken up their arms.

They yanked, pulled, prodded, dragged the old and young, growled at the rest to hurry them along. To the south! It was the only direction of escape left them.

In that frightening confusion a few ponies reared, and some went down screaming as bullets smacked into them. A few women struggled to control what animals were in camp. Because most horses were out grazing with the herd, those Shahiyena who fled the carnage did so on foot—clutching a young one beneath an arm, perhaps snatching up a weapon or a blanket before darting through the hellish smoke and dust, heading for places of safety and hiding in the sandy bluffs hard by the river.

The old shamans had spelled doom for the band! Trusting as they did to the blood congealing at the bottom of a badger carcass! Yet—in the end it was Tall Bull who had decided to believe the old medicine men.

Porcupine was already hollering for the warriors to follow him into the teeth of the charge, there to make a stand only as long as it would take to clear the camp. Then they would escape.

Until then, their weapons and their brown bodies were all that stood between the white pony soldiers and this camp of fleeing women, children, and old ones.

A streak of blond hair and a swirl of greasy, smoke-stained cloth swept past the young warrior. It meant one of the white women had escaped and was fleeing toward the soldiers.

Bull wanted to find Tall Bull—to see where he himself had run to escape this destruction he and the old ones had brought down on this warrior band. Angrily Bull rubbed the grit from his eyes and strained into the yellow dust that stung his mouth and nose. Then he found the war chief beside his lodge, the white woman suspended at the end of his brown arm by her blond hair. Her hands gripped his wrist, her face turned upward, imploring Tall Bull. Raised in his other hand was a silver-bladed tomahawk.

Her mouth opened, a huge black hole in her face, as the woman screamed inhumanly.

"Kill her!" Bull screamed at the chief through the din of rifle fire and war cries. "Kill the white woman!"

Without hesitation Tall Bull hurled the tomahawk downward into the woman's face.

"Yes! Yes!" cried the young warrior as he watched the blood and gore splatter the war chief.

Her body convulsed, falling to the side, where it trembled for a moment. Then Tall Bull was gone.

He left unaware that the young warrior came to stand over the woman's splattered body. To stare down at her, stare at that crimson and gore, feeling the flush of overwhelming triumph wash through him.

22

SHAD'S THROAT BURNED in torment each time he hollered out his own death song.

In the thick of it, his hot-blooded fury drove him to carry death to the door of every lodge in this camp of kidnappers, thieves, and murderers. He swore that by himself he would cut a swath through the Dog Soldier camp until he found every last one of the warriors who had burned and maimed, mutilated, raped, and butchered white folk across the whole of Kansas and Nebraska.

And a part of him hoped, prayed fervently, that he would find his son before anyone else.

Shad knew the boy was here.

As a shadow burst from behind a lodge, he fired the Spencer on instinct.

Yet High-Backed Bull was no longer a boy. He was a full-grown man. But thinking that in his head had never helped Shad's heart deal with what had become of his shattered family. For this father, Bull would always, forever and always, be a boy. His boy. His father's only son.

Before he realized it, Shad was hurtling through the air, heels over head, landing on his belly, sliding across the grass and sand, then slamming the side of a lodge. Behind him his horse struggled to rise, one leg broken, flopping wildly, where the animal had stumbled in a hole. Perhaps a fire pit.

A scream aroused his blood as he came slowly to his senses, making him whirl around to pull the Spencer's trigger, finding he had not chambered a fresh cartridge. He took the warrior's charge there, where he lay sprawled on the ground, raising the rifle in two hands to blunt the blow from the youngster's war club.

Driving his big foot into the warrior's groin, sending the Cheyenne reeling backward in pain, Shad clumsily levered another round into the Spencer's action and fired.

For a moment he stared at the warrior collapsing before his eyes, studying the face, the war paint, the way he wore his hair. He sickened for an instant—believing he had killed his son.

In grief he careened over to kneel beside the body. Sweete used some of the Cheyenne's loose hair to smear a patch of the greasy earth-paint from the young warrior's face. This dead one's skin was too dark to be Bull. Still, he was nearly the same age as his boy, if that old. So young to die—

The terror-filled screams were not those of a man. Not those even of a Cheyenne woman. Such blood-chilling cries for help came only from one of the white women.

Out of the swirling dust and gun smoke curling serpentine on the dry breezes among the lodges emerged a white woman, babbling incoherently in a foreign tongue. She hurled herself toward him for a moment, then skidded to a stop, bringing a hand up to her mouth when she gazed at his buckskinned frame up and down. Eyes wide as saucers, she shot away from him—careening toward some mounted soldiers.

The Pawnee darted through the thick of it, screaming at the top of their lungs, sating themselves with long-awaited blood lust. Exacting revenge on their old enemies. Hacking, butchering men and women who had fallen with the soldier onslaught.

Fifty yards away a small group of warriors held out from a ravine, drawing the white man's fire away from their families fleeing into the sandhills. Small platoons of soldiers raced after other knots of resolute warriors who steadfastly continued to fight from horseback, but most fought their struggle on foot. These small bands would retreat for some distance before suddenly wheeling to fire at their white pursuers while the women and children doggedly made for the tall grass in the marsh, some for the sandy bluffs nearby.

It was but a moment before Sweete and an old sergeant gathered enough soldiers to lay down some blistering fire on that ravine running through the Cheyenne camp. Without thought, nothing but courage and foolhardy bravado to power their legs, the sergeant led his squad in an infantry charge on the ravine, pouring enough lead into the enemy to drive the warriors who could still move clawing up the far side of the sandy defile.

One by one the defenders went down—those brave enough to stay behind and cover the retreat of the others. Now the soldiers and Shad were among the sweat-slicked brown bodies, both dead and wounded, kneeling quickly to rechamber another cartridge spat from the spring-loaded butt-mounted tube, firing at the retreating brown backs.

"Lookee here, Sergeant Dickson!"

Shad watched a young, thin soldier come up to the old sergeant, opening his palm. In it lay the shiny crimson-and-gold badge of distinction worn by a Royal Arch Mason. On the white enamel of the banner stretched across the bottom of the badge were emblazoned the words: *West Springfield, Illinois.*

"Where in hell you get that, Lorrett?" demanded the sergeant.

"Yonder," and he threw a thumb up the ravine at the copper-skinned bodies of the enemy.

"Some white settler gave his life for that goddamned badge," grumbled another soldier come up to join the group as he shoved more cartridges into his Blakeslee loading tube.

"Lookit there," Private Lorrett said, pointing into the village.

At least a dozen of the Pawnee trackers herded some captured ponies ahead of them, making quickly for the north and away from the fiercest of the action.

"Goddamned Pawnee every bit as bloody bad as these here Cheyenne," grumbled a middle-aged corporal sporting greasy, smoke-stained stripes sewn at the sleeves of his sweat-soaked blouse.

"Damn right, Walsh," replied Dickson. "I ain't seen a one of them Pawnee scouts down here mixing it up with the Cheyenne bucks like us."

"Chicken-shit Pawnee sonsabitches went running in to rub out the women and children," Walsh growled. "Yellow-backed redskins . . . no one's ever gonna convince me they can face the music like a white man."

"Sergeant Dickson!" an officer's voice hollered from the dust and gun smoke. "Bring your squad over here!"

"Let's go, bunkies!" Dickson hollered. "Fill them tubes if you ain't already."

Shad watched them go, headed south toward a ravine with more steadfast defenders.

The clatter of the Pawnee trackers skidding to a stop captured his attention. Five of them dismounted, most already wearing some captured necklaces and bracelets, each of them sporting at least a pair of bloody scalps hung at their belts, where they had stuffed captured pistols and axes. Into the ravine they pitched, crouching over the dead Cheyenne warriors. With the toes of their moccasins, the scouts rolled the Dog Soldiers onto their backs, slashing loose belt pouches, yanking necklaces of elk milk teeth or mummified fingers from the dead, stripping the enemy's bodies of anything worth stealing.

Shad couldn't stay for the rest of it. It had been how many years now since he had seen his first scalping—that first mutilation? The fur trade had been in its infancy . . . Shad shook his head as he clambered to the side of the ravine. Too damned many winters to remember right now. It wasn't as if mutilation—even jamming a dead man's pecker in his mouth—were something new to Shad Sweete. He turned away and planted a foot up the side of the grassy slope.

Then he stopped. And turned to look back at the dead warrior sprawled in the grass at the lip of the ravine—one of those who had refused to budge, refused to attempt escape before the soldier guns.

That meadowlark, stuffed and tied in the warrior's hair.

Slowly Sweete took a step, then another toward the body. At the same time one of the trackers descended on the dead Cheyenne, who appeared to have nothing of any value but his big Walker pistol. Wrenching it from the dead man's belt, the Pawnee jammed the captured weapon in his own belt as he knelt beside the Cheyenne's head. Shad kept walking, walking toward the body, his eyes fixed on the meadowlark.

With a flick of his wrist the Pawnee brought his knife from his belt, then yanked back on the long black hair, cutting free the thin whang that had bound the stuffed, mummified meadowlark to the warrior's single braid.

"You shouldn't done that," Shad declared quietly. "Put it back."

The Pawnee looked up, a quizzical light in his eyes. Then, as if recognizing the tall white scout, he smiled in a friendly sort of way. And went back about his business, laying his knife blade behind the dead Cheyenne's ear. He plunged the blade into the flesh—

Then stopped as he heard the click of the hammer on the Spencer rifle, felt the carbine's muzzle pressed against his head, just back of his ear. Slowly the tracker turned, finding the white man's rifle less than an inch from his nose.

"I told you: shouldn't done that. For the last time . . . tie it back."

Shad was amazed the words had gotten across his tongue, as dry as his mouth had gone suddenly. For him the battle for Tall Bull's village at Summit Springs was something far away and fading, most of the remaining gunfire concentrated now at a deep ravine south of camp where Cody and the North brothers had gone when a dozen warriors holed themselves up and were making a stand of it.

For Sweete, this fight was over.

"Mine," the tracker said, mimicking in poor English, trying out his ready grin on the white man. "Mine hair."

Shad shook his head, fighting the stinging boil of rage. It wouldn't take much just to pull the trigger in the tracker's face.

"Listen, you no-count stupid nigger!" he roared. "I'm gonna give you your worthless life—if you want it. Now . . . get up!" And he motioned with a couple swings of the Spencer's muzzle. "Get the hell away from my . . . the body."

He saw the Pawnee's eyes flick left, then right, about the same time Shad heard the tumbling clicks of several belt weapons. Not anything near as loud as the Spencer's action—so he instinctively figured them to be the trackers' pistols. He sensed the Pawnee drawing near more than he could hear them. Like a burning he sensed their muzzles trained on his back, pointed at his ribs, aimed for his gut. Years of staying alive out here plainly told the old plainsman that the rest had turned their sights on him. His ears burned as they jabbered among themselves in confusion and anger.

"Leave him be," one of them finally spoke. "His coup. Leave be. His hair."

Shad turned his head slightly, seeking the one who talked something he could understand from this bunch. "You speak English. So I'll say this in English. Get this worthless sonofabitch off that Cheyenne—or I'm gonna kill him. Here and now."

"You shoot him, you won't—"

Shad roared, "Listen—I'm gonna splatter his goddamned face all over the ground!"

His eyes went immediately to the tracker on the ground over the body when the Pawnee shifted a bit, then bent over to resume his taking of the scalp.

Uncorking his fury, Sweete swung the muzzle of his Spencer against the side of the tracker's head to send him sprawling backward and clawing for his own belt weapon. In a whirl of motion the old plainsman brought up his big moccasin, connecting below the chin, hurling the tracker backward again, watching the blood squirt from the Pawnee's mouth.

He had begun to whirl back on the rest, but not before he felt the searing slash of the blade along his ribs. The pain came white-hot as the knife tip entered, then skittered along a rib with a sound like someone drawing rusty iron across a flat sheet of granite. That turn he had started likely saved the old man's life, that act of bringing the elbow up, making contact with the slasher. Like the solid ring of an iron ladle brought down hard on an oak table, his arm sent the Pawnee into the air. The rest were coming now.

Too close to fire the Spencer, he slapped it into his left hand, gripping the barrel midlength to continue his swing in one unstoppable arc. It cracked against a skull, splattering some blood as the Pawnee went down in a heap, as heavily as a burlap hundredweight of wet oats.

Shad took a long step toward the others. Now he stood over the body, ready to defend it—flailing away with the Spencer in the left hand as he yanked the big knife from his belt with his right, ready to fling it as the rest suddenly drew back, their eyes as wide as frightened coyotes suddenly interrupted at a feeding frenzy.

They jabbered among themselves quickly. Shad wished Hook were here: he knew enough of the Pawnee tongue. Then one spoke.

"We shoot you—or you kill us," the Pawnee said.

From the tremulous edge to the tracker's voice, Sweete somehow did not quite believe it. "If you're to be about killing me—let's have at it, you red niggers."

Tossing the Spencer with a spin into the air a few inches, Sweete caught it, thumbing back the hammer. Not knowing if there was a loaded cartridge under that hammer or not.

"No bullet in gun," the Pawnee sneered. "We shoot you—"

"Just what the shit is going on here?"

At the corner of his eye Shad watched an officer appear, coming to a halt with more than a dozen soldiers.

"Likely I can get a couple more of you before I can't pull the trigger on this here rifle no more. Maybeso gut a bunch of you niggers before I go under," Sweete growled.

The soldier plunged down the side of the ravine, landing in front of Sweete that next moment. Major Royall.

"Mr. Sweete, isn't it?"

"Out of my way, Major. Don't want you to get hurt."

"Hurt?" William B. Royall asked. "Looks to me like you're the one about to be hurt by this bunch of North's trackers." The officer's eyes fell to the two groggy Pawnee on the ground, then quickly narrowed on the dark, wet slash along Sweete's ribs. "Tell me what started this blood-letting."

"Told this bunch of niggers to leave the body alone."

"We've got Cheyenne to fight, Mr. Sweete. We're not supposed to be drawing down on our own Pawnee."

"I'll kill them—I'll even kill any soldier of your'n what touches this body."

For a moment the major studied the scout's face. Then Royall glanced down at the dead warrior. Slowly he wiped his dusty, gloved hand across the back of his mouth. "Never will get used to using Indians against Indians. It's something I think makes us just as savage as—"

"You gonna get these sonsabitches away from me, Major? Or am I going to have to spill a little more blood here?"

With a wag of his head the officer asked, "What in blue blazes makes this one so damned special to you, Mr. Sweete?"

The salty sting at his eyes made it hard to look down into the face of this dark-headed officer. Not really such a bad sort, this Royall.

"Put your guns away!" the major suddenly turned and snapped at the Pawnee.

Their leader grumbled, then passed the order along in their tongue. The trackers angrily stuffed weapons away, but refused to move off. Instead, they clustered around the one of their number Sweete had hammered with his Spencer.

"Now," Royall said as he turned back to the plainsman, "are you going to tell me?"

"You get these goddamned turkey buzzards away from here!" Sweete bellowed with all the rage of a wounded bear. "Far away from me!" The rifle in his hands shook, still pointed at the chest of the English-speaking tracker.

"Mr. Sweete—these guides are allies of ours—"

Shad spat his words. "Pawnee no better'n vultures feeding on dead meat."

The soldier sighed, then cleared his throat. "Lieutenant—go ahead and get these trackers out of here."

"Major?"

"Now!" Royall snapped like a man gone too long without sleep. "We'll sort the damned thing out later."

It took some threats from the lieutenant's soldiers before Royall got the trackers herded on their way out of the ravine. Reluctantly the sullen Pawnee left with their escort, yet not without some nasty grumbling that Major North would have a lot to say about the soldiers interfering with his Pawnee having their revenge on the enemy dead. As tense as it was for a few minutes, in the end Royall's soldiers did get them on their way toward the ravine to the south where a withering gunfire still rattled above the last of the Cheyenne holdouts.

Royall sighed as he watched them leave, hands balled on his hips. When he turned, he strode back to confront the tall gray-head. For a few wordless moments, the major studied Sweete's face, as if searching there for some clue.

Choking on his grief, Shad didn't trust himself to move, not just yet. Then as he blinked, the first tear spilled in a streak through the dust caked on his cheek.

"It's all right. It's gonna be all right, Mr. Sweete," he said quietly, clearly bewildered by the big man's violent actions. "Now, please—just tell me what the devil was going on here? Why were you so all-fired ready to get yourself killed over some dead buck—over this dead particular Cheyenne bastard here?"

Royall waited for what seemed like a hot, endless moment, watching the tall plainsman's face.

"Mr. Sweete?" he asked again. "Just what in blazes is one dead Dog Soldier over another to you?"

"My . . . my boy."

23

H E SAW THE figure in the distance. On that big buckskin, it had to be Cody.

The far-off rider reined the pale horse in Shad Sweete's direction and brought the buckskin into an easy lope. He watched the young blond-haired scout eat through that shimmering summer countryside. When Cody was ten yards out, he slowed the animal to a walk, then brought the buckskin to a halt where the old plainsman had waited with his two extra ponies atop the low hill that looked down on the South Platte.

"Been worried about you, Shad."

Sweete's eyes found the distant serpent of blue crawling over the tan carpet of rolling, sandy plains, following the riverbank north.

He looked at Cody, smiled. "Where away you bound, Bill?"

"Carr's got us headed in to Fort Sedgwick," Cody replied. "We got one of the women out of that camp alive. Gonna take her on in to the fort, where the army can dig around and try to find her people back in Kansas. Seems the right thing to do: get her back to her own folk, to her family. The other woman . . . damn, but we found her butchered just like we figured them Dog Soldiers would do."

"You say some words over her—bury her?"

"Back there at the springs."

Shad only nodded, his eyes leaving Cody's face to stare into the distance.

Cody sighed, almost contentedly, as he studied the old man's face a moment. "I was really worried about you."

With a shrug Shad asked, "Got any chew about you?"

"Pipe tobaccy."

"It'll do, if'n you can spare some for this ol' nigger."

Cody flashed that even-toothed grin of his that seemed to light up the whole of his handsome face as he stuffed a hand into a saddlebag, fished about, and came forth with a dark lump wrapped in oiled paper. "You're entitled to as much as you want to take, Shad."

"Just a chew," he replied, taking a wad from the paper and stuffing the coarse-cut shag inside his cheek. "Damn," he said quietly as he handed the bundle back to Cody. "Ain't had no tobaccy in more'n three days. It does taste good. Thanks."

"Keep the rest?"

He shook his head. "I'll get some on down the way, I s'pose."

A cloud crossed Cody's face. "You . . . why, I thought you was here because you was joining the column to go on in to Sedgwick with us."

Squarely looking at the young scout, Shad said, "Don't think so, Bill. Have Carr send my pay voucher up to Laramie. Care of the post commander there."

"But—this campaign ain't over yet, Shad. We're just getting—"

"It's over for me, Bill."

Cody swallowed, then stuffed the oiled paper back into the saddlebag. "What with them Dog Soldiers we scattered over hell's half acre, why all this time I been thinking on you, Shad—worried ever since you left the springs, pulled away with the . . . with your boy."

Shad straightened, wincing as if shot through with a burning pain. "You know?"

"Royall told me."

"A good man, the major," Sweete replied, staring down at his hands crossed over the big-dished saddle horn.

"Was it, Shad? You sure it was . . ."

He nodded. "It were my boy."

Cody nudged his buckskin a little closer, coming up alongside the big scout on the strawberry roan. "You can't blame yourself for it."

"I ain't, Bill. Really I ain't. Leastways, I'm not blaming myself for him getting killed in that fight. He was his own man. Been so . . . for some time now too." Sweete looked at Cody, his puffy eyes gone sad as a doe gone dry. "What's that they say the good book tells us: them that lives by the sword gonna die by the sword?"

All Cody did was nod, his lips drawn into a straight line as if determined not to betray himself with emotion. He flicked a glance over his shoulder at the distant column pulling farther away to the north.

"You buried him proper, Shad?"

"He was a Cheyenne warrior, Bill," Sweete said proudly, his eyes stinging and his lips trembling so slightly only he would know. "A Dog Soldier what died defending his people. His . . . his chosen people."

"I'm . . . proud of you, Shad."

Sweete snorted, trying a smile. "I made mistakes a'times—"

"Any man does."

With a wag of his head, Sweete stilled the young scout. "His mother's gonna be proud of him."

"Shad—that bunch has been murdering and—"

"His people gonna be proud of him too."

"They killed and raped and kidnapped from Nebraska down into Kansas, Shad. You can't forget that."

His eyes got a cold fire behind them as he glared at Cody. "I ain't gonna forget none of it."

Then Sweete thought on Bull, remembering times he had been driven to lash his willful son's thumbs to the lodgepoles, just as a Cheyenne father would do, to let the boy hang there awhile and settle his high spirits.

Then he sighed with the sting of remembrance. "I did of a time forget something, Bill. Forgot that white is white and red is red. And 'cause I forgot and fell in love with a Cheyenne woman—my boy did everything in his power to wash away what he had of me inside him."

"Goddammit, Shad—don't blame yourself for what he turned out to be. You said yourself he was—"

"Bill, a man finds he made a mistake, he can do one of two things to right it. He can curse himself the rest of his days, reminding himself of what wrong he's done. Or—" And Shad stared off at the wagon drag of the far, dark column of Carr's march.

"Or?"

"Or he can do what he can to help another man keep from making a mistake, maybe the same mistake."

"Another man?"

"A friend," Sweete replied quietly.

"Somebody you've knowed for a long time?"

Sweete shook his head. "No. Not very long at all. Got to help him— so I can help myself in the bargain."

"I don't understand, Shad. You help this friend of yours—how are you gonna help yourself?"

"I help him, then I can forgive myself, Bill. That's the hardest thing I have to do right now. To forgive myself."

Cody glanced over his shoulder at the distant column. "If you're headed north to Laramie, why not ride with us far as Sedgwick? It's on the way."

Shad wagged his head and tried a wan smile. "No, my friend. Gonna cross over the river down there. Head north by west. Ride up along the foothills toward the Laramie plain. Gonna be . . . all right to be alone for a while."

"Will the woman be there?"

"Bull's mother? She should be. If not, I'll find out where. She deserves to know how he come to die. Where he's buried."

"I figured you took off from the springs to bury him."

"The Cheyenne way: put back in the rocks where the ground and water spirits own his body now."

"And after that? You'll come on back to McPherson to work with me?"

Sweete held out his hand. Cody stared at it for a moment, then smiled and took it. When they finished shaking, Shad kept hold of the young scout's. "After I tell Shell Woman about the boy, and she's had time to grieve—a person needs someone there with 'em when they grieve . . . then I gotta ride off to find someone else."

"Someone else should know about your boy?"

"No. Find the friend I want to help. The one I got to help now. Before it's too late for the two of us."

Cody finally took his hand from Sweete's. "You . . . you need anything? Cartridges? Jerky? Some of the army's goddamned rotten hard-bread? I got plenty of that."

Shad grinned a little to show some measure of his appreciation, then the smile was gone. "Don't need nothing else now but to be on my way, Bill."

"You're sure I can't do nothing else for you, Shad?"

Sweete brought his old, gnarled hand up to his brow and saluted the young scout. "Well done, soldier. Well done."

Cody choked a little, swallowing hard. His eyes seemed to brim as he forced a smile onto his lips and his own hand came up for a salute. "Well done yourself, old friend."

Shad reined away abruptly, nudging his roan into a walk. "Watch your hair, Bill Cody. It'd look mighty fine on some buck's coup-stick. Damn, but it's awful pretty!"

Cody forced a quick laugh, watching the big plainsman's back as Sweete moved away down the slope toward the wide silver band of river. "You . . . you watch your backtrail, Shad Sweete. By God, you watch your backtrail!"

It had been many, many miles, this travel they had undertaken after the soldier attack on their village at White Bluff Creek. Porcupine's heart weighed heavy as a stone in his chest.

So total a surprise, so terrible a disaster. So complete their loss of nearly everything—all of it burned by the soldiers, all that had not been looted by the Shaved-Heads before the lodges were put to the torch. Meat and flour, blankets and robes. Weapons and powder and the wealth they had collected from the white homesteads across many moons of raiding. All of it—gone in the time it took for the sun to cross half the sky above.

And those bodies mutilated by the Shaved-Heads and left for the predators that always came, drawn by the smell of blood on the winds. Porcupine and many of the other warriors had returned to that smoking camp when the soldiers withdrew. Come to bury their own: fathers and sons, brothers and uncles, friends.

The bodies were all there, most still recognizable despite the butchery of the Pawnee trackers—identified by a fragment of clothing or quillwork, some body paint or a particular weapon, perhaps a necklace or hair orna-ment.

After the soldiers had gone, Porcupine had looked and looked, unable to find the body of his young friend who had stayed behind in the grassy ravine as the war chief and others clawed their way up the far side and escaped before the soldiers overran them. Bull's body was not among those at the ravine near the village, nor among those who had taken refuge with Tall Bull in another deep ravine south of camp where the war chief and the rest had died bravely rather than run. Tall Bull had even killed his favorite war pony there at the mouth of the ravine—to show the Shaved-Heads that he would go no farther, that he would attempt no escape.

Like Bull, a handful of the Dog Soldiers had stayed behind to cover the retreat of the women and children and old ones. To give their lives for their people.

Inside his breast, Porcupine's heart felt chilled and prickly, hollow as a buffalo horn, black as the far side of night. Having hoped against hope, praying as he waited until he could return to the devastated camp, unable to mount a counterattack, Porcupine and some of the others had angrily watched the Shaved-Heads mutilate the dead Shahiyena scattered throughout the village. From a nearby hill he had seen the tall white man approach the grassy ravine where Bull fell, saw the tall one guard the fallen warrior's body with his own life—fighting off the Shaved-Heads until soldiers arrived.

Porcupine sensed in his heart what his thoughts had tried to tell him a long time ago—that the one Bull hunted now in fact grieved a great loss.

The white man wrapped the body in a blanket, then bound it in a buffalo robe. He took from one of the lodges soon to be torched those special possessions with which to bury a warrior: weapons and parfleches, food and finery. Binding it all inside the buffalo robe with the body, lashing it tight with rawhide whangs he cut from the bottom of a seasoned lodge, he tied the body across the back of one of the handsomest of the captured Shahiyena ponies and moved slowly out of that camp as the destruction of Tall Bull's village began.

He had followed the old gray-head toward the river and beyond, heading south by southwest toward the tall, chalky river bluffs in that wild, austere wilderness that had long been the hunting ground of the Shahiyena. Each time Porcupine had turned around to look behind him at the site of destruction, it had sickened him to watch another tall spiral of greasy black smoke rising in the distance beyond the hills, where once the camp of Tall Bull's people had waited beside the spring.

Into the second day the old one had pushed on with the two extra ponies strung out behind him on picket ropes, riding below the river bluffs slowly, looking carefully before he finally stopped—having selected the right crevice below the shade of both juniper and cedar, there above the quiet murmur of the great river fed by distant mountain snows.

In a struggle up the sharp, sandy slope, the old one had dragged the buffalo-hide bundle to its final resting place, taken one last look around, then placed the body of High-Backed Bull within the darkness of eternity. It took the rest of that second day and into the fading twilight for the old man to lumber up that slope with enough rocks gathered along the riverbank, enough to seal up the crevice forever and all time to come.

As the sun had sunk like a bloody benediction over those faraway mountains, Porcupine watched the white man bring the reluctant war pony up that loose and shifting slope, right to the base of the bluff, to the very foot of the rock-enclosed crevice where High Backed Bull lay. There the old man raised his hand to the sky and began singing. Not the words of the white man's prayer medicine—but the words of the Shahiyena air spirits song.

The song over, its last notes falling away from the bluffs to echo across the river below, the old man pulled free his pistol, rubbing the neck of one of Bull's favorite ponies.

That single shot reverberated for the longest time, carried back and forth along the river.

Just before dark the old gray-headed one finally rose and made his way down the slope, leaving behind the carcass of the war pony to guard the entrance to the rock cairn.

That rainy night icy hail lashed the white man's cheerless camp as he softly sang over and over the traditional song that wished the departed one a safe and quick journey across the Star Road, into the far, far land of Seyan. With no drum, he beat a hand on the bottom of a much-used copper kettle.

When the hail was done with them, passing on to the east with its white fury, the white man stripped himself naked to the chilling night. At his deep fire pit the man lit some white sage and smudged his body in the sacred and healing smoke. All the while he mumbled prayers that Porcupine could not make sense of from his hiding place in the willows.

Prayers spoken not in the white man's foreign tongue—but in the language of High-Backed Bull.

In the gray of sun-coming that next morning, Porcupine awoke cold and stiff in his rain-soaked blanket beside the river, blinking against the sleep-grit matting his eyes, rubbing them quickly before he peered through the willow to find the old one gone, disappeared some time in the night.

He wished the gray one a safe journey now that the white man rode all the more alone, rode without his son. Feeling sorry, Porcupine himself felt empty still, realizing the old one had journeyed far too many miles already without having the love of his son. The one born of his flesh, blood of his blood.

Yet Porcupine's spirit sang as he rode below that river bluff one last time that glorious dawn, stopping to gaze above at the carcass of the war pony, at the vertical scar in the bluff, a dark slash filled with river stones of every size.

High-Backed Bull had gone where he had wanted to be.

And the one who had fathered him was now traveling a road to seek his own redemption.

For knowing them both, Porcupine felt stronger still as he moved away from the river. Resolved more now than before to help White Horse once again gather the Dog Soldiers and their families into a fighting force that High-Backed Bull would be proud of.

Porcupine sensed his own spirit renewed, knowing the struggle continued.

—— Book III

Blood

Atonement

24

THE TRAIL HAD gone cold.

Two winters came and passed; each day they hoped against hope that some clue would turn up, some slip of a tongue, some word of Jubilee Usher's Danites passing through the country. But, nothing.

Back that October of sixty-eight, Two Sleep had taken Jonah on west from the land of the red desert beside the Sandy, crossing Green River, then pushing on to Fort Bridger. Like the back of his leathery, walnut-colored hand, the Shoshone knew the lay of that land and the caliber of those men in army blue. Jonah stayed quiet for the most part, letting the Indian ask the questions needing answers.

But none of the soldiers stationed at Bridger could remember a big outfit of horsemen, wagons, and an ambulance coming through of recent. Anything on the order of that many armed men would have surely caused that undermanned garrison at the frontier outpost to stand right up and take notice, what with so few civilian travelers moving east or west out in this infernal country. As it was, for the most part the soldiers said things had gone quiet to the north: up where the Sioux and Cheyenne had appeared to settle down after wrenching the big treaty of 1868, and the abandonment of the forts along the Bozeman Road, from the white man's army. With that summer of sixty-eight fading into history, the troops assigned the Montana Road had filed back down toward Laramie, for all time quitting the hunting ground granted the wild tribes.

"We just got tired of fighting," explained an aging captain commanding at Bridger. "After that four years of hell fighting the secesh back east, we were ordered out here to pacify this land, make it safe for the California argonauts, safe for business trade and what settlers was to move in."

As Jonah and Two Sleep listened, the captain sighed in the autumn shade of that brushy porch awning outside his mud-walled office. "We're taking a well-deserved retreat right now—this army that just got tired of fighting. You're aware this land along the great immigrant road once was ruled by the Cheyenne and Sioux, you know? Still, they haven't deviled us in a long time."

"Wasn't always that way," Jonah said, feeling the captain's eyes shift in his direction. "I fought them—the Cheyenne and the Lakota—to keep this road open."

"You with the galvanized volunteers, were you?"

"Sixty-five."

"Serve at Platte Bridge?"

Jonah only nodded, remembering Lieutenant Caspar Collins's brave ride across the bridge to break through a cordon of a thousand warriors and rescue an incoming squad of soldiers.

The aging captain had gone back to staring at the sun setting beyond Utah and that land of Brigham Young, lighting the leaves in the trees with fall's gold and crimson fire. "Yes, Mr. Hook. For a while now, the army got tired of fighting."

"Can't say as I fault 'em," Hook replied quietly.

Jonah ended up selling to the army four of those horses taken from the Danites, keeping what they needed for packing. And with the credit the outpost's commander gave them in trade for the animals, Fort Bridger's contract sutler resupplied Jonah and Two Sleep with cartridges and powder, coffee and sugar, flour and a few looking glasses, along with a modest amount of some Indian trade goods the man had been a long time in getting shet of. Hook was anxious to push on after a matter of days.

But pushing on southwest into the land of Zion had been as big a waste of time as Jonah could ever remember.

The closer he rode toward the City of the Saints, the more Hook felt he was treading on foreign ground. He had been north of a time in his life, twice he could remember as a youngster crossing what became the Mason-Dixon. And he had been hauled to the land of the Yankees after his capture at Corinth. That had been war—and he a prisoner of that bloody struggle. Yet even then, with the exception of a few sadistic guards who beat their prisoners for the manic love of seeing the pain and blood and suffering, Jonah remembered being treated better at the hands of the blue-belly civilians than in the land of Brigham Young's Saints.

No more was he merely a southern boy come north with his kin to conduct some commerce. No longer was he a Confederate soldier captured in the vain, brutal struggle waged by the South against a far mightier North. Now with the coming of another winter, Jonah Hook all the more felt like nothing less than a feared and distrusted stranger come to this foreign land. Not one with the religion of these quietly industrious people, he found himself treated civilly in few places, with cool indifference in most others, and outright hostility at many stops he and Two Sleep made.

A plainsman in tattered, trail-worn clothing, riding in the company of an aging Indian warrior, found himself nothing less than suspect of all color of crimes against the State of Deseret. Clearly a man of the prairie, and most certainly a Gentile, his companion none other than a member of a dark, heathen race of Lamanites said to be fallen from the grace of God—Hook was regarded more with pitying curiosity than with any desire on the Saints' part to offer anything in the way of assistance.

Already he had steeled himself, prepared to find the Mormons closing ranks around their own, this Danite, this leader of avenging gunmen, this mongol lord of the plains. Instead, what Jonah discovered was that Jubilee Usher might actually be one Prophet too many in his own land.

"Who was it you said you were looking for again?"

"Jubilee Usher's the man's name," Hook would answer those he would stop along the road, those who would come to the edge of the manicured fields long enough to listen as Jonah prodded for information. "Leader of the Danites."

Hearing that, most of the shopkeepers and farmers eyed him severely before they moved off without so much as answering. Most, but not all.

"And why would you be looking for this Jubilee Usher?" asked the rare one.

"Heard of the man by reputation," Jonah would say.

"Never met him, have you?"

"No, never," Jonah answered truthfully, remembering to recite the keys he had learned while riding with Boothog Wiser's Mormon battalion, keys he had sworn himself to use when at last the time had come to unlock the mysteries of Zion. "Rode with Lemuel Wiser—Usher's right hand. Decided I'd come here to Zion. Aim to join Usher's Danites."

That shopkeeper in a small agricultural settlement northeast of Salt Lake City flicked his eyes over at his wife as she swept the plank floor of their dusty establishment that frosty November day in 1868. What he had to say, he said guardedly, almost under his breath: "You got that right, stranger. That's Usher's band of Danites. Not Brigham's no more, they're not. That bunch belonged to Jubilee Usher for some time now."

The woman cleared her throat loudly above her busy broom, as if to utter a warning. And kept on sweeping without once raising her eyes to look at her husband.

Hook had summoned up the patience to keep asking. "Then I suppose this Brigham Young you spoke of would know where I might find Jubilee Usher?"

The Mormon's dark eyes moved to the window, beyond which the Indian waited in the autumn cold with their animals, clearly an Indian who knew and kept to his place among these whites who practiced a strict theocratic pecking order.

The shopkeeper said, "The Prophet would be most happy to know where Jubilee Usher is, stranger—if you're one to know yourself."

"I wouldn't have to ask you if I knew where to find Usher my own self," Jonah said.

"That much is clear. Still, it would be well worth your while to let Prophet Young know anything you might be privy to about Jubilee Usher."

"Said I was just looking for the man."

A cool smile darkened the face of the shopkeeper. "So is Young— looking for Usher, that is." He eyed his wife quickly again, then whispered to the counter secretively, "You take the offer of my help: you'll not go join up with that bunch."

"Why shouldn't a man be about God's work with Jubilee Usher?" Hook asked, a bit too loud.

He shook his head, whispering, "Usher ain't all that—"

"William!" the woman called out, standing there midfloor with her waxy hands draped over the top of her corn broom. "There's lots of work you could be doing in the back if our customer is finished buying what he needs so he and that Indian can be on their way."

Jonah would learn no more from that one.

The closer he drew to the seat of Mormon power, the colder the trail felt to that unnamed lightning rod he carried in his belly. It grew colder all the time until on the outskirts of Salt Lake City itself, Jonah decided he was likely riding into a blind canyon. The horsemen passed on through the City of the Saints without stopping, swinging south and east toward the Green once more, marching through Zion's outlying communities, their neatly platted streets and arithmetically plowed fields becoming more and more sparse as the horsemen pushed deeper into the southwest while November's sweet taste of autumn unraveled into the first bitter days of winter.

At one settlement Jonah asked how far the Church's settlements stretched toward the Mexican provinces.

"On deep into Arizona Territory. Down yonder to New Mexico too," came the answer given him from beneath the shading of a hat brim, where the eyes peered up at the horsemen in cool suspicion.

Women worked these fields beside their men. Indeed, lots of women. More than once Jonah found himself unconsciously studying the faces and figures of those most lanky, those fair of hair, those who best fit the dimming remembrance of a particular female. A gamble, it was, to hope with so much of his fiber, to discover himself yearning for her all the more in this land of the Saints—here, where a man found so many white women. And he gone so long without his eyes blessed with the sight of any pale skinned female, any white-skinned woman at all.

And now came this sudden feast of setting a hungry man down before all these who belonged to the polygamists, laboring in the fields for their husbands and the greater glory of their God.

So used his eyes were to the frontier garden of dark-skinned females. To Jonah it seemed that damned near all of the alabaster-skinned ones a man would run into in making his way back and forth across the West were businesswomen. The painted, perfumed, softer, and whiter sex had followed the gamblers and gamers, the saloon keepers and drummers, to make their share where a fortune might not be guaranteed, but where there would never be a shortage of eager customers.

The cold emptiness gnawed through Jonah's belly. How he felt starved of a sudden, his eyes looking over those fair-of-skin women. His rage returned, robbed as he was of these years with her: the months and days and fleeting moments stolen from them both, never to share again. And as he sat looking out upon those busy in their fields, or as he gazed at all the industrious of the gentle sex he saw moving up and down the streets of the small communities founded by these Saints, Jonah sensed the first stirrings of doubt.

Was he chasing so much wind? Hadn't Gritta's trail gone just about as cold as the boys' trail had in drifting off toward Mexico?

For the first time he considered giving up the chase while he still had time to make some kind of life for himself. Maybe, he told himself, he should beggar his losses and give up the trail, lonely and unforgiving as it was. Close this dark chapter of his life and start anew—make a life for Hattie and perhaps find a widow for himself, someone who could cool the burning rage and pain he suffered, who could take away the hurt and fill this hole gnawing in his chest. Yes, Hattie would finish her schooling, then come live with him and her new stepmother. . . .

A vision of Hattie swam before him. Almost four years back he had found her in Nebraska. Lord, how she had grown into a young woman who looked more like her mother now than he ever had imagined she could. When he'd wrenched her from the clutches of the Danites, Hattie was damn near the same age as Gritta when he had married her. Jonah's only daughter had grown to be every bit as beautiful and smitten with life as her mother.

No, he realized he would never be able to look at Hattie again without seeing Gritta's face. Never able to gaze into his daughter's eyes without cursing himself for quitting the chase.

"Goddamn you," he grumbled aloud that evening as the black-bellied clouds quickly shut down the last shreds of fading light left in the sky. "Damn you if you go and give up when this ride gets hardest. Remember how you lost the trail before? But still you never lost hope, Jonah. Never give up before."

He was of this life to suffer the pain—one sort or another. He had decided this was his lot to bear. And if he was called upon to endure, then his choice was simple: the pain of pushing on until he found them or could push on no more—that hurt seemed much, much easier to bear than the pain of living with himself knowing he had played out, folded, and given up.

He would not fool himself into thinking he deserved a better hand, nor cash in his chips and back away from the table. No, he would play out the hand dealt him. A man would, that.

As Two Sleep became Jonah's brother of the blanket, they inched over the first heavy snows carpeting the passes of the Uintahs, then eased down the east slopes pushing on south. From time to time they crossed freight roads the Mormons used, choosing whether or not to follow them into the distance toward a small community of clapboard shacks, more usually of sod or adobe, settlements of fields and irrigation ditches and laundered clothes hung on a line behind the dirty shacks where dim trails of smoke rose into the cold air of that first winter in the land of the Mormons.

Only once more did he ever allow himself the sweet luxury of wanting to give up—halting the Indian as they gazed upon a cluster of mud homes in a nameless little settlement appearing all the more squalid with the early coming of winter night, dark of shadow and gray of twilight snow, the small windows in each shack lit with the warm beacons of light, figures passing between the light and those two lonely sojourners out in the cold. Back and forth the shadows moved as the fish-belly gray of evening descended to night upon that naked land of red escarpment and ancient geologic upheaval.

A warmth beckoned him in from the cold, those shadows no more than suggestions of ghosts from his past, ghosts of happier days calling the lost and wayward one to join them at the fire of remembrance on brighter times and lighter cares.

"Come, Jonah Hook," Two Sleep said finally.

Eventually he tore his eyes away from the window and its seductive corona of light and found the Shoshone staring at him with what the plainsman took to be sympathy.

"You don't gotta feel sorry for me, Injun." He looked back at the distant windows now that twilight's purple had faded to winter's cold squeeze of black. "Never, never feel sorry for me. You hear?"

"Make camp. Food, then sleep. Tomorrow we go."

"Always tomorrow, Two Sleep. How many more will there be?"

"Every morning I think we find them," the Indian replied quietly, following the white man's gaze at the distant spots of saffron light.

"You tell yourself that too?" Jonah asked, then sighed. "At times I just feel like . . ."

When Hook's voice drifted off without finish, Two Sleep said, "You give up this trail, Two Sleep stay on it. This trail no more just for you, Jonah Hook. It mine too now."

He finally nodded, feeling his shoulders sag, reluctant to release the anticipation of giving in to his fondest dream. Here at last vowing that he would never again grant himself the delicious ecstasy of the dream that took him down a far different path.

"Sometimes it feels like there's just too damn much trail left to cover, Injun."

"Tomorrow is the day," Two Sleep reminded.

"Yes," Jonah replied, urging his horse off gently. Once and for all he struggled to convince himself he had the patience of the eternal rocks themselves. "Tomorrow morning is the day."

It was weeks later as they followed a course slightly east of south that the riders no longer came across any outflung settlements of white men. Instead, they rode toward the distant, gleaming, snow-draped walls of the adobe huts that seemed to squat on the valley floor, what proved to be a settlement of farmers and sheep herders nestled among steep-sided bluffs on one side, those buttes and canyon walls taking the unwilling eye and leading it upward toward the clouds and peaks mantled in white one upon the other.

"You s'pose we're in Mexico already?" Jonah asked.

With a shrug Two Sleep replied, "Never ride this far. Ute country. Far into Ute country. Don't know, Jonah Hook."

"Long as it's been since we left Brigham Young's City, it still don't seem we've come far enough to be in Mexico. Maybe these here Mexicans live north of Mexico."

"No matter, Jonah Hook. We still go south—still ride till the land of the traders who buy your sons."

"Comancheros."

"Yes, comancheros. We ride into land of the comancheros."

They had pushed off the *sangre*-hued hills, colored by the blood of infinite sunsets spread prayerfully on this ancient land, wending their way down, down to that village of adobe shacks, mud-and-wattle jacales, cramped streets of solid-wheeled *carretas,* a village where farmers and shepherds knew little English. But unlike Brigham Young's Mormon settlers, these brown-skinned people would in their own way try to help the stranger come among them that waning winter as Jonah learned 1868 had died and 1869 had already ushered itself in.

There would be days and weeks, months and seasons to come learning more and more of the language as he and Two Sleep pushed on east of south, struggling over mountains and crossing valley floors, only to recross and return time and again to familiar villages and ranchos when a fickle clue or rumor ran itself out like the trickle of water in this arid land. As the miles became years, Jonah knew more of the right words to use, better to pose his questions while the seasons turned and the winds cleansed the land with each unfathomable tilt of the earth away from the sun.

As they had realized that first winter afternoon riding into that first village where nothing but Spanish was spoken, the two strangers come from the land of the north had long known the one word that was sure to get a map drawn with a stick in the dirt, perhaps scratched on a table or stone hearth with a chunk of charcoal—or only as simple a gesture as a nod and a pointing of the arm with the name of a new village to try.

That lone, powerful word never changed across the last four winters as Jonah Hook asked his one question—his first and last question in this distant, sunny land.

"Comancheros?"

25

H E HATED THE taste of tequila.

Like someone had boiled down a winter-old pair of long-handles in a copper kettle as they distilled the cactus juice. It turned his stomach just hitting his tongue. Not like the corn whiskey a man got back home in Virginia, even Missouri. Corn whiskey betrayed its punch and potency behind a taste more genteel on the tongue. Like a proper southern gentleman who could shake your hand with civility or kick you in the head like a mule.

But not this tequila. It was a drink as crude as the people who brewed it behind every poor mud-and-wattle jacal huddled beneath the never-changing sky like trail droppings from the passing of the sun itself. Some varieties proved to be more bitter than others, but the best of them no better than sour. He hated having nothing else to drink—the warm, milky water, or this goddamned tequila.

But that never stopped Jonah from pouring more of the saddle varnish from the *garrafas,* the pitchers of fired clay. Never stopped him from bringing the glazed cups to his lips at every stop, every village and cantina, every brothel or barn. More times than he cared to remember, Jonah and

Two Sleep had spent nights in any sort of dosshouse where they might lie with the whores for the cost of a few centavos. When there were no beds to be had, no matter the price, sleeping with their animals among the fragrant hay of barns and liveries at no cost at all had done nicely.

Eventually he gave up sleeping in the brothels. Too often had he carried away on his flesh and in his clothing the biting torment infesting those beds and those who made their living in them. Bitterly Jonah remembered the cursed lice up at Rock Island, remembered how that prison vermin tortured a man so that he never really slept soundly, how a man was forced to make a truce with weary sleeplessness. Back then he had wished the lice would freeze to death simply to stop the incessant biting at his whiskers, down in his groin, across his unwashed scalp. Back in that death hold of a prison he scratched himself till he bled, and still the lice lived on. Vermin that moved from the dead men the guards dragged from the cells each morning, and migrated to the living still left in those cages of rotting humanity.

Squashing those painful, bitter memories, Jonah Hook sensed the warmth of the cactus juice spread from his belly, radiating out in spidering fingers of comfort, amazed that he already felt a lightness come to his forehead, his nose seemingly grown bigger. It always swelled on his face with the cactus juice. He hoped he would not suffer the cactus thorns before morning. Just get a bellyful of beans and some of that goat meat down—keep it down—then a night's sleep. This could be one of those rare nights under a roof and out of the howling cold: small respite for a man who hadn't been home for ten years.

Oh, he had gone back to Missouri, to the valley, to the cabin he had built for Gritta, of a time in sixty-seven. But Jonah would never count that as going home. Not with nothing there he could call home. Everything was gone, even the window glazing stole. He hadn't stayed long.

No, Jonah had been on this trail away from his family for ten years now come spring. Spring? If winter ever released its grip from this desert land.

Such different country from southwestern Missouri, different still from that heady richness of the Shenandoah Valley. Fleeing the land of the Mormons, they had kept their noses pointed south into the land of the Navaho in New Mexico Territory. For the most part the Navaho kept off by themselves and weren't at all curious enough to cross the path of the two horsemen, perhaps content now that they were a defeated people not to know the mission of any sojourner.

Plunging farther still into the land of the sun, they marched past the feet of the emerald mountain peaks of Sierra de Tunecha and on to little clusters of the mud huts, where the jacales knotted around a common spring or well dug from the hardpan desert. Watering holes and villages with names that rang off the tongue: Bernalita and Corrales. Wandering farther east out of the mountains and onto the beginning of the great southern plains, they eventually turned back to the north again, sensing that their answers lay west of the Llano Estacado, on west of the Journada del Muerto itself, that high, hard-baked land the comancheros crossed in plying their profitable trade. The two horsemen rode on past the villages of Pacos and Vermilla, past Ojo de Nicolas and Salina de San Andres, stopping to ask for word at Joya and Cachilla and Albiquira.

Without fail Jonah gave voice to the same question that seemed to rise from the hope that some day would bring him the answer he sought.

Always he asked where a man might find the comancheros.

Instead, the poor folk of those little towns, gathered around the common spring or dusty square, would shrug, point off in a meaningless direction, and gaze back with passionless faces, their black eyes reflecting the glare of the bright sun, or shaded beneath the protection of straw hat brims. All about Jonah were the mouths that said nothing to help, the faces that hid even more.

"Just tell me where I can talk with comancheros who trade into Tejas," he would plead in his halting Spanish.

And always the poor of those towns went back to their work at the stunted corn they watered frugally, driving their bleating sheep from one patch of burned grass to another beneath an omnipresent cloud of gray dust that turned pink, then orange, and finally red with every sunset. Smiling, these people apologized with their shoulders, sorry they could not be of any help to the sojourners.

Down at the settlement of Santa Fe they were told the nearby river would take them south into Mexico. Perhaps if there were no answers to be found up here, it was suggested, then south where the comancheros lived is where a man might go.

"What river?" he had asked.

One after another of the peons pointed. "That river."

They followed, staying with the Rio Grande south past the sprawling settlement of Albuquerque and on to the tiny ranchos of Belen, Sabina, Lumitar and Parida, Fra Cristobal and Valverde. Told they had only to follow the well-beaten path south, farther still, on across the Gadsden Purchase, where they would come to the old town of El Paso. The place crawled with army and border profiteers, every man suspicious of all whom he had not bought with his money.

Still, by simply watching the constant activity along the road heading south, they had learned enough to know that Chihuahua was where they needed next to go. They were lured to that great center of commerce, that hub of riches from which manifold trade routes radiated like the spokes on the wheels of the crude *carretas* that carried forth all that was shiny and new, glittering and painted, hauling back the wealth of distant ports.

"You ain't got shit for a chance to find nobody the comancheros brung down here," the Irishman told Jonah.

It was in a tiny Chihuahua cantina that Hook ran across the fair-skinned, red-headed Irishman with the wild blue-gray eyes split by his swollen red nose. Jonah had been more than eager to lubricate the man's tongue once he found out the Irishman might know something about the trade flowing back and forth across the Rio Grande into American territory. While the Irishman drank, Jonah and Two Sleep wolfed down steamy bowls of cornmeal porridge mulled by little chunks of raw brown *peloncillo* sugar.

Hook wiped his mouth, suspicious that he'd been taken by the red-eyed drunk. "Maybe you can tell me who some of these comancheros are. Names. Where I can find them. That's all I need. Nothing else from you."

The fleshy, corpulent Irishman weaved to his feet, a cup of the potent, homemade *aguardiente* in his hand, then crooked a finger for Hook to follow him from the table. When Two Sleep started to rise, the Irishman motioned the Indian to sit.

Stopping at the open doorway, the Irishman swayed against Jonah, then swung an arm slowly across the scene.

"Look there, Mr. Hook," he said. "And say to me that you'll find two boys in all of that dark, smelly nest of vermin. Unpossible."

"I aim to find the comancheros first."

"Look, I told you!" snapped the Irishman. "You come to the wrong place looking for help."

"Just the name of one," Hook asked, slipping out from beneath the fat one's fleshy arm.

He drank, then dragged the dribble from his chin. "What do you see there, American? Look carefully and tell me."

Hook studied the street throbbing with the comings and goings of all sorts of poor. Occasionally a vaquero rode by, resplendent in dress and horse trappings, forcing his way through the crowds of peons by his sheer presence. Only now did Jonah see a carriage roll by, matched fours pulling along the landed aristocracy of Mexico.

"There—that one," Jonah said eagerly. "He's a rich man. Bound to know some comancheros who trade into Texas, into Indian Territory."

"Him?" the Irishman asked, pointing with a slosh of his cup. A pair of Mexicans entered the cantina, forced to duck beneath the Irishman's outstretched arm. "You see a rich man there, no?"

"He will know the names of some comancheros—is that what you're telling me?"

The mottled cheeks were flushed with the blush of tequila. "You have been looking in the wrong place, Mr. Hook. Looking for the wrong men."

In angry confusion Jonah watched the Irishman turn away from the doorway and stumble back to ease himself into the chair once more. He dashed back to the table himself, slamming his two palms down on it as he sat.

"I'm here in Chihuahua—where the comancheros trade from, goddammit. Don't drink my tequila, then play a riddle on me . . . telling us I've been looking the wrong place for the wrong folks."

"See at the bar?" he asked, leaning in close to Jonah.

Hook turned, finding some vaqueros with their arms laced around several women in their blousy skirts and shiny high-heeled shoes that clacked along the plank floor. Near them were more well-dressed men. He grew weary of the game. "Them? That rich-looking bunch. You're telling me they're comanchero traders?"

"No. Not the obvious, my dear Mr. Hook. The others. There. See? And there. Look carefully and behold. And over there too."

Jonah shook his head. It made no sense. Every man the drunk pointed out was as poor a dirt farmer or craftsman as a man would care to meet. Not a successful comanchero. Not like the vaqueros dressed so exquisitely as they drank with the whores at the bar.

"C'mon, Two Sleep," he said with disgust and frustration as he rose.

"We go?"

"We're going. This bastard's drunk our tequila and spit back nothing in return. Hope you wake with your head pounding like a carpenter's hammer."

With a slap the Irishman dropped his soft, empty hand over Jonah's wrist, pinning it to the table. "Listen, you fool—I am telling you everything you need to know short of what actually became of your boys."

Slowly Hook disentangled himself. "You ain't told me shit."

He chuckled, wagging his big head, the flaming hair disheveled and uncombed for the better part of his three-day drunk. "Go back north to find out about your boys, Mr. Hook. Talk to the comancheros."

"I come here to Chihuahua to talk to the comancheros."

"That's what I been trying to tell you!" he snorted, upending Hook's bottle to refill his cup. "There's no comancheros here."

Jonah squinted. "They're up north?"

With a nod the man answered, "North is where they trade. North is where they work."

"So who the hell are those fancy-dressed fellas you pointed out to me?"

"Them—they're called *ricos*."

"Rich men."

"Right. Their kind are the money men. They run the operations out of Chihuahua. That's all they do—never soiling their hands with work. Maybe once in a while one of them will want to amuse himself and take a long vacation, ride north with a caravan, joining his hired vaqueros and the comanchero traders for a diversion one trading season or another."

He squeezed it in his mind. Had he been looking all this time— month after month, season after season—for the wrong sort of man? Looking for him in the wrong place?

Jonah sensed his heart hammering with self-anger ready to boil over in tears of helpless rage. "You're telling me there's no comancheros here? They're back up north?"

"*Ricos,* not comancheros. Not here."

"Back up north, goddammit?" Jonah growled.

He licked the drops of tequila from the red hairs of his mustache. "Yeah. Chihuahua is where you'll come when you find out which *rico* train brought your boys in. Here is where you'll come to get some idea where the boys were taken once they were brought down here. Until then, you got to go back north and find some answers."

"Back . . . back to El Paso?"

With a wag of his big head, the Irishman said, "No. Out there. To the

northeast is the trail you need to take. It's wide and well beaten. Used
every autumn trading season for years. Centuries, likely."

"Northeast?"

"To Portrillo and beyond the river."

"Beyond the river, you say? Texas."

"Texas."

So now Jonah drank in this dark, smoky hovel of a cantina in a village
he thought the locals called Vieja. Another one of the miserable, stinking
jacales squatting somewhere north of the Rio Grande.

With Two Sleep he crossed back into the States at a place called
Presidio, angling north by east from there, staying clear of the mountains
that hugged the distant skyline here, there, and on almost every side of
their line of march. It was a hostile land peopled with too few gringos and
too many Mexicans, where a growing population of Texans were protected
as best they could be upriver by Fort Quitman on the west, by Fort Davis
to the north and Fort Stockton on farther east of there, outposts strung so
far apart in that long, desperately thin line of frontier defense the army had
been establishing ever since the end of the South's bid for independence
from the Union.

"You got the right idea," the old man declared to Jonah. "But your
line's off some."

At a settlement called Marfa a bartender had suggested that Hook
scare up one of John Bell Hood's faithful—an old Confederate soldier who
might be able to help point the two sojourners in some likely direction or
another. For reasons he could not explain, Jonah trusted the old man more
than he had trusted most others come across in the years since leaving Shad
Sweete and Fort Laramie behind. It came hard for Jonah Hook to trust
others. So much already lay crushed and trampled inside him. Hard anymore to trust, to hope.

The old soldier dragged out a rumpled map with few lines scratched
across its dark surface, a parchment given a rich buckskin patina of time
and smoke and the grease of many fires.

"There," Jonah said again. "I draw a line from Chihuahua north by
east," and he slowly traced his fingernail northeast across the Rio Grande
the way he and Two Sleep had come, heading on east into the open ground
east of Fort Davis and west of Camp Hudson and Fort McKavett.

"Like I said—appears your thinking is on the right track when you
head out from Chihuahua. But trick now is you gotta think like a co-

manchero, friend. Think like someone going north to trade with the Comanch'.''

Jonah's eyes studied the map, smarting in the dim light and the smoke of cheap tobacco, the smudge of tallow candles that gave this cold, stinking, low-roofed room its only glow of life. The far northern edge of the old Confederate's map had the words *Indian Territory* scratched across it in bold letters, while the tracings of rivers were barely more evident than the many wrinkles aging the old parchment.

"I come this far from the plains because I was told that the co-mancheros trade outta New Mexico. Went down there the long way from Fort Laramie, wandered around and found out I needed to head south to Chihuahua. That was where I was told to come back north, into Texas."

"And here you are," the old man said softly, his rheumy eyes lit with the candles' glow and the cheap *aguardiente*. "When'd you leave that north country? Fort Laramie, you said?"

"Right," he answered. "End of summer, sixty-eight."

Jonah watched the old man's eyes flick from him to the Shoshone and back again, widening in pure wonder as he whistled low. "You got any idea what month and year it be, son?"

With a shrug Jonah replied, "Didn't keep track. S'pose it never mattered. Why?"

"Man has a job to do—he just does it, right?" He wagged his head in amazement. "Got the patience of the Eternal Himself, you do. Why, don't you have any idea you been wandering over four year, friend?"

In ways, it felt like more than four years. In another way, Jonah was just as certain the old man was having sport with him. "Four years. You're crazed, mister. It can't be seventy-two."

"No, friend, it ain't."

Jonah grinned, smiling at Two Sleep. "See? Told you. Knew you was having fun with me."

With a shrug of his shoulder, the old man explained. "It ain't seventy-two. It's winter of 1873. Already two months gone past the new year."

For a long moment he stared down at his hands, in a way wishing he hadn't come to know that so much time had slipped under him wandering through the land of the Mormons before he plodded back and forth through season after season begging for and scratching out information in New Mexico, time fooled away before they ever wandered south to Chihuahua. All that time had stacked up solid as cordwood behind him, one piece at a time. He hadn't noticed because there had always been another village to visit, another trail rumored to hold promise. In the end every day, week, month, and year had come at him and flowed on past in such small, unobserved pieces. So much of his life, and he hadn't noticed it gone.

Of a sudden Jonah's thoughts turned on something peculiar: that he would turn thirty-six this approaching summer. And owning up to that only meant that Gritta had grown much, much older too. Some ten years' worth of older from the time Jonah had last held her against him.

And the boys. They weren't really boys no more. Grown into men without him.

As much as he wanted to cry or lash out and hit something, someone, Jonah stoically turned back to the old soldier. Then gazed back down at the map, his heart thrumming in his ears, his breath come shallow like the flight of moth's wings. "All right, old soldier. You want me think like a comanchero."

The old man wiped some tobacco juice out of his gray chin whiskers before he asked, "Lookee there and tell me where you gonna go to trade, friend?"

Jonah's eyes rose to the Shoshone's, then slowly moved over to the old man's. "I'm gonna go where the Injuns are."

"Good! But—not just any Injuns."

"The Comanche."

There was that gap-toothed smile of triumph. "Doggedy—now you got it!"

With a slash of a grin, feeling the hot hammer of blood at his ears, Jonah gazed back down at that old, faded map in the candlelight. "All right. Show me where the comancheros go to trade with the Comanche."

Without a word the wrinkled one licked his lips in the glow and wispy faint smoke of those tallow candles, then dragged his long fingernail across the parchment . . . slowly up from Chihuahua, across the Rio Grande west of Presidio, ever on as his fingertip neatly split the seventy-odd miles of wilderness lying between forts Quitman and Davis.

Jonah looked up and asked, "What's out there?"

26

THERE WASN'T MUCH out there.

Like the old soldier told him, "Jackrabbits and desert. A few Mex squatters. And the Pecos River. North of there—ever'thing—the hull durn country belongs to the Comanch'."

Into the bitter cold of winter's last gasp on the southern plains they plunged, crossing low mountains, peeling their way over rough country like all that they had pierced coming to Comancheria. This was a waterless chaparral where only the creosote brush and spear grass grew to break up the harsh monotony of the rise and fall of a sinister land. That, and the cactus. Always the cactus.

Reluctantly winter relinquished its brief hold on this southern land—making for a muddy time of things.

Over Jonah's head the low roof leaked, drops of cold mud smacking the back of his neck as he scooped the refried beans, what he had come to call Mexican strawberries, from the earthen bowl with the crude iron spoon. Across from Jonah sat the Indian, smearing a load of the *refritos* into a swab of tortilla that Two Sleep stuffed into the side of his mouth. The Shoshone called fewer teeth his own nowadays than he had four and a

half years before, beside the red desert country where the two had first
met. In their time together he had been forced to let Jonah pull three of
them from one side alone. Two yanked from the other. It was crude, hard
work with the small field pliers Hook packed along for gun repair: messy,
bloody work, and damned painful too. But after a day or so of walking
around with a small swab of his shirttail stuffed down in the bloody hole,
the Shoshone had never failed to smile again, poking his tongue through
the new gap, the glaze of pain finally gone from his eyes, that singular ache
of a rotting tooth now nothing but a dimming memory.

Some three years wandering among the Mex had taught Hook what
he needed of their simple language, absorbing enough of a smattering of
verbs and nouns and idioms that allowed him to learn even more as the
seasons turned, ever turned.

Most every day it never failed to amaze him that these dirt-poor
people had stayed in this unforgiving country, nailed down in this land of
sunburned offerings, blessed with little shade and even less sweet water.

Water—that was the one thing worth more than gold in this country.
Most of what the two horsemen and their stock had been forced to drink
across the slow whirl of the seasons had been squeezed from the drying,
death-laced water holes and muddy seeps they ran across on their travels.
And whenever the pair found themselves in a mud-and-wattle settlement
like this very one, Jonah had come to count himself fortunate that the
milky water proved thin enough to drink. His prayer had been answered
long ago: the earth-colored fluid so predominate in this land no longer
troubled his bowels the way it had when first they had begun their sojourn
into this land of the sun long, long ago.

A long time back he had tried the Mexicans' beer—thick as syrup but
shy on flavor. So still he drank the tequila, the Mexicans' pulque, as much
as he hated it. And here in this cantina, as in practically every jacal where
they had stopped across the years, there was little but that fermented juice
of the agave to drink, its sour and ropy taste barely softened by the warm,
earth-rich water a man used to chase the cactus juice, to mellow the racy
sting of the green chiles set before him at every meal, hot as a spoonful of
red ants.

The hanging lamps cast a light the color of a dull tropical orange over
everything, especially the deep-brown hide stretched over the back of
Jonah's hands busy above his bowl. From the corner table arose a quick
spate of muffled laughter as men gambled with a greasy deck of flare-red

pasteboards. Smoke from their cigarillos hung in wispy spiders' veils just below the lamplight.

His nostrils came alive, flaring slightly as Jonah smelled her—even before he actually heard her, before he felt her arm rope loosely over his shoulder. The peculiar odor of these cantina women, ripe with the fragrance of pomegranate and *penole* meant to mask the stench of unwashed flesh, bean wind, and the previous customer, had long ago become as recognizable as the smell of his own horse. Back came the memory of that first of these dark-skinned whores he had taken in a squalid little settlement they reached in New Mexico, he grown so anxious for her that there in the dark corner of that low-roofed hovel, out of the firelight, Jonah had let her unbutton his canvas britches and tantalize him, stroking his hot and swollen flesh until he exploded in her hand. Like music he had been starved from hearing in so long—the music of a woman's laughter—the whore had laughed at his eagerness as she led the gringo back to a dark room where she showed him to a chair, worked him once more into readiness with her tongue and lips, then sat down upon him.

Gazing up now at this new one in the flickering light shed by the tallow candle that dripped and sputtered in its pool of heady grease at the center of his table, Jonah discovered his lips and the end of his tongue already gone mushy, numbing from the potent cactus juice. Something in his mind made him wonder if this whore was really as good-looking as the tequila made him think she was. Bending low over him, she tantalized him, brushing his shoulder with one of her breasts, her fingers raking through his long hair as she luringly moved the breast past his cheek before settling in the chair at the corner of Hook's table.

Immediately his eyes fell to her loose blouse, hidden partially beneath the folds of a coarse woollen shawl she had knotted against the depth of her cleavage. In the way she thrust those breasts at him, she made it plain that there was nothing else beneath the blouse, nothing but her brown flesh that rose and fell with her every breath as she poured herself a drink from Hook's bottle.

"Help yourself," he said with a wry grin, already sensing his hands on those breasts, willing his lips to suck at their warm aureoles.

There was something playful around her big eyes. Jonah supposed it was the fact that she wanted him, had abandoned the Mex at the bar and came over to show the gringo that she wanted him. She seemed so young, though, so likely that look in her eye was only something practiced, for someone so young would not really know how to share herself with a man. He tugged down the last shred of woman-loneliness left in him, hungering to recognize those small, furtive changes in a woman's face when she draws close to the one she wants to sink her claws in, if only for a night, if only for an hour, if only for as long as it will take the man to seize his satisfaction.

When he spoke his English, she looked at him quizzically, the cup stopped at her chin. *"Señor?"*

He hadn't meant to say it in English. "Don't matter. Drink up." Jonah took his cup from the table and clacked it against hers, motioning for Two Sleep to toast with them.

She was woman enough and he had been without long enough, she put the blood so thick in his throat that he could scarcely swallow the ribbon of fire the tequila made descending from his tongue. The pulque didn't possess the reassuring and familiar formaldehyde stench of frontier whiskey.

She smiled like sunrise calm in the autumntime, something smoky and warm to it, and tossed back the hot tequila in one gulp, hammering the table once as she set her clay cup back down and poured more of the fiery cactus juice into it. That teasing, taunting look in her eyes had probably condemned many a hapless, helpless man to doom in this same stinking cesspool of a cantina.

From the corner of his eye Hook noticed the tall vaquero at the bar for the first time, a young dandy who stood a head above his companions, their faces shrouded in smoke rising from their corn-shuck cigarillos, voices clanging sharp-edged like tiny cymbals. The handsome horseman was dressed in creamy leather all lashed together with stamped conchos and roped in gilt braid. In the dim candlelight Hook could barely make out the man, not much more than a foggy blur of the vaquero's face as the Mexican glared flints in his direction, and for a minute his tequila-dulled mind argued on which one of them the Mex was looking at. Perhaps the vaquero simply did not like Two Sleep. No matter, really. There would always be those who didn't take to Injuns.

But that did not quite fit, either, the more Jonah's slow mind kneaded it while he kept on eating, his teeth tearing at the chiles and the tortilla, sucking back the softened beans, then gazed up at the vaquero again and decided the man was glaring at the woman. That was it, he decided. She had come over from the bar, where he remembered seeing her looped beneath the vaquero's arm when he and Two Sleep had blown in and slammed the crude door behind them, the fine powder from the trail settling like gold dust in the pale, yellow candlelight. Ever since Jonah had felt her hot black eyes on him.

The way he now sensed the Mex's eyes burning a hole of hate in his left shoulder.

From where Jonah sat, he faced the door and the room's only window, his back for the most part turned on the bar and half of the room. His partner watched the rest of that low-roofed hovel.

"How many's the others?" he asked Two Sleep, grumbling it in English.

The Indian did not answer at first. Instead, he swabbed some more beans and chiles into his tortilla and stuffed it in his mouth. As he wiped the back of a hand across his lips, only then did the Shoshone's eyes quickly rake the half of the room under his gaze.

"Five," he replied in English. Then moving his hands quickly, but casually, in the ballet of plains sign language, Two Sleep told Hook the rest.

Three of them do not belong to the rest of the poor ones. Three of them are for us.

"Three with him?"

The Shoshone nodded his head.

When Hook began to look back to the woman, he watched the Indian's eyes climb and narrow. Jonah smelled the man before he heard the leather-heeled boots clatter to a halt beside his chair.

"You may be only a slut," he told the woman gruffly. "But tonight you are my slut. Come with me."

Her black eyes went to Jonah's, perhaps to search for hope, to plea for help, to find a hero.

"Come!" he roared at her.

Jonah's eyes climbed to the vaquero's now. Blinking, clearing them of the tequila-and-chile tears, he found the Mexican's eyes shining like those of some despised, creeping night animal. The man's breath rose and fell in great gusts, sweetened with agave

"Time enough for you to have her, friend," Hook told the man in Spanish. "Go and leave her for now. Go back to the bodega and your friends. Time enough for you."

With a smooth movement the vaquero brought his right hand to rest on the handle of the long knife stuffed in the colorful sash at his waist. The left hand seized the whore's wrist and yanked it up.

"Come, I said!"

She began to babble in pain, gripping the hand that imprisoned her. Her head was thrown back as he kicked the chair out from beneath her, yanking her roughly to her feet, yanking her back from the table.

"No cause to do that," Jonah said quietly, in his own tongue. "Leave the woman be."

As the vaquero's three companions inched toward them, the bar at their backs and the massive rowels on their Mexican spurs jangling like tambourines, Hook thought he heard the click of two hammers coming to full-cock.

"Two Sleep?" he asked as he rose slowly from his chair, without looking at the Shoshone.

The Indian whispered, "They are dead men—they move on you."

Jonah turned back to the vaquero. "I will say it for the last time," he spoke in Spanish. "Leave the woman be."

With a laugh the vaquero whirled the whore backward out of the way, pulling his knife as Hook's arm swung, bringing up the cup filled with tequila. It splashed into the Mexican's face at the same moment the knife glinted candlelight across the distance at the end of the vaquero's arm. It moved like quicksilver sliding off an upended piece of isinglass.

Numbed by the liquor, Hook didn't feel the pain of the blade's slash along his left arm. Yet he knew in that primitive way of the animal that his flesh had been opened. A moment later he sensed the hot, sticky beading along the slash. The Mexican stood smirking at him, wiping the tequila off his smooth brown face.

For a moment Hook stood transfixed by his blood-slicked arm, his glazed eyes crawling past the three others at the bar, then coming to stop on the vaquero's face as Jonah's right hand went to his belt for his own knife. It came into the candlelight slowly, a dull glint reflected off the long blade that had scalped more than one of the Danites he hunted with a vengeance.

"No. Shoot him and we go," Two Sleep snapped, pushing his wobbly chair back slightly. "Put the goddamned knife away. Shoot him now."

Hook wagged his head, shaking loose wispy webs as his eyes crawled across the men gathered at the bar, stopping once on the fat bartender, his brown neck plopped atop his shoulders in unwashed rolls like a turkey's wattle, long *ristras* of dried chiles hung behind him like crimson curtains. The man's hands were out of sight. Danger pricked Jonah as he looked back at the shrieking woman, the back of her hand over her mouth, her eyes wide in terror.

He sensed she had seen enough blood spilled on her account. Women like her drew trouble, like flecks of iron to a lodestone. Yet knowing it did not help. Here he was, his own knife drawn against the young vaquero, who again pushed the whore back out of his way and turned sideways, crouching slightly at the knees.

There was no grace, no finesse in Hook's sudden, drunken lunge for the Mexican. The only thing that saved him was the surprising suddenness of it, closing before the vaquero could slash out at his enemy.

A cry of shock, a yelp of pain reverberated in Jonah's ear as he slid his knife along the Mexican's ribs, dragging the man close with his free arm. He felt the warmth ooze over his blade hand. With all the strength he had, Hook held the vaquero close, continuing to dance from beneath the man's wild swings with that knife, knowing that if the Mexican broke free . . .

His breath exploded from him when the vaquero spun Hook and pushed him backward against the bar. The Mexican's free hand clamped around Jonah's wrist, repeatedly hammering the arm and hand against the edge of the bar. Unable to maintain his grip, the knife popped free, sent spinning down the bar.

As quickly Jonah brought both hands up, seizing the vaquero's wrist, holding his red-tainted knife high overhead. There they struggled, pitching their weight against the other, spinning and each trying to throw his opponent off balance. Hook lunged for the vaquero's ear, catching it between his teeth, squeezing down until he felt the salty, thick syrup trickle over his tongue. With a squeal of pain followed by a grunt of effort the Mexican drove his knee into Jonah's groin.

Down Hook tumbled, the sudden pain radiating out from the core of him like exploding stars.

In triumph the vaquero stood over his vanquished enemy, rotating the knife handle as he dropped to his knees on top of Hook so that he could plunge it into the gringo's heart. He smiled, then as suddenly as he had descended on his enemy, the vaquero wore a look of utter surprise, a pinched look of panic as he rocked back to gaze down at his chest where the American released a second knife.

Staring dumbfounded, the Mexican struggled to rise. But his legs had gone to water and would not hold him.

Hook shoved the Mexican off. The vaquero tumbled to the floor, his legs beginning to draw up as Jonah pulled his knife free from the man's chest—then savagely plunged it into the red-stained white shirt again and a third time, splattering flecks of blood across the creamy buckskin jacket.

"*Donde?*" the vaquero asked with a gasp, blood on his lips.

"Where? Where'd I get the knife?" Jonah asked in reply, slowly pulling the blade from the man's chest, then holding the sharp tip against the vaquero's Adam's apple. "Where I come from, a man never carries just one knife, *Señor*. Never just one."

With a jerk Jonah fell to the side as the bunched gunshots boomed in the low-roofed earthen room. A last one rang in his ears before Jonah rolled over to find Two Sleep still sitting, his pistol muzzle smoking, and two of the vaquero's companions crumpling slowly, a third clawing desperately at the edge of the bar, their own guns tumbling from their hands to clatter dully onto the pounded clay floor.

"Watch the drink man," Jonah snarled at Two Sleep, his head nodding at the bartender.

Two Sleep leveled one of the pistols at the Mexican behind the bar as Jonah crabbed back to the vaquero, who lay wreathed in blood, his breath coming ragged. He put the tip of his knife blade back against the Mexican's throat, then gazed up into the flickering candlelight, eventually finding her.

"C'mere!" he ordered her in English. When she did not obey immediately, he called her gruffly in Spanish.

Whimpering, the whore stood over him, tears having streaked the *alegría* she had used to rouge her cheeks.

"You want me to kill him quick?"

She shook her head, then nodded yes. "*Sí.* No, no—leave him be."

"You love him, eh?" Jonah asked as he slowly drew the bloody knife from the vaquero's throat, wiping it off on the buckskin jacket.

"No—I could not love him. He is trouble to me every time he comes in," she said quietly in the hushed cantina. "But there would be more trouble for me if you kill him."

Hook peered down at the Mexican and sighed, then gazed up at the whore. "It doesn't matter now, *Señorita.*"

"He is dead too?" growled the bartender.

As he rose, Jonah stuffed the second knife away inside his boot. "These others, they should have minded their own business. How about you? Will you mind your own business?"

The man's puffy black eyes were like a frightened, caged animal's as they darted here and there, then eventually landed back on Hook's face. He slid Jonah's knife down the bar toward the American. "*Sí.* Just go. Go now and never come back."

Two Sleep still had his pistols drawn, covering the room as Jonah dragged up the Winchester propped against their table. Hook reached over to clamp his right hand around the woman's wrist, holding his left forearm protectively in front of him.

"You owe me, *Señorita.* You better help me stop this bleeding—for saving your life."

Her eyes climbed from his bloody shirt, softening as they peered into his. "Yes. I owe you, *Señor.*"

27

S HE SMELLED MORE of dust than anything else. It wasn't that the woman was dirty. Just this land, the mud houses, what with the wind that blew night and day—it seemed natural for her to have the same sweet, musky smell of the land.

That, and the slightly damp feel to her sere-colored flesh as she worked herself into a frenzy, throbbing like a steam piston up and down atop him. Her breasts quivered inches from his eyes, the nipples coming rigid and rosy against the dusky hue of her skin. Jonah reached up and brought one round melon to his mouth as she trembled atop her perch in his lap. Throwing her head back, the high Indian cheekbones firing her eyes with an even brighter flame and her long black hair slithering over the curve of her shoulder, she shuddered from chin to toe.

The whore whimpered softly as her mouth came forward toward his, then slid off his lips, tantalizing him as her teeth sought the side of his neck. She bit him, hard enough to make Hook wince.

He hadn't been bitten like that in . . . Jonah couldn't remember a woman ever biting him before. Not in anger. Nor in passion.

Hurriedly leaving the smoky cantina, the whore led the two horsemen across the alameda, a tree-lined walk, then on down the muddy street pocked with the holes cut by recent hooves and streaked with greasy rivulets carved by iron-rimmed wheels, each silvery, moonlit sliver of water afloat with the day's refuse tossed from most every door leading into the rain-drenched darkness. On she took them to the poorest part of this squalid village, where the houses squatted like colorless mud toads amid the low-hanging smoke of cedar fires.

First she took them to a small stable, where they stripped their horses and pack animals. It was there the woman told the Indian to make himself a bed of straw. When Hook had loosened the lashes that held his bedroll behind his saddle and dropped it atop some hay in an empty stall, the whore shook her head.

"Oh, no, *Señor*. You will come with me," she had told Hook, beckoning not just with her finger, but with those black eyes like evil a'light.

Telling the Indian that they would be in the small hut across the muddy street, she led Jonah back into the storm and darkness, dodging puddles and piles of droppings gone cold with spring's onslaught before ducking out of the rain. In the tiny room she lit a single candle. When he straightened there beside the short doorway, the crude door hung awap on its loose leather hinges, Jonah had to remove his hat to keep it from brushing against the low ceiling, his shadow cavorting across the near wall in the dance of flame thrown out by that tallow candle.

She had turned then, her black hair dripping with rain, catching the flicker of the single flame like a red mirror, hair strands hung in dark tendrils over her eyes as she pulled his coat from his arms, gently nudging him back toward one of the only two chairs in the room. It sat opposite the narrow rope-and-timber bed. She turned away and went to a small table, where he heard her tear a strip of cloth. His eyes danced across the walls— carved in the mud wall over the bed was a niche where stood a small painted saint, hands folded before him, a gilt halo perched on the crown of his head. Beside the door hung a figure he supposed was the Christ—this one fashioned poorly of corn straw and shucks. On its hand-carved head lay a wreath of bramble thorns, drops of bright red blood stained the brow.

She came to him, gently tore open the slash in his sleeve, and dabbed cold water onto the wound. He didn't think it deep enough to worry over as she snapped a cactus leaf in two and squeezed its milky juice onto his arm, working it down into the long wound. That complete, the woman took the pieces of cloth she had torn from one of her own garments and wrapped Jonah's forearm. Turning it this way and that, she inspected her work and her knot, then knelt before his knees.

Reaching for his belt, she hurriedly opened his britches. Jonah rose off the chair slightly as she took his flesh in her hands. He was the dry tinder, she the flame licking him into fire. He was rigid by the time she broke away to pull off his boots, then yanked his trail-stiffened canvas britches off his legs. In a damp trail of puddles tracked clear across the clay floor, she carelessly threw his coat and shirt.

His breath came short, in heavy gushes, spiraling in clouds of hot vapor in the cold room as she tucked her arms inside her chemise and pushed it down to her waist, exposing the small, firm breasts. With one hand she again took hold of his rigid flesh, the other hand encircling the back of his neck to pull him toward the dark aureole of her breast.

He hadn't sucked long when he found the warm, sweetish liquid spilling across his tongue. That unforgettable taste compelled him to draw at the breast harder still, more insistently as she locked him against her, drove her hand up and down the length of him like a ramrod. Jonah moved his mouth to the other breast and found the nipple already dripping in milky readiness.

It was then that she drew away from him and said, "No, *Señor*. Do not take everything."

She stood, right before him, pushing the chemise, skirt and all, down over her hips, stepped out of them, and flung it all to the low bed. Now she wore only the crude moccasins that were all most cantina women had to wear—nothing so rich as shoes imported from Madrid or Barcelona. Not even a pair of high-heeled dancing shoes brought up the trade routes from Chihuahua.

When at last she returned to Jonah, she took one of his hands and put it between her thighs, massaging herself on him, working his fingers back and forth over her warm cleft, into the very moistness of her. When she finally pulled his hand free and came astraddle him, settling slowly while he groaned in exquisite, delicious torment, Jonah wanted to explode.

She felt it, his readiness, and immediately stopped her moving atop him. Reaching beneath her with one hand, the whore gently cupped his scrotum in her palm and pulled ever so slightly. Again and again she milked him until she felt she had done enough to delay his climax.

Then she resumed her work atop his rigid shaft.

Twice she performed that same magic on him, delaying his release, and twice more she thrust herself atop him, trembling and whimpering, reaching her own climax with him still firm and unspent inside her.

When she finally brought her teeth away from the side of his neck, Jonah sensed a temporary relief wash over him as that exquisite pain diminished. Once more he could concentrate on the woman. Laying his hands along either side of her face, Jonah laid a middle finger across her rouged lips. Instantly, eagerly, she opened and swallowed the finger whole, sucking on it playfully as she drew his heated flesh back and forth into that deepest part of her.

Her black eyes smoldered, shiny and as dark as chimney soot. With a growing frenzy of whimpers come to growls, the woman climbed and climbed evermore until he spent himself in her, causing the whore to cry out as she shuddered savagely atop his lap each time he pulled her hips downward atop him brutally.

"Sí! Sí! Ahora, Señor—sí!"

She sat huddled against him as he grew soft, murmuring something unintelligible into the side of his neck not bruised by the passionate clamp of her crooked teeth. When at last Jonah felt he could trust his knees not to turn to water beneath him, he rose unsteadily, still holding her against him, and carried the woman to the small bed. There he dragged back the musty, threadbare blankets and laid her atop the bare tick mattress.

He tried to stand, to look for his clothes, but she pulled insistently on his hand, bringing him down beside her before pulling the blankets over them both. She fell asleep quickly, her head nestled in the curve of his shoulder, his now-soft flesh curled protectively between her two hands.

When Jonah awoke, it came of something easy: moving only his eyelids, and those barely opening, sorting his place in things. Through those gritty slits he first saw the fading of the night's darkness and the graying of the light. It was raining again and he was warm here beside the woman, in her blankets, sensing the rise and fall, the slight rasp of her breathing. So he closed his eyes again, knowing after all this time on this trail, there was nowhere he needed to go in any great rush.

The next time he awoke, Hook found her gone. The damp air chilled him as he sat up, the blankets sliding away. He dressed quickly, listening to what few distant sounds announced the village coming awake. As Jonah pulled on his last boot, the woman pushed open the door and reached down, ushering in a small child, who heaved herself over the doorsill, then immediately stopped in fright, wide eyes locked on the gringo. In the crook of the whore's arm she carried a second child, a bundled infant.

She closed the crude door behind her, shutting off some of the chill, shutting out the rain-soaked breeze, and pulled the long black rebozo from her head, shaking the drops from it as she asked, "You go before breakfast?"

He glanced at the small earthen oven built into the corner of this mud-and-wattle hut. It would serve as oven, stove, and fireplace, easily heating the small jacal.

"I have miles to go," he said quietly, gazing down at the small child, a girl, who squeezed up against her mother's leg with a thumb pressed against her lower lip, gazing up at the stranger with doe-eyed fright.

"Please, *Señor.* You can eat. Go get your friend. He will want something hot to eat too. Go, get him and I will heat up some coffee."

Hers was a smile that warmed him from the inside out. Jonah finally relented. "Yes. I will let you cook us breakfast . . . if you let me give you what you will cook in your pots."

She nodded at last. "It is settled. Go get your friend and I will settle my children."

As he pulled on his coat and set his hat down upon his hair, the woman laid the sleeping infant in the bed, then motioned the older child over. She was taking the thin, crudely sewn coat from the girl's arms as Hook ducked from the door and crossed the muddy street to claim Two Sleep from his warm, fragrant bed atop the stable hay. While the Indian climbed from his blankets, Jonah stepped to the jakes out back, a stinking room made of thin tree limbs daubed with mud to hold back the wind and rain.

Returning to the mud hut with the Shoshone, Hook shut her small door behind him. She knelt at the corner fireplace, a small fire already warming the tiny room. Motioning for the Indian to sit in one of the two chairs beside a narrow table, the woman went back to her work over the blackened skillet. Jonah dropped his oiled canvas bag beside her. From it the woman pulled some hard-bread, a small sack of cornmeal, and an oiled paper wrapped about nondescript strips of dried meat, as black as the bottom of that skillet of hers.

Jonah turned back to look over the rest of the room and noticed the small child again. His heart went to her as quickly, those big eyes so filled with fright of him and the tall Indian. She stood frozen at the edge of the firelight, there at the foot of the bed, gazing anxiously at the two strangers.

"She is afraid of men?" he asked the woman. "That is a good thing, perhaps."

Turning her head slightly, the woman said, "No. I think she is most afraid of your friend. Indians."

"*Sí,*" the little girl responded, her voice a'quaver. "Comancherias! Comancherias!"

"No, no," the woman soothed, rising and going to the child. She took the girl in her arms and lifted her, stroking her black hair. "Not Co-mancheria. From far, far away to the north is where the Comancheria live."

When she brought her daughter into the greasy light of that flickering candle, into the spreading glow of the fireplace's warmth, Jonah was not immediately struck with the child's garb. Yet as he watched the whore calm her daughter, explaining that there were many tribes of Indians and they were not all the feared and hated Comanche, who rode back and forth through this country plying their seasonal raids into Sonora before they returned to their homes in the southern reaches of the Staked Plain— Hook was eventually taken by something strange in the girl's clothing. Rather than dressing the child in a small chemise and skirt, smaller copies of adult clothing, the woman had instead draped her daughter in what appeared to be a boy's shirt, long enough to reach the crude, wet moc-casins the child wore. It was plainly a pullover, three-button style, the sort to be found among most households on the southern plains, the sort offered for sale in any sutler's or mercantile.

Yet this was not a white settlement, his thoughts boiled as he studied the child again.

"Step over here," he told the woman gruffly, with roughness taking her elbow in his hand.

"*Señor?*"

"Come over here to the light," he said, his voice low. "I don't mean to frighten you."

Her eyes pleaded with him. "My child, *Señor.*"

"Yes, I know," he replied, trying to smile at the young girl. "Just . . . just bring her into the light."

That look of fear still captured on her face, the whore did as Hook demanded, reluctantly bringing her young daughter closer to the light.

When he reached out to touch the long hem of the shirt, the child shrieked and the woman pulled back. "No. Just tell her not to be afraid. I won't hurt her. Only want to look at this shirt."

"She grows so fast, *Señor*," the woman began to explain, apologetically. "I can't keep her in nice things—a child that plays in the streets when my mother watches her. I go to work and my mother watches—"

"All right," he interrupted the whore, having inspected the dingy, faded hem of the shirt. "Turn her around. I want to see in the back of the dress, *Señorita*. Please, turn your daughter around so that I can look."

In curiosity the woman turned her daughter's back toward Hook. He gently pushed aside the child's long hair and twisted open the back of the collar.

"Over here—to the light more."

She cooperated by leaning the child more into the candlelight on the narrow table where Two Sleep sat watching the whole process with curious eyes of his own.

Jonah felt it rush over him as he let go the collar of the shirt. He touched it with his fingertips, running his hand down the full length of the child's back until his hand rested on the woman's bare forearm.

"What do you want for the dress?"

Her eyes narrowed. *"Señor?"*

"How much will you take for the child's dress?"

"I do not understand—"

He turned abruptly and dragged up his outer coat, stuffing his hand into a small inside pocket. Pulling out a small skin pouch, Jonah brought forth a single eagle into the candlelight. She gasped slightly at the sight of the gold piece, her eyes grown even bigger while the frightened child buried her face in the crook of her mother's shoulder.

"I'll pay for the dress."

"*Señor*, I do not know what to say—"

"Say yes," he interrupted, his mind scratching for more of the Spanish words to express it. All of it was coming so hard—staring at that scrap of shirting hung over the small child like a simple sack dress . . . how dingy, dirty, sun faded, and stained. Across all these years.

Then he thought to remind her, "You won't earn this kind of money in a week. In a month. Will you?"

Reluctantly, the whore shook her head, clutching her daughter ever tighter. "I . . . I am not sure I should—"

Dragging out another single eagle, Jonah told her with a low, even voice, "All right, I'll give you the two of them. For that dress your daughter wears. With this you can buy her, and yourself, many dresses now."

She swallowed, as if something dry and unforgiving were lodged in her throat, then reached out for the two shiny coins.

Jonah pulled them back, just out of reach—tantalizing. "But first, you tell me if there are any comancheros in this village."

Her brow knitted in concern. *"Sí."* She nodded. "There are a few. Why do you—"

"Good." He glanced at Two Sleep, seeing the interest there lighting the Shoshone's face. "Now we are making ground. I think you got this dress from one of the comancheros, yes?"

She nodded again. "Yes."

"Take it off your daughter and give it to me."

"I have . . . don't have nothing else to put her in. Not another dress."

"Put her coat on her now and give me the dress . . . that shirt."

As her eyes fell away, the woman sought to apologize. "Yes, *Señor*—it is a shirt. The only thing I could afford when the comancheros bring clothing to sell."

As she set the girl on the hearth beside the fire and took up the threadbare coat, preparing to pull the thin, faded garment from the child's skinny frame, the woman gazed up at Hook, her eyes pleading. "You are really . . . really going to give us those coins?"

"Yes," he answered, holding them out to her. "I am an honest man. I will never steal from a mother. Never would I steal from a child."

As she pulled the garment over her daughter's head and quickly put the thin coat on the child, Jonah felt Two Sleep step up beside him in the firelight. Hook asked the woman, "How do the comancheros have clothing to sell?"

Her eyes went to the floor again as she rose and handed him the limp, much-washed shirting. "It was so dirty when I bought it. But I knew it was big enough, it would fit her for some time to come."

He pressed the two coins into her hand. "How did the comancheros have this?"

With abject apology in her eyes, the woman looked up from the coins in her palm and replied, "They take the clothing from the American children they buy from the Comancherias."

His mouth went dry, his tongue almost pasty, slow and clumsy to move of a sudden. "Where did the comancheros go with the child who wore this?" He held its faded shadows out before him, as if beckoning for her to answer.

Instead, she shook her head, her lips trembling. "Please, *Señor.* Take that and go. Give me your money, or no. But just go."

Jonah took a step closer to her, towering over the small woman now. "I will go, but only when I have your answer. Where did the comancheros take the child who wore this shirt?"

Again she shook her head, gazing up at his face, her eyes swimming with tears, imploring him, her words coming hard. "There was no . . . no child. Only this." She touched the garment, then knotted her hands in the front of her chemise, beginning to sob. "I think I know now why you came here. To our village."

He was slow putting it into order in his mind. "You are telling me you don't know of the child the comancheros took this from? The child who wore this shirt?"

"All I know," she answered, dragging a hand beneath her nose, "I heard them tell a story that they had bought that with some other clothes from a band of Comancheria." She pointed. "To the north in the forbidden land where the comancheros go to trade with the Indians."

"Wait," he said angrily, confused. "You are telling me there was no child sold to the comancheros? Only the shirt?"

She nodded, her eyes fluttering to the old Indian before she answered. "That is right. The story the Comancheria told the traders was that their warriors had killed another band of bad comancheros—distrusted ones— then the Indians took the white children from the traders they killed. When the children outgrew the clothing, the Comancheria decided to trade it to other comancheros, as they did with other things the traders wanted."

"Did the traders say . . . did anyone say anything about the children? How old they were? Boys?"

She wagged her head in resignation. "Nothing like that, *Señor.*"

"All right," Jonah finally said, his tone softened now. Looking quickly at Two Sleep, he said in English, "We got a fresh trail to follow now, my friend."

When the Shoshone had nodded, Hook turned back to the woman. He reached for her hand and laid another gleaming coin in the charcoal-stained palm. Then spoke in Spanish, "I have been waiting a long time to give this money to someone who can help me find someone I love."

Her damp eyes filled to brimming as her lips sought words, but found none.

Folding her fingers over the three coins, Jonah continued, "Buy your children clothes to wear. Fill their bellies and keep them warm, woman. It matters not what you do to feed them—for there is no shame in doing what you must in caring for your children."

Her face filled with hope. "You . . . will you ever come back, *Señor?*"

He shrugged. "It is not likely that I will ever ride this way again." Looking quickly at the infant asleep on the bed, at the young daughter clutching her mother's leg, Jonah spoke. "I never asked you: is your youngest another girl?"

She shook her head. "No. He is a boy."

With a single nod Hook turned, went to the doorway. In opening it, Two Sleep slipped out into the drizzling rain of that gray spring morning. The breeze freshened, tossing a shaft of rain onto the pounded clay floor at the portal. Jonah turned to the woman, sensing suddenly the warmth on one side of his body beckoning from the little hut with its fireplace and family within. On the other side he sensed the cold already clutching for him, ready to embrace him fully—the rain ready to swallow him on the shelterless plains, leading him on a joyless trail as he shivered in the saddle, on to fireless camps and curling up in soggy wool blankets, fighting off the nightmares that he knew were now to return.

Now that he had a fresh trail to follow. Now that he knew his own flesh and blood had not been sold into slavery by the comancheros.

Now that Jonah Hook knew part of his family might still be alive . . . among the Comanche.

"Take care of them both," he told her softly as he stood there framed in the tiny doorway, half-warm, the other half of him grown suddenly cold in the leave-taking. "Your girl . . . and the boy. They are both, both so very special. Watch over them, as God would watch over them in your absence."

A gust of wind followed his prayer into that tiny mud hut as Jonah Hook closed the door, turning into the lancing sheets of rain.

Hurrying into the cold once more.

28

"THE DRESS. WHAT of that dress?"

When the Shoshone first asked Jonah that question, Hook hadn't looked back at the Indian. Instead, he sat there in the shadows of their cheerless camp that first night riding north toward the land of the Comanche, surrounded by the immense prairie and soggy darkness, hulking buttes rising like ominous shadows against the sodden, seeping sky. Theirs had been a hard ride pointing their noses into that forbidden country, a long day of hardly ten words spoken between them after saddling and dragging their pack animals out of the tiny, nameless village in southwest Texas.

All day they had watched low black clouds swirling out of the west like smoke off a greasewood fire, and now the rain fell from gray sky gone mushy with twilight. Just before they had been forced to make camp, the wind came up, spitting a thin, driving rain between its snapping teeth. With night coming down, that wind became an ugly thing on these southern plains, whistling and whining like death's own hollow bones.

Hook sighed quietly. "It weren't a dress, Injun."

"Did not look like no dress," Two Sleep replied, wagging his head as he tried to sound out his best English. "A shirt, yes."

Finally, Jonah nodded. "A boy's shirt."

"Sure it your boy's?"

Staring into the icy darkness of that sodden, moonless night, watching the grayish, ghostly curl of his own breathsmoke rise before his face, Jonah explained, "That shirt may be faded and old, for certain. But I knowed right off from the way the front placket was sewed that Gritta made it. Never in my days did I see another like it. The woman's mother taught her to sew like that. Only folks in all the Shenandoah. But not just that—it were the cloth of it too. Gritta made our children clothes from her old worn-out dresses. That woman never let anything go to waste. Not Gritta."

"You sure, I trust you," Two Sleep replied.

"It ain't just a matter of you trusting me." Then Jonah wagged his head, saying, "Besides, until I looked back of the collar, I couldn't be absolute certain it come from one of my boys."

Two Sleep reached up to tap the back of his own shirt. "Collar?"

"Gritta sewed the boys' names in their shirts. I imagine it were handed down from the older boy to his brother."

"What name you see in the collar?"

"Ezekiel. That's my youngest. Ezekiel Hook."

But as he spoke his son's name, Jonah sensed again that unrequited pang of doubt. The gnaw of something so tangible it felt real. Yet there was nothing to fight, nothing to grapple with, nothing he could get his hands on so as to settle the doubt then and there.

Little Zeke hadn't been much older than the Mexican whore's daughter when Jonah last saw him, when Jonah marched off with Sterling Price's volunteers to drive the Yankee army back north. Three years old was all he had been. Only six when he was taken from his home by Usher and his gunmen.

Like old Seth would chaw on a big bone, Jonah worked over it in his mind, scratching hard for an image of the boy, trying to see how he just might age that mental picture of Zeke he had been carrying so that when the time came, he would recognize his own son: older, taller, filling out as boys always did.

What was it John Bell Hood's old soldier had told him? Was it really eighteen and seventy-three already? If Zeke was born in the spring of fifty-nine, that would mean Jonah's youngest was already fourteen. A time to set aside childhood things, time to take up the mantle of a man.

And Jeremiah. A dim, wispy portrait of his eldest son swam before him in that frosty darkness by their smoky fire. He was two years older than Zeke. Sixteen now and almost a full-growed man. Would either of his boys know him as their daddy?

What pierced him with all the more pain was his own self-doubt. Would he recognize his own sons, the flesh and blood of his own body, when at last the time came to find them? So many, many years gone. So much doubt lay waiting there in the cold darkness, enough to make him wonder if the time ever would come to find them both.

Huddled beneath his cold, wet blanket steaming beside the fire, Jonah counted off the years on his fingers. Eight of them gone. That meant Jeremiah had spent half of his life with the Comanche. Even more than half of little Zeke's life was with the savages.

It had been even longer since last he had laid eyes on his boys. An eternity since they had last known their father.

His eyes grew hot despite the cold drizzle of early-spring rain come to bring its resurrection to this winter-starved southern prairie, here on the precipice of what many had called the most dangerous country in the whole of the continent.

His lips moving silently within the dark curl of his beard, Jonah cursed this land for granting these poor people so little of life that they fell easy prey for the *ricos*. And he cursed the rich ones who funded the expeditions into the land of the Comanche that traded in human misery.

The wealthy hired the poor wastrels—turning them into drivers, wagon packers, cooks, guards, and even gun handlers for the dangerous plunge into enemy territory, the last two brought along as some minimal insurance against the terror of what lay ahead in Comancheria. In this land blessed with little hope, between the poverty of Mexico and the far edge of nowhere, a *rico* could buy what and who he wanted to put together his wagon train bound for Indian country, and not only buy the services of a man who might want nothing more than to earn enough to feed his family for one more season—the *rico* bought as well that poor man himself, body and soul.

Many times, Jonah had learned, the poor and expendable hadn't returned from Comancheria. No matter to the *ricos,* though. There were always a dozen or more out there, each one eager to step into those empty tracks and embark on the next trip out come trading season.

When he thought on it, Jonah had to admit he really knew little more than he had four or five years ago. Only now Jonah was certain that the boys were not among those Mexicans—they were held by a band of Comanche. Every bit as bewildering, perhaps, as looking for a particular outfit of comanchero traders was looking across this trackless waste for the comings and goings of a particular band of horse Indians. True, he had learned to track and read sign, to tell if he was following a village on the move fleeing soldiers or a war party riding out to avenge themselves on far-flung settlements.

Later that spring Jonah finally admitted to himself that he did not know how to find any one single band of the Comanche.

Spring slipped into the first warming days of early summer as they left Fort Concho and crossed the Rio Colorado, moving north for the headwaters of the Brazos. The two were traveling lighter now, trading a Danite saddle if they could, a belt gun if they had to, to buy beans and bacon, flour and coffee, along with those twists and plugs of tobacco gone black as sorghum molasses in the tin cases sutlers opened for smoke-hungry travelers come in from the sun and the dust of the western prairie.

The Fort Concho trader had eyed Jonah's rifle with envy as he stacked the horseman's provisions on the counter to begin his total. He was a pie-faced man of simple features, most certainly a face nothing usually happened to. "That a sixty-six Winchester, ain't it?"

"Yes, it is. But it ain't for sale." Jonah had long hesitated selling his own, or a single one of the rifles taken from the Danites years before.

The trader shifted his approving gaze at the Spencer carbine Two Sleep carried. "Give you top dollar for that repeater the Indian's carrying. Ask anyone in these parts—they'll tell you. I give a man top dollar for good weapons."

Hook wagged his head, determined not to be taken in. The pistols they could let go for the food and cartridges and smoke, if need be and they ran out of scrip money. "Gonna hang on to our saddle guns, mister. Trade you some army belt guns if the price works out."

"Got enough belt guns to do me," the Concho sutler replied sourly, his mouth pinched up in sudden anger. "Just remember, you'll never get a better price for them rifles than I'll give you here, and now."

"Just tell me what these here provisions gonna cost—and I'll pay you in coin."

The trader leaned back a bit in admiration, the furrows between his eyes softening. "Not in army scrip, eh?"

"No paper money: so take your cut off what you usually charge for scrip. I got a few pieces of gold."

With a smack of his lips, the sutler put his pencil to work on his pad. Jonah wanted to pay and be gone, getting farther north where someone might be more willing to answer questions about what lay out there in the immense beyond, where a man would likely find the wandering warrior bands, which creeks and streams and rivers they haunted. Hereabouts the soldiers spent a lot of tongue wagging telling him much of nothing useful. Seemed the army was every bit as intent on keeping white folks out of the Llano Estacado as were those Comanche horsemen.

What with them pushing north just like the tribes that were following the buffalo herds into the summer winds, to be gone from the forts and still have all those rifles strapped behind them on the pack animals, it was a wise thing, having those weapons that might well come in handy one day, Hook figured. Might well make the difference between him wearing his hair or losing it if things came down to making a fight with a band of these elusive Comanche. Might and firepower it was, the language of these southern plains: a matter of simply having more lead and powder and repeating weapons than a man's unseen enemy.

When it came down to a real fight of it, Jonah figured to be ready.

By midsummer they had left Fort Concho behind, having crossed and recrossed the southern half of west Texas. By then Hook had finally come of the conclusion that it would take a stroke of real luck for him to run across the path of that particular band holding his two boys prisoner. Perhaps, he decided, it would take more than any pure gut-strung, man-made luck from here on out.

Bound to take something more on the order of a godsent miracle.

The long green pods suspended in the trees were ripe. Whenever the village camped in these river valleys and deep canyons, the women picked them, loading blankets and shawls with the beans that would be pounded and mixed with water to make a delicious paste. Something cooked on hot stones beside the fires, to be served with the meat the men brought into camp.

Tall One was clearly a man now: in his sixteenth summer already, lean and gangly, made all of sinew and bone and wrapped with skin cured to a rich brown hue. He liked the way some of the girls looked at him behind their black eyelashes. But he would wait. Enough time for marrying, he thought.

Antelope, now he was another matter altogether. Tall One's younger brother had eyes for the girls and talked incessantly about girls, about marrying, about starting a family and raising his children in the way of the Kwahadi.

Perhaps to marry and have children would be Antelope's way of proving himself to the band, in that way to show that he had truly become one of them, had married one of their daughters and begun fathering Kwahadi children. More important, he was fathering Kwahadi warriors to keep up the struggle against the white man. Yes, perhaps Antelope wanted to begin having sons of his own to prove to the rest that he was no longer white.

Or perhaps it was nothing more than Antelope liked girls.

Tall One himself would grow hard at times thinking about girls, looking at their bodies when he came upon some of them bathing in a river pool. This past spring Antelope had coupled with an older girl who desired him as a partner. Tall One had laughed at that, until the girl also presented herself to Antelope's big brother.

He had been more than a little afraid of the girl, of her father, of this coupling and what it meant to father a child. Frightened, Tall One had run away from her and ever since had never failed to believe Antelope's stories about the girls in camp. Only fourteen summers and Antelope was already possessed with the prowess of a man. It was whispered among the boys that many girls boasted that Antelope was an admirable lover.

Still, Tall One was the fighter. He had already killed two men. Funny to think about it, but Antelope was the one who sang his praises even more than Tall One sang of his own exploits in battle against the Tonkawa and the Caddo, against the white man and his pony soldiers. His young brother bragged on him more than he would have ever boasted on himself. Riding into battle was something Antelope had not yet done, though he had accompanied many a raiding party. Instead of scalps, Antelope had returned with ponies and some of the white man's cattle to his credit.

"I want a scalp," Antelope said many times.

"Here, take mine." Tall One tried joking his brother, gathering his hair in one hand and pulling it upward, straight over the crown of his head. He drew the index finger on the other hand around the scalp lock as if slashing it off with a knife.

At first it had been funny to offer his own hair to his brother. Then, sometime this past winter, it had ceased being something to laugh at. Antelope had lost his sense of humor. He had even swung his short bow at Tall One, catching his older brother across the cheek and laying open the skin in a long gash where the browned skin lay taut over the bone. Still, it was more the wounded look on Antelope's face that brought pain to Tall One.

He never joked about taking scalps again. No more did he offer his own to Antelope.

Whereas Tall One could wait to become a man in the blankets with one of these squat Comanche women, young Antelope was impatient to fully become a man by taking the scalp of the enemy.

"No, I don't want to go with you to find a Tonkawa," Antelope snarled when Tall One suggested the two of them go on their own raid into the land of the tribe that served as guides and trackers for the pony soldiers.

"You want to wait to go with many others?" Tall One had asked, wondering if his young brother might still be frightened.

"No," Antelope said severely. "I don't want an Indian scalp. I want the hair of a white man to hang from my belt."

It would be the last time, Tall One vowed, that he would offer to take his brother on a raid. Better that someone else go with Antelope when he took his scalp. Perhaps his young brother did not remember much of what had gone before after all this time. More than eight summers now might make him forget. After all, they had been so young. Antelope . . . Zeke, yes! Zeke had been so young.

Tall One sensed the warming joy that it brought him to remember his brother's white name: so long unthought, so long unspoken.

"Zeke," he murmured it quietly, the sound sent into the wind in his face.

Far to his right his younger brother stalked through the brush, tracking deer into the wind. These last few years with the Kwahadi they had become proficient in riding the short-backed ponies, slipping to the side to hook a hand in a loop of rawhide lashed to the mane, one foot hung over a bony rump. Now they both handled the short sinew-backed bows as well as any Comanche boys their age. And Tall One could not remember the last time he had experienced any trouble in following the Comanche tongue. After all this time, both he and Antelope were proficient in their adopted language.

Long, long ago had they ceased speaking in English. There for a while, in private, stolen moments only, had they conversed in their birth tongue. Yet as the days grew into moons and the moons turned into seasons, then one winter after another drove this warrior band into the shelter of the deep canyons, the two brothers had spoken less and less of that birth tongue to one another.

No more did he find himself even thinking in that foreign language of a bygone time. It had been so long now, in fact, that Tall One genuinely surprised himself by remembering his brother's name.

"Ezekiel," he said unconsciously.

Antelope shushed him sternly from afar, pointing into the brush, making a hook of his right-hand fingers, setting the hand beside his head to show he was in range of their prey.

Thinking the name in English, more so saying something in that old tongue, immediately washed over him with some of the old longings he had buried in those ancient days when he first came to live with those people. They were mostly impressions. Nothing really remained clear enough to remember anymore.

True, what wispy memories there were flooded up to the surface from time to time, from season to season when certain smells reminded him of a life lived long, long ago. The feel of a blanket laid against his cheek in a certain way, the manner in which firelight fell on his brother's face, casting shadows and flickering highlights, made his heart leap for an instant in unconscious recognition of someone important from that dim past, knowing he should remember a man who had the same nose, the same curve of the lips or the same solid, square chin—much of the same features as he and Zeke shared.

Antelope stopped suddenly and threw up his bow, releasing the arrow in a fluid movement. Out of the brush bounded a doe, the shaft deep behind a foreleg. She took a fourth and fifth bounce, then crumpled, thrashing briefly, then lay still, only her side heaving.

They both hurried to the doe, where Tall One knelt and dragged his iron knife across the soft underside of her neck. As the ground beneath the deep wound grew dark and moist, Antelope stuffed his bow away in the quiver and brought out his own knife. With it he opened the animal's belly, then bloodied himself to his elbows gutting her.

When he was done, Antelope rose, red nearly to the shoulders, standing there between the deer and the gut pile. What he had to say surprised

Tall One—for his young brother talked not of hunting, nor of the dinner on such fresh and tender meat they would have this night.

Antelope looked squarely at his brother. "I am going to marry."

Caught by surprise, he could only ask, "Prairie Night is the one?"

The young brother nodded.

He was a little afraid for his brother, so young he was to become a man so soon. "Can't you wait?"

"I could," he replied with a shrug. "After all, there are so many other ones every bit as pretty and firm and willing."

"Then wait." He tried smiling at his little brother, who had so serious a look on his face.

"I cannot, brother. Prairie Night . . . her father says we must marry."

"Let me go talk with him, tell him you have only been flirting with his daughter. Explain that you are not ready."

He wagged his head. "That will do no good. Not now. He knows I am ready."

"How can he know this? Look at you! You cannot marry Prairie Night. And her father cannot make you!"

"His daughter is big with child," Antelope explained, some sadness, some loss of innocence around every word. "My child."

"You are sure it . . . this is your child?"

"She hasn't been with another," Antelope sighed. "Everyone in camp knows that."

Tall One put a hand on his short brother's shoulder, wanting to embrace him—remembering that such a thing was a white man's custom. Like the touching of hands. They two, they were no longer white men. They were Comanche hunters. Kwahadi warriors.

Instead of hugging his young brother to tell him of his feelings, to tell him of all that made his heart brim over, Tall One said, "Then you must become a man and marry Prairie Night."

"Yes," Antelope nodded with resignation. "I will marry to become a man in the eyes of our village. And one day, one day very soon, I will take a white scalp. Then—only then—can I become a man in my own eyes."

29

MORE THAN THREE years had passed since the U.S. Army had crushed the resistance of Apache chief Cochise down in Arizona Territory. It had been some time since the Navaho and Zuni and the other quiet tribes had been all stirred up by the Apache.

But that hadn't stopped Colonel Jubilee Usher and his army from loading their Murphy prairie wagons and making their frequent forays down into northern Sonora.

From time to time the Mexican officials were willing to part with gold and guns, bullets and whores, if only Usher's *pistoleros* would rid a certain province of its Apache threat.

Jubilee thought of himself as a royal cat: sustained by the royal and the wealthy to keep their domains free of troublesome mice.

Over the past three years the Apache had become more a threat to the Sonorans than they had ever been before, thanks to the efficiency of the U.S. Army and its crushing defeat of Cochise. The Chiricahua and Mescalero, even some White Mountain renegades, all had bolted from Arizona Territory, fleeing south across the border into the mountains of northern Sonora. It was down there that those American Apaches preyed on the tiny Mexican settlements, forcing the provincial governors to offer rich bounties for Apache scalps.

How quickly Usher had learned the way of the scalp hunter: the Sonoran officials would pay handsomely for any black scalp. It was that simple. Be it Apache warrior, woman, or child—be it Mexican peon, woman, or child, the ruins of those sundered villages made to appear the work of the Apache in turn renewing the call for some action to be taken against the marauding savages.

The gold and specie the Mexican officials paid for those burlap sacks Usher's army stuffed with stiffened, grisly, red-hued trophies had been more than enough revenue for Jubilee to keep his small army together. In fact, the Danite leader had discovered just how easy it was to recruit more volunteers in Arizona Territory: a few breeds and Mexicans, to be sure— but mostly those who had been drawn to Usher's band of zealots were men in need of steady work with a gun.

Jubilee kept them up to their elbows in steady work. And blood. And scalps.

When he grew weary of the hunt and the carnage, Usher ordered his army back to one of the larger provincial towns to present his bags to the local officials: Cibuta, or Magdalena, Cananea, and Turicachi. There the debt was always paid promptly, and without fail, from local treasuries. Those officials knew they were sure to be reimbursed from the provincial capital of Hermosillo. It had not always been so.

One failure to pay the promised bounty, seasons ago—and the Mexican officials came to realize just how great a mistake it would be to loose Usher's carnivorous brigands on the countryside.

Furious that he had been refused his money, Jubilee released his hounds of war. They had pillaged, raped, and killed, burning to the ground a small village of farmers and shepherds just the way Usher's army rode through Indian camps dotting the scrub in the distant foothills and mountains. When the government sent its soldiers against the invading army of Jubilee Usher, his gunmen turned the Mexicans around, then made slow work of the hapless soldiers over three days of a running fight, chasing the Mexicans back toward the valley towns and settlements. Although they were outnumbered by the provincial soldiers, Usher's men clearly had their enemy outgunned. These bounty hunters enjoyed prolonging the inevitable end—eventually killing all but one, a major who spoke a smattering of English.

Leaving the man barefoot and in his underwear, Usher dispatched the major back to Hermosillo with a message for the governor and all the venal officials around him who had refused to pay the offered bounty that first time.

"Your soldiers cannot prevent the Apache from banging on your doors. If you do not pay—your soldiers will not be able to keep my army from the walls of your cities and towns and villages. If you will not give me what you guaranteed me—I will take it out in blood, crossing and recrossing your land, leveling it all with a clean swath of my bloody sword!"

It had been a message not lost on the Mexican officials.

In seventy-two Usher had expanded his operations as the Apache, no respecters of any boundary, crossed over the mountains into the province of Chihuahua, making things hard on outflung villages like Nacori, Chico, and Madera, Huachinera and Huasabas, over to Sahuaripa and down to Yepachic. Back and forth across that continental divide his gunmen rode, driving the Apache before them and in the end taking all that they wanted as a virtual army of occupation. They used the sheep herded by the poor villagers for target practice. They took girls and women with them whenever they left a jacal, using their prisoners as long as the women served their purpose—then leaving them behind in the desert to find their own way back to what was left of their dusty, bloodstained villages, or die alone and forgotten.

After the first real cold rain of autumn that clearly announced the coming of winter, Jubilee had collected the Mexican bounty and turned his army north in triumph. As always, they rode wide around Fort Bowie and Fort Thomas, especially Fort Apache. To fight the puny Mexican army was one thing. But Usher would hardly be fool enough to prod the might of the U.S. Army against him.

No less than Brigham Young himself might tempt the fates, pushing and goading the federal government to find out just how far he could go before he had to back down. But Jubilee Usher was a different sort. He knew enough about fighting and killing, enough of the blood sport of war, to stay clear of the army.

After all, such just might prove to be an admirable alliance come a day when Usher needed the help of the U.S. Army to pry that heretic Brigham Young out of his throne in Deseret.

Once more winter settled down on the central basin, and those last, short days of December waned. Again Jubilee led his long column of weary, bloodied gunmen back to the security of John Doyle Lee's settlement at Cedar City. It was here his army rested and recruited itself each winter, celebrating their victories and spending hard-earned blood money, waiting again for the advent of spring when they could ride south, to determine if the cowed officials of Mexico were once more in need of their specialized services.

"Where else is an army such as this to go, brother?" Usher had asked the double-dyed pious Lee for the first time that autumn of sixty-nine.

Among the polygamist's faithful the Danite gunmen had wintered until that spring of seventy, when they rode out to the south and discovered the rich cornucopia to be made in Apache scalps. Usher knew Lee was relieved to see his army of gunmen depart.

But when the raiding season ended, Jubilee had needed a place to post his brigands until the following spring allowed them to take to the blood trail once more.

"John Doyle," he had replied in that soft rumble of his cannonlike voice, "these are Saints. My Saints. Like you, like me. How well you know we are not of the mold Brigham would want of us. But instead, we are born of the mold Almighty God has Himself made—formed us of its dust and clay—then shattered that mold into an infinite number of pieces. Charging us to go forth and do His work. You," Usher said, snatching up Lee's black wool lapel and leaning his big face inches from the polygamist's, "you and me are destined to control the fate of the Church, of the faithful, of this whole earthly Empire!"

Lee had removed Usher's hand from his coat, slowly, his fiery eyes narrowing as they rose from the grisly necklace of human ears interlaced with blackened, shriveled penises once pendant between the legs of Usher's victims, worn front and back like a medieval church scapular.

His eyes turned up in an owlish frown, Lee told the Danite leader, "Only so long as your soldiers walk the path of righteousness. Only so long as that, Jubilee—will you be allowed to commune among us. These are gentle folk and you, your men—"

"Are rough-hewn, yes," Jubilee had interrupted. "They are fodder only, Lee. Don't you see? Among them are the makings of our greatness. Yours and mine."

"Count me out of your blood work, Jubilee," Lee had protested, wagging his head meaningfully, his Adam's apple as big as a turkey's egg.

Usher had laughed, a caustic sound, like ice breaking apart in northern rivers. When he spoke, his words came sharp, filled with bile, cutting with a lasting sting. "Seems I recall a great deal of blood work done at the behest of John Doyle Lee back to 1857," he said more softly then, theatrically. "That train of Gentiles, wanting nothing more than to make their way to California. You slaughtered them all—man, woman, and child at Mountain Meadows—didn't you?"

"What of it!" he protested in a voice as tart as pickling brine, the rangy dance of his big Adam's apple bobbing up and down his stringy neck.

He had rocked back into Lee's face, the venom returned to his words, licking a fleck of spittle from the fleshy curve of his lower lip as he said, "Don't seek to preach to me about blood work, John Doyle Lee! We know where we each stand, whereof the call from on high comes. And now we share the same dream of seeing that false prophet Brigham Young removed from his temporal throne."

"The years have brought a change in . . . circumstances, shall we say?" Lee replied, his face as dreary as a priest's at a sacrifice. "I want nothing more than to live out my life—"

"The old fires dying in you, my friend?" Jubilee had asked. Then sighed. "All right. I think we understand one another. For the time, I only ask you and yours to help me embrace these men within the folds of your faithful for the coming winter. Help me teach them the true faith, John Doyle—and in return you and yours will be paid handsomely for all that we are fed, for the roofs put over our heads."

"I cannot escape the feeling that you have brought to my doorstep an army of occupation," Lee protested softly, his arms swung out wide as if submitting to crucifixion. "These are gentle, common people—"

"But we both know it will take an army, its arm raised in vengeance, to seize this land from the heretic. That army then to wield its sword to wrest our kingdom away from the Gentiles and their federalized government so far away in Washington City. Look out that window, John Doyle! Out there I have the beginnings of just such an army. And if you stand beside me, together we will not fail Almighty God!"

So Usher led them north to Utah again in seventy, there to sojourn another winter in the bosom of Lee's Mormon faithful. And what was all the better, Jubilee wintered right under the nose of that heretic prophet, Brigham Young himself! Winter after winter Jubilee returned them here, leading them up from the blood plain of Arizona and New Mexico, Sonora and Chihuahua. From here in Cedar City, Jubilee could keep a watchful eye on the development of affairs among the Prophet's insiders, the political machinations of the Quorum of Twelve, the pulse of the rock-solid membership from Stake to Stake. He sent those he could trust the most to be his eyes and ears among Young's faithful. In the end the Danite chose emissaries who had never been known to associate with Jubilee Usher, new men recruited across the past few years and taught the requisite theology at Usher's knee, told who to find and who to talk to, who to trust and who to keep at arm's length. It was always a winter's task, this grooming of a handful of his crude hellions, making of them men of the cloth, men the likes of Lemuel Wiser.

There were cracks in that solid wall Brigham Young had fortified about himself, cracks through which Usher made his patient, dogged inroads: waiting, waiting, waiting for the moment to bring that unsteady wall down around the Prophet. It would not be long, he told himself now as he washed the woman's back with hot, soapy water. Steady progress could be measured, progress in the crumbling of Young's hold on the Church and its Empire.

"And you will stand at my side, dear woman," he told her, dragging the coarse cloth back and forth over her white shoulders. How he loved women untouched by the discoloring rays of the sun. "A most fitting lifemate for the new Prophet. How the faithful will rejoice in our happiness."

She always sat quiet and unmoving at these times, also taking refuge in the warmth of this small room and the heady steam rising from the tub of soapy water Negro George had prepared for them. Twice a week Jubilee ordered a bath drawn, filling this large cedar tub that was itself long enough for even a man of Usher's height to stretch out and fully immerse himself. It was Lee's old baptismal pool, relegated to a stall of a little-used barn years ago when a new and larger one had been constructed for the polygamist by Usher's winter soldiers. It was then that Jubilee adopted the tub and discovered its most savory use.

While other Saints might not practice the healthful properties of regular bathing, Jubilee Usher was a man who believed in the periodic, methodical cleansing of the body as much as he believed in that periodic and seasonal cleansing of his soul: the release of pent-up lusts and furies on the heathen populations with which this land was so cursed.

"If Lee ever discovers what delicious, what randy use I have made of his old baptismal," he murmured to her as he drew the soapy cloth across the woman's shoulders, "I'm afraid even he would raise his hand against me. To think—the blasphemy, he would cry!"

Seated outside the tub behind the woman, Jubilee gently pulled her head back and kissed her, hard and moist and long. She did not resist when he forced open her mouth. But neither did she kiss him back. He let the back of the woman's head rest against the gunwale of the cedar tub. His cheek lying against hers, strands of her soppy hair dripped over his shoulder as he murmured warmly into the dampness of her ear. Jubilee brushed the coarse cloth up and down the round softness of her breasts, enjoying the reddening, rigid response of her nipples as he excited them. Lightly he kissed them, sucking on her breasts, as sweet as scorched honey.

Outside his bathhouse each spring arose the tremulous squeals of baby frogs in the marsh, reminding him it was time for another season of renewal. Soon would come his appointed hour to march south. Killing savages and Mexicans alike, wiping them off the face of God's kingdom, was nothing less than ripping good fun.

He raked his teeth down the side of her neck, shifted himself, and came round to settle where he could bring one of her breasts to his mouth. How he liked this too—the way her breath caught in her throat when his hand plunged into the water and dallied between her thighs. Still, each time she composed herself after that initial surprise. Nonetheless, after so many years, he still waited for her to lose herself in him.

But he would be patient with her. The same way he had become patient with the pace of events in Deseret. Five years ago he had returned in what he then hoped would be triumph, only to find that his loyalty had been discarded, torn asunder and thrown aside by the powers of the Church. But he would be patient a little longer.

Usher rose at the side of the tub, laid aside the washing cloth, and began to push the pearl buttons through their holes in his shirt, then hung it on the back of a chair.

His faithful soldiers always left their victims sprawled in blackened pools of their own crimson and excrement, each man, woman, and child lying in their horrific wig of dried blood where the flies and beetles and winged creatures began to gather moments after his gunmen ripped the hair off the gaping skulls and stood to hang their trophies red-raw at their belts like profane pendants above the warm bodies the men would then take their pleasure on.

276 *Terry C. Johnston*

Jubilee took one button at a time from its buttonhole in his britches, savoring his growing desire for her, the delicious way his flesh anticipated hers.

Indeed, the cracks in Young's defense were widening. Through them one day soon he would ride at the head of a mighty army to wrest power from that pretender to the throne.

Laying his wool britches over the back of another chair, Jubilee stepped out of his temple garments. He straightened them on a hanger. They were all he wore for underwear. Like the other faithful, Usher believed no clothing was to touch his body—nothing but these ordained and sacred garments, which served as a shield, much as the strength of his soul shielded him from the harm of evil so rife and rampant in the Church itself.

Outside he heard the rise of some laughter, a snippet of a song, and knew the men enjoyed themselves here, as they regained their spiritual strength for spring's coming sojourn into the land of the heathen. From time to time each winter, he regaled his soldiers with flip made with imported rum and John Doyle Lee's own home-brewed potato beer, the heady concoction flavored with cinnamon and blended with a hot poker.

He turned from smoothing the garments and looked at her reclining there in the soapy water, curls of steam rising from the tub's still surface, soppy ringlets of her blond hair turned dark, pasted against the side of her face as her eyes watched him approach, then looked away to stare at the ceiling.

Yes, he thought, the Mormon faithful. They would once more respond to a charismatic leader. They could not fail to respond to his power once he made his play against Young.

As big a man of towering bulk as he was, Usher slipped into the tub with barely a ripple, settling back against the side, where he took up one of her feet and kneaded the sole of it with his thumbs. Her eyelids always fell when he did that—perhaps in some hedonistic response to the sheer pleasure of it, perhaps because she realized what always came next.

After kneading the sole of her other foot, Jubilee brought the woman's feet together at his groin, stroking his soft underbelly with her wrinkled toes, working the feet downward, ever downward until he had them both pressed around his hardening flesh. Up and down, slowly, deliciously slow he moved her feet along his shaft in that warming womb of soapy water, studying her half-lidded eyes as he brought himself to a full erection.

Most Mormon women were flannel-mouthed and all too often kept their legs locked together so that a man could never have any randy fun for fun's own sake. But not this one.

He could never think of giving her up.

A year after Jubilee's army first came to winter in Cedar City, Brigham Young himself had given Usher's father the directive to forward a message for the elder's son, in whatever manner he could contact Jubilee:

> *Give up the woman. Give her back. Sell her if you must. She is nothing more than a slave for your carnal needs and will never belong in the holy company of the Saints.*

Little did the Prophet know what needs this woman truly satisfied in Jubilee Usher.

Oh, Young made much of the fact that in February of 1870 Utah had followed Wyoming's 1869 lead in granting women full suffrage rights. But in this realm of the Church Empire women served their greatest function not as political tools in the electoral process—but as repositories of future Saints. It was through the woman's power to conceive, carry, and give birth to babies that the Mormon faithful grew. Evermore were the disembodied spiritual star-seeds required to find earthly, temporal homes among the Latter-day Saints. A woman's greatest role on this earth, her spiritual gift, lay in giving birth to a baby where would rest another wandering, disembodied soul come home at last to Zion.

What, after all, was more important now? Jubilee wondered. After all these years of building and grooming his army? Should he obey Brigham Young and abandon the woman?

Damn that heretic who had allowed his feet to wander away from the path that led to the throne of Almighty God!

Usher took one of the woman's hands and wrapped the soft, wrinkled fingers around his oak-hard shaft, holding that hand in both of his as he worked hers up and down, sensing the approach of climax.

Or, Usher thought as he brought himself to full arousal, in the end was he called upon by the Almighty Himself to challenge the false Prophet?

This woman was here of a purpose. And here she would stay.

There would come a day when he had it all: the throne of power in Zion and this woman there beside him.

Closing his eyes as he began to erupt in the warm, soapy water, furiously dragging her hand up and down the length of his hardened flesh, Usher trembled slightly.

She was the only weakness he allowed himself.

His flesh throbbed at the boiling surface of the bath water.

He would kill all who attempted to take her from him.

His heart hammered at his temples.

Jubilee Usher would strip away all obstacles that stood in his road to achieving leadership of the Church of Jesus Christ of Latter-day Saints.

And he would joyfully kill any man—Prophet or no—who dared separate him from the woman he loved.

Not just kill him . . . but revel in that man's destruction.

30

I T SEEMED THE wind had howled for days, the frozen icy snow driven against the crusty side of the buffalo-hide lodge, rattling like hailstones against a hollowed log.

It was February. The heart of winter on the central plains.

She was alone again.

Long before last winter young Pipe Woman had bundled up her few possessions and rode off with Porcupine and his band of Dog Soldiers, heading north into the land of Two Moon and the rest of the wild tribes. It was said Sitting Bull's Hunkpapa and Crazy Horse's Hunkpatilla Oglalla roamed that land up there. Shell Woman remembered that country from her childhood. With the fondness of those memories, she had allowed her daughter to go with the young Hotamitanyo warriors hurrying north to the last great hunting ground of the roaming bands.

After all, she had reasoned with herself, what else could she do? No one believed the thin one called Hook would be coming back. Gone more than four winters, with no word of where he was, when he would return. Pipe Woman was growing old waiting for a ghost to return. Reluctantly, with a real pain in the parting, Shell Woman let her daughter go, to roam the north country with the bands wandering in the footprints of the nomadic old ones.

She had not let her daughter see the tears. But that was more than a winter ago and long enough to get over it.

So now she was alone again.

Six sleeps ago Shell Woman had watched her husband ride off to find work, called to the place called Kan-sas by the army, to guide the Bear Coat General.

Outside her lodge the rattling, bare-bones wind was finally dying, like a living creature itself, slowing its raging howl into a keening whine. For a night it had lowed like a snuffling rodent outside the frozen lodge walls. And now the wind whimpered in its last gasps of the blizzard.

Miles: the American name her husband used when he spoke of the soldier chief. Her man had gone off to find work in a faraway place he said was called Kan-sas, where he said the army was preparing to crush the southern tribes. Kiowa. Comanche. And her own people too—the Sha-hiyena. All those who would not come back in to register themselves on the reservations staked out for them in Indian Territory. It was common knowledge that many bands had never ventured in to the reservations, had vowed they never would.

The army knew they were out there raiding, stealing, killing—kidnapping again. And the Bear Coat General was gathering his warriors to take up the war road against the southern tribes one last time. He needed scouts: eyes and ears and noses—wolves to track the scent of his enemy, the warrior bands.

Her man, the one her people had named Rising Fire, had held her body close against his through that last long winter night before riding off of a cold gray dawn that grew no brighter for Shell Woman.

For the most part he hadn't left her side ever since that autumn day four winters ago when he returned to her camp in the shady copse of trees where she had raised her lodge. Already the cottonwood had begun changing, going to gold when the man named Sweete had come riding slowly into her camp where she waited, there near the soldier fort called Laramie. He had an extra pony with him: a gift for High-Backed Bull's mother that he said came from Porcupine.

"Why does Porcupine send me a gift of this pony?" she had asked the big white man who stood over her, reaching to take her in his arms.

In his eyes Shell Woman had seen the answer.

Through the days of her grief that followed, time and again her husband repeated the story. Telling and retelling the details to give them permanence in the heart of Shell Woman. It was there in the heart of a mother that High-Backed Bull would live on.

It was the scars she touched now, running her callused fingertips slowly, gently over the long, stiffened worms of discolored flesh that laddered up the length of her arms the way the ancient rivers made a lattice across the great plains on their relentless march to the big water she had only heard stories of, but had never seen. In time her hair had grown after she hacked off the long braids in mourning the loss of one born of her womb. Now it hung nearly gray, streaked with the iron of more and more snow come every winter. So old now, she thought—and never would she see the children her son might have fathered.

Had he not hated his own blood. His own father.

Shell Woman lay back down, resting her head on an arm, and closed her eyes. Time enough to venture into the cold for more firewood. Enough left there by the door if she was frugal—for she ate so little anymore. And if she stayed wrapped in her buffalo robe, she would not need to keep a big fire burning day and night like those in other lodges. Only what was needed to drive most of the frost from the inside of the dewcloth.

Time enough to look outside at the world. She had seen many, many snows in her lifetime—remembering how it was to be a child and push aside the hide door flap after a blizzard, to gaze outside happily at the dazzlingly white world that stretched pristine and unbroken clear to the horizon in all directions. Overhead would dome the inside of that virginal blue bowl, so close and pure that she was sure this was how the world must have looked the day after the Everywhere Spirit had created all things.

A world not yet marred by the tracks of man nor disturbed by the passing of animals—it was so new it made her heart ache looking at it. Beneath that white blanket of winter's might lay the renewal of life that throbbed in the endless flow of the seasons.

And now she chose to lie here instead of going out to look upon the new world. Shell Woman had seen it before. Instead, she would sleep and think about the renewal of the world another time.

Outside, the commotion of the loafer camp told her the others were moving about. Poking her head from beneath the robe, Shell Woman saw her breath in the murky darkness of her lodge. With the door flap closed and the smoke flaps laid one over the other, little light penetrated the thick, smoke-cured buffalo hides. From the texture of the sky above and quality of what light snaked in at the top fan of lodgepoles, she knew it must be late afternoon. That meant she had slept again for more than a day without waking.

A night and another day come and gone.

She heard voices of women and children, the yips of camp dogs, and occasionally the sound of young men. Burnt Thigh of Spotted Tail's clan: these people who hugged close to the soldier fort at Laramie. They were Lakota words, and most she understood.

"Shell Woman."

The scratch came at the antelope hide over the lodge entrance. After a moment they called out her name again. It was a voice she had not heard before. And it spoke to her in her own tongue: Shahiyena.

Though she did not allow herself to hope, she had to ask, anyway. "Rising Fire?"

"No, Shell Woman," the man answered. "It is Porcupine."

"Is Pipe Woman with you?"

"No. Your daughter did not come south with us."

Her heart cracked, as did her voice when she replied, "Come . . . come in."

The setting sun's light seeped in through the east-facing lodge door as the warrior pulled back the stiffened antelope hide and stepped into the dark interior. She sat up, clutching the buffalo robe to her with a cold shudder.

"Porcupine," she said, a smile adding its light to her face. "It is good to see you. The rest? They come with you?"

He wagged his head and came to sit at her left hand. "No. Not all. A few rode with me. To see family. Visit old friends."

"The storm."

"Yes," he replied, and smiled. "The skies were very angry for many days, weren't they? We waited them out at the forks of a stream a day's ride west of here. Had to kill one of our ponies for food. But we kept warm, and out of the wind. And our bellies were full enough that we sang and told stories and made fun of one another."

"Young men," she said with a sigh.

"You are all right?" he asked, his eyes falling to the cold ash mound in the fire pit.

"I am well. Warm and fed."

His eyes bounded over the dewcloth rope strung the circumference of the lodge, in search of what might hang from it. "Is the white man here?"

Her eyes dropped from his as she answered. "Six . . . no, seven suns now. He went to . . ." Then Shell Woman decided not to say any more about her husband to the warrior. That they fought, she knew. That these two had clashed at the springs where Tall Bull's village had been destroyed—that much was certain. But she had vowed not to let either of them put her between her people and her husband.

"Yes. I see," Porcupine replied. "The army is thinking of marching again. It is no secret."

"You have been fighting?"

"Not since last summer—far to the north on the Elk River.* The pony-soldier chief called Yellow Hair by the Shahiyena, he led his warriors along the river for a long time while the days grew hot."

"Yellow Hair. The same who rode into Black Kettle's camp on the Washita?"

"The same," he answered. "My small numbers joined Crazy Horse, Gall, and others as we followed the pony soldiers and the ones they escorted. The Lakota grow very angry, for it appears the white man will bring the tracks for his smoking horse across those northern lands."

"Will the Lakota stop the white man?"

"With the help of the Shahiyena, they will stop the white man for all time."

"You scared the soldiers off?"

"Yes—I think we drove them off, back to the east they fled."

"For now, Porcupine," she sighed. "The day is coming when—"

"Do not tell me, Shell Woman," he interrupted. "I do not believe it will happen."

She sensed the raw, open nerve she had dragged a fingernail across and sought to talk of something else. "Where do you go from here?"

"We will move east, then north once more. Back to the Paha Sapa, the black-timbered hills—where we can worship at Bear Butte, praying for strength before the coming of the shortgrass time."

"Before the coming of another raiding season."

* Yellowstone River

"Yes."

How well she knew this cycle of the seasons of war. "From time to time here at this Laramie fort, I see white men coming through, marching north to the black-timbered hills."

"More soldiers?"

"No. These are not the army. Just white men with their horses and supplies and tools. What do you think they are looking for in that land north of here?"

He shrugged, rustling his one rattail warrior braid. "I do not know what they are looking for, Shell Woman. I only know what the white man will find if he trespasses in those sacred hills. For a long, long time that has been medicine ground to both the Lakota and the Shahiyena. A white man would be very foolish indeed to trespass on that sacred land. If they are stupid enough to come into our hunting and medicine grounds, they will find only death."

"Perhaps you only fight the inevitable." And as she said it, Shell Woman was sorry, watching the gray cloud cross the warrior's face, his brow knitting in a deep furrow as he glared at the dead fire pit.

Then with even, thoughtful words, Porcupine asked, "Do you speak those words as a Shahiyena, a mother to a brave warrior? Or do you say that as the wife of a white man, one who first leads the pony soldiers to attack our villages and the next day buries the body of his son as only a Shahiyena father would do?"

With surprise she looked up, staring evenly at him. "You know what Rising Fire did to protect the body of his son?"

"I saw everything from the hills overlooking the ruin of Tall Bull's camp, where your husband protected his son's body from the Shaved-Heads who wanted a brave warrior's scalp. I followed, to watch him bury Bull in the crevice of a great ledge that faces the rising sun."

"Above the river that will always flow at his feet."

"Yes. I am sure he told you that Bull is safe for all time to come."

She nodded. "He told me. And brought me the pony you gave him as a gift for me."

Porcupine tilted his head, eyes narrowing as he asked, "A pony I gave him for you?"

The first teasing tickle of confusion arose in her. "You did not have a pony brought to the mother of High-Backed Bull?"

He swallowed and straightened, his mouth a thin, grim line on his otherwise impassive face. "May I see this pony I sent you?"

"If you did not send the gift for my grieving, then why—"

"Will you show me this pony?" he interrupted.

"It has been many winters, Porcupine. The pony—"

"It lives?"

"Yes," she answered finally.

"Take me to see it. Now," he directed, standing in the deepening darkness of that cold, shadowy lodge.

Without saying another word, Shell Woman dragged up a blanket and wrapped it about herself, lashing at the waist with a wide belt studded with many brass tacks. The cold shocked her as she stepped from the lodge. How quickly the warmth left the earth when the sky cleared the day following a terrible storm. The snow lay trampled in most every direction she looked, except along the narrow trail leading down to the riverbank itself. Here only a few feet had troubled the surface of the deep, wind-driven snow. She listened to his deep, rhythmic breathing as he followed her into the bare cottonwoods, down to the small corral where some of the Brule kept their special breeding stock separated from the herds allowed to pasture in the river bottoms.

It was there she had built her own small pen for the three ponies: the young gelding that pulled everything she owned on her travois, the old mare she rode, and the present from Porcupine that autumn day long ago, when she learned she was no more the mother of a warrior son.

The three animals had fared the blizzard well enough. In the beginning hours of the storm, as the wind began to rise with the icy bite of snow in the air, Shell Woman took the ponies cottonwood branches and bark shavings to eat, not knowing how long the sky would remain tormented. Now she was relieved to find them still there, a bit cramped against one side of the pole corral for the tall snowdrift that iced over a good half of their pen.

"It is the gray one?" Porcupine asked.

"No," and she pointed.

"The red one?"

Shell Woman nodded, watching him approach the pole corral and climb through onto the snow trampled by those unshod hooves. The old mare came up to nuzzle against the warrior. He stroked her long gray muzzle, then sidled around her. The gray gelding bobbed its head, eyes widening as the man approached, but stood its ground, scenting the warrior. He patted its neck, then ran a hand down the length of its spine, crossing behind it for the corner of the corral.

"Yes, I remember this pony," he told her quietly as he approached the strawberry roan.

"It is a beautiful animal, Porcupine. I thank you for remembering the mother of High-Backed Bull in such a way. My son would be proud to own such a pony."

At first the roan wanted to have nothing to do with the warrior, trotting first this way, then that, moving along the short corral fence walls. Finally Porcupine reached inside his woollen capote and took something out. Holding it aloft and speaking soothingly to the pony at the same time, he gradually moved closer and closer.

She could not tell what it was at first, until the warrior finally reached the pony, looped an arm over its short neck, and stroked its mane. Then she recognized what Porcupine held in his hand—the horse medicine. A small skin bundle, trimmed with red wool, two small hawk's feathers strung from the drawstring at the top.

High-Backed Bull's horse medicine.

Her hands gripped the top pole of the pen to keep from falling. "Where did you get my son's horse bundle?"

"From his pony."

"The pony his father killed at the entrance to Bull's resting place?"

He nodded, still stroking under the jaw of the pony, then tied the bundle into the roan's mane before walking back across the trampled snow to stand near her, on the inside of the corral.

"Shell Woman," he began, laying a hand atop one of hers, "this pony was not mine to give."

Already her eyes had filled with tears from the cruel slash of the wind as the light died behind the mountains far to the west and twilight failed in this cottonwood grove beside the river. But more than the sting of the wind, she sensed the sting of something else rising within her.

Porcupine continued. "My friend's father buried his son as only a Shahiyena father could treat his warrior son."

"You told me. But why did you follow him?"

"I followed, afraid of what a white man might do to the body of my best friend." He bowed his head. "Soon I was sorry that I had doubted the father of High-Backed Bull."

"This is why you took the horse medicine from the pony Rising Fire killed by our son's resting place?"

"Yes. And I kept it all these years, wanting to bring it to you—but not knowing what to say to you."

"You have been here many times since my son was killed. And still you did not give it to me—even when Pipe Woman took her things and rode off to the north with you!" The anger and sadness rumbled through her belly.

With a wag of his head Porcupine answered, "Only because I selfishly wanted to keep Bull with me—not wanting to give him back to you. Not just yet. If I kept something special of him—something of his love for ponies and the special way the animals loved him back—then maybe I could in some way keep Bull alive."

"If you remember him, he will always be alive in your heart."

"Yes, Shell Woman." He stared off into the darkening sky to the east. Perhaps conjuring up those places whence the enemy came. "Bull died hating the white man."

"No, Porcupine. My son died only because he hated the white man in himself."

He seemed to contemplate on that, then bent and came through the corral poles to stand beside her. "Perhaps you are right. Many times Bull told me he would rather die than father any children who would carry the white man's blood in his veins. He vowed he would never marry, never have a child of his own. To do so, he said, would be to stop cursing the man who was his father. To have his own child would be to accept his own legacy."

"Then, tell me—is it true you did not send the pony to me with my husband?"

He shook his head and looked directly at the woman beside the pole corral in the growing darkness.

"No."

"But it is one of your ponies, is it not?"

"No, Shell Woman. It belonged to High-Backed Bull."

"I don't . . . understand. The one Rising Fire says he killed beside the resting place—"

"Was a favorite of your son's."

She gazed at the strawberry roan, its thick winter coat a dark umber

against the snowy ground and white-shawled tree branches illuminated
with the dim starshine come of a winter evening.

"And this red one . . . if not yours—why did my husband bring it to
the mother of High-Backed Bull?"

"This one," Porcupine explained softly, "he is the animal Bull always
rode into battle against the white man."

31

To some this was the Moon of Popping Trees. To those Lakota and Cheyenne who stalked the northern plains.

But down here in the panhandle country where the southern tribes had for generations followed the migrations of the buffalo, Jonah figured they would call it something on the order of the freeze-up moon. Lord, was it cold. And it didn't take a farmer to know a brutal winter always made for one miserable summer. Jonah was too frozen, and summer was still too far away for him really to dread July and August on the southern plains, anyway.

Last summer had grown old as the two horsemen marched north from Fort Concho, stopping to ask for any fragment of news at Fort Griffin on the Brazos. The most he could muster of any word was that up at the Fort Sill Agency, where some of the Comanche were watched, might be a place a man could start. Stories always ran free about the Comanche, stories that the army had more reports of white children among the wild tribes than you could shake a stick at. Stories, that is. Lots of goddamned stories.

Autumn was seeping down the central plains, coming in its relentless crawl to mark the end of another season, working its way across the Arkansas and Cimarron, on over the Canadian and then to the Red River by the time they heaved away from Fort Richardson and headed north to Indian Territory carrying Colonel Ranald Mackenzie's handwritten pass for Two Sleep.

"It wouldn't do for an Indian to be caught wandering around off his reservation in this part of the country," the commanding officer of the Fourth U.S. Cavalry had said to Hook. "A Shoshone at that."

"But this ain't Snake country, Colonel."

Mackenzie's brow had wrinkled. "To most folks in Texas, Mr. Hook—an Injun is an Injun. And if an Injun isn't on his reservation . . . he's fair game. Take my pass for your friend here, with my hope that it will serve you well. I commend you to your good sense, and may God bless your search. Watch your backtrail."

The hardwoods had been illuminated with autumn's fire by the time Jonah and Two Sleep crossed the Red River into Indian Territory. That first night back in that country Jonah spoke of tracking the Mormons into the land of the Creek.

"Sixty-six was it?" Hook asked himself thoughtfully. "Or was it sixty-seven?" He had wagged his head. "The Creeks were a good people—farmers, raised some horses too. I had my cousin at my side. Artus."

For a long time he was deep in himself, mucking around in the memories of those first bygone days spent searching for family, on the trail of blood kin. Better it was to have blood kin beside you when you set upon that trail.

Cousin Artus, who came home to Missouri from the war to find his mother already in the grave while he was off fighting Yankees. Soon to put his father in the ground beside her final resting place. When Jonah showed up to discover his family took and his place gone to ruin—why, it became clear neither of them had anything better than to leave behind all their loss and say farewell to that Missouri valley.

Following the recollections of old man Boatwright, the one the Mormons had tortured, Jonah and Artus tramped west into the land of the Creek before Usher's trail went cold. They moseyed north out of Indian Territory and found work supplying buffalo for the railroad crews laying ties and track along the Smoky Hill in Kansas. When Jonah later went to work as a scout for the army, cousin Artus was left behind to continue working for the westbound railroad.

Jonah had often joked how safe Artus had it—while Jonah seemed to be riding out there on the point, pushing his luck at the head of soldier columns searching for the warrior bands.

Still, it was the railroad and the great smoking horse that drew much of the red fury back then, the way the high points in country like this would draw the most lightning strikes.

There by that fire, his first night back in Indian Territory, shivering from the cold autumn wind gnashing its teeth at his back, Jonah remembered how he first saw the scene of the derailment—how the crumpled cars lay askew on both sides of the twisted track like a child's toys. At first glimpse from that distance the cars seemed like something he had of a time carved for Jeremiah and little Zeke.

Trying his best to control his panic as he drove his horse into a gallop along the ravaged rail bed, Jonah had eventually stood over the second bloated, burned body, thinking it had to be his cousin. When he had tried to turn the blackened body over, the swollen skin burst with a sickening hiss, releasing a horrid gas that made Jonah stumble back from the corpse. After losing what breakfast he had left in his belly, Hook had turned back to what remained of his cousin after the warriors got done with the railroad men.

He had wished he remembered more of the words he should have said over the shallow grave he dug there beside the twisted tracks. Words of love and forgiveness and everlasting peace. But in the past seven years since his cousin's death, Jonah had come to realize all the more that he knew very, very little of love and forgiveness. And had long ago come to the conclusion he would likely never know a damned thing of everlasting peace.

Pushing on into autumn Jonah and Two Sleep had reached Fort Sill. They spent time among the bands gathered at the Kiowa and Comanche agency. Talking with Indian agent James Haworth, they picked the man's brain for all that Jonah hoped to learn. In the end they saw a handful of white children waiting to be claimed, were shown crinkled daguerreotypes of others—pictures that had been taken by a photographer out of Topeka, photographs to be circulated among the forts and towns of Kansas in hopes that relatives might come to claim these orphans of the Indian war.

As much as Jonah wanted any of those boys to be his, as much as he strained and squinted, trying to make those dim, sepia-toned tintypes into something he might recognize, he finally had to admit he had come up with a busted flush again. What hurt even more was his growing fear that in the end he would never recognize his grown-up boys, even if by that unadulterated God-ordained miracle he ever came across Jeremiah and Ezekiel.

In taking his leave from the Kiowa-Comanche agency, Jonah stopped for a moment with Haworth outside the door of the small clapboard shack topped by a hip roof that served as the agent's office. A few yards away on a patch of bare ground, a young man was using a long branch to pick up dirty, greasy clothing. Those worn and torn garments were fed to a smoky fire, one at a time. Jonah watched as britches and shirts, pantaloons and dresses, coats and even Indian clothing, were fed onto the smoldering, smoky flames.

"What's he doing?" Hook asked Haworth.

"The children's clothes."

"You burn what they got to wear?"

"We give the recaptured children a bath, cut their hair, and purge them of the body lice before we give them new clothes donated by Friends back east."

Hook's eyes narrowed as he turned away from the fire. "Your work should give you satisfaction, Mr. Haworth. What you do makes these poor children white again."

The agent wagged his head. "Not so simple as that, Mr. Hook. Some of these young wretches will live with their horrors the balance of their natural lives."

"And the rest?"

He tried a smile. "They'll do fine. Just a matter of getting them back to their own people."

Jonah turned his back on the fire and asked, "How about a child, took when he was five or six?"

Haworth tried to put a cheerful face on it, but it turned out to be nothing more than a wan smile. "Who is to say?" And he shrugged.

"No," Jonah forced the question. "I want to know. What are the chances?"

The agent's face went as gray as old oatmeal. "Perhaps that child will heal in time. Any younger, a child—well, it depends on how long the child is held by his captors. Still . . ."

"Still . . . what, Mr. Haworth?"

"Any younger than that, Mr. Hook—truth is, I'm afraid there is little hope of fully recovering the child to a life among a God-fearing white culture."

He turned back to watch the fire, watch the smudge of smoke rise among the trees losing their autumn-tinged leaves that chilly afternoon. Finally he asked, "So where does a man go from here?"

"You might move north. To Anadarko on the Washita. If you find no help there, you can check with John Miles, agent at the Darlington Agency up on the Canadian."

"What tribe?"

"Cheyenne, Mr. Hook."

"I know something of the Cheyenne," he replied too quietly, two fingers brushing the long scar at his hairline where a warrior's bullet had grazed him seven long years gone. Then he stared directly at the agent, saying, "These Indians will never make farmers, Mr. Haworth. Scratching at the ground is something for the white man who wants to dig like a burrow mouse."

"I must still try, Mr. Hook. Like you, I must keep on trying." Haworth held out his hand, hope in his eyes. "I wish you God's speed in your search."

Perhaps it would have been better if they had never tried Anadarko and Darlington. About that time another Christmas passed and with it his unenthusiastic greeting of another new year. Just a waste of time. Slowly they made their way through each camp dotting the two agencies, looking, talking in sign with those who would talk. For the most part, the old men stood around their lodges as Jonah and Two Sleep came through, old men who talked in furtive whispers with their heads bent together. Jonah thought of those on the free prairies to the north when he looked at these beaten people. These old warriors so much like gaunt prairie wolves caught and trapped in this cage—grown suspicious, cautious, anxious, and frightened of the white man who holds their spirits prisoner. Yet saddest of all were the starving, sunken-cheeked children peering up at the two horsemen, each one in his ill-fitted, cast-off clothing from a benevolent white society back east.

He talked as best he could with the old men who did not turn away when he made sign, asking them about two boys—one who soon would be fifteen, and the other seventeen. And as he talked with the old warriors gathered around smudgy fires on those cold early-winter days, a piece of Jonah's mind snagged on a thought the way a man's coat might catch on a

nail worked loose from barn wood by the torment of the wind: these were
no longer boys he was looking for. They were young men now. Going on a
dozen years since he walked away down that narrow, rutted lane, stopping
to turn one last time and wave back at those three children and their
mother, before he marched off to fight the war. A war he had yet to come
home from.

He hated these Cheyenne and Kiowa, hated them even more for what
they kept hidden behind their unmoving, gaunt faces and the hollow looks
in their black, sunken eyes. Hated them for ever riding with the Comanche. He hated them most for giving up and coming in to feed their
families on the infested flour and moldy salt pork now that the buffalo were
disappearing from the southern plains. In those cloudy, angry eyes and
sullen faces Jonah caught a glimpse of himself—like dark light sliding off a
broken shard of mirror.

In their eyes he saw the hopelessness that grew daily inside his own
breast. Their hopelessness now become a way of life. His, a hopelessness
for two boys and their mother. In reality no less a way of life for Jonah
Hook.

In late January he raked off his chips and turned their trail south once
more, back across the Red River to Fort Richardson. From there he
planned to strike out to the northwest, pointing into the deepest reaches of
the Llano Estacado. A land where the trickles of rainfall grew and gathered
into creeks and streams and then the meandering forks of the great rivers
like the spreading of a great many-fingered hand. Among those canyons
and austere, sere-colored bluffs Jonah Hook decided he would stake
himself one last turn of the cards.

And came up with a hand that would not force him to fold.

"You a resident of the state of Texas?"

Hook looked at the tall, skeletal old man who had asked him the
question. The skin fell in folds over the gaunt cheeks, dark rings of sleeplessness gouging liver-colored pockets below the eyes lit with some distant, yet
bright inquisitional fire. His white mustache and much of his chin whiskers
were yellow, stained with dribbles of tobacco juice. His clothes seemed of
the wrong size, too big for the bony frame—yet there was a sinewy strength
and assurance about the elder one, something that gave an intangible bulk
to his otherwise wispy stance: that aura of rock-solid resolution there in the
jut of his jaw, that and the butt of the big Walker Colt's pistol that rode in
front of the man's left hip as if it hung there from birth.

"Missouri."

"If I get this right—you're telling us you'd join up just to hunt Comanche?" asked the second man at the table, a civilian as well.

He was younger than the first, clean-shaven except for the bushy black mustache that fell from the severe crimp of his face to hide his lower lip. The tip of his tongue repeatedly combed the long brush aside as the man gave voice to the deep concerns seen in his blue eyes. They were as blue as a good trout hole, all tracked up with crinkles that made him seem real sociable.

"I would. You're hunting Comanche I was told."

The younger of the two flicked his trout-hole eyes at his partner. "This company is commissioned to keep the peace, Mr. Hook. We don't set out a'purpose to hunt down Comanche. If they are raiders—we'll follow their trail wherever it leads."

"Out there," Jonah asked, pointing. "To the Staked Plain."

The old man nodded his gray head, his face so old and creased, it looked like a frost-bitten apple. "We go to that savage land on the trail of the heathens, and snag the feet of murderers if God so wills it."

"Then I want to join."

The younger one quickly eyed Two Sleep. "I'm not so sure we can use you."

"But you said you needed men—any man who could use a gun."

The civilian nodded, his blue eyes squinted as if they perpetually squinted against the high plains sun and wind. "True, that's what I said and I stand by it. I must recruit where I can, Mr. Hook. If that means to take our fighters from the watering holes and the knocking shops here across the way from Fort Richardson, so be it."

"Poxy sluts," the old man grumbled miserably, "sluts what don't know nothing but how to prop a man up for minutes at a time."

The younger one stared at Two Sleep, as if studying the Indian. "Deacon—we'll recruit where we can."

"Told you—I want to join," Jonah repeated.

"And the Indian?" asked the younger, eyeing Two Sleep again.

"He'll ride with me."

Leaning back with a sigh, the bushy mustache said, "We are a paramilitary organization, sir. Men who have volunteered to undertake great privations to protect their families and homelands against outlaws of all color. And frankly—a lot of that job right now requires us to kill Indians. Your friend here, he's a . . ."

"Shoshone."

He cleared his throat diplomatically. "I'm concerned that he might be mistaken for the enemy in the heat of battle." Jonah wagged his head, spreading both his hands on the small café table where he sat with the two white men. The winter sun was sinking fast on the small town of Jacksboro, a frontier settlement erected not far from Fort Richardson, state of Texas. It was to this smoky café that Hook had been told he might come to meet men who best knew the Staked Plain. Men who knew the Comanche, knew where the warrior bands might be hiding.

Finally Hook nodded toward Two Sleep, who stood with his back against a far wall, away from the ring of conversation, but with his eyes never leaving the three at the table.

"Look at him. Then you tell me that Injun's gonna get mistook for a Comanch'."

Reluctantly the two eyed the Shoshone, dressed the most part in the clothing of a white man. Most everything had come from traders over the years, all of it the dress of a white man, but those long braids spilling over his shoulder, along with the medicine pouch hung at midchest. The younger of the two civilians took his eyes from the warrior to glance at the rawhide-wrapped amulet hung around Jonah Hook's neck.

"You spent time among the Injuns, you said?"

"Not the Comanch'. But I'll bet my ass I been scrubbing leather a damn sight longer than most of the boys you two are toting along, boys swaybacked under all their iron and tin badges."

"The Comanch're the devil's own handiwork, my friend," spouted the older man, his ire suddenly pricked. "Pure murdering fornicators, them are."

"See that Spencer the Indian's packing?" Jonah asked the two, turning to throw a thumb at Two Sleep.

"What of it?" asked the young one.

"That Snake there is handier with that Spencer of his than a Comanche with a new scalping knife."

They looked at each other, then the bushy mustache wagged his head. "Just don't know about enlisting a—"

"Listen," Hook said, quieter now as he leaned forward on the table. "He's been riding with me for more'n five year now. Been through one scrape and another. Just say he can ride with me and you won't have to pay him. And what you get is two good guns for the price of one."

Hook watched the two men look quickly at one another, and if there was some exchange there between them, Jonah could not say what it was. Perhaps only something in the cast of the eyes. When next the younger man spoke, the die had been cast.

"You'll provision him on your own, Mr. Hook. From your own rations. And I will expect him to keep himself to himself. For the sake of my command. Is that understood?"

"Perfectly."

"You both have horses, I take it?"

"And two pack animals."

"Sell one of 'em," the old man ordered.

"Where?" he asked.

"To the fort. Army always needs horses—the way them brunette troops and Mackenzie's cavalry going through good riding stock the way they are."

"You won't need but one pack animal for the two of you, Mr. Hook," the younger man explained, the muscles along his clean-shaven jaw making little ripples just beneath the surface of the tanned skin. "We travel light and fast."

"You got to," Hook agreed. "If you're going to track a war party what's moving light and fast. More times'n not, the army moves too damned slow."

"Amen to that!" the old man exclaimed, animation brought to that face sharp-stitched with lines of hard living.

Hook asked eagerly, "When we go?"

"Two days. At dawn. Front of the sheriff's office down the street," answered the younger, his blue eyes become narrow points of light. "But drop by there tomorrow sometime, and the deacon will get you signed on proper."

"Papers?"

The younger man eyed Hook with another hard-eyed cast of appraisal. "You ain't got a reputation to hide, do you?"

"Nothing what would keep me from signing my name to your paper, no," Jonah answered. "Nothing what would keep me from hunting Comanche neither."

"Good," he replied, and stood, putting a hand on the old man's shoulder as they rose together. "This is Deacon Johns."

"Mr. Johns," Jonah repeated, putting out his hand and shaking with the gray-headed one.

"Deacon. I'm lieutenant of this company—but you can call me Deacon. It's what I figure is my God-give title. And such as that carries more weight than any temporal military rank."

The younger man took Jonah's hand and shook. "And I'm Lamar Lockhart. Captain of the company you have just joined."

"What company is that?" Hook asked Lockhart.

"Company C. Texas Rangers."

32

WINTER STILL HELD the plains in its death grip.
        While there hadn't been any snow of late, the cold had kept
the warriors near the village, and the ponies worked harder to find some
graze worth the work. High scurrying clouds looking suspiciously like
clots of ice crystals shined beneath a dull pewter dish of a sun. Only the
deep canyons offered shelter from the brutal, incessant wind that ravaged
the prairie above.

Down here they could find more grass for the herd. And more firewood to keep the lodges warm. Still, the children cried with empty bellies.

Antelope was a father already—his son born early last autumn. And
now Prairie Night thought she carried her husband's second child. Tall
One knew the young ones always suffered the most.

Time and again he watched the gray-eyed war chief send scouting
parties out into the cold, dispatched this way and that, to the south mostly,
to look for sign of the great herds. What was left of the once-great herds,
that is.

More and more the big shaggy animals hung to the south, away from
the banks of the Arkansas River, even south of the Cimarron of late. The

buffalo hunters with their big guns riding out of the white man's settle-ments in Kan-saw had seen to that. Those hairy-faced hunters would now have to push farther and farther south still if they were to continue their slaughter of the humped masses. And by pushing across the Canadian, the hide men would march right into the heart of the Kwahadi hunting ground.

Tall One could not wait for the air to warm and the grass to raise its green head on the prairie, for the ponies to grow sleek and the dancing to begin once more. The calls would go out from one war chief or another—asking for young men to ride in search of the white men. Come shortgrass time, Tall One would ride with the war parties. And this season Antelope would be at his side.

The air blew racy with the fragrance of winter's decay, last autumn's leaves hurling along the ground ahead of the brutal wind moaning out of the west like a death song upon this high, barren land given its Spanish name, Llano Estacado. Spring and renewal come to resurrect the land. But for now Tall One thought only of the band's last search for meat. How the hunters had to go farther, search longer. The Kwahadi were running dangerously low on meat they had dried to last them the winter, forced to venture out on the hunt much earlier this winter than they had in winters come and gone.

It was during one of those hunts last fall that Tall One had gone with the war chief, when he and the older warriors had killed a few white hide hunters they discovered far south of the "dead line," that place where the *tai-bos'* government treaty-talkers declared white buffalo men were not to cross.

The white man's government and its guarantees seemed to matter little to the white men intent on plunging farther and farther south of the Arkansas River, come now to the last hunting ground promised the south-ern nations as their own.

"A waste of time, this talking treaty with the white man," the war chief growled at Tall One that night at their small fire after they had killed the buffalo hunters. There were scalps to dance over, clothing and mirrors, and the guns—those big buffalo guns taken from the dead men.

Tall One asked, "Is it true the old men give away to the white treaty-talkers all that we young men have fought to hold on to?"

He touched the rangy youth with those gray eyes as he said, "Six winters ago, ever since the autumn when the old chiefs of the Kiowa,

Cheyenne—and Comanche too—all signed that talking paper up on Medicine Lodge Creek, the white hunters have been pushing into our buffalo country in greater and greater numbers."

"These buffalo hunters with the big guns who you and the others speak of more often these days—you are afraid they will slaughter their way through the herds?"

"I fear these white men will soon cross the Canadian River—the river that is the northern boundary of our sacred buffalo ground. And when they do, I fear this coming fight will prove to be the last stand for our people."

From all that Tall One had learned from Wolf Walking Alone he knew that killing soldiers carried nothing but a curse for the Kwahadi. If they had learned anything since the first white man set foot in this country, the Comanche had learned that the yellow-leg soldiers would strike back with a vengeance—sending even more of their number against the Kwahadi next time.

"No matter," protested young Antelope. "Because we should strike and strike again. The yellow-legs never find our roaming warriors." He had made his first, bloody kill that day. And at long last had his first white scalp.

Sadly Tall One could only reply, "My brother, don't you understand that the white man's Tonkawa trackers seek out our villages where stay the women and children, the old ones who cannot flee?"

Antelope laughed without mirth. "I am the one with a woman, brother! I am the one with children. Don't talk to me about the villages where the women and little ones are trapped by the yellow-legs!"

Indeed, rarely were the young warriors punished by the *tai-bo* soldiers. It was the Kwahadi families who were made to suffer—losing lodges and blankets and robes, clothing and meat and weapons when they fled quickly enough to escape the soldiers. Losing their lives, falling prey to the Tonkawa scouts and yellow-leg soldiers when they did not run faster than the white man's bullets.

A person crippled by an empty belly, weakened because there was simply too little food for all to eat—he or she would stand little chance of outrunning the hissing bullets when the *tai-bos* came.

With a shudder Tall One ducked out of Old Owl Man's lodge and stood feeling the sting of great cold. A terrible storm had rumbled down the very gut of the plains, rolling in on the hoary, marrow-numbing breath of Winter Man. In its wake on the prairie above, the storm left behind icy snowdrifts, and many children cried out with hungry bellies. Old ones as well wailed in want. As hungry as he might be, Tall One had vowed not to complain with the gnawing pain. The warriors must be brave, the men reminded themselves. It was up to them and them alone to find meat—and thereby exorcise the ghost of starvation from the Kwahadi.

Their last hunt had taken them far, far from this canyon where the village waited. After riding south for many days, the gray-eyed war chief and his hunters found themselves at the southernmost extent of the Llano Estacado. Without sign of buffalo or promise of other game.

"It is as if Winter Man has wiped all before him with his great cleansing, cold breath," Tall One said quietly to his brother.

"Have the white men killed them all?" asked Antelope with a hiss of hatred in his question.

As those first cold days of searching stretched into many, the hunters had finally come across a few old bulls partially buried in a coulee here, then some more frozen in a snowdrift against a ridge—no longer strong enough to march on with the rest of the herd.

"These are what the Great Mystery offers us, to keep our families from starving," their war chief explained. "These few left to rot by the passing of Winter Man's storm."

Antelope snarled, "We get these poor animals, while the white hide hunters leave the carcasses of the rest to rot in the sun!"

With nothing more to hope for, having reached the southern frontier of their hunting grounds, the Kwahadi warriors turned their noses north, limping back to their winter village.

"Where have the rest of the herds gone?" asked some.

"Farther and farther south still," answered the few.

"To the land of the summer winds?" worried a growing number.

If the buffalo had indeed fled as far to the south as the tribe was beginning to fear, the herds would likely not return until the shortgrass time came to the prairies—not until that shift in the great season of things, when the winds blew soft and the Great Mystery once again compelled the great buffalo herds to nose around to the north in their annual migrations.

The terrible, cold breath of Winter Man whipped hot tears at his eyes as he remembered, and heard the low keening, the cries from the lodges huddled in this canyon, sheltered from the strongest of the winds.

In the waning days of winter the rains came to soften the hard breast of the land. Spring arrived, with little letup in the rain. It was a time of cold, gray, never-ending days. The ground sucked at a pony's hooves. Yanked at a man's moccasins. And still the little ones, the sick and dying, whimpered in their lodges.

The buffalo had yet to return. And the old men prayed over their drums and rattles and notched sticks.

And when despair seemed the darkest, news of a new shaman arrived from another band, a shaman who was said to perform wonderful miracles. He had promised to make war on the white man: those the Comanche did not kill would turn and flee from this land, their hearts gone to water, soiling their pants as they ran.

Tall One prayed this new medicine man would prove the answer to so many doubts.

His name was Isatai.

"The ass of a wolf?" Antelope asked, barely able to keep from laughing out loud. He had to keep a hand over his mouth.

"Some say his name means coyote droppings," Tall One explained.

Born of a different band of Comanche, nearly the same age as their own gray-eyed war chief, this young shaman was already a rising star among his Penateka people. When two of his major predictions came to pass, news of Isatai spread like prairie fire across the southern plains. A year ago when a fiery comet had burned its first path across the springtime night sky for three days, the medicine man predicted the star would perform five more times, then return no more.

It amazed the Kwahadi to find no comet in the heavens on that sixth night. The fireball in the sky had obeyed Isatai.

Not long afterward the shaman predicted the beginning of a great drought that would parch the southern prairie and especially the Staked Plain.

True to his prediction, the creeks dried up last summer. Normally in abundance, the game wandered far away, gone in search of water. Suspended overhead, the sun seemed like a dull brass button as each new day of torture seeped into the next with no relief from the blistering heat. Isatai told his people to persevere, that winter would bring rain—but that respite would not last: they would suffer another time of great dryness.

The rains had come as predicted. The Comanche bands praised the power of Isatai. And all but the most hardened cynics believed when they were told that the shaman had vomited up a wagonload of cartridges right before the eyes of his most faithful believers.

"Our prayers are answered!" cheered Antelope. "A man to lead us in wiping out the white man."

"I too want to see the bullets—then I will believe," Tall One said. "Without question, then I will believe in Isatai."

But the messengers exclaimed that Isatai had swallowed the bullets again.

"So there is nothing left for us to use killing the yellow-leg soldiers?" demanded Antelope.

Sheepishly the messengers replied, "The whole wagonload is gone."

Tall One shivered again as the wind knifed through the canyon, its striated red walls rising eight hundred feet above the creekbed where his people camped. Very soon, when winter at last released its tight hold on these prairies, the gray-eyed chief would send pipe bearers among all the bands of Comanche still roaming the Llano Estacado. Others would carry his message on to the Cheyenne and Kiowa reservations. If the chiefs took up the gray-eyed chief's pipe and smoked it, they vowed to join the Kwahadi in war.

If, however, the chiefs decided not to touch that offer of the pipe, then they would be told to step out of the way. War was coming with the spring winds.

The mere thought of it made Tall One's blood run hot. Like Antelope, he too hungered for this chance to prove himself against the *tai-bos*. To prove once and for all that he was no longer white. That he had become a Comanche.

War.

"*Ricos and whiskey. Ricos* and guns," grumbled June Callicott, one of the Rangers with Company C, as they loosened cinches and pulled saddles, blankets too, from their weary horses the evening of that late spring day. He constantly chewed his cud like a glassy-eyed cow, his teeth the size and color of pin-oak acorns beneath an unkempt mustache that bent like a small black horseshoe over his mouth.

"*Ricos* and their blood money," piped up Deacon Elijah Johns.

"Scum-bellied fornicators. Satan's blasphemers we need to put in the ground."

"You said you spent time among the comancheros?" asked Captain Lamar Lockhart, stepping over to the brush where Jonah Hook dropped his saddle and blanket.

"For a long time I had reason to believe my boys was sold off to traders headed for Mexico."

Most of the company had quietly turned to listen in. With his Indian partner, the new man had ridden with the Rangers for the better part of two months now—a long time without opening up and pouring out all that much of himself.

Lockhart nodded. "Cattle and horses, Mr. Hook. The *ricos* will buy furniture and clothing and mirrors and even family Bibles—"

"Satan's handiwork, they are!" Johns snapped. "Good and kind Jesus—help these sinners see the error of their ways!"

The company captain pulled off his hat, the print of his hatband lying across his forehead like a wide scar as he pressed ahead. "Those traders will take anything the Comanches bring them what they got off the settlers they murdered. Anything worth stealing, that is. Only what the *ricos'* comancheros will pay for in whiskey and in guns."

"A bad combination, that one," June Callicott added, his face as hard as a war shield, his cheeks flaring red as if he sweated chinaberry juice. "Whiskey and guns."

For as long as there had been this ground called Texas, there had been Comanches and whiskey and guns. A deadly mix for those who wanted nothing more than to bring the fruitful hand of civilized man to these plains. Come here with a wagon and a milk cow and a family, come here to raise crops and cattle and a passel of children.

As far back as the Texas Revolution there had been Rangers—first organized in 1835 as local committees of safety and correspondence, right in the midst of their war with Mexico. Silas M. Parker was empowered to engage the services of three companies of Rangers whose business would be to range and guard the frontiers between the Brazos and Trinity rivers. From then on, in one incarnation or another, the Ranger existed on that high, wild prairie where he was first given birth to meet the outlaws of three races: American desperado, Mexican bandit, and Indian warrior. Down through the years the function these few men served might have changed in detail, but never did the Ranger cease standing as a bulwark between the lawless, savage elements and the coming of civilization.

No matter what other description might be given of him, the Ranger was a fighting man.

It took a lot of doing in the years after the revolution, but the few eventually subdued many of the tribes—formerly warlike—such as the Tonkawa and Caddo. The Rangers began pushing back their wilder cousins like the Kiowa and Comanche just before Texas went from being a republic to joining the Union itself, when Texans disbanded their Rangers, believing that it was now the duty of the federal government to protect them.

After more than a half-dozen years of waiting for the troops to come make a stand against the renewed raids of the wild tribes, Texans figured they had endured enough. In the late fifties the Rangers flourished once more. Again they issued the call, and young men rode in to answer the clarion. Again they sent out the companies to construct their modest outposts strung like distant beads on a strand of spiderweb, all the way from the Brazos on the north clear down to the Rio Grande flowing against the border of Mexico itself. Small bands of a dozen or more were scattered to live among the far-flung pioneer families tenaciously dug in like hermit bugs out there in that brutal, beautiful country. The Rangers were ready to ride out at a moment's notice—to track down and punish any and all who cast a shadow of lawlessness and savagery across the whole of west Texas.

Years later when the South ripped itself away from the Union, the call went out for men to join the likes of John Bell Hood. Fighting men answered that resounding trumpet, leaving gaping holes in the fabric of Texas's frontier defense. Quickly sensing the change, the wild tribes brought out their drums once more and danced over the scalps. Again the red tide savagely pushed against the scattered white settlers, reversing all the good the Rangers had accomplished.

When the men of Texas returned home after Appomattox, they found they had been defeated on two fronts. Not only had the Yankees whipped them in those four bloody years of war back east, but while they were gone, off to save the Confederacy, the savage horsemen of the southern plains had risen up to reclaim their buffalo ground. While some of the sons of the South continued to cry out that they would never surrender, a few even fleeing across the Rio Grande to continue their war, most accepted their defeat and rode home to put family and life back together once more.

And wound up staring right into the blood-flecked eye of another war.

How could a man think of plowing and planting when there were warriors roaming about, ready to undo everything a man might accomplish?

The Rangers offered a private $1.25 per day for pay, rations, clothing, and the services of his own mount. To sign on, each of them had to be ready with a trail-worthy horse, saddle, bridle, and blanket, along with a hundred rounds of powder and ball. Officers—the captain and his lieutenants, in addition to the sergeant of each company—were paid a pittance more. For most the pay did not really matter.

No more were these men mere green recruits. While most were young, very few weren't proficient with a gun—most had been proven in battle.

To Hook it seemed that most of the men who rode with Company C were hard-wintered and humped in the loin. Seemed too that they could stare eyeball to eyeball with death itself, ride for days in the saddle and gallop straight-up into daunting odds.

So it was that Jonah found comfort in this irregular company of men. Nothing like Sterling Price's Missouri Confederates. Further still from the galvanized U.S. Volunteers he had joined to fight Indians in Dakota Territory after the Great War. Probably as far from the Army of the West as any civilians could be, the Rangers still weren't anything like militia. No matter, their captain stood them to a grueling inspection each morning. While Company C did not dress in uniform, their captain nonetheless did expect the men to wear clothing that was clean and functional, demanding that the men keep their horses fit and their weapons in fighting trim.

"We may not be military," Lamar Lockhart had reminded them before they rode out from Jacksboro. "We may be nothing more than irregulars—but we have no need of looking like bobtails, do we?"

Irregulars indeed: a Ranger furnished all his own needs and arms. Never did these men ride beneath any flag, nor with a surgeon along. And all matters of rank came about through a man's ability to lead and inspire his own company of staunch individualists—not through some political appointment or timely graduation from the U.S. Military Academy.

It did not take long for Jonah to come to admire the saddle-hardened men in this crude bunch he rode with, marching northwest from Fort

Richardson toward the Staked Plain of the Penateka and Kwahadi Co-manche.

No—not for pay, nor for glory did this company of Rangers ride into the breach.

For most of these it might be but the memory of a loved one killed, scalped, and savagely mutilated that spurred them to join. Mothers and fathers, perhaps a sister or brother. Blood kin captured and enslaved, outraged or butchered.

This was something that Jonah Hook understood right down to the very core of him.

These were men who rode into Comanche country with a score to settle.

33

S UMMER'S LONG DAYS of oppressive heat were almost more than
Gritta Hook could bear.

Year after year her days flowed like this, agonizingly slow from one to
the next. Season after season Usher marched them north when autumn
kissed the trees with color, south again when those trees bloomed in
spring—into the land of desert and cactus and dark-skinned, raven-haired
people who stared at her from the side of the dusty roads where rumbled
the ambulance George drove.

It was good she remembered. She tried so hard to remember names
nowadays. Jubilee Usher . . . and the old colored man called George and
. . . her name was Gritta.

The big man never called her by her name. How she wished he would.
If only once. To say her Christian name. Not the one she took when she
married long, long ago. But her own name. Gritta.

So she said it to herself when the days grew long and the nights
became lonely. She devised conversations between herself and Usher,
between herself and the old colored man, long conversations about
nothing of any great consequence. Something—anything at all—to keep

her mind from slipping over the edge where she already teetered precariously.

And so many times she came back to recalling snips and snatches of Bible verses, remembrances of things faceless folks had said to her of a dim time long ago, perhaps fragments of a song heard on a hot Sunday morning as a child, lullabies sung as a mother to children of her own.

Sunday-morning sunlight had always poured like creamy white butter in through the isinglass windows of that tiny church—just the way the sun's light was magnified as it penetrated the creamy white canvas of this wall tent where she was imprisoned most every day while Usher's men roamed the deserts and mountains. Horses and men coming and going. Celebrating their bloody work, then taking their leave once again in a new direction.

Here in the tent the air began to hum like a hot summer Sunday at church, listening to the preacher drone on and on. The way Usher droned on and on, ranting before his faithful.

Gritta began to whisper, faintly caressing each bright note belonging to the melody of an old Baptist hymn.

Do not wait until
Some deed of greatness you may do.
Do not wait
To shed your light afar.
To the many duties
Ever near you now be true:
Brighten the corner where you are.

Brighten the corner where you are!
Brighten the corner where you are!
Someone far from harbor
You may guide across the bar.
Brighten the corner where you are!

Her eyes found the corner where the canvas seams came together, bunched to make for a shadowy place. How she longed to be there, where it would be cool. Right where a spider hung in the dark midst of her web. She had hung there, balled up for the better part of two days, likely hibernating after a feast on the moth snared in her sticky trap day before last.

Up there in the shadows, where things looked all the cooler.

They had learned the old songs from her, the three children had. Learned to say grace before their meals. No matter that they might eat nothing but plain food, there was always some meat on the table, along with potatoes and an abundance of other vegetables in season. Always plenty of food for their growing bodies to eat. That is, until Jonah marched off to fight that war he never come back from.

Grace. Thanking God for all His bounty. For what the Lord had seen fit to bless them with.

Gagging, she physically swallowed down the sour bile as she fought the nausea, slowing her hand at work with the smooth, peeled twig between her legs.

It made her as sick to think of what blessings had been given her family as it did to plunge the twig deep inside herself, searching out the demon seed that had attached itself to her womb.

"Dear heavenly Father, we are grateful for the bounty Thou hast set before us this day. Thy gifts are the fruit of our hands. Bless this plentiful harvest to nourishing our bodies, and Your holy word to nourishing our hungry souls," Gritta whispered quietly, her lips barely moving as she fought back the waves of nausea bordering on pain.

What needed doing now had needed doing more than once since that bright day the man had come and took her from the home she had made for her family.

"Watch over and protect these three children of ours, the youngest of your creation," she continued her recitation of grace. "May we never turn from Your face, our heavenly Father—forever praising You in the name of the Savior of man, Jesus Christ our Lord. Amen."

She felt the warm, sticky flow over her hand then. Hoping she had torn Usher's seed from her womb, praying her body would flush it as she had each time before.

Exhausted, Gritta sought out something more to hang her thoughts on as the pain rose low in her belly. Slowly she dragged the smooth twig from her body and lay panting, sensing in some dull, primitive way that she was bleeding again. That was good. Only through the bleeding would she flush the demon seed.

"Now I lay me down to sleep," her voice came from deep within her, as deep perhaps as she had been probing with the twig. It was a child's voice that rose quiet and eerily from her throat. "I pray the Lord my soul to keep. If I should die . . . if I should die . . ."

Gritta clenched her eyes shut, trying to hold back the hot tears of pain, of failure at her attempts to kill herself.

"Before I wake," she sobbed. "I pray the Lord my soul to take."

She knew God would not take her now. Not after what she had done with Usher. Not after all this time. How she wanted to die and have it done with—just how much worse could hell be than where she was right now?

Pulling her closer and closer to death was Gritta's belief that her children had gone on to a better place. Too long since she last saw the boys.

"Now I lay me down to sleep."

Remembering how she always got down on her knees beside the bed the boys shared, kneeling between them. Each night Hattie knelt at her small bed nearby.

"I pray the Lord my soul to keep."

She hadn't seen her daughter in almost as long as she had missed the boys. Couldn't remember—Hattie's face. For so many years there it had been like looking back on her own childhood, so much did Hattie look like her mother.

"If I should die before I wake."

But she would never see them again. Not living. Not in death. They had gone on to heaven, and she was going to hell for all that she had done with Usher.

"I pray the Lord my soul to take."

How fervently she prayed that last line, repeating it over and over as she grew more and more faint, without the strength to hide the smooth, peeled twig beneath one of the table's leg supports. It was there she had kept it over all these seasons and miles and operations she performed on herself.

Cursing her womb that had given birth to three children who now lived with God. Cursing her womb, desiring to scar it irrevocably so that no chance would the devil's own seed stand of finding sustenance there and growing.

How long had it been? She dug at the thought the way her fingers dug at the hard, flaky soil.

She sensed again that fleeting remembrance of being bedside with the children, saying the prayer before diving between the cold sheets and blankets and the thick comforter.

Then Gritta was struck with the fact so cold and smooth, it was like the limestone walls of the springhouse where they kept the milk and butter cool. She could not say where she was, how long it had been, nor how old she had become. Nothing to relate to space and time.

The warmth between her legs was turning slightly colder now.

None of the rest mattered anymore, for the children were all gone and with God now. Only her regrets that she would not live for eternity with them in the glory of the Lord's love. And J— . . . Jonah himself must surely be dead. Not come home from the war for so long. Not come after her. He was surely dead. Killed by the Yankee soldiers Sterling Price wanted to drive out of Missouri. How much longer would they be fighting?

She knew these men who rode with Usher fought and then marched back north to spend the winter. It must be a long, long war for the fighting to go on and on and on this way.

When the war ended, would she no longer be Usher's slave? How that made her battered soul rejoice, sending tiny shards of light against all the darkness of her gloom. Not that she saw anything to change in the way things had worked out for her: getting took off that farm of theirs in Missouri was probably the best thing after all—what with Jonah killed by the Yankees and her unable to do a lot of the work it took a man to do. Better that she was took by Usher now that Jonah was dead.

Only regret she had was those children of hers dying so young.

As sure as she was about anything, she would be going to hell eventually—if this wasn't it already.

This heat. This singing, buzzing, hot air. This endlessness. This despair and lack of any hope. Where she was, it must surely be hell.

"I pray the Lord my soul to take."

The first day of the Moon of Green Grass. Already the endless, rolling waves of it were growing tall against the legs of their ponies.

Tall One had never dreamed he would see so many warriors together, all riding north by west, nearing the earth-lodge settlement where the buffalo hunters gathered. A wildly independent tribe, never before had the Comanche banded together in numbers anywhere near these. And with them rode the fiercest of the Kiowa and Cheyenne.

First they would strike the buffalo hunters there at the earth lodges, then spread out like the fanning tail feathers of an eagle as war parties leveled one after another of the white settlements they found trespassing on buffalo ground. How glorious would be this ride behind the war chiefs for him and Antelope!

It was to be the last summer of the white man in the land of the Comanche.

They were timing their arrival at the white man's earth-lodge settlement, wanting to get there when this first moon of the summer had grown full and fat. Beneath the silver light of that moon they would charge in and club the hide hunters while the white men slept in their beds.

As decided by the war chiefs, the many wandering bands came together a few days ago at the mouth of Elk Creek on the North Fork of the Red River. It was there, within the boundaries of the Kiowa-Comanche Reservation itself, that the shaman Isatai had commanded a sun-dance lodge be erected. By the hundreds The People had come until there were more than any could ever remember celebrating this ancient ritual. Even avowed peace chiefs Horseback and Elk Chewing came south to the great sun—praying with their bands.

And after that celebration of dancing to the sun for renewal of their People, the chiefs of those warrior bands held their council of war. Kiowa under Satanta and Lone Wolf. Shahiyena under Medicine Water, Iron Shirt, and Gray Beard. Each of them came carrying the war pipes sent them by the gray-eyed Kwahadi war chief.

Still, there were holdouts. Like the Shahiyena Little Robe, who upon hearing the talk of war immediately fled with his people back to the agency. Fearing most what everyone knew was coming, the Shahiyena Stone Eagle sat arguing with himself about what path he should set his feet upon.

For the rest, the path lay clear and straight.

They had come to believe in the prophet called Isatai, come to believe that this shaman might truly be more than a mere magician. Perhaps through this powerful medicine man the Comanche finally could drive the white man from their ancient hunting ground, for all time to come.

So it had seemed most fitting, before they undertook the bloody work of war, that the Comanche chose to immerse themselves in more of the frenetic symbolism of the sun dance, excusing themselves from most of the "formalities" practiced by the Kiowa and Shahiyena. That symbolism of the sun dance had for many generations been unequivocally tied to the buffalo. And now more than ever the threat posed by the white buffalo hunters had become most real.

If the buffalo disappeared—the Comanche would be next.

At Elk Creek the bands had gathered the poles and branches for the great sun-dance arbor. At the center they raised a tall, forked ridgepole, and ringing the outer circle stood the twelve shorter poles, each one connected to the center with long streamers decorated with scalps of their enemies and scraps of fluttering calico and trade cloth. A newly killed buffalo calf, its body cavity emptied, then stuffed with willow branches, was raised to the top of the huge center pole. There it would gaze down upon the dancers, granting them its buffalo magic.

Masked clowns smeared with mud cavorted and swirled among the gathered villages, throwing mud balls at the unsuspecting and lending a carnival atmosphere to this important undertaking. These were the Comanche "Mud Men," the *sekwitsit puhitsit,* a comical diversion to an otherwise deadly serious occasion: invoking the power of the supernatural to bring about the salvation of a dying way of life.

Four days of searing sun and short, chilly nights filled with the endless drumming and prayer singing by the old men. For Tall One and Antelope it proved to be a frighteningly beautiful celebration to watch. While dancers among the northern tribes hung themselves from the rawhide tethers or dragged buffalo skulls from skewers driven beneath the muscles of their backs, the Comanche did not believe it necessary to torture themselves to be heard by the Spirit Above. Still, the dancers allowed themselves no food nor water for the duration of the celebration of the sun. While these warriors danced, men and women came forward and hung small offerings of food and tobacco and scalps from the center pole. Young boys hoping one day to become full-fledged warriors tied their gifts to their tiny arrows and shot them into the sun-dance tree, far above the dancers.

And when the celebration to the sun was over, the voices of the hundreds were raised exultantly to the heavens. Never before had there been such a gathering on the southern plains: Kiowa, Shahiyena, Kiowa-Apache, and Comanche. The hot summer breeze toyed with Tall One's single feather lashed to one of his braids. His heart filled standing there, witnessing that grand union of fighting men.

"We want to follow the buffalo herds as in days of old!" the chiefs bellowed.

"We wish to stay a strong people, needing nothing from the white man!" cried others.

Isatai had harangued the chiefs, bellowing, "The strong of heart will prevail in the coming war. If we take to the warpath and wipe our land clear of the white man—only then will the buffalo return to blanket our hunting ground."

"Unless we drive the white man out now, the buffalo will disappear!" shouted one.

"The white man must go!" agreed another in the same fervor.

"No!" Isatai barked at them, worked into his own blood frenzy. "The white man must die! All of them. Man. Woman. Child!"

Tall One sensed what the rest felt: that magnetic charisma of the shaman, able to think of nothing else at that moment but slaughtering all whites where the warriors would find them. Amid the great noise of celebration and the fury of the war council, he paid little heed to the quiet voice inside that reminded Tall One he had of a time been white.

In the end it was the old and proven chiefs of the Shahiyena Nation who decided what would be their first objective.

"We think the Kwahadi need first to wipe out the buffalo hunters gathered on the Canadian River," White Wolf told the gathering. "Kwahadi go accomplish that first. Then I think your hearts will be ready for war. You kill all the buffalo hunters—then we follow you to make war on Texas."

Another Shahiyena, Otter Belt, agreed. "The real threat to the survival of our peoples remains the buffalo hunters. If we stop them—we stop the white man."

"Those hunters have guns that shoot a long, long way," came a voice from the council ring, filled with doubt.

Isatai whipped round on the doubter, banging a fist against his own chest. "Let them empty their guns shooting at me!" the shaman shrieked, scuffling around the center of the gathering, spitting his words into the faces of the gathered war chiefs. "Do any of you doubt that I can make medicine so powerful that it will protect our warriors as they charge down on the white man's earth lodges? Do you doubt the power of my medicine to turn their bullets into water?"

In the end not one of them doubted Isatai's power. Not even the tall, handsome, gray-eyed Kwahadi war chief.

"When the white man wanted to put us all on a reservation six winters ago—he wanted us to live in one place as he does," he had told the hushed assembly. "I was born of the prairie, where the wind blows free. Where there is nothing to bend the light of the sun. I was born where every living thing draws a free breath. I want to die in my own country—free—and not within the walls of the white man."

That night as many of the Kwahadi were rolling into their blankets, anticipating an early departure at dawn, Tall One and Antelope hung close to the gray-eyed chief, hanging on his every word as he continued to exhort his faithful.

To Tall One it seemed the war chief was even more a mystic than Isatai. Even more perhaps a man who believed in the power of the human spirit over the powers of magic.

"No Comanche will ever again die a captive of the white man," he promised his warriors at that late-night fire. "A warrior dies riding the prairie. A Kwahadi dies charging into the face of his enemy. We will take the power of our people to the buffalo hunters' settlement. The white man's days on this prairie are numbered."

The war chief had made a tight fist he held up before them all as he concluded, "I hold the last days of the white man in my hand!"

34

T HINGS WOULD HAVE been hot in Comanche country even if it had been down in the deep days of January.

It wasn't only the weather.

The southern plains had exploded in full-scale war.

First came the rumors of some of the bands moving off from the agencies, heading southwest to Elk Creek to attend a big war-talk. But by the time any of the army got around to checking out what sounded like the wildest of stories—the Comanche holding a sun dance and crazy whispers of a powerful shaman whipping the tribes into a blood lust against the white man—the whole affair was yesterday's news. Why, just about the time the army was getting set to check out the rumors, word out of the Territories was that some of the Cheyenne were even coming back to their agency after the big medicine stomp of the war bands.

Still, that left the Kiowa and Comanche out there roaming about, adding their numbers to the Kwahadi, who had never come in to their assigned reservation.

"Kwahadis led by one of Satan's own," Deacon Johns told Jonah. "The devil's own whelp, that one."

The old fellow with iron-crusted hair wore a set of dentures that gave Johns a pretty smile but were not too good for talking, what with all the clacking. He got in the habit of slipping them from his mouth behind his hand when he had a big piece to say. Which was most of the time with the deacon, his slack jaws at work like a well-used, wrinkled blacksmith's bellows.

"Quanah Parker's his name," explained Lamar Lockhart.

"Got a English name, does he?" Hook inquired. "So the bastard's a renegade, eh? Back to sixty-five, I rubbed up against my first half-breed renegade. North to the Platte Bridge fight. A Cheyenne name of Charlie Bent."

"This one's a half-breed too," Lockhart replied. "His mother was took by the Comanch' almost twenty-eight-some years ago, just a girl as I remember the story of it. Her seed's turned out about as bad as they come, with a reputation as smelly as his breechclout."

"He's spilled blood from down on the Pecos all the way past the Prairie Dog Town Fork," offered Niles Coffee, sergeant of Company C, his tanned, wind-seamed face a java color beneath a crop of red whiskers that gave the Ranger an air of raffish gaiety.

"We'll get him," Lockhart said sternly at the fire. "It's only a matter of time."

"Wanna see him swing," murmured John Corn, one of Hook's messmates. His nose seemed oversized, it and his cheeks perpetually red, scored over with little chicken-track blood vessels. He was a walking barrel of a man, with toothpicks for legs.

"Shooting's too good for that heathen fornicator," Johns grumbled.

"Rest assured, he doesn't have long to roam free," Lockhart repeated.

Over the past months he had been riding with this company of Rangers, Jonah had come to have a real respect for the quiet captain of Company C. A year younger than Hook, Lockhart had been born late in the autumn of 1838.

"My parents came to Texas from Georgia when all this still belonged to Mexico," Lockhart had explained one of those quiet prairie nights when men gathered at their cook fires just like this, watching the embers die slow at their feet, the stars dusting the dark canopy like coal water flecked with diamonds.

"My father came west to Texas like many of the rest in those days, intent on finding the length of his own stride. He fought in the revolution that drove out Santa Anna. When Mirabeau Buonaparte Lamar was first elected president of the Republic of Texas in thirty-eight, my folks named me after him—a man they both admired. He come from Georgia too, matter of fact. A dreamer, a poet—besides hating Injuns to the bottom of his craw. Probably why my father liked Lamar so much."

"You hate Injuns as much as your father?"

"No. Not anymore," the captain admitted thoughtfully. "Last couple of years I've been trying real hard to understand Injuns more than hate 'em. Hate will eat you up until you got nothing to feed on but it, Jonah. Still, I do understand men like my father. Men like Mirabeau Lamar. Neither one of them give a inch."

"Tough on the Injuns?"

"President Lamar tough on Injuns!" Coffee hooted.

"These Comanche bands, yes," Lockhart replied. "Lamar wasn't in office a little over a year when three Comanche chiefs come riding into the village of San Antonio, saying they were sent by the rest of the chiefs to make arrangement for some treaty talks with the Texans. *Tehannos* they called us—probably from the Mexican tongue."

"Comancheros?" Jonah asked, his interest growing more piqued as Lockhart went on with the story.

"Likely that's where the Comanche learned the word," the captain answered. "Seeing a chance to free some of the white captives held by the Comanches suddenly dropped in their lap, the Texans agreed to treaty-talks to be held at the Council House there in San Antonio—if . . . if the Comanche would bring in all their white captives to sell to the peace commissioners."

"But them Texans weren't about to buy the captives back, were they?"

Lockhart shook his head. "Plan was to capture all the chiefs and hold them prisoner. Exchange 'em for the white captives even up."

"What came of it?"

"That meeting come to be—but the sixty-five Comanche chiefs, with all their women and kids that come in, brought only one white prisoner with them."

"It was Matilda Lockhart," Deacon Johns broke in.

Hook brought his eyes back to the captain. "She kin to you?"

He nodded. "My father's sister-in-law. My uncle had been killed in a raid on the Trinity. Folks who watched her brought in said she had been starved down to hide and bone. Bruised and cut up something bad." And the captain swallowed hard in its telling, the cold-banked fires glowing behind the man's eyes. "When Matilda was brought into the Council House, she told the others there were several others at the big camp only three days away. The bastards brought her in to see if they could get a high price for her—planning to ransom each prisoner separately to get the most they could for each one."

"But them God-fearing folk at San Antone took up the sword of the righteous!" exclaimed the deacon. "Rangers, they was. The ones closed the trap on those Comanch'."

"Colonel William Cooke, our republic's secretary of war, got his Rangers spread out around the walls inside that Council House while the peace-talkers tried to find out about the other prisoners. Red bastards claimed the other captives were with bands far, far off. So Cooke told the chiefs they were prisoners of the Texans and would be exchanged, one for one, for the whites."

"That's when the hoedown was called!" said Niles Coffee, his red hair lit with life in the fire's glow.

Lockhart nodded. "When the chiefs and their women pulled out knives and bows, rushing the doors, Cooke gave his order and the Rangers opened fire."

"Damn—but that would have been a sight!" marveled Johns, with a big smile dancing across the war-map wrinkles of his face.

"What come of it? How many dead?" Jonah asked.

"Half the Comanche were killed on the spot: thirty-five, including three women and two children."

"The seed of the devil will suffer the gall and wormwood!" growled Johns.

"Twenty-seven women and children—plus two old men—were captured when the shooting stopped."

"And the Rangers—what of them?"

"Seven died," Harley Pettis said, the veins in his neck bulging like a river boatman's hemp rope. He was a clip-tongued sort with a dark broom of burr-length hair sprouting from the top of his head. "Another eight was wounded."

Jonah shook his head in wonder. "Can't believe there wasn't more Rangers killed in all that gunplay."

"The deacon here might tell you it was God's own hand helping the Rangers against the devil's children," Lockhart said. "Whatever we are, Jonah—this is a flint-hard bunch you've sworn allegiance to and joined, my friend."

Hook squirmed anxiously on the stump where he sat. "So tell me—they ever get them other prisoners back?"

"Colonel Hugh McLeod of the Rangers sent one of the squaws out on a pony to tell the rest what bargain they could strike."

Jonah looked sour at that, saying, "They didn't come in, did they?"

Lockhart gazed at Hook a moment. "No. Not these Comanche. Maybe Lipans or Caddos or Tonkawas would've seen the writing on the wall. But not these Comanche."

"Them heathens gathered up and marched south to the gulf coast," Deacon Johns took up the story now. "Made their famous raid on Linnville, a tiny port village of Christians!"

"Looted all they could," Sergeant Coffee added. "Burned everything to the ground."

"But McLeod's Rangers went after 'em," Lockhart continued, staring into the fire. "Four days later they caught those Comanche moving north. At a place called Plum Creek. First and only time we know of those red sonsabitches fighting a pitched battle."

"They made a real stand-up fight of it," Wig Danville said, speaking for the first time. He had a high forehead that said something of his great even-mindedness and ready sense of humor. "Not like usual: hit and then run off when things get tight for 'em."

"Eighty warriors killed that day," Lockhart said, that slash of his mouth beneath the bushy black mustache. "Stock recovered, along with three more white captives abandoned when the fight turned bad."

"An amazing miracle from the Lord!" Johns cheered, dribbling the front of his old ticking shirt with some tobacco juice. "Most normal the Comanche kill their prisoners if they can't take 'em along with the fleeing village."

"Was the tribe whipped for a while?" Jonah asked.

"Not by a long chalk," Deacon Johns grumbled.

"Those what got away went right back to raiding the small settlements, same as always," said Coffee. "Stealing, burning, killing, and kidnapping."

"Ranger Captain John Moore caught another bunch down on the

Red Fork of the Colorado later that fall," Lockhart explained. "Caught them asleep. One hundred thirty Comanche killed, and one more white person freed from terror."

Jonah leaned back, studying the faces of these men gathered around the embers left by the evening cook fire. Nearby, two other mess fires had gone to a red glow, circled by other Rangers.

"This the way it's been ever since?" Hook asked. "They raid—you go try to even the score. They raid again—you ride out again to kill more of 'em."

Lockhart only nodded.

"They strike when and where they choose—especially that bunch of Kwahadis with the half-breed," Coffee said, scratching at his red whiskers.

"In their hearts still burns a rage against white folk for what those red fornicators suffered at the Council House all these decades gone," Johns added, his steely eyes aglow in the dying flames.

"Things got no better during the war, Jonah," Lockhart said. "Especially afterward, when we all figured that since we were part of the Union, that the goddamned federal government would now take care of the Injun problem for us."

"Instead, the carpetbaggers come in to run our government for us," Coffee snarled.

"A carpetbagger governor named Davis sat on his thumbs while the Injuns just got all the bolder too," June Callicott added.

"That scalawag disbanded the Rangers for nine ever-loving years!" Johns bellowed.

"Not until seventy-one did the army finally get the idea that there was a serious problem down here," Lockhart continued. "Back in Washington someone finally got some ears and started to believe that the Comanche were actually raiding. That spring the Sixth Cavalry was moved to Kansas, and Mackenzie's Fourth Cavalry was assigned to Texas—anticipating a bloody spring."

"Gotta give 'em credit," Coffee said. "Mackenzie kept his boys in the saddle for the better part of seventy-one and seventy-two, chasing them red bastards."

Lockhart scratched his crop of three-day whiskers, saying, "An uneasy peace came of things last year, so that scalawag Governor Davis cut back the money, meaning Ranger companies dropped from a thousand to just over three hundred men. And now this year Davis has gone and pardoned a couple of Kiowa chiefs who have the blood of white folks on their hands—why, the whole southern plains has took fire all over again."

"Less'n three hundred Rangers—with all this ground to cover?" Hook looked at Lockhart, wagging his head.

"That's why we had us another revolution here in Texas this past spring, Jonah," Lockhart said, a wry smile below that bushy black mustache. "Bunch of Rangers went in and threw that copper-backed Davis right out of office—put in a good man, Richard Coke."

"First Democrat since the war," Johns declared.

"If there's only about three hundred of us—what's the army doing now?" Jonah asked.

Pettis shrugged, his jaw muscles working like the current of a river, and said, "Mackenzie's down on the border, told to chase the Kickapoos back into Mexico."

"And all the while—up here the devil goes on the prowl!" added Deacon Johns.

Lockhart gazed steadily at Hook. "Isn't that the reason you joined us, Jonah? Instead of signing up with the army?"

"The army chases Injuns a lot. They don't always find what they go after," Jonah admitted. "I've seen enough of that with my own eyes to know it's the truth."

"The Gospel, that is!" Johns exclaimed.

"So you took the oath because you know the Rangers find what they go after," Coffee said.

Jonah gazed around the group sitting with their feet to the last glowing of the low flames. Most of the rest from the other fires had come over to join the circle. "I fought in the war. Fought Injuns in Dakota Territory too. I know good men when I see 'em. I took you fellas to be good men what didn't give up."

"That's why I decided to sign you on, Jonah Hook," Lockhart replied. "From what I've come to know of you—you're a good man who doesn't give up."

"Besides," crowed Deacon Johns, "you're a good southern boy!"

Lockhart nodded, waiting while some of the rest quietly hooted their approval. "There's a lot to be said for all that Texas gave to the Confederacy during the war, Jonah. Why, when hostilities broke out back east, even General Con Terry, an old Ranger himself from the days of the revolution, organized his own damned regiment of former Rangers and frontiersmen."

"They was called Terry's Texas Rangers," Coffee said with admiration.

"From Bull Run clear down to Appomattox—Rangers fought agin the Yankees," Johns added, just as proud.

"By Appomattox, Terry's regiment had lost nigh onto eight of every ten who had mustered into the general's bunch," Wig Danville said.

"God bless their souls," Johns said, removing his hat to place it over his heart as he gazed up into the night sky.

"God bless the Texas Rangers," Niles Coffee repeated.

Lockhart knelt by the dim glow of the embers and consulted his big turnip watch, its gold turned as red as a Spanish doubloon. Standing, he slipped it back into a vest pocket. "Time for second watch to relieve our pickets."

Hook watched a handful of men off into the darkness without a grumble, only the faint crunch of their boots fading on the flaky ground.

"You always prefer last watch, Jonah?"

He turned back to Lockhart. "Don't mind rising early—not at all."

"How about when there's snow on the ground?"

Hook smiled. "Just gets me an early start on the day."

Lockhart nodded with a grin of his own. "That's the sort of man we have in the Rangers."

"I'm waiting to find some sign, a trail—track down a village . . . anything: that's what I'm waiting on," Jonah replied.

"You travel light and lean as this bunch does—you're bound to come up with some Comanche sooner or later."

"Can't be soon enough for me."

"Remember what they say about good things coming to all those who wait. Good night, Jonah."

He watched the company commander turn and move off into the dim light toward his bedroll. "G'night, cap'n."

The next morning after the men had wolfed down a cold breakfast and loaded the company's two pack mules, Lockhart had Sergeant Coffee hold roll call as the Rangers stood by their mounts. June Callicott, a man as homely as blue sin and skinny as rack-bone crowbait, stood beside Jonah, waiting through inspection.

"Full moon was two nights back, men," the captain began, striding the front of his company. "Most of you know what that means. We can figure the savages were out in force."

"Comanche moon," Callicott whispered from the corner of his mouth.

Ever since last spring Jonah had heard the term mentioned enough: the full of the moon when the Kiowa and Comanche and Cheyenne, too, all timed their biggest raids to take advantage of the light while they plundered and pillaged at night, able to escape before many of their thefts were discovered, before any pursuers would take up their trail.

"With that sobering thought in mind," Lockhart went on, "we best be about covering our assigned territory—even more closely now than we have for the past three weeks. I'm doubling the outriders, hoping we can cross some sign between the headwaters of McClellan Creek and the far end of the Palo Duro."

"With the captain's permission?" John Corn inquired.

"What is it, Corn?"

"We gonna work down to the Palo Duro on the double, sir?"

"I figured we would," Lockhart replied.

"Thank you, Captain. Pleased of that because we all know the red bastards cross and recross this country by the same trails they use whenever they been out raiding."

"But this time there's something more afoot than just plain raiding, Private Corn," Lockhart said, coming to a stop near Corn and Hook. "This time the stories say the Comanche have gone and held a sun dance. Their first ever."

"Godless heathen fornicators!" grumbled Deacon Johns. "Praying to the sun! The wrath of God lies barely sleeping, boys—hid from the days of Abraham himself, and them red-baked sinners got the power to awake the wrath of the Almighty, they do. Hell ain't half-full yet!"

"I say let hell open up and swallow all them red bastards!" growled Harley Pettis.

When they were done, Lockhart looked back at Private Corn. "This time the bands are gathering up. That tells me the hostiles in our assigned territory aren't going to be content with raiding for a handful of horses here or a dozen cows there."

"What do you figure is on the wind, Captain?" Jonah asked.

"I think what we have staring us in the eye is out-and-out war, Private Hook," Lockhart answered. "Nothing less than a full-scale uprising."

35

July 1874

"RIDER COMING IN, Captain!"

Up ahead of Jonah Hook one of the Rangers pointed into the distance. North and east, in the general direction Lamar Lockhart had been pushing them for the past three days. It was a land of steep-side arroyos sloping down in garlands of red and yellow rimrock, a country of hard-running creeks come spring's runoff dance, bottomless canyons, scrub pine and cedar stands on every knobby sandstone outcrop, all scratched up like turkey tracks with shallow, shadowy gulches. Out here in all this immensity, Jonah figured the space inside a man seemed a lot less crowded.

Into the brutal light of that summer afternoon more of them were pointing now, murmuring among themselves as Lockhart threw up an arm and ordered a halt.

"Whoever he is, that man's tacked his poor beast into a lather," Deacon Johns said. He sat the saddle beside Jonah in their column of twos, the short gray whiskers that ran around the edges of his gaunt jaws bristled, reminding Hook of the raised hackles on an angry dog's neck.

The outriders on the point escorted in the civilian. He looked to be a dour, flavorless man, as though the high plains sun had gone and boiled all the good juices right out of him. His eyes ran over the Rangers quickly as he raked a hand across his mouth and pulled up the leather-wrapped canteen lashed to his saddle horn when he came to a stop in front of Lockhart.

"You fellas scouting for the army?" the newcomer asked before he even brought the canteen to his dry lips.

Jonah had the man figured for a buffalo hunter, what with his saddle rig, that big-bore Sharps rifle resting across the pommel, and the blood-crusted, sweat-stained clothes the rider wore. Especially from that pale-eyed, loafer-wolf look about him as he eyed the captain.

"Texas Rangers," Lockhart replied. "Company C. I'm Captain Lockhart. What's your name?"

He pulled the canteen away from his glistening lips, still as gray-gilled as alkali dust. "Schmalsle. William, Captain. Most call me Billy."

"Why the hurry?"

"Big hurraw of red bastards hit Adobe Walls a few days back."

"A few days?"

"Maybe a week at most."

"What Injuns?" Coffee asked.

Schmalsle shrugged, a grin coming easily to his face, making it crinkle into a pleasant smile. "Well, now—I don't think any of them hunters up there at that meadow stopped to ask questions."

"Comanche?" Lockhart inquired as Coffee started to grumble.

"Didn't mean no offense, mister," Schmalsle apologized to Coffee, then turned back to Lockhart. "Yep. Them and some Kiowa. Likely some Cheyenne too."

"You were there?"

"No. Rode in from my hunting camp couple days after they attacked the meadow."

"How many were there?" Johns asked now, easing his horse up with the others, who had the newcomer nearly surrounded, starved for news the way they all were.

"Some figure there was eight hundred. Others claim as many as a thousand or more."

Behind Jonah one of the Rangers whistled low in exclamation.

"A goddamned thousand of the heathen niggers!" Johns said, clapping his dusty, trail-worn gloves together in a joyous, prayerful attitude, chin tilted heavenward. "Dear Lord, would I love to set the table for those sinners. Just look the other way if ever I get these hands of mine on that saint-forsaken hell chief Quanah Parker!"

"You might get the chance, Deacon," Lockhart said with that wry grin of his beneath the bushy mustache, then turned back to the civilian. "Where away are you bound?"

"Me and a few other boys each riding a circuit to warn other hunters that the devils are up to no good."

"They've let out the wolf now and are bound to howl for a long time," growled Niles Coffee.

"How many white men killed?"

"Only one hunter. Two teamsters got et up on the first attack, though. S'pose that makes three all count."

"So how many of the red bastards did you make good Injuns?" Johns demanded before spitting a brown stream into the dust.

"Fifteen maybe. All the bodies what was left when the Injuns pulled out. Seems the rest couldn't ride in any closer and fetch out them bodies 'cause of the big guns. So we don't really know how many was killed and hauled off to be buried."

"Pagan ceremonies, no doubt!" Johns added. "Dear Lord, raise your hand and smite these the unholy."

Lockhart took his hat off and wiped his brow with a single finger, the scar of that hatband lying like a wide strip of new skin along his forehead. "You said there are more of you dispatched to spread the word, Mr. Schmalsle?"

The man nodded. "Less'n you need me, I best be making my swing round toward the divide above the Washita. Head on into Camp Supply and let the army know about the attack."

"They'll know already," Jonah said quietly.

"How's that?" Deacon Johns asked, swabbing a dribble of juice squeezed into a deep cleft at the corner of his mouth with a thumb.

Lockhart turned in the saddle too. The rest had all turned to hear what Hook had to say.

"The Injuns up there at Camp Supply—they'll know before this fella ever gets there," Jonah explained. "Word always travels fast on the moccasin telegraph."

Lockhart nodded with approval, then turned back to Schmalsle. "How far out are you from Adobe Walls?"

"The bunch of us rode out last night soon as it growed dark. I been pushing ever since, without a stop. Good God but did you boys give me the jump, till I could see you was riding in twos."

"Very well, Mr. Schmalsle. We appreciate your news."

He peered at the captain and then swiped his chin with the sweaty bandanna he had looped loosely around his neck. "You figuring to head in to Adobe Walls yourself with this bunch?"

Lockhart shook his head. "No. We've got some territory to cover and cover fast. If there are truly a thousand warriors roaming this country, then we damned well ought to run across at least one fresh backtrail we can follow that will take us right to one of their villages. We find that village— Company C of the Frontier Battalion will do more damage to the Comanche than fifty buffalo hunters could do."

"Twenty-eight, Cap'n," Schmalsle corrected.

Lockhart tipped his head slightly, asking, "How's that?"

"There was only twenty-eight men there at Adobe Walls," Schmalsle said a bit defensively. "Twenty-eight agin them thousand red sons-abitches."

"Twenty-eight against a thousand," Lockhart repeated with respect, a light ignited behind his dark eyes. "Sounds like the sort of odds tailor-made for a company of Texas Rangers."

It had been the full of the Moon of Fat Horses when the Kwahadi struck the hide hunters' earth-lodge settlement.

On the way there from the great sun dance, Tall One had counted ten-times-ten on eight of his fingers when he gave up counting any more of the horsemen.

And began thinking on little else but the coming fight. They ultimately came to that place where they would kill white men.

He had asked to go along as one of the seven young scouts who accompanied the old Shahiyena chief White Wolf—those seven to find the exact location of the meadow where stood the white hunters' earth lodges. The gray-eyed Kwahadi chief had agreed, but held back the young brother. Antelope had been angry enough to spit bees, but was told that soon enough he too would see the hide men's settlement, and close up. Very soon they would all get to see the looks on the buffalo hunters' faces as these warriors rode among them, smashing clubs into their faces, pummeling their heads to crimson jelly.

With the graying of the sky at dawn, they would make that meadow reek with blood.

The scouts located the four earth lodges. Some ponies and the white man's slow and lumbering spotted buffalo used to pull his high-walled wagons.

"How many *tai-bos*?" asked the gray-eyed war chief.

The leader of the scouting party held up five fingers, then struck his other arm six times.

"Three-times-ten. And they will all be asleep. With their bullets useless and their guns like limp manhood unable to answer our challenge!" the chief had roared. Then he laughed loud, the hundreds laughing with him.

It was not the first time Tall One and Antelope had made their toilet together, helping one another paint themselves for battle, stringing an owl or turkey feather in their hair, hopeful that the coming battle would earn Antelope his first eagle coup. Every man—Comanche, Kiowa, and Shahiyena—prepared himself for this great victory, smearing on his bullet-proof medicine before a fragment of a mirror stolen from a settler's soddy. Black braids were loosened, then retied with trade cloth or animal skins. Gleaming conchos traded off the comancheros were again polished and woven into scalp locks, lashed to clothing. A nervous tension ran through that camp waiting for the order to move downstream toward the meadow. War ponies were given attention: a sprinkling of puffball dust was rubbed on an animal's muzzle, or red mud from the creekbank was smeared around a pony's nostrils to give it extra wind for the coming fight, bear grease streaked up and down each of the four long legs to give the pony speed for what would be required of it in the coming hours.

It was then that the war chief instructed them all to put their saddles and extra baggage in the trees. The branches hung heavy with all that they would not carry into battle. Up there, it was explained to Tall One, badgers and skunks and other scavengers could not drag off their belongings before the warriors returned, victorious in battle.

For but a moment Tall One and Antelope caught a glimpse of Isatai, always escorted by those who wished to be seen in the company of the powerful young shaman as he strutted through camp on foot, leading his pony. He did so completely naked except for a special pair of yellow-painted moccasins, his skin carefully covered with yellow earth-paint. His pony had been smeared a dull yellow as well. In his hair the medicine man stuffed sprigs of gray sage.

"I need nothing—no clothing to stop the white man's bullets!" he harangued them. "My medicine will turn the bullets to water!"

When darkness came to court the short summer night, the gray-eyed war chief gave the order for the warriors to move out without mounting their ponies. They walked for a long time until reaching the edge of the valley where stood the white man's earth lodges. Here they were told to sleep with the reins in their hands until it was time to attack.

Tall One did not sleep. How could he—come this greatest of all his days as a Kwahadi warrior! How could any man sleep?

When the command came to mount the attack, the tall war chief rode his gray horse before the hundreds, reminding these hot-blooded young men they must remain in a solid, unbroken line until he gave his order to charge.

"We walk slow at first," he told them. "When the earth lodges come into view—then I will order the charge."

In the murky, graying light of dawn-coming, Tall One barely made out the dark shadows of the four buildings where the *tai-bos* were sleeping. It was then the war chief had ordered the warriors spread for the coming charge. Quietly the hundreds shuffled to the right and left, forming an immense but compact phalanx. Hundreds of ponies grew restless. Warriors murmured their war songs. The air hummed with death-coming. Like the swinging of a club so heavy, it could not be slowed nor stopped.

His heart had pounded in his throat, threatening to choke Tall One as he waited those last moments until the war chief had finally screeched his call for the charge.

From the hundreds of throats erupted war cries that rumbled across the river valley, causing a thousand birds to take wing from the nearby trees. In that instant thousands of hooves hammered the dry, flaky earth as the entire line burst into ragged motion. The noise of the charge fell deafening on Tall One's ears. Never before had he heard anything like this: the hammering of the hooves like a hailstorm on a buffalo-hide lodge; the keening voices like the crying of a deadly wind.

Around him several of the horsemen went down as their ponies stumbled across a prairie-dog town. Horses cried out with the pain of broken legs, riders screeching as the rest careened over them in the new light shredded with streamers of gray dust.

Still the hundreds rode down on the earth lodges, gathering speed as they brought terror and death for the *tai-bos*.

But they had failed. Isatai's prophecies had simply not come true: the white men were not asleep in their beds; the bullets from their big buffalo-killing guns did not turn to water; the shaman's medicine did not protect warriors from dying at the hands of the *tai-bos* who hid inside their earth lodges through that long morning as the sun rose across the meadow where the blood of brave horsemen and war ponies stained the thirsty ground.

To the voices of the many Tall One added his own, crying out in rage as the first charge was turned back. Crying out in frustration at the failure of the famous Comanche wheel that flew in a fury around the earth lodges, hoping to grind down the enemy as it had for so many raiding seasons. Around and around they had circled in a tight red noose of screaming warriors, while the white man knocked horsemen from the backs of their ponies, even spilling many of the animals into the dusty meadow.

"Isatai lied to us!" shouted Antelope as he reined up beside Tall One at the far edge of the meadow where more and more of the warriors milled about, confused, frightened, and ultimately sucking on their deepest rage. Leaving their ponies and the Comanche wheel behind, more and more warriors chose to sprint forward on foot and fight behind the *tai-bos'* wagons and the tall stacks the hide hunters had made of their dried buffalo hides.

There was a moment when it seemed the gray-eyed war chief was the only one of them still mounted. Alone he charged one of the earth lodges. But his pony too was thrown, shot by the powerful medicine of those big buffalo guns. Their bravest—this war chief—made to crawl for his life, forced to seek cover behind a stack of buffalo hides, slaughtered by the white man.

As the sun climbed ever higher toward its summer zenith, the battle became a long-distance waiting game. Out in the meadow after they had killed all the *tai-bos'* horses and mules, the warriors took to sniping at the windows and doors while Tall One listened to the white men yell to one another, back and forth from one earth lodge to another. Behind that wide stack of hides, the young warrior sat, listening to the sounds those strange words made in his ears, feeling the tug of something uncomfortable in his heart as more and more of the foreign tongue made all the more sense.

Over and over he wished it did not. Hoping he could shut out what became more and more familiar—shut out what he wished was not a language he remembered. His eyes smarting, Tall One had grown angry with himself for crying. So instead he made himself angry at the *tai-bos* for yelling loud enough that he could hear them use the words spoken by his father and mother, by his sister.

It had been so long since he had thought of her—remembering now the curve of her sunburned cheeks, the pretty nose beneath the shade of that bonnet brim as they worked up the weeds in the field.

Tall One gazed down at the soil where he knelt, the ground gone dry and thirsty. He scooped up a handful, allowing it to run through his fingers as the big bullets sang through the super-heated summer air of that meadow. And he remembered a time he had planted row upon row of seed in ground rich and dark, soil made fertile with the embrace of sun and the blessing of rain, where the old mules dragged the single-shovel plow behind them, turning the soil over in black, steamy curls where little Zeke would trundle behind, struggling beneath the huge shoulder bag filled with seed.

Zeke. He hadn't remembered his brother's name in . . . many seasons. And now these *tai-bos* had brought it all welling to the surface again. Try as he might to squeeze them out, their voices still echoed in his ears. Not the hide hunters' shouts of encouragement to one another. No, what tormented Tall One then were the voices of those who had loved him, the voices of those he had loved.

Near the end of that terrible, bloody day, he had looked at the sun falling to the west, sensing in the old core of him that this time of the year was well past the season for planting. Instead of crops, here in this meadow all that had been sown was blood and terror and death. What else could the Kwahadi now reap but more blood and terror and death?

That morning as the sky had lightened in the east, the hundreds of horsemen had been filled with great heart to overrun this place of the *tai-bo* hide men. But now as that sun sank in despair, the hundreds had found the white hunters awake and not to be clubbed in their sleep, found the enemy's big guns shooting far and accurately, discovered the white men tenaciously clinging to the shadows of their earth-walled burrows. Every bit of fight had seeped out of the warriors.

Like translucent milk oozing from the old sow's teats as one of her piglets came loose, the fight had gone out of these hundreds. Like that milk gone bad, their sun-dance war medicine had gone sour in the mouths of the Kwahadi.

By sundown Lone Wolf rode away with the Kiowa. No man tried to stop them.

That next morning Tall One awoke in the gray stillness to see the Shahiyena of Medicine Water and Rock Forehead and the rest mounting up. They said they were going to ride north, raid settlements where there were no *tai-bo* hide hunters with their far-shooting guns.

Eventually the moon shrank from its former grandeur. The same way the hope that Tall One had once recognized on the face of the gray-eyed war chief faded in those days after the fight at the earth lodges. What man would not feel some despair, having watched so many warriors hurl themselves against the might of the buffalo hunters' guns, and still call himself a man who cared for his people?

In those first days of frustration and rage as the war chief reluctantly turned his back on the meadow and led his horsemen away from that place of blood and defeat, there had been much angry talk, for most had yet to sort through the confusion borne of loss of hope.

Some believed their sin had been to hold Isatai's sun dance.

"Other tribes hold their annual sun-gazing dances—but the Comanche have never celebrated in that fashion," they said.

"Yes! We must never again follow the ways of the Shahiyena or the Kiowa. We must put our feet only on the path walked by the ancient ones."

Once again the gray-eyed war chief and the headmen decided that The People were to avoid the white man just as they had attempted to do for far back in the generations. Only when it proved wise for the young men to attack outlying settlements to reap horses and scalps and plunder would the old men approve of such contact with the *tai-bos*. Yet those leaders grappled with the new reality that these days every raid brought out the yellow-leg soldiers who crossed and recrossed the Llano Estacado, hunting for the Kwahadi. And instead of the warriors who always disappeared onto the Staked Plain like breathsmoke gone in a winter gale, the Tonkawa trackers and yellow leg soldiers preferred to attack the villages of the women and children and old ones.

Already Tall One knew that whenever the soldiers went in search of those villages, they always found what they were looking for.

36

Day after endless day Company C probed deeper, rode longer, yet came up with empty hands. Tides of heat and dust and distant thunderstorms brought one day after the next washing over them, taking each day away in the same order. Summer waned and grew weary, one of the hottest any man on these plains could remember. Steamy nights swirled overhead with a million old stars flecked behind gray rain-heads, and this land once more grew old before its time. These final days of August came up clear and green-skied and hotter than the last, then imperceptibly the sun's path grew shorter, a man unable to notice until it was too late and autumn was upon him.

Closing fast with the odor of things dying, turning, changing—never to be the same again.

Come this cooling of the nights, come this season of the yellow leaf, Jonah was told by the others. That's what they said the Comanche called autumn.

All he knew was that soon enough another winter would be closing in, and once more he had all too little to show for the miles crossed since the first green break of spring when he had decided to ride with Lamar Lockhart's company of poorly paid Texas Rangers.

From time to time they circled back to re-provision, backtracking east to Camp Supply, using vouchers to draw on the treasury of the great State of Texas. It was there these men caught up on the momentous news following the bloodletting at Adobe Walls. The southern plains were indeed on fire—and from the sounds of it, the government was finally determined to put an end to Indian problems down here once and for all. William Tecumseh Sherman's War Department had ordered no less than five columns into the field, all to converge on the Staked Plain, home of the holdouts: the Kwahadi Comanche.

Trouble was, right in the middle of it all lay the territory assigned Major John B. Jones's Frontier Battalion of Texas Rangers. And at the heart of that was a piece of ground marked out for patrol by Captain Lamar Lockhart's company of horsemen. Them, and some of the most skillful nomadic red raiders of the Llano Estacado.

Back in late August when Company C rode in to Camp Supply, they learned that Colonel John W. Davidson's four companies of brunettes had already cut the deck. Those buffalo soldiers had forced the issue—scattering some of the fiercer bands, driving others back to their agencies. Seemed the government had demanded a roll to be made of all the peaceful bands on the reservations. Those not answering the roll call were deemed clearly hostile and would be hunted down, then driven back to their agency if possible.

"If that ain't possible," Niles Coffee was explaining what had been told him by friends he knew among Camp Supply's soldiers, "then the army's got orders to exterminate 'em."

"Praise God!" Deacon Johns wailed. "Them savages are purely onhuman. Separate the wheat from the chaff, sayeth the Lord."

"Trouble is," Lamar Lockhart cautioned, "all those warrior bands that didn't answer the roll at Fort Sill, or over at Anadarko and up at Darlington—they've all gone off and scurried west toward the headwaters of the Red River, the Brazos—who the hell knows how far they'll scatter now."

"The Kwahadi . . . they're scattering?" Jonah asked anxiously.

"Chances are that's what they're doing—and why we haven't found a sign one of all that bunch that went and hit the buffalo hunters at Adobe Walls," Coffee answered.

"You think we'll find any Comanche?" Jonah inquired, his cheeks growing hot in angry frustration. "Or we gonna keep riding back and forth till we're old men?"

Lockhart turned to Hook. "You took an oath when you joined up, Jonah Hook."

"I don't give a goddamn about Texas!"

"No," Lockhart replied all too quietly as the company of men moved close. "Maybe you don't. But the rest of these men do. So I want you to think of one thing before you decide on booking in and giving up on this company's duty. Think about the fact that of all these men here—I don't know a one of them who positively knows they have a member of their family among the Comanche."

Jonah's eyes moved slowly across the more than two dozen men standing quietly nearby, every last one of them watching him with intense interest. "I don't understand what you mean, Cap'n."

"Jonah—it's as simple as this: these men ride out with me into the unknown every morning for less than a dollar a day, hoping to find the scattered hostile villages, praying they'll find white captives in those villages we do run onto. But not a one of these brave men has kin among the Kwahadi. But you do, Jonah Hook. By damned, you do."

He felt the sting of the words slap him with the force of a flat hand across his jaw.

Lockhart stepped closer, his eyes gone as black as gun bores. "Jonah, I don't know a bunch of men you could ride with who could pray any harder than this outfit has that it will be them that finds your boys for you."

The colicky harshness, the utter truth of the captain's words made Hook tremble inwardly. "I . . . I'm sorry, Cap'n Lockhart." He snorted back some of his unrequited anger. "I'm riding with you. Riding with all of you."

"Give us time, Jonah," Niles Coffee said, "time and a little luck— we'll find 'em for you. By God—we're bound to find 'em."

That night, their last at Camp Supply for some time to come, Jonah lay awake for the longest time as the rest of them snored. Unable to sleep, he could not tear his mind loose from what war machinery the soldiers told Coffee was already in motion. If by some kind of luck his two boys were still alive and still with the hostile Kwahadi of Quanah Parker out there on the Staked Plain, there now existed the very real possibility that they would soon be in the very path of that hungry war machine.

Two small boys . . .

But he had stopped, forcing himself to remember they were no longer little. Grown to young men already. Old enough to be . . . soldiers themselves.

How he had prayed for sleep to come soothe him as his fevered mind dwelt on nothing else but those five columns that would converge on the Llano Estacado to effect the final cleanup of the southern plains before winter set in. Major William R. Price was said to be marching east along the Canadian River out of Fort Union in New Mexico with eight companies of the Eighth Cavalry to effect a junction with Colonel Nelson Miles.

Lieutenant Colonel George P. Buell, leading four troops of the Ninth U.S. Negro Cavalry and two troops from the Tenth, along with two companies of the Eleventh Infantry and thirty scouts, was moving northwest across the Brazos from Fort Griffin, Texas.

Lieutenant Colonel John W. "Black Jack" Davidson was leading six troops of his Tenth U.S. Negro Cavalry, three companies of the Eleventh Infantry, and forty-four scouts west from Fort Sill.

On south of the austere caprock of the Staked Plain, Colonel Ranald S. Mackenzie was probing north out of Fort Concho at the head of his column comprising the largest prong of the attack: eight companies of his battle-tough Fourth Cavalry, four more of the famous buffalo soldiers from the Tenth Cavalry, one company from the Eleventh Infantry, in addition to some thirty scouts.

Then there was Colonel Nelson A. Miles himself, who was marching southwest at the van of eight troops of the Sixth Cavalry, four companies of the colonel's own Fifth Infantry, along with one Parrot ten-pounder and two Gatling guns.

It boggled Jonah's mind to think that those five columns made for more than three thousand soldiers converging on the ancient buffalo ground of the Kiowa and Comanche. The war those hostiles had started with the white man would soon be over, every man was saying. Only a matter of weeks now. Then he thought of a bitch in heat, and all the town dogs yammering around her, tails up and whipping with great excitement. That female finally left with nowhere to run—only to turn and snap back at the frenzied pack.

Sure enough, the army was going to go out and give those red heathens a bellyful of war. Whip the lords of the southern plains back to their reservations. That, or wipe them off the earth.

At sunrise the next morning, Lockhart turned their noses west again for another swing across the North Fork of the Red River. With this second summer of horrid drought, no man could say he relished the thought of more miles and saddle galls, riding all day through the stifling dust and searing heat to find nothing more than a parched pucker of ground where they had expected to find a water hole to slake the thirst of their animals. No water, and only stunted, sun-parched grass to offer those lathered horses.

With a vengeance summer had gripped the plains in its dry and lifeless paw, refusing to release the land. Until the second week of September, when the skies clouded, frothed, then boiled over, drenching the thirsty killing ground.

But with the rains came a whole new set of problems. Now the horses had trouble pulling each hoof out of the thick red gumbo that sucked at man and beast alike. Day and night the thunder rolled, rattling like dice bones in a horn cup. Storms that gave the men little relief, and no time for any of them to dry out. They slept wet and cold, if they slept at all. They rode soaked to the skin, shivering clear to the marrow, teeth chattering as the first winds of autumn hissed out of the west with a wiry whine, hurrying before them those whispered hints of winter.

Somewhere beneath this same low sky, he repeatedly told himself, his two boys slept and ate. And rode, prisoners of the Kwahadi. Just out of reach. Somewhere out there in all this tangle of creeks and streams and river systems, this land haunted by the holdout Comanche. He had to remind himself that they walked beneath this same sky. Under this same unforgiving sky.

Jonah grew thinner still. Hard for a man to keep his appetite about him when there was little in the way of cooked food to eat. Few fires allowed, by order of Captain Lockhart. So instead Jonah fed himself on his renewed hopes. Those, and his fervent prayers.

Beneath that unforgiving sky, filled horizon to horizon with slate-colored sheets of bone-numbing rain, Jonah Hook prayed for his boys harder than he had in the six years since he last left Fort Laramie behind him.

Prayed he would find them both before the army cornered Quanah Parker.

This season of the year the air freshened, cooled quickly, after the sun went down. It felt good on Tall One's face as he and the others loped toward the east, driving their great pony herd before them. They hoped to lure away the yellow-legs who rode with Three-Finger Kinzie, draw the pony soldiers away from the village as it marched to the north.

"The tracks of our herd will serve as the bait," explained the gray-eyed war chief. "Kinzie cannot resist the chance to follow so wide a trail."

In the past five days the soldiers had drawn ever closer to the village that hurried to the canyon where they would join Lone Wolf's Kiowa in safety until Kinzie passed on by. But they needed meat to feed their people. Of late too many days had passed without time taken to hunt. And if they were to wait out the soldiers at the bottom of the dark canyon, then the Kwahadi desperately needed meat. Reluctantly the war chief had allowed a small band of hunters to go in search of the buffalo said to be just south of the canyon.

He hoped this wide, scoured trail of the pony herd would be enough to draw the army scouts from discovering the trail of their meat hunters. Drawing so close to the canyon where his people would hide, the war chief had come up with what all the Kwahadi prayed would be a successful diversion.

Many of the warriors had even tied bundles of lodgepoles to some of the herd ponies, the better to scratch the ground in shallow furrows, to fool the Tonkawa trackers into thinking this was indeed the trail of a great village fleeing to the east, back to the reservation.

Surely, the lure of so fresh a trail could not be denied by the pony soldiers and their scouts.

But if their diversion failed, Kinzie's Tonkawa would bring the yellow-legs right to the canyon, once more to the very doorstep of the Kwahadi.

So to confuse the soldiers all the more, to make Kinzie think the Comanche warriors were acting as a rear guard to their fleeing village, to draw Kinzie's scouts off the scent of the chase, the Kwahadi war chief ordered a large-scale night raid on the yellow-leg camp.

Hours after sunset, when the sky had darkened from rose to twilight's deep hues, more than 250 horsemen lashed their ponies in among Three-Finger Kinzie's herd. Only to find the soldiers ready for them.

In the midst of the confusion, yelling, and gunfire, the war chief rallied his warriors. If the soldiers would not scatter with surprise, then the Kwahadi would fall back on what always worked: the grinding of the Comanche wheel. Around and around Tall One and Antelope galloped with the rest, firing into the herd, working in and out, looking for a weak

Terry C. Johnston

spot in the soldier lines where they could drive the frightened soldier horses. From time to time, Tall One barely heard Antelope's familiar war song against the rattle of gunfire, the rumble of hammering hooves, and the shouts of men at battle.

Then as quickly as he had come and found the soldiers prepared for their attack, the war chief called off his warriors. They drew back and sniped here and there on the perimeter of the yellow-leg camp throughout the rest of that cold night. Just before dawn, when the soldiers finally gathered up the courage to make their own counterattack, the gray-eyed one ordered his warriors back atop their ponies, telling them to withdraw as he led them in a circle to the east, riding away into the bright, rosy-gold autumnal sunrise, their backs to a falling, overturned sliver of a moon—a route determined all the better to confirm for the soldiers and their Tonkawa trackers that the village lay to the east. Only after that great war party had covered many hours and that many more miles did the gray-eyed one finally rein about to the north. Back toward the deep canyon where their families waited.

Every man of them prayed their buffalo hunters had been successful. Every man of them prayed for the success of their costly ruse.

Riding with the ten chosen to stay behind atop the ridges, where they would keep an eye on the yellow-legs, Tall One watched Kinzie march his soldier column to the northeast, along the outbound trail they had made with their pony herd.

"Our plan is working!" one said as the soldiers plodded below them.

"We can go tell the others," agreed another.

"Shouldn't we follow the yellow-legs a while longer?" asked Tall One of the warrior who led the scouting party.

"I remember you as a boy, Tall One," Dives Backward chided. "You always refused to listen to the rest of us. Always wanted to go your own way."

Standing laughed. "He didn't learn his lesson then. And it seems he still hasn't learned!"

"How long are you going to think like a white man?" demanded Tortoise Shell.

The burn of embarrassment fired Tall One's face. "I only want to be sure. To know that the yellow-legs are really going to march on to the east, away from our village."

"You have eyes, Tall One!" Dives Backward roared. "Look!"

He felt their eyes on the back of his shoulders, burning holes in his flesh with their disapproval. He wanted to belong to them more than just about anything, wanted their approval. What hurt him most at that moment was that he still hungered to belong just as he had when he had first come to the Kwahadi. Thirsted for their approval like a man many days in the desert. To belong, he would now shove aside his gnawing suspicion.

"Let us . . . let's go tell our war chief his plan has worked," Tall One eventually said, turning away from watching the soldier column, back to the smirking faces of the others.

"For all their looking, those stupid Tonkawa haven't come up with a feather, not one Kwahadi pony, much less a single lodge," Tortoise Shell said. "We give them tracks to follow, to follow clear to the end of yesterday! As for what they will think, let them think we have disappeared into the air."

"Come," Standing said. "We'll ride back to the canyon, where the earth can swallow us whole!"

Dives Backward laughed, his head thrown back. "To the canyon, where the white man's trackers will never find us!"

37

T HIS GREAT CREVASSE in the austere tabletop prairie of the Llano Estacado was nothing less than one of the wonders of the Grandfather's hand. Old men attempted to explain how the canyon had grown so deep, yet remained so fertile, lush with many varieties of trees and plant life, along with the rich grasses that fed their great pony herd.

"Grandfather dragged his fingernail along the face of the ground," said the old ones. "He carved this place of safety out for The People. Here: away from the eyes of the Tonkawa, away from the guns of the pony soldiers."

That morning Tall One lay wrapped in the furry warmth of his buffalo robe, listening to the silence in the camp. Above him the smoke hole of Bridge's lodge showed that sunrise was not long in coming. Here he lay a thousand feet below the surface of the prairie, where already the sun would be warming the earth. But this far down the shadows hung deep, the cold persisted, and a young man's thoughts turned on autumn.

It was a time he remembered in some visceral way, more than any clear and distinct memories. More some beads of recollections turning on sensations and smells, or the feel of the cool air against his skin as he pushed aside the buffalo robe and pulled on his shirt, breechclout, and leggings. When his moccasins were tied, Tall One glanced at Bridge, saw that the man's eyes were open, smiling at his adopted son.

With a smile of his own for the aging warrior, Tall One turned and ducked from the lodge as silent as a sliver of night itself.

He drank deep of the morning coolness, sensing its tang deep in his lungs. It was there the memories resided. Not so much his lungs, but deep, deeper still within him where his blood coursed and his heart pounded in anticipation of this autumn morning.

What beauty this place held for those who came here season after season, he thought. Many times before the Kwahadi had traveled to this canyon—what the Comanche called the "Place of the Chinaberry Trees"—a sanctuary of safety from the soldiers, a place of shelter from the battering of winter blizzards. This season the Shahiyena of Stone Calf, the Kiowa of Lone Wolf and Mamanti and Poor Buffalo, had come to join them, off the reservation and away from the many soldier columns rumored to be out and moving this season before the coming of winter. Their camps lay upstream where their herds grazed. This village of the Kwahadi was the last of the five circles.

Above him the narrow walls rose abruptly toward the prairie beyond, where the rose tinted gold of dawn's light illuminated a narrow strip of deep azure sky strung raggedly with dispersing clouds, there between the reds and ochers, pinks and buff-creams that striated the canyon in brilliant layers. Here at the bottom lay the lush greens in many hues: stands of cedar and cottonwood, the mesquite and willow that all drank their fill from the Prairie Dog Town Fork of the Red River.

The prospect of a day filled with sun excited Tall One. There had been too many long, endless days of rain and mud, of numbing cold and chill winds as they lured the soldiers away, feinted, attacked, then lured the soldiers some more. The thought of having the sun caress his skin made the young man feel more alive than he had in a long time.

Overhead the world must surely be alive already. Down here the day still awaited its awakening. Only the most industrious would be up, he thought, his nostrils pricked with the pungent, earthy fragrance of cedar smoke. In among the deep green and the bright yellows of the changing cottonwood leaves, wisps of gray hung in tattered streamers. The smoke reminded him of breakfast, and that in turn caused his stomach to growl.

The rumble sent from deep within him reminded Tall One of cold autumn mornings like this one, rising in the darkness with the others, quickly pulling on his clothing as he had done, his nose filled with the smells of a mother's labors over her stove and skillets. Sweet wood smoke and slices of sugar-cured ham. Hominy at the boil and the coffeepot steaming. He had learned to drink coffee early as a child. A good warmth to carry in one's belly on those days the whole family tramped off to the fields before sunrise, together.

"Bring in the crops," he said aloud. Startled that he had said it in English.

Autumn—a time he remembered working his young muscles alongside the others from those moments before dawn until every last sliver of light had been pushed from the evening sky, then eating his supper although he was half-asleep. Stumbling off to bed where his weary, joyous muscles sang in praise of a long night's rest before they would get up and do it all over again. Day after long autumn day, until the crops were in and his father would once more turn the ground in anticipation of winter.

One final turn, the man had taught them. The better to soak up what moisture winter's snows brought them.

He recalled how the ground would often steam, the warm undersoil resurrected into the cool air of a chill autumn morning much like this one. Just the way the belly of a slain buffalo would steam into the frosty air of a winter morning as the men and women set about butchering their kill.

It was then that Tall One remembered with his own seeing the great, incomprehensible litter of rotting carcasses that stretched mile after endless mile across the rolling prairie now far above him. Those great piles of bones and skulls where gathered the carrion eaters always brought a great pain to him—this dying of something without its chance to regenerate. Up there on the buffalo ground, the grasshoppers and locusts and other winged ones had descended from the pale autumn skies to seize dominion over the tall, withered grasses. Fewer of the shaggy beasts now to graze upon that land.

Those white hide men. Come to take without returning something in the great cycle of life.

His first father had been a white man. Yet for a reason he could not name, Tall One sensed that the man in some unspoken way understood that mystical circle of life. If for no other reason than his father always turned the soil, Tall One believed that his first father did indeed understand that he must return something back to the soil for what he had taken from it. So it was the man had turned over the warm, fertile ground, and with it turned under the stalks and roots, the stems and leaves, all of it to nourish once more the dark loam as it lay under the white breast of winter, where it would once more await the call of spring's awakening.

At the edge of the creek he knelt, bent forward, and leaned far out over the water by supporting himself on his elbows. There he drank of the cold water, then drew back and wiped his mouth. Staring down at his rippling reflection. Something about it—the eyes, maybe the nose. Tall One gathered his long hair in one hand and pulled it behind his neck. Staring, studying that reflection intently. Uncanny, how it made him think of his father.

No, his first father.

Sensing now the teasing recollection, the dim memory of so many people telling a boy how much he favored his pa.

Memories were dim, had for the most part remained very dim over the years—until he really studied his reflection in the smooth surface of that stream. Would now the man have hair touched with the iron of many winters? Or like his second father—Bridge—would his first father have only a touch of gray at the temples?

And how many wrinkles would he have? Would the seams carve themselves deeply into his face, like the faces of the old ones in this camp in the canyon?

What of his hands—those hands that had brought calves and piglets and foals into the world, those hands that had struck out as he corrected his children, hands that had also caressed his sons and daughter with his crude, unsteady love. Would those hands now be gnarled and deformed as he had seen the hands of the old warriors become? Or would they still be strong and sure, unshaken as he took the reins of a team and moved them toward the field in need of planting?

Hands that would remain forever young with the elixir of a young boy's dream.

Try as he might, even staring down at this wavering reflection in the cold stream, Tall One could not make himself believe this was a true picture of his father. The man would surely be much, much older now. After all, Tall One was himself.

Suddenly a cautious part of him reminded Tall One that it likely did not matter. Something mocked him—saying the man who had been his first father no longer existed. He had not come home from that war he marched off to fight, leaving his family behind. And even if in the realm of slim possibilities that man did survive the war . . . in the end his first father had simply ceased to exist.

No more did that life on that farm mean anything to him. It was something too remote, too foreign, too long ago to matter anymore. And those dimly focused people from his memories, the people who had shared his long-ago days and nights, the fights and the loving, the laughter and the tears—they too had simply ceased to exist in this new world of the Antelope People. That is, every one of those memory people except his brother, Antelope.

Antelope had always been, and always would be, Tall One's brother.

It was that single handhold gripping something lasting and eternal that allowed Tall One to feel secure.

Over the seasons of wandering from camp to camp, from stream to stream, hunting and raiding, sleeping and eating in an endless cycle of nomadic wanderings, the boy had eventually grown accustomed to this life of change. Still, coming to accept it was nowhere like feeling secure. The way he had sensed a rock-steady security of day after day, season after season on that farm his family carved out of a valley so far, far away now. Secure in knowing what was expected of him by those he loved. Secure in knowing what to expect out of the turning of the seasons shared with those who loved him.

As much as the boy in him had reveled in the life of these nomads, the young man in him came to yearn every bit as much for something solid and lasting. To count on the rains of spring and the sun in summer, the chill of autumn's harvest and the season of rest given a farmer come winter's short days. If only . . .

It could not be! His life had changed irrevocably. The silly chores of a white man scratching at the earth no longer made any real sense to him. He was a warrior now—

Angrily Tall One plunged his hand into the cold stream; all the way to the muddy bottom he stirred savagely, his fury bringing the once-placid surface to a froth. Doing so, he churned the reflection as quickly as he dispatched all those memories recalled over all those seasons.

He would not allow himself to miss the life he had lived back then. For he never would live it again—

Turning at the distant sound, Tall One felt the sense of being out of place. If not he, then some thing.

A sound sullying the stillness of this morning. Low, rumbling, rolling downstream between the high canyon walls. Perhaps a warrior's gun. Hunting—

The next crack in the pristine morning raised the hair on his neck. Another gunshot. And a third.

Then as Tall One rose on the muddy bank of the stream, there came a flurry of gunfire from upstream where the Kiowa and Cheyenne had camped. The medicine of those old Kiowa shamans had guaranteed this would be a sanctuary for them all—safe from attack by the pony soldiers.

Behind him the Kwahadi camp came to life. Men sprang from their lodges, pulling on clothing. Women began to drag sleepy children from the lodges, everyone clutching something important beneath an arm as they scurried downstream like a covey of frightened quail, away from the shooting. Into the noise and confusion Tall One raced, dodging little ones and old ones with big, frightened eyes, hurling himself around lodges and favored war ponies. Bridge stood outside the lodge, buckling on a belt shiny with cartridges.

"Your weapons—inside!"

Tall One plunged past him, finding the interior in disarray. He was alone. The rest of the family already gone in those first moments of gunfire up-canyon. From the dewcloth liner the young man tore free his medicine bag, which he draped over his left shoulder, then pulled down the wolf-skin quiver that rattled, heavy with arrows, and his short cherrywood bow. He dived through the doorway as Bridge turned to him.

"Take this, Tall One!" he ordered, shoving an old pistol into the young warrior's hand.

"It is loaded?"

"Yes," the old warrior said.

"I . . . I never shot this before—"

"It does not matter. You will learn how to shoot it well before the sun rises to midsky," he replied sternly, his eyes narrowing on the youth. "Fight well this day, Tall One. And remember: you are Kwahadi!"

Bridge whirled, setting off.

Tall One called out. "Four Spirits Woman? She and the children?"

Bridge turned, his face grim in determination. "I have sent them on downstream with the others. Into the rocks to hide."

In the distance rose the brass-throated eruption of a soldier bugle echoing off the blood-red walls of this canyon.

Bridge stared for a moment as the sound echoed from the canyon walls. "They will be safe, Tall One. Be strong this day—we Kwahadi must not fall!"

He watched his second father wheel and disappear, melding into the confusion as people and ponies swept past him.

"Bridge, let me fight beside you!" he shouted. But it was too late. Already the man was gone too far, and the noise too great for Bridge to hear him.

The Comanche village was cleaving itself asunder: women and children, along with the old ones, all headed downstream while the warriors rushed upstream toward the sound of the gunfire becoming more general now. As the women wailed and keened their mourning and death songs, men raised their voices in anger, rage, fury—in the terrible mocking of death.

Where was Antelope?

He feared fighting alone, perhaps even dying alone. Not having his brother by his side when they finally clashed with the soldiers. Grudgingly he admitted that his brother might be more Comanche than he was. Might be more Kwahadi than Tall One ever would be.

It had always helped to have Antelope beside him as they rode with the others, caught up in the swirl of things before he had time to think, to feel, to fear. To doubt.

He dared not allow himself any doubt—

Crying out with his own war cry, Tall One dived into the rush and blur with the others as they hurried, most on foot, some on horseback, to the sound of the fight upstream. Sharp cracks of the Indian weapons punctuated the low booming of the soldier rifles in a two-note symphony reverberating down the twisting path of the Prairie Dog Town Fork. The simple act of crying out, letting his lungs roar against what residue of fear he might still hide in his heart, helped Tall One once more shed the last paralyzing hold that fear itself had on him. It had always been easier to hurl himself in with the others, let them sweep him along, let them do the leading so that he did not have to think. Only follow.

As he joined them, Tall One was struck with a singular thought: that none of the men, young warriors or old, had painted themselves or taken any time to put on their hair ornaments. He fretted, creating an ever-tightening knot in his belly that this absence of ritual, this forfeiture of the tribe's spiritual power, would spell disaster for them this day. Yet he calmed himself, reminded that all they had to do was what they had done so many, many times before: just cover the retreat of their families with their own lives until it came time they too could escape downstream.

Just cover the retreat with their own lives.

"Tall One!"

Far ahead one of them stood against the rest, waving Tall One on as the others rushed by him. The warrior's face flushed with excitement. Eyes lit with the flame of passion.

"Antelope!"

"Come, brother—we have *tai-bos* to kill! At long last—we have *tai-bos* to kill!"

When together they reached a bend in the canyon where their progress slowed, then ground to a halt, they found Lone Wolf's Kiowa stalled among the rocks, taking cover behind the trees on the outer perimeter of their village, firing back at not-so-distant targets. Here and there a white face swam through the gun smoke and wispy trails of abandoned fires. Still, most of the faces of those making this attack were dark. Many times they had been told to expect that the first wave they might encounter in an attack on their village would be the Seminole and Tonkawa trackers. This day these were dressed in the same dark-blue shirts as the yellow-legs themselves, their hair tied up provocatively for battle. It was disturbing to see that many of those dark faces had been mockingly painted . . . while the Kwahadi had no time for their medicine toilet.

"Look!" Antelope shouted in his ear, nudging him sharply and pointing to their left.

Against the far side of the canyon wall snaked a dark column of more soldiers, leading their horses, winding their way down the thousand-foot descent from the prairie above. As fast as they could inch along the narrow footpath, the yellow-legs were coming to augment the Indian scouts who pressed the point of the attack.

Abruptly it seemed the Kiowa were up and moving, coming back toward the Kwahadi now. More noise crashed ahead of them in echoing reverberations as Lone Wolf's warriors fell back first at a walk, then one by one broke into a run past the Comanche who had just arrived on the battle line.

Then he saw them clearly—the Tonkawa trackers and soldiers draped in blue, down here in the cool, dark shadows, their horses snorting wispy streamers of gauze into the autumn air, horses' legs like throbbing pistons hammering the streambanks as they charged among the rocks and trees the Kiowa were abandoning helter-skelter.

"Come, Tall One!"

Antelope hollered at him a second time, tugging on his elbow. Around them the rest of the Kwahadi and Kiowa were backtracking now like bits of ghostly flotsam adrift on the mist and canyon shadow— stopping hurriedly to turn and fire from behind a boulder, next time stopping behind a wide cottonwood, wheeling off again to reload quickly on the run before they would wheel and fire another shot at the pursuing soldiers and their Indian trackers.

Tall One found the pistol in hand, his arm outstretched without thinking, yanking back the hammer with the other hand before he squeezed the trigger—pointing the muzzle at one of the Tonkawa riding down on him. The tracker's horse skidded stiff-legged to a halt, twisting its head savagely to the side, heaving its rider off in a tumultuous shudder, pitching the tracker into the brush as it went down in a heap, legs flaying.

Its unearthly cry sent shivers up from the base of Tall One's spine.

A bullet's snarl cut the air beside his ear angrily. He felt it pass so close, it smelled of brimstone and death. Suddenly the cold air hissed through the icy furrow along his neck where the bullet had creased him. Some of his long hair stung the open wound, matted in the first beading ooze of that raw tissue.

As quickly as he saw the puff of smoke from the enemy's weapon, Tall One whirled on his heel and sprinted off, his heart singing. He could not claim killing one of the enemy trackers—but there was little doubt he had spilled the rider and killed the Tonkawa's horse.

To put an enemy afoot was a great coup!

But just as his heart began to soar with his brave feat, Tall One's heart sank. Beneath his feet he felt the ground tremble. Around him the air reverberated with the thunder of hooves. Hundreds of hooves rising to a great, raucous crescendo as they charged ever on down the canyon, following the throaty call of those bugles.

While he had unhorsed one—there remained more than he and the rest could ever knock from their saddles.

Glancing over his shoulder as he ran, heedless of the brush he stumbled over, tripping only to pick himself back up and rush off again, Tall One sprinted along with the last of them, the warriors heading for the rocks against the side of the canyon where the women and children had gone to climb upward toward the prairie, toward the sun, to safety.

Where the thundering of those yellow-leg horses would not find them.

Where no man might know of Tall One's doubts.

38

THE MONTH WAS growing old. In less than a week, someone had said, it would be February.

February. Jonah laughed humorlessly. Why, he was still far from accepting the fact that another year had thrust itself upon him!

Still, five days ago there had come a break in the weather that imprisoned these southern plains, and Captain Lockhart had given them three hours to make ready for the trail.

They had left their station at the headwaters of the South Fork of the Pease River at sundown four of those days ago, riding the moon down that long winter's night, marching west at a hand-lope, the hard breast of the wind fresh in their faces, so cold it brought tears to a man's eyes without letup.

West toward the great monolithic wall of the Staked Plain.

Into the caprock of that barren buffalo ground they rode down the second and into their third day, stopping long enough to water the stock when they were lucky enough to run onto sinks and springs, unsaddling for a spare six hours each successive night—just long enough for the men to grab three solid hours of sleep, the captain having his men stand two watches at guard.

"If we're up and moving now that the weather's gone and broke," Niles Coffee explained, "it's bound to reason the Comanch' are up and roaming too."

From the look on Two Sleep's face, it seemed the Shoshone wanted to ask the same question Jonah had posed of the Ranger.

"You got any idea where we're heading, Sergeant?"

"There's a place out there," Coffee replied, pointing with the blade of his folding knife he used to curl a sliver of chew from a dark plug he shoved back into the pocket of his canvas mackinaw. "We get on up where the White River comes in—you can sit there and keep an eye on a whole bunch of country."

"That's what the cap'n wants to do, you figure? Damned cold for a man to do nothing more than keep an eye on things."

Coffee grinned, his tongue noisily slipping the sliver of chaw to the side of his red-whiskered cheek. "It's country the Comanch' gotta go through if they're on the move, Jonah. If they been wintering down south of us where Heck Peters's Ranger company runs their territory, then the Comanche gotta come back north through that White River country. And if the red bastards been wintering up farther north in Cap'n Roberts's country after Mackenzie's Fourth give 'em the rout back at Palo Duro Canyon . . . then we'll catch 'em traipsing south again. Either way, I see it through the same keyhole as Cap'n Lockhart does."

"You can't mean you think there's only one way in or out of this piece of country!" Jonah exclaimed.

"I know you got scars and experience hunting Injuns up north, Jonah," Deacon Johns said quietly in that way of his as he eased down beside Hook beneath the cold starshine. "But you gotta remember we been fighting *these* heathens most all our lives. Every gray hair on this ol' head is a day I've suffered hunting Comanch'—days grave with fret and frazzle, trouble all."

"That may be so, Deacon. But one thing I've learned about the Injuns I've tracked and fought," Jonah said, "is that when you figure you've got an Injun figured out—he's already one jump ahead and bound to outsmart you."

"Maybeso these Comanch' ain't really any different from other Injuns," Coffee said.

Johns nodded. "Could be. But what we do know of these godforsaken fornicators—the Comanch' are creatures of habit. For generations they been moving up and down their buffalo ground, following the trails the buffalo use. Don't matter if they're moving their village, gone hunting for hides and meat, or taking out on the warpath. The Comanch' follow the old trails they know, trails going into and out of a piece of country."

"If they come onto the ground this company of Rangers is sworn to protect," Coffee said, his voice low, laden with resolve, "by God they'll have to come through a narrow door in the caprock less'n three mile wide."

Jonah followed where the Ranger pointed, Coffee's arm extended toward the last rose tint to the twilit sky. Against the pale pink of that aging sunset stood the rising bulk of the caprock that surrounded the immensity of the Staked Plain, swathed boldly in black as all light drained from day. Back to the east a few first stars blinked on. But here, looking toward the west and all that wild, open country ruled by the red lords of these southern plains—it was the raw, ragged edge of the earth itself thrown against the far sky.

Where they were heading, the ground itself seemed to swallow the heavens in huge, hungry, ripping gulps.

As long as he had been out here in this country, riding with these men—never before had Jonah ever experienced such a feeling staring at all that jagged, savage immensity. A land every bit as big as the sky itself. And someplace in that primitive, ragged country, these men seemed cocksure of waiting out the Comanche, of being there in the right place when the Kwahadi up and decided to move out with the break in the winter weather.

Lockhart had them up and scrubbing leather before sunrise, after coffee and a breakfast of what leavings they could find among the skillets from last night's feast. Niles Coffee said they'd make the White River portal by nightfall if they humped it and got high behind. And with the way the captain let his big gelding have his head, Company C had their tails high behind and covering ground.

"This is real country for a real man, Jonah Hook," Johns said to him that morning not long after sunrise. "A land for a man who loves nature and all God's finest handiworks. Bet you've seen some tall mountains out where you been."

"I have, that."

"They must be something, Jonah," he replied in imagined awe. "But nothing could possible compare with the savage beauty of what God Himself has took up and made for the critters out here," Deacon Johns said, admiration closing on reverence in his voice as he gazed side to side. "Hill and valley and canyon teeming with deer and buffalo and turkey and antelope. Streams so full of fish, we don't have to use a line—only that seine the captain carries along. Bear caves and bee trees—Lord, what bee country this is! Why, in the spring a man can ride for near three hundred miles on a solid bed of flowers the color of the rainbow."

Jonah replied, "And for generations it belonged to these here Comanche."

Johns squared his eyes at Hook, his face souring a bit as he answered. "Yep. It did belong to them. But God Almighty Himself set the way of nature when He created this world in six days, Jonah Hook. God Himself made it the first law of nature that in the wilds the strong shall always hold sway over the weak."

"So these Comanche are about to find out which of us is stronger?"

The deacon nodded. "It's the way of nature. The way of all things under God's own heaven. They submit and move aside of the progress of white Christian civilization—or we'll crush 'em underfoot on our way past."

"Praise God, eh?"

Johns drew himself up and replied, "Praise God for making things right in His world, Jonah. *His* world. Not man's. This is God's world, and it's herein He reigns."

That evening when Lockhart brought them to a halt in the first cold caress of winter's darkness after the sun had fallen, he explained that this was likely to be their last night together as a company for some time to come. They had permission to build fires for boiling coffee, but only if those fires were set at the bottom of pits scooped out of the hard, flinty ground. The captain did not have to waste his breath explaining that the light from any fire was likely to travel a great distance in country such as this.

Sergeant Coffee mustered out his three watches, then sent out the first after the men had picketed and sidelined mounts. Then the camp fell quiet as the rest lay down two by two to share body warmth and their scant issue of blankets. Above them lacy silver clouds scudded across the growing moon. Jonah figured it would reach full plug in something less than two weeks. And then they could count on the Comanche moving.

If they weren't already.

Their breath came frosty, the hairs of his mustache and beard matted icy film that next morning as the captain stood them to inspection and broke them into squads in that predawn darkness. Four, each with one of those who had long served with Lockhart, to act as squad leader.

"We'll rotate duty at this base camp," the captain explained. "Two different squads will move out every morning. The first to make a wide sweep to the west, nosing around to the north, then east before coming back in here just after nightfall. And the other will begin their sweep heading east, moving around to the south, then up into the west before reporting in by sundown."

"And the next day the other two squads will make the same patrols?" asked Coffee.

Lockhart nodded. "Those of us remaining in camp will keep the country both north and south glassed throughout the day, laying low and resting the stock. I want this unit to be in fighting trim when it will be required of us. Not if—*when.*"

"Them bloody fornicators will show up, Captain," Johns cheered.

"I'm counting on it, Deacon," Lockhart replied, easing over toward Jonah. "I'm sure Mr. Hook is counting on it as well."

"I am, Cap'n."

Lockhart turned away, his hands laced behind him as he paced before those two squads chosen for the first day's scout. Continuing, he told them, "We may not see anything for a few days, perhaps a week or better. But you will cut sign. Keep your eyes moving when you're out. This is naked, open country. Each squad will stand out like a four-bit whore in church—excuse me, Deacon . . . but so will a Comanche war party."

"We'll keep our eyes on the horizon, Captain," Coffee promised.

"Very well, Sergeant," he said, eyeing the east. "Let's get squads one and three out before the sun comes up."

No one had to awaken Jonah that second morning.

The rest of the men of Company C lay about him as dawn came up slow as winter's own pull, Rangers cocooned in blankets around their fire pits like obsidian chips at the floor of a dark stream in the cold moonlight. He had hardly slept that night before their first patrol, his back against the wide bulk of the Shoshone who rarely left Hook's shadow. The two ate, slept, and now would again ride together with Second Sergeant Clyde Yoakam's squad. After gulping down the scalding coffee that would serve as his breakfast, Jonah saddled the horse, then returned to the fire pits dug deep to smother the flames' tattling glow, where he stood and waited, rocking boot to boot anxiously.

After standing his squad to inspection, Yoakam settled down between the high wishbone pommel and rounded cantle upon the open-slot seat of his McClellan saddle and moved them out. Most of those riders turned to look back at least once before their camp disappeared from view in that broken land of bare, buzzard-bone ridges streaked red, yellow, and white, waving at those friends and compatriots they were leaving in camp, those who would recoup and rest: repairing saddles, bridles, even reshoeing if necessary. All the while Lockhart would debrief yesterday's squad leaders and those men most familiar with this ground. No man wanted to know more about this country and where the Comanche might turn up than Lamar Lockhart.

No man, besides Jonah Hook.

Especially after that first long day in the saddle, riding back at nightfall empty-handed and with nothing of import to tell Lockhart. No trails crossed. No smoke seen. Even the small, normally unobserved things: they had spotted ample game throughout the day; the water holes and springs remained untrammeled. Only the crusty snow atop the flaky ground betrayed the passing of yesterday's scout.

The Rangers moved in and out and around that country for the better part of the next ten days, on into the first week of February. Camp became a familiar haven with its odors of gun oil and soaped leather, the pungent aroma of men and animals about this business of waiting for war. What few decks of cards they had packed along grew dog-eared as those decks were passed from squad to squad to squad, the men funning themselves playing seven-up or rowdy games of monte. A few precious sets of checkers also served to break up some of the camp monotony, played on limber game boards of gingham-checked cloth a man could roll up around the scuffed black and red checker pieces, then stuff the whole of it away into a saddlebag.

Former barber Enoch Harmony gave a trim to all those who desired a haircut. Slade Rule, a brands inspector, gave every horse a good going-over at least once every third day to determine if the pounding of their patrols was wearing down the company's stock. And Lockhart himself held the outgoing squads to inspection every morning: their outfits, belt guns and carbines, in addition to each individual's saddle and tack.

"When it comes time for this company to fight," the captain preached with regularity, "the success of the whole must not be hampered by the failure of the one to see to the readiness of his outfit."

"A worn cinch strap, a shoddy stirrup latch, maybe even a loose bit chain—anything," explained Sergeant Coffee, "sure as tarnal sin it could mean the difference between life and death when we finally run down these Comanch'."

Over the past fall and into the winter grown old, Lockhart's company had kept up with what old news drifted off the agencies or out of the army's posts. After the War Department had caught the last hostile bands between the five jaws of their mighty clamp, most of the Kiowa and Cheyenne, and even some of the Comanche bands, had wearily marched into Darlington, Anadarko, and Fort Sill itself. Mackenzie and Davidson and Buell and Miles had pulled a victory out of their collective hat. The hostiles were coming in. Slowly, for sure—but they were coming in to surrender and be counted, even knowing that their headmen were to be arrested and herded off to a faraway prison.

Agents Miles up at Darlington and Connell at Anadarko, especially Haworth at Fort Sill, all three knew how to send word to Jonah if one of their bands showed up with two white boys . . . two young men the age Jeremiah and Ezekiel would be that winter. They had promised to send a rider with the news, no matter the cost—just get a rider moving for Texas and Company C of the Frontier Battalion.

But after October came and went with the surrender of the first bands to give up after Mackenzie whipped them at Palo Duro Canyon, then November faded into December with no news . . . something began to twist inside of Jonah, roll over and shrivel a little more each day. Hope it was. What he had left of hope that got him into December and through until late in January when Lockhart had marched them out here to the Llano for the White River country. But now they had been out patrolling close to a month without any news from the Territories about what the warrior bands were doing or what the army was continuing to accomplish.

All anyone knew was that the most irrevocably savage of the Comanche, the band that called themselves the Antelope People, the warriors who rode under a half-breed named Quanah Parker—that bunch was still out. No one, army nor civilian, had seen sign of them since Palo Duro.

Word had it they had been in the canyon when Mackenzie struck last September. The story was that about half of the fourteen hundred ponies Mackenzie's men had captured, then slaughtered, on the prairie had belonged to Parker's Kwahadi.

"There's them that says Mackenzie got himself something personal for Quanah Parker—wants that one red bastard more'n all the rest put together," John Corn had said, the liver-colored bags under his eyes the same as the rest, telling the tale of too little sleep.

The inveterate worrier Harley Pettis agreed, two deep vertical lines marking the flesh between his bushy eyebrows. "Mackenzie won't stop till he gets Parker and strings him up for what he done."

"Back in the times of Abraham," Deacon Johns exhorted, his eyes like smoldering slits, "vengeance might have been the Lord's. But not here in Texas! Here on this ground, vengeance belongs to us as has a call to take it!"

"There's more blood of white folks on the hands of those Kwahadi warriors than can ever be washed away with all the absolution and forgiveness in the world," said Lamar Lockhart with a cold fire behind his eyes. "We don't get Quanah Parker before Mackenzie does, men—the Rangers won't ever have another chance to try to even the debt."

"Them Parker's bunch—and only them is what we hunt," swore Deacon Johns, all wrinkled, dried, and smoked of hide. "Pray God delivers them to us . . . and we'll take care of the rest."

"Make them red-bellies all good Injuns!" shouted June Callicott, the owner of a homely, narrow, overlong face.

"Buck, squaw, and nit," growled Harley Pettis. "Company C will see there's a few less to feed at the reservation come spring!"

The deacon closed his eyes, raised his face and arms to the diamond-dusted sky, saying, "Oh, Lord—deliver us from evil, and Quanah Parker to this outfit."

The icy rains continued nearly every day, usually approaching from the west in the midafternoon when a man and his animal had grown most weary from the ride, bored with the monotony of covering the same ground week in and week out with nothing to show for Company C's patrols. Driving, bone-numbing rains. By the middle of February most of the men suffered one malady or another. Some sniffled, others battled a persistent dry hack. And nearly all looked out from those red-rimmed, sunken eyes showing the first telltale signs of despair. Wasn't a one whose disposition hadn't become about as ragged and sharp as shards of broken bottle glass.

Behind Lockhart's back a few were even beginning to whisper of the unthinkable. They murmured of leaving the White River country, talked of heading back into the settlements for a spell. Then as if the captain had heard them through their despair, Lockhart waited until late one afternoon when all but one late-arriving patrol was in their camp among the jagged rocks.

Sergeant Coffee called that sullen bunch together, but it was the captain who strode up and stopped before those restive men who stood or squatted among the damp, scattered baggage of Company C.

"I won't stir a lot of dust with this, fellas. Want to come to the point of it fast," Lockhart began. "I truly thought I had it figured out as soon as the weather broke and winter seemed to withdraw. But my hunch has gone and clabbered up on me."

In the uneasy silence that followed Lockhart working up to things on a crawl, two of the men coughed that dry, unproductive hack that could trouble a man many times soaked and dried out in a cold wind blowing across country such as this.

"Thought we'd find sign of the Comanche, cross a trail, see smoke or something. I want the Kwahadi as bad as any of you. Even as much as Jonah there."

Hook felt some of the others look his way for a moment before they shifted anxiously again, ready to have this meet over and done.

"But we've pushed rations about as far as I can. For the past five days I've had us on half rations, boys. No other jump to it: we'll have to go in soon to re-provision . . . anyway." The captain sighed, gazing at the ground.

There was an oversized silk kerchief tied loose around Lockhart's neck, a grimy swatch of cloth as brightly colored as the sweet williams that Gritta had planted in the bed at the front of the cabin back in that Missouri valley.

Able again to look his men in the eye, their leader continued. "So what's hardest to take is that I was wrong about running across Parker's bunch."

"It weren't just you, Captain," Deacon Johns said softly. "Rest of us had it figured same way you did. Ain't you what failed alone."

"What you figure to do?" asked John Corn, his sun-browned skin shriveled up like last year's potato.

"We'll recoup one more day here. Not sending patrols out tomorrow. Following morning we'll head back for Dickinson's place. From there on in to our post. Time I sent word to Major Jones." He scratched his sparse black whiskers. It had been four days since last he had shaved, enough of a clue for any man to see that the captain was not in the best of humors. "The major will be expecting a full report on our extended scout."

In Jonah's belly lay a cold stone of growing uneasiness.

"You really figure us to go in?" inquired Coffee, his hair and beard as red as a rooster's comb.

"Isn't that what you boys want? Get out of this heathen country?" Johns snapped at them, turning round on that group.

His words cut at them, forcing those rawhide-tough bravos to stare at their boots or the ground like scolded schoolboys, their eyes furtively glancing at one another.

Until Hook finally spoke.

As much as he might have held against them long ago back there at Jacksboro and Fort Richardson, when he signed on to protect the citizens of west Texas, Jonah now knew the men of Company C were every one and all something more than ordinary men.

"Don't really wanna go in, Deacon," Hook told them. "I was figuring on staying out as long as it took. Live off the land, we have to. Where I was brought up, I was always taught you stayed with a job till it was done."

"Hook might have a good idea there," June Callicott said. "This bunch could live off the land."

"Maybe we just need to find a different place to set up a base camp, Cap'n," offered Wig Danville.

"True enough," Johns echoed. "The foxes have their holes and the birds of the air have their nests—but the Son of Man ain't got the where to lay his head across all of this wild creation!"

Lockhart drew himself up, his chin jutting. He turned like some of the rest, seeing that last patrol come easing in out of the east. They all saw the way the horses bobbed their heads, the way the men sagged in the saddles. No one had to spell it out plain, that theirs had been nothing more than a repeat of the weeks gone before.

The captain sighed. "Thank you for your suggestion, Jonah. However, I'm the leader of this company and my decision is made. Day after tomorrow, we light out for Dickinson's Station."

39

A T DICKINSON'S PLACE the settler and his three sons greeted Company C with nothing less than flat-out celebration as the Rangers legged down off their weary mounts. That family of stockmen and farmers eking out its existence at the edge of the west Texas frontier hadn't seen different faces for going on three months.

It was either in the barn, or outside in the barn's sun-striped winter shadows, that Jonah Hook and Two Sleep stayed across those next thirty hours as Ezra Dickinson and his boys helped Lamar Lockhart's Rangers recoup from their patrol. It was a barn built at no cost to the old stockman, raised free by the State of Texas in return for allowing Ranger patrols to use it to store feed, tack, supplies, and provender. A hundred of these barns cast their shadows across the caprock fringe of the Staked Plain.

While the celebration of men and the talk of weather and stock and horseflesh was one thing Jonah hoped to avoid, it was the Dickinson women that Jonah tried most to stay clear of. Too much did they remind him of those once a part of his own life. Both gone: one off to St. Louis and Miss Emily Rupert's Seminary; the other . . . just gone.

Memories of her were the bitterest water Jonah had been forced to drink in those years lost and gone. But drink he did, forcing himself to taste a little more of her remembrance each day. Sad glimpses of what he once had, triggered ofttimes by smells, delicious smells coming from the kitchen where the three Dickinson women cooked supper for that bunch. As the others joked and sang and arm wrestled, Jonah remembered the smells of snap beans and carrots set on a pale-blue plate next to a mound of Gritta's mashed potatoes, them that she boiled and mashed, then served up skins and all.

So as much as Jonah yearned to study the face of a white woman, to stand just close enough to determine how a white woman might smell, as much as he felt a need to be in the company of such genteel farming folk of the earth like those he was raised among, Hook of a sudden felt ill at ease, ill-mannered, rough, and more coarse than he ever had in all his life. And downright afraid of making a damned fool of himself.

So he stayed to himself, there in the barn with Two Sleep while the younger Rangers flirted with the three Dickinson girls and the missus baked dried apple pies for her guests. The merry sounds of men at their fun, the tinkle of women's laughter, made Jonah recall the days of camp meetings back to the Shenandoah—religious tent revivals that got so frolicsome, the long-coated preachers had to keep women off the grounds between sunset and sunrise.

"Peel your ears back, Jonah—I got some news!" bellowed Niles Coffee as he strode up through the deepening shadows that first night after the company had come in to the ranch.

"What news?"

Coffee settled, his back against the rough-plank barn wall where Hook leaned. "Dickinson says Mackenzie's figuring he's got the Comanche whipped bad enough so he's gonna offer the Kwahadi a chance to make peace."

"What's his peace offer mean to us?"

Sucking on the chewed and fractured stem of his old pipe, Coffee answered. "Mackenzie offers peace to Parker's bunch to come in—that means the war's over."

Hook studied the flame-headed Ranger beside him a moment there in the last glow of the day, the sun having slid beyond the far rim of the prairie, beyond a small piece of ground above the barn where he had frequently gone to sit, staring, wondering.

Jonah asked, "Ain't that what you boys wanted to do all along? Get the war over with?"

With a wag of his red head, Coffee said, "Not exactly. Those of us I can speak for, we took the oath so we could get us a crack at the Comanche. Captain Lockhart ain't leading no rag-tailed bunch of splay-footed farmers now. To the last man we joined the Rangers to fight those sonsabitching red-bellies. Never counted on the army coming behind us and making it unpossible to hunt down Comanche."

"That what Mackenzie will do? Keep us from hunting?"

He dug at the ground with a sliver of weathered barnwood. "Not likely the army can keep us from hunting, Jonah. Just keep us from . . . killing Comanche."

"You want to get your licks in first—don't you, Coffee?"

The sergeant's dark, larval eyes narrowed on Hook. "Don't you? Seeing how the Kwahadi are the bunch that stole your boys?"

"Just want my boys. That's all."

Coffee snorted quietly. "Can't believe you could just ride in there, fetch back your boys, and ride off without taking blood from them that stole your kin."

"My boys is all . . . all I need," Jonah repeated, his words coming hard. Hot flecks began to sting his eyes, and something sour and thick clogged his throat.

They fell silent for a few minutes as Coffee sucked on his pipe and the sky they watched wheeled from orange to rose, then faded to the deeper hues of twilight.

"Major Jones sent out the word," Coffee said.

"Word that Mackenzie was gonna make peace with the Comanche?"

"Yep. Sent a rider through here a few days back with the major's dispatch for the captain. Jones wants all his company captains to meet him at Griffin in a couple weeks to plan our final campaign."

"What're you talking about—a *final* campaign? You just said the army's making peace with the Comanche. It's over, Sergeant. Your goddamned war is over!"

"Not my war, Jonah," Coffee growled. "Not the war we Texans been fighting since the days before we tore free from Mexico. No, sir—by god-bloody-damned! This war ain't over till Texas says it's over. Those are *our* Comanches—not the army's. And sure as hell they ain't Mackenzie's." He raised his arm, pointing at the house porch where many of the Rangers lounged. "See them boys? Not a one of them ready to say their war is over, Jonah. *Their* war. *My* war. I lost kin! Goddammit—I lost kin!"

"All right," Hook said quietly as Coffee shuddered with that jolt of passion. "So what you aim to do?"

The fire-headed sergeant composed himself and turned back to look at Jonah. "Lockhart figures from Jones's dispatch that the major is going to send his Frontier Battalion out in force. To make a real campaign of it. All the companies in a grand fight of it: loop up from Fort Griffin, north, clear to the Canadian. Sweep the country clear before the army goes and herds all them Comanche onto the reservations at last—before Kwahadi get about as scarce as a harpsychord in a whorehouse."

"Sweep the country clear?"

"Goddammit, Jonah!" Coffee growled. "Major Jones wants what Lockhart and the rest of us want. One final push against them red bastards."

"The Rangers gonna make your own war?"

"A bloodletting the likes of which no Texan has seen in the history of the Lone Star Republic."

"I'll bet you get your licks in too."

"Look, Jonah. We all of us got a hunting permit the good people of Texas give us the day we signed on with the Rangers." Coffee reached into a pocket inside his heavy coat and pulled out the star into the dimming light. "Here's my six-pointed hunting license, Jonah. Each man of us carries it, 'cause we take this war serious."

"I got something else other'n Comanche bucks to hunt." He pushed himself back against the barn and stood slowly.

"Ain't you with us, Jonah? They got your boys. And now you can even things up. Looks like we'll have this one last chance to wipe out all them stragglers what don't go in to their agency."

He wagged his head. "Sergeant, I don't need to even things up, because there ain't no way on God's green earth things ever will get even for me."

"No matter if you find your boys—you won't be even?"

"No. I lost so much—time, years, miles . . . just living—ain't nothing nobody can do to ever get Jonah Hook even again."

He started off down the side of the barn, hearing the Shoshone rise from the winter-parched stubble to shadow him. Then Coffee's voice caught Hook again.

"I want to try, Jonah. Good Lord knows I had kin took and killed," Coffee tried his best to explain in that darkness. "So the Good Lord knows my heart when I stand here now and I vow to try to help you even things up. Once and for all."

Jonah had walked on without stopping, slipping on out of the dimming, translucent light of that sunset and disappeared into the shadows of twilight. For the rest of that evening until well past moonrise, the sounds of laughter and loud talk trickled out to him from the rifle ports in Dickinson's two sod houses that squatted here on the prairie, the both of them joined by the low-roofed dogtrot. For so long he remained afraid of dawn coming, afraid that someone would light a candle or bring a lamp looking for him. Not even wanting to look into the light of a fire that night— simply for the fear that he might be forced to look into his own thoughts, like shadowed corners of a sudden given light.

Lockhart ordered them back to the saddle at midmorning, marching them a little east of due south, aiming for Fort Griffin and the war council called by the commander of the Frontier Battalion. And while they rode the sun down that day, Jonah Hook wondered what he would do now, come this last push against the Comanche—the ones said to hold his boys.

Had he eaten up too much time that he didn't have? Time and again did he just up and ride after a ruse, believing in smoke on the wind, hoping against his better judgment? Following one hunch after another that had clabbered up like Lamar Lockhart's White River patrols?

Had the time come for him to leave Texas and head southwest? Go back where he had the last—and really the first—solid evidence of what had happened to his boys? At least that dingy, grayed, washed-out shirt had been more solid than any cantina rumor or wild comanchero tale he had listened to over the years. Perhaps to go back there to New Mexico, maybe back south to Sonora once more—there to pick up more of a solid thread. Something to cling to, even if it was only a thread as thin as spider's silk.

The captain halted the company when the sun had touched the top margin of the caprock to the west, turning the slopes of braided cedar to a rusty band of gold beneath the dark, gut-colored clouds. Lockhart instructed them to build only three small fires, then dismissed the Rangers. Some gathered and tied off the horses. Others sought out firewood. A few got out cups and knives to scoop and dig at the flint-hard soil, the better to hide the tattletale flames of their fires. And when the water had been poured from canteens into the blackened pots and set to boil for coffee, a drink the trail-weary men would use to soften the thick, wide strips of dried beef Lockhart had bought off Dickinson, Jonah moved out of the circle and sought a place to relieve himself.

Seemed such a simple thing as taking a pee was getting harder every year. His body growing older, the pounding his kidneys took of the trail felt more magnified with each successive season.

On the far side of camp from where the animals had been hobbled, Hook stopped near some clumps of winter-brittle grass and unbuttoned his fly. On a scout like this in country where they would likely come quickly on the enemy, a plainsman had to practice all varieties of precaution: even to using the heel and toe of his tall stovepipe boots to scoop out a shallow hole quickly at the base of some stunted scrub. He would then pee in that hole. Done, Jonah used his scarred boot to cover up best he could the sign, and that telltale odor, of a white man's passing. Buttoning up as—

"Jonah."

He turned with a jerk, finding Lockhart and Coffee. "Surprised me, Cap'n."

There was no nonsense on that face with its bushy black mustache. "Want you to come with us. Get that Snake—Two Sleep—to come with you."

Following the two Rangers back into the midst of the camp, Jonah motioned for the Shoshone to follow. Through the scrub where the herders had hobbled the stock and were cross-lining the pack mules, Lockhart and his sergeant moved on into the waning light. As they rounded the base of one of the rolling hills, Jonah saw Billy Benton. The man rose when he heard the rest coming.

"You find anything more of interest, Billy?" Lockhart asked.

"Nothing but the tracks, Cap'n." His was a pointed, prying type of nose set between friendly eyes. The man dusted his hands off on the front of his britches, then straightened.

"Billy here came out to have himself a look around before he took up his guard post 'top that hill," Lockhart explained, turning to Hook and the Shoshone. "And in the late light he came upon something I want you both to have a look at."

"You got sign?"

"Look for yourself, Jonah. Tell me what you fellas think."

The graying man pointed at the ground, his beard and mustache tobacco-stained like Deacon Johns's. Benton moved his hand back and forth, then once around in a circle, before he stepped back out of the way as Jonah nodded for Two Sleep to join him. Side by side they knelt, studying the ground.

After a moment the Shoshone rose and moved off a few yards in the direction taken by the trail. Jonah glanced at the sky. The tracks headed north. Hook stood and turned to the three Rangers.

"What's south of here? Maybe not far as Griffin."

"You know, Sergeant—that's what I like about Mr. Hook here," the captain began. "I'm glad you're still with us, Jonah. So what's south of here? And well this side of Fort Griffin . . . why, it's Cedar Lake."

As Coffee and Benton grunted what sounded like approval, Jonah asked, "What's Cedar Lake?"

Lockhart grinned slightly, some of his teeth showing. "Seems it's an ancient place the Comanche go. They wander there from time to time over the years."

Coffee nodded, removing his hat and scratching that red scalp of his. "It's a place that the interpreter up to Fort Sill, fella named Phil McCusker, says the half-breed Quanah Parker his own self claims he was borned."

"They're moving north," Jonah said, again looking into the distance where Two Sleep rose from the ground and began heading back slowly.

"Back to the White River gate," Coffee added. "Like we figured all along. You was right, Cap'n."

"I guess we were, Sergeant," Lockhart said. "Only thing we had wrong was we got there way too early. How old are those tracks, Jonah?"

Hook turned to Two Sleep, moved his hands in the question at the same time he asked it in English of his saddle partner. "How old the tracks?"

"A week. Maybe little more."

Lockhart nodded, moving forward a step, motioning along the ground. "From what I see, doesn't seem they were in any hurry."

"Nope. No rush."

"How many you figure on?" asked Niles Coffee.

"Eight. Maybe ten," he answered, looking at Two Sleep. The Shoshone nodded to confirm it.

"No travois, though," Lockhart grumbled.

"Likely a raiding party," Jonah ventured. "Maybe out hunting."

"Scouting the way north, out ahead of the whole village?" Coffee inquired.

"Could be," Jonah said, looking at the deepening sky. "We can tell more come morning."

"C'mon, then," Lockhart ordered. "Let's get back and get supper in our bellies. I've made my decision to move on a few miles after we eat and before we bed down."

"Makes more sense to have a cold camp now," Jonah replied.

"Damn right, Captain," Coffee agreed. "This ground rightly swarms with Comanch'. If them Kwahadi are up and about at long last, I don't want no wandering scalp party finding sign of us. Them sons-abitches worse'n red ants swarming over my mama's slop bucket back of her stove."

Company C soaked their hard-bread and jerky in their coffee, for the most part eating silently, each man down in his own thoughts now that they had fresh sign. It was not a sullen bunch that emptied the blackened pots in the fire holes, kicked dirt back to fill the depressions, then walked their horses back and forth over that ground before mounting and moving out at a lope behind Captain Lamar Lockhart. This time, however, he turned them about, turned them into the wind. Instead of pointing their noses south for Fort Griffin and the earthy recreation offered by St. Angela, the fleshpot across the river from the post, the Rangers were coming about to the north.

Deacon Johns had grumbled his praise as they went to saddle in the dark. "Praise God you boys are forced to go a while longer before you lie fornicating with some likely, oily-tongued slattern what has her seven kinds of pox!"

Lockhart had them backtracking for the White River portal, on a fresh trail that just might mean a payday come at last for Company C.

In the gray of dawn's first awakening that next morning, Jonah and Two Sleep led Lockhart and Coffee in a wide swing to the south for insurance's sake while the rest of the Rangers waited in a cold camp for their return. In little more than an hour, it looked like they had their answer.

Jonah reined them up and dropped once more to the new tracks they had just come across.

"I don't think this bunch is scouts for a village on the move, Cap'n," he said, rising and slapping his glove against his britches silvered with dust.

Jonah pulled the glove on, saying, "We should've found something by now, sweeping around like we done. No outriders would be pushing this far out from the village moving to new ground."

"Like I said, it's a scalping party," Coffee replied, assuredly.

"Sorry, Sergeant," Jonah said. "This bunch ain't on the lope—it's moving too slow to be making a war trail. They might just be hunters. But that ain't the who of it."

"What else, Jonah?" Lockhart asked.

"They've run onto friends out here."

The captain's eyes narrowed sharply, a deep furrow dug between his bushy black eyebrows. "Friends?"

"Another bunch," Jonah replied, his arm motioning over the new tracks, then pointing north.

"These are the prints of the war party we found last night?"

With a shake of his head, Jonah said, "No. Different. One of these bucks riding a pony got a hoof I ain't see before. A mustang with a split hoof. Back a ways you can see where they stopped while one of the riders changed mounts. Took the weight off the pony with the split hoof."

"I'll be go to hell," admired Lockhart, smiling in his black mustache. "What else you tell me about this bunch? How many now?"

"Probably a couple dozen by now—what with this second outfit joined up."

"What's all that tell you, Jonah?"

"Says this ain't a hunting party. Probably not a real scalp raid neither."

"What then?"

"Likely the village split up to move across a big piece of ground, coming out of that Cedar Lake country you say is down there. Split up because of what you fellas told me—with the soldiers patrolling out of Fort Concho and all."

Lockhart worked his hands anxiously over the saddle horn. "Which means they're re-forming ranks?"

"If you mean they're coming back together—you can bet the bank of Texas on it, Cap'n."

"By damned!" he exclaimed. "We've got a fresh trail—and it will lead us right to their village."

"Cap'n Lockhart," Jonah said soberingly, "remember this bunch of Comanche is on the move."

Coffee leaned forward, his face suddenly gone serious in that red beard of his. Concerned, he asked, "They don't know we're behind them, do they?"

"No," Hook said. "They don't know we're back here—yet. But that's only a matter of time."

40

THEIR ESCAPE FROM the yellow-leg soldiers at Palo Duro Canyon seemed like an eternity ago. More than four moons had come and gone since the Shahiyena and Kiowa, and the Comanche themselves, had torn themselves apart into smaller bands, scattering before the winds and Three-Finger Kinzie's pony soldiers.

It had worked. Once more the Kwahadi had survived the winter undiscovered. As brutal as the weather had been, as hard as it was to find the buffalo that would prolong the life of the band, as often as they had been compelled to uproot and move to a new camp, they had survived.

The fight in the canyon had shown Tall One what few others were ready to admit. The white man and his army were not about to rest until they had driven the red man into the squalor of the agencies, until all the rest who remained out on the free prairie were ground under the heels of the *tai-bos'* boots.

What a fight it had been. Something that lived on in the bitter recollections of the warriors who recounted their bravery in covering the retreat of their people against the overwhelming numbers and the total surprise of the yellow-leg attack. From their hiding places behind trees and boulders, the Kwahadi men disappeared, melting into the chill dawn mist strung in a gauzy veil over the narrow creek, flitting away like cave bats come the rising of the sun. With their women and children climbing out of the canyon, with the Tonkawa and Seminole trackers in full possession of most of the Kwahadi pony herd—there was nothing left to do but flee. To escape so they could fight another day.

So the gall of their defeat kept gnawing away at the men through that fall and into the time of cold. There in the canyon that morning they had been given no time for the women to gather up the travois ponies, to drag down lodges, to pack clothing and utensils, dried meat and robes, to ward off the coming winds of winter. Most everything had been lost to Three-Finger Kinzie.

Doing what they had done time and again against this same soldier chief, Tall One and Antelope had joined the Kwahadi men in falling back slowly, firing, holding the soldiers at bay while they could. From every crevice in the canyon walls, behind every rock and tree big enough to give them cover, the warriors dogged and deviled that solid blue phalanx.

Through the heated minutes of that fight the gray-eyed war chief was among them—Kiowa and Shahiyena as well as his own Kwahadi. He had exhorted them, rallied them, bolstered them as they fell back—urging them to hold the line a little longer. Many times during that hard winter Tall One recalled with great pride how he had stood with the war chief, he and Antelope some of the last to retreat.

"For our women and children!" the gray-eyed one cheered first in one tongue, then in another. "For our families! For them we leave our bodies here to protect the ones who flee!"

Back, back across the yucca and tiny prickly pear, across the white quartz studded in the red earth, the last holdouts had retreated, slowly scaling the upvaulted rock formations as red-tailed and swainson's hawks drifted overhead on the morning's warming air currents. For more than four twisted, tortured miles of that snaking canyon they had held the soldiers back. From afar Tall One had recognized the low, grumbling charge of the cavalry washing their way, so much like the sound of an old mare with her paunch filled with bad water. In the end it came time for the last of the warriors to disappear into the narrow washes and bent-finger arroyos like so many eye-corner wrinkles off the main canyon.

"Flee!" the war chief hollered at them there at the last, waving his warriors away with his rifle. "We will regroup at the top."

It was there at the top of the canyon walls as that autumn day's sun grew weary and desirous of seeking its rest beyond the far mountains that Tall One watched the gray-eyed war chief confront the headmen of the Kiowa and Shahiyena who said their people had suffered enough, who said they were turning away from the struggle. Would at last the Kwahadi join them on their road back to the agencies?

"No, I will not join you in turning my back on my country. I will never join you in giving up the life of my father on the free prairie," he told them. "How can you presume to ask that of me—the one who had never taken a mouthful of the white man's food! How could I ever consider the reservation my last option? When I am the lone chief here who has never set my foot on the white man's agencies—never held out my hand to accept one of his thin blankets, or his rotten pig meat, or his bug-infested flour."

The end had come there on the lip of that great crevasse as the Kwahadi war chief asked of those who were going in, "In your wisdom, tell me what my people are to do now. Is it better for me to lead them into the reservations now? Or better for us to continue this fight?"

In the cold, bitter, hungry days that followed, many more voices took up the questions as the Antelope People argued among themselves.

"Should now we be forced to walk the road those Shahiyena and Kiowa take? To follow their steps to the reservation, where the Kwahadi have never retreated, forced to turn over our weapons just so our starving women and children have something to fill their empty bellies now that these winter winds come slashing across the cold breast of our land? How do we expect the little ones, the old ones, and those who are sick to face this onslaught of winter bravely without lodges and blankets and robes, even spare moccasins for their frozen feet—when all was left behind?"

Time had altered their way of life as much as had the white man.

In the nine winters Tall One had spent with the Kwahadi, he had seen the tribe teeter, then slip, from their one-time greatness. No more did they roam in such numbers. Summer after summer of warfare against the growing legions of yellow-legs, winter after winter as they hunted the disappearing buffalo—it took its toll year after year after year. One had only to look around him to see that the number of lodges had been whittled down by nearly half. Yet something in these proud people kept them alive and off the reservation that winter.

They raised their crude shelters in the arroyos, out of the wind, until they could find enough old bulls to begin curing lodge skins once more.

Again they hunted antelope and deer for clothing and moccasins. The few ponies they had escaped with had to be cared for more watchfully than ever, for those animals would allow the tribe's finest horse thieves to strike once more come spring. Soon they would ride out as the grass shoved its first green shoots from the winter-weary ground.

Once the weather began to moderate, they broke into six small groups, Antelope riding with one of the four scouting parties sent off to wander in search of buffalo and to clear the path for those to come. The other two warrior societies escorted the women and old ones, stayed with the children who rode atop the few drags they had left. The strongest of the women pulled the travois now, the ponies gone with the warriors, gone with the hunters. Antelope's wife struggled as best she could, young and strong as she was with one child barely walking, another infant lashed in a blanket at her back as they plodded north, waiting for spring.

Because he had chosen to stay with the village, Tall One too used the growing strength of his back to drag a travois across the cold ground. Atop the bundles on that travois sat his young nephew, wide-eyed and silent. More and more the face of Antelope's firstborn reminded Tall One of his mother.

And because the village traveled so slow those last cold days of winter, Tall One was one of the last to know. It was Antelope who brought the news late of an early spring day as his warrior society rode back to rejoin the main village. What news they carried proved momentous.

"Soldiers?" asked Tall One.

"No," Antelope answered his brother's question. "But they are white men. Three-times-ten. With two mules along and many, many guns."

"How close are they from catching us?"

"Two, maybe three days at the most."

Over the days that followed their discovery of the Comanche trail, Company C watched the spoor of their enemy freshen, found the camp fires and their beds, watched as here and there more trails converged.

"Another bunch come in from the west, Cap'n," Jonah told Lockhart.

"That makes how many now, Sergeant?"

Coffee consulted the small hand-stitched, leather-bound tablet he carried inside a vest pocket. "Near as we can count the tracks of them parties we've run across—we're closing on seventy-five or eighty warriors now."

"Sniffing up their hind ends you mean!" roared June Callicott.

Most of the rest laughed uneasily. It was better to laugh, Jonah knew, knowing they were already outnumbered three to one if things came down to a fight of it. And why wouldn't things end up just that way? That was, after all, why Captain Lockhart's men were trailing these Kwahadi, wasn't it? To make a fight of it? But no one said anything of the odds. Though it might be there plain as paint on their faces if a man looked hard enough, long enough—no one said a goddamned thing about the odds that grew more stacked against them every day they dogged that Comanche trail.

"How many more you figure on joining up?" Lockhart asked.

Hook shrugged. "No telling. This could be most of the warriors. Could be just a small scouting party sent out to roam over this country."

"What's your guess?"

"I'd hate to hazard a guess, Cap'n."

"Hazard one, Mr. Hook," Lockhart snapped, the tension of trailing the Comanche finally placing cracks in the captain's implacable exterior.

"All right. Were it up to me, I'd figure this is about half of what warriors there be in the village."

"This half meaning seventy-five or eighty?"

"Yes, Cap'n." As he said it, Jonah felt the palpable hush fall over the rest of those men as they sat their saddles stoically.

"We might face maybe as many as a hundred fifty, Mr. Hook?"

"Maybe."

Lockhart swallowed that one like he had been given a woolly worm to eat. Still, he straightened, and tugged down the front of his wide-brimmed hat before he said, "Men, if we prepare for the worst that things could possibly be, then nothing can deter us from the success of our mission."

The captain had looked at Jonah for a moment, as if measuring the plainsman one more time, as if to ascertain something before committing Company C to the do or die of it.

Then Lamar Lockhart quietly said, "Sergeant Coffee—we have Comanche to track. Put out our scouts and let's get moving."

There wasn't a grumble, not a word one as Coffee put that outfit into motion again. Nothing but the creak of saddle and holster leather, the plodding of hooves and the silence of men in their own thoughts of what lay ahead. Still, one thing was plain as the sky overhead: Hook could see that this bunch would follow their captain not only to hell and back again, but six times around the devil on the way.

A good leader was like that, able to lead men against daunting odds where a lesser man couldn't budge his troops. It was just the way a certain gentleman general had led the fight of the Confederacy through all its battles, over all those years. In the end these sons of Texas shared the same feelings about just such a leader as Robert E. Lee, gone peacefully to the ages barely five years after he had handed U.S. Grant his sword at McLean's farmhouse. These sons of Texas followed a good man in Lamar Lockhart. Bound to follow him now into the jaws of hell.

A February sun continued its climb toward midsky, then fell back to their left as they pressed on, the trail they were following become fresher, the fire pits a bit warmer, the pony dung not near so dry. It was late afternoon when Two Sleep rode up, doing his best not to bring attention to himself, and signaled Jonah in the sign dance of the plains.

Hook in turn pushed his horse ahead until he rode beside Lockhart. "Cap'n, seems we've found something ahead."

"Your Snake?"

"He run onto a Comanche pony. Calls the Comanche 'yellow jackets.' "

"Let's go have ourselves a look, Jonah."

After crossing the crest of that last hill, Hook spotted the animal more than half a mile away, even before Two Sleep pointed.

"I see him," Lockhart said without being asked.

The miserable creature stood with its head hung among the refuse of an old campsite: a pitiful few rings, many fire pits, scraps of meat and hide and ruddled bone the porcupines and magpies continued to work over until the white men drew too close and stopped. Only then did the predators and scavengers scatter, and all was silent again, save for the hiss of the wind in the scrub cedar and the bare, skeletal branches of the mesquite.

Jonah's eyes followed the moccasin tracks, the growing number of hoofprints. Another bunch had evidently joined up here at this campsite. And still the village moved north, rejoining in anticipation of the spring hunt. He gazed off at the path scoured in their leaving this place: a trail more than thirty feet wide pointing toward the Pease River country. Slowly he moved back and forth across the site with Two Sleep, absorbing every ring and pit, every gnawed bone and scrap of hide or discarded moccasin.

He had to admire them—no matter they were savages. If this was truly the bunch caught in the Palo Duro by Mackenzie's Fourth Cavalry more than four months back, then Quanah Parker's Kwahadi were something, all right. Starting the winter with next to nothing, for them to come out this well the following spring. How he prayed the boys were alive. Prayed they were with Parker's fierce and hearty holdouts.

Eventually he walked back to the old pony the village had abandoned there when it had put to the trail once more. The animal suffered what looked to be a festering bullet wound low in the neck. The way the pus and blood had clotted and oozed around the bullet hole told the story.

"This bunch been fighting its way north, Cap'n," Jonah explained. "Likely this pony got hit on a raid and stayed strong enough to carry its warrior back to the village. But the Comanche plainly saw what you and me can see: this critter's dying."

As Hook inched over to the pony, it vainly tried to move away, although it had strength to do little more than stay on its four wobbly legs. Carefully, moving slowly, Jonah inched up to stroke one of the forelegs before picking it up to inspect the hoof. He set it back down, patting the animal's neck with one hand as he brought his pistol out.

That country proved flat enough that it swallowed his gunshot in the time it took the pony to fall without a struggle.

"What did the hoof tell you, Hook?"

He gazed up at Lockhart. "This bunch has been running. That hoof was sore and bleeding. Near worn out. Some of their stock didn't fare the winter so well. And still, this bunch is fighting on."

"Kwahadi, Mr. Hook," Lockhart said respectfully.

"Yes, Cap'n. I've come to know just what you mean."

"How long since they broke camp?"

He returned to the pony, rubbing his hand along the inside of the rear flanks, under the neck. The dampness of the hide and the heat of the animal gave him something to make his best guess.

"We're behind 'em less'n two days now."

Two Sleep came up. "Two days," he agreed.

"They find out we're back here, they'll bolt," Lockhart said to no one in particular.

Jonah shook his head. "I don't expect this bunch will get worried all that much about our outfit."

"You don't think they'll make a run for it—try to outdistance us?"

"No. From what all I've been learning about Comanche—I figure soon enough they just might turn around and wait for us to come right to 'em."

41

TALL ONE'S EIGHTEENTH summer was not that far away. Already Antelope was eager for his sixteenth spring. Together they had fought and killed Mexicans, Lipan, and Tonkawa. Black scalp locks hung from their war shirts, from their clubs and at the end of their bows. And both had struggled against the yellow-leg soldiers at the bottom of the red canyon. Still, their belts held no white man's scalp from that battle.

It would be only a matter of time now.

That small party of white men dogging their trail had the Kwahadi making no preparations for war. When the time came to turn about and strike, it would be nothing more than a brief inconvenience, a momentary interruption in their march north. To think that three-times-ten would have the gall to throw themselves against four times their number. It was nothing short of utter foolishness: these white men wanting to die so badly that they hurled themselves into sheer suicide.

On its way north one of the warrior societies had bumped into a roving soldier patrol. Antelope's hunting party had been of equal strength, so they had charged into the yellow-legs and made a fight of it. Two of the soldiers had been wounded, maybe bad enough to die. And one of Antelope's young friends had been knocked from his pony.

Antelope had joined another rider rushing in to pick the young warrior from the prairie and sling him to the back of his wounded pony. They turned about and headed across the rolling plain, in the direction they hoped to find the migrating village. By the time the warriors returned, the pony was clearly dying, its rider faring little better. The village war chief said they would have to abandon the animal. All the while the shamans continued to shake their gut rattles and beat on their hand drums—praying that the bullets left inside Antelope's friend would disappear and he would come back from the near-dead.

Antelope had grieved like never before when his friend failed to return to the land of the living. His spirit went on to cross the great Sky Road. That was the closest the lightning bolt of death had ever struck near Antelope. Like a passing spring thunderstorm, the death of his best friend heated the air and charged the ground where young Antelope stood, frightened him into greater resolve against the white man.

"What about our mother?" Tall One asked one morning.

"Big Mule's wife? What of her?"

"No. I am not talking about the mother who adopted you. I am talking about the woman who gave us birth."

Antelope stared at the ground, squeezing his eyes as if something must surely come of kneading his memory so hard. "I cannot remember her. There are no pictures anymore."

"Our sister?"

The young brother eventually shook his head. "No. Do you remember them?"

"Some things. If I try—I can remember."

"Pictures only?" Antelope asked, a little suspicion in his voice. "Or do you remember . . . words?"

Tall One could not lie to his brother. Keeping silent about it was like being turned wrong side out, just like a snake shedding its skin, from the inside out. "The more I try, looking at things, thinking on it hard—I remember some of the words. I remember other things too."

Antelope's eyes had darted back and forth like night birds, looking for anyone who might overhear. "Tell me."

"The touch of our mother's hand." He watched Antelope stare into the distance. Out there might prove to be his memories of her, of the life they once had. "Brother, can you remember how good it felt when she held us against her, rocked us to sleep?"

With a wag of his head he answered, "No. I can only remember Rain Woman and how she cradled me when I grew frightened."

"We were frightened a lot those first days, Antelope. Rain Woman was a good mother to you."

"She is the only mother I remember. And Big Mule is the only father I know."

He bit his lip a moment, then grew determined to say it. "You were too young, perhaps. But we both had the same father long, long ago. A tall, thin man with a long face."

"Like many of the *tai-bos*, did he have hair on his face?"

"Yes. I remember how loud his voice would get when I did something wrong. And I've been remembering how safe and secure I felt sitting in his lap when the sun had gone down at the end of a day, when he moved back and forth in a chair that rocked."

"I cannot remember such a thing. I know I have seen a chair—but not one that moves back and forth."

Tall One squatted slightly, then swayed forward and back in panto-mime. Then he stood again and sighed. "A few days ago I remembered how it felt to lay my ear against Mother's breast and hear her heart beating as she ran her fingers over my cheek. It was hard, and it took some time, but I remembered too the smell of our father—that fragrance of tobacco smoke from his pipe, and the rich smell of moist black earth that clung to him always."

"He was an earth-scratcher?"

"Yes. Like these settlers who are moving into our buffalo ground," he answered. "And just this morning before the camp awoke, I lay in my blanket thinking on those memories. Trying for more. And I did have a new one come to me: remembering the feel of his strong hands wrapped around mine as he taught me to shoot his rifle."

Antelope wagged his head, looking into his brother's face. "I never learned to shoot a rifle." Then his eyes brightened. "But I can use the lance, throw the tomahawk, use my knife, and shoot the bow as well as any."

He touched his younger brother on the shoulder. "Yes, you are as good as any Kwahadi warrior. But don't you see? It was not the learning of the rifle that I remembered most, Antelope. It was the safe, secure feel I had when that man took my hands in his and wrapped them around the gun, or the handle of a hoe, or held me in front of him in the saddle, or even let me handle the two horses hitched to our wagon."

A sudden wave of excitement was heard washing its way across the camp that morning. Antelope turned to see what caused the noise, then looked back at Tall One.

"I don't know what to think, my brother—except that maybe these memories are not so good to have so often. Better that you think of the Kwahadi. These are our people now. Try as I might, I cannot remember being anything else but Kwahadi."

"You want me to forget? Forget all that is good in my memories?"

Antelope nodded as they noticed some other young warriors hurrying their way. "You are strong enough to keep yourself from remembering. The *tai-bos* we lived among long ago are now our enemies. We belong to The People. You must tell yourself that the white people we once were are our enemies now."

"You mean our own white selves are now our enemies?"

"Perhaps, I do not know for sure. But what I am certain of is that your memories of that life are as evil as anything can be to our way of life with the Kwahadi."

"Antelope!" cried one of the arriving warriors rushing up in a swirl of noise and excitement.

Tall One's younger brother turned away, but not without whispering, "You are a Kwahadi warrior now."

"Tall One! Our war chief has given the word!" said Burns Red.

"Yes," cheered Old Owl Man. "We are to paint ourselves and make ready."

"For what?" Antelope asked.

"The white men," Burns Red replied. "They are not far behind us, say the scouts."

"Won't we pack up our belongings and move the village this morning?" Tall One inquired.

"No. The war council says we will wait right here for the three-times-ten to put their foot into the trap."

"What trap?" Antelope asked.

Old Owl Man chuckled, then said, "Not a real trap. Just that we are not running, not going anywhere. We know there are only a few *tai-bos* behind us—and their scalps will look good on our weapons, to decorate our war ponies."

"I want one of those big horses for my own," said Burns Red.

Antelope agreed. "My brother needs a horse."

Old Owl Man laughed. "I know—but Tall One has been pulling a travois and acting like a horse for so long, I am afraid he won't remember how to ride a horse!"

"I remember how to ride a horse—"

"Can you still fight from horseback?" demanded Burns Red.

His blood was warming. There was something about this friend of Antelope's that Tall One did not like. Never had. He was a cocky one. "I fight on a horse. I can fight on my own two feet. Would you like to fight me here and now, Burns Red?" Tall One growled.

The youth laughed, throwing his chin back and puffing up his chest. "No, Tall One. I want you to join us when we go fight these *tai-bos*."

"How close are they?" Antelope asked.

"If we wait for them right here, the scouts believe the white men will arrive by the time the sun reaches the top of its climb today."

"I must make ready," Antelope said, stepping away toward his friends.

"Aren't you going to make ready to fight the *tai-bos*, Tall One?" asked Burns Red.

How he wanted to pound the smirk from the young man's face. "Yes. I will go to my lodge now and ask Bridge for some of his paints and grease."

"You can use some of mine, Tall One," Antelope offered.

He shook his head, never taking his eyes off Old Owl Man and Burns Red. "Thank you, brother. But I will ask Bridge for some of his."

"It is good!" Burns Red mocked. "Dragging a travois is work worthy of only an old pony . . . work done only by a *tai-bo* who tries to be a Kwahadi. Will Tall One be a warrior today? Or will he fail and still be a *tai-bo* pony dragging a travois?"

Antelope tried to protest, saying, "He helped move the village each day like many of the others—"

Tall One put his hand out against his young brother's chest to interrupt him. "I did then what my people needed of me. And this morning I will make ready to fight these *tai-bos*. Because that is what my people need of me. Then—when we have killed these white men, and their scalps hang from our belts—I will call for you, Burns Red."

"Why will you call for me, Tall One?" Burns Red demanded haughtily. "You want to carry my belongings and be my *tai-bo* pony?"

The small group laughed with Burns Red and Old Owl Man.

"No. Because at long last, after all this time, I will see you take back all the insults you have heaped on me for so many seasons."

Burns Red laughed, and most of the others there laughed with him. "How are you going to make me take back these insults, Tall One, the *tai-bo* pony?"

"You will take them back—or I will kill you."

Captain Lockhart had kept the marches of the last two days as short as he could while still gaining some ground on the village moving before them. The Rangers were closing in, and their weary, broken-down stock had to be as ready as those men could make them.

Jonah felt proud to be among these men. Not one of them seemed concerned they were narrowing the lead on a force of proven warriors at least three, perhaps four times their own number. Instead of worrying about the coming fight, the Rangers instead talked about everything else but. Girls they left behind back home. What the coming spring meant to them as they were growing up. The smell of laundered sheets taken off the line by their mother and spread atop their tick mattresses with that once-a-week cleaning. The proper cutting of a male colt that made for the least amount of bleeding, hence narrowing the possibility of infection after doping the wound. How best to judge the fine qualities of a colt to know if you were going to geld him or leave him stand to stud.

As well as talking about which weapons were better than others there among Company C as it went through the last hours before those thirty-some men rode into war with Quanah Parker's Comanche.

That last day they had covered a minimum of twenty-five miles without unduly punishing their horses, but Lockhart urged them on just so they could reach this great depression in the prairie where cold rainwater had been trapped in the passing of a storm two nights back. It had been a damp dying of winter, cold and chill, and the Staked Plain was now dotted with many ponds, some as wide as a hundred yards or more.

The pond where the Rangers spent last night had been muddied by the village they were trailing. If the sediment hadn't settled, Lockhart explained to men who really needed little explanation, then the village could not be more than a half day's ride ahead.

They didn't light fires, nor did the captain allow any of the men to charge their pipes. That was perhaps the biggest loss to many of them—in Indian country a bowl of tobacco was so often a man's only consolation when he could not have a cheery fire at his feet, bringing his coffeepot to boil.

Instead, Lockhart would not allow the men to brood on what they were going to do without. He put them out in messes, separating the men as well as the horses they kept saddled in the event some of the Comanche had become aware of the Rangers on their backtrail and returned after nightfall to stir up trouble, attempting to run off their stock or make a night scalp raid. The wind grew ugly, and already there was a cold spit to it that served to let no man sleep. Throughout the long hours of cold darkness beneath a crooked strip of sky filled with whirling stars above that rolling tableland, the men had for the most part kept to themselves. Few talked at all, and if they did, it was only to let others know they were moving off for a minute or so to relieve themselves.

Somewhere in the middle of the night as the sky swung around the north star, the wind swung down around them from the north. It tasted now of snow, guffawing around their cheerless camp like mocking swirls of Comanche laughter. Then the first of the icy snow began in that hour past midnight, pattering against the canvas and leather and wool felt of their hats like little feet come to steal away every vestige of their hope of catching the enemy.

The cold, utter silence of that high, barren land seemed to swallow all sound in huge, hungry draughts . . . the darkness of that sky overhead graced with but the thinnest rind of moon behind the icy clouds, and that steady, incomprehensible rhythm of the wind, all made for one of the longest nights in Jonah's life. Without the talk of other men, without the luxury of being called to action, Hook was forced to talk to himself, forced to stay in one place where he could not flee his bitter memories. Bittersweet thoughts of the past, painful thoughts of what might have been, once more came to darken his mind like the spilling of a tin of lampblack.

What should have been.

Hattie was back there in the East, as safe as any man could make his daughter now. Learning about books and manners and cultured things and

. . . great Lord! he thought. Hattie would turn twenty this spring. Was it still February? No sure idea what month it was—he would have to find out from Coffee. The sergeant kept his log for Lockhart. And when they got down to Fort Concho, Jonah vowed to go in to the sutler's there and find something to send his daughter. Maybe a dress he could have posted to the seminary school he sent money to regular. Maybe he could even find a music box. He remembered how she had always wanted one of those. The perfect gift for a girl her age.

Twenty—he marveled. She was near five years older than her mama was when he and Gritta had married back in the Shenandoah. So Hattie wasn't a girl no more. She'd be a full-blown woman when at last he went back to get her.

As soon as he had his two boys back, as soon as he got back on Jubilee Usher's trail. He'd find Gritta. He'd find her. He'd find her.

He had found Hattie.

And now they were only a matter of hours from this village of Quanah Parker's Kwahadi who held white prisoners.

Jonah knew he had found his boys.

This done and his young'uns took back to Cassville, where they could likely stay with old Boatwright and help the old sheriff about his place . . . Hook would set out again, back to the land of the Mormons. How swiftly faded the dead from people's minds, he brooded. It was the living lost that haunted a man.

But he'd find her. He would find her.

The wind died a little as the east seeped into gray, then a murky crimson behind the fleeing snow clouds. For a moment it reminded him of the birth opening on one of the old cows back to Missouri. Helping the old girls work their calves out into this world, a struggle of cow pushing and man pulling, the calf all spindly of leg and refusing Jonah a dry place for a grip. It was all a part of life, that. So much of life a person damned well had to do on his own.

No one else to do it for him. Like this hunt. As much as Shad Sweete and Riley Fordham and now Two Sleep had come along to ride this trail with him—it was in the end his trail alone to ride this last mile.

Like these last minutes as Lockhart motioned them up to shake out the kinks from sitting out the passing storm, knock the ice off their blankets and shelter halves they had wrapped around themselves in that silent, icy darkness; told to roll them up and lash them behind saddles as they each and all shivered in that cold crunching of the predawn wilderness. Tightening cinches, warming bits before slipping them back into horses' mouths, loosening cold weapons in stiffened holsters and saddle boots.

With only a wave of his hand to give voice to his command, Captain Lamar Lockhart signaled Company C of the Texas Rangers into the saddle, and pointed that brave band of thirty into the dawn's cruel slash of whispering wind.

42

A FEW DAYS BACK one of them had told him what season this was. Said the Comanche called this the Moon of the Last Cold. Something like that. They also said next month was called the Moon of Geese Returning.

Could be, Jonah thought now as a cold, cheerless sun rose on that small band of white men moving north at an easy lope across the icy snow gathered in crusted fans around the stubble of dead prairie grass. Not so hard a pace that it would take any more than necessary out of the horses.

The ice crystals in the wind flew against his canvas mackinaw, pecked at the brim of his hat the way Gritta's chickens had pecked at the yard outside their cabin.

His eyes crawled from horizon to horizon. Maybe it was so, in a few weeks they might actually get to see the big longnecks stretching their great wings out in wide vees across the bright spring blue of the sky overhead. It was always a sight to behold, he told himself. No sight to match it, those longnecks coming and going, spring or autumn.

To think on how those birds made a circuit of their seasons, great loops encompassing thousands of miles with every flight. They would be moving around to the north soon, come the spring. Then back around, retracing those same thousands of miles with the first halloo of autumn. Hell, just like the buffalo. The numberless that wandered into the winds with the countless, ageless seasons.

Those animals no different from the wind itself that worked around a man in great loops that likely meant a journey of thousands of miles too, a journey that eventually brought the wind right back where it began.

How Jonah prayed the wind and this great endless cycle of the seasons would take him back to where he had started.

Prayed it, as Company C rode the cold sun up into that late winter sky unsullied by a single cloud, save for the east, where the storm had blown.

What a perfect day for a man to go hunting or fishing, to work his fields, to repair harness or fix that ill-hung door on the barn. Or a perfect day for a man to do nothing at all but lie on his back among the bounty of his fields and stare up at the great endless immensity of all God's handi-works. Wondering where he fit, in all that had been wrought of the seasons and sculpted by the wind around him.

A damned cold day as well, one fit for spilling blood. Then at last he could start back home with his boys.

This was turning out to be one of those late winter days when the sun hung high, dull as a pewter button, when the air would never really grow warm—when John Corn, who was riding point, suddenly wheeled his mount around in a tight, haunch-sliding circle and skedaddled back for the column. Reaching those in the lead, the Ranger pointed ahead, talking in hushed tones to the captain, then led Lockhart, Johns, and Coffee ahead a ways where all three stopped in view of the rest. Lockhart reached about and took his field glasses from a saddlebag, then sat staring, likely adjusting on something Jonah could not see with the naked eye, something lost in all that immensity of snowy brilliance.

"You think they've spotted the village?" Hook quietly asked Two Sleep beside him in the column.

The old Shoshone nodded. "Yellow jackets."

"Comanche? That what you figure?"

"That what I see."

Hook glared again, squinting into the shimmering distance of the icy plain, trying to make out anything that Two Sleep could claim would be Comanche.

Lockhart reined about, hurriedly stuffing the field glasses away. He slowed his horse to a walk as he reached the company and began by giving them what sounded like his first real order in many days as he rode down their line.

"Dismount."

They obeyed him instantly without question, without muttering a word. The only sounds among those thirty were those of the restive horses, the squeak of soaped leather, the rattle of buckle and chain, the squeak of holster and rifle boot. Their captain had news for them fit to singe the hair even in a Ranger's ears.

"If your cinches need tightening, now's the time," Lockhart instructed. "We've spotted the enemy ahead."

"The Comanch'?" Clyde Yoakam asked.

"No doubt, Sergeant," Lockhart said, wheeling his horse and walking it back up the line of men, who stood flipping stirrups over their saddles, tugging and tightening on cinches and cruppers, drawing up their own britches, taking belts up a notch or so. That done, some men pulled rifles from their boots with a noise like tired buggy springs, chambering a cartridge into the breech. Others broke open the action of their pistols, exposing cylinders, slipping a sixth round beneath the finely honed hammers.

"You see how many, Captain?" asked June Callicott.

"Not certain how many. Not really sure that they've seen us just yet either. If it weren't for the glasses I used, that camp'd still be just a black dot on the edge of the horizon. So it's not likely they know we're here just yet."

"You saw 'em still in camp?" Jonah asked, his eyes going to fix a cold, milk-pale sun against midsky.

"We've caught them sitting."

Hook wagged his head. "We didn't catch 'em, Cap'n. They ought to be up and on the move long before now. Only reason we got 'em sitting is those Comanche are waiting for us."

Lockhart's face went dark as scorched wood behind his bushy black mustache and that week's growth of shadow over his cheeks. He jutted his chin at Hook's severe appraisal of their situation. "So be it, men. Remount—and form into line for inspection."

Jonah had to admire the captain for that. Lockhart wasn't about to be bullied into fearing this bunch of warriors. He could be a cool one when it came down to cutting the deck with the whole night's game resting on this one last hand they were about to play.

The entire company came into the saddle and settled almost noiselessly, jostling their mounts left-about into one long line stretching right and left, facing their stiff-jawed captain. Clearly holding his horse in check, Lockhart eased down that formation, appraising each one of them from their sun-faded hat to the toes of their high-heeled boots stuffed clear to the insteps in the stirrups. Nearly every last one of them wore two belts, one looped over the other around their outer coats in a lazy X, all brass and lead that looked damned near as impressive as a crown of feathers would atop a proven Kwahadi warrior.

The captain slowed before Two Sleep and Hook, and stopped. "I'm a little concerned about your Snake here, Jonah. Going into battle now, things are likely to get a bit confusing for the rest of the men. Perhaps he should stay behind."

"I go fight with you," Two Sleep said evenly, his eyes held straight ahead, as unwavering and military as any soldier's.

Jonah felt more proud of him at that moment than he had since that morning in the red desert when they jumped Usher's Mormons. He stared straight ahead too as he said, "He'll do fine, Cap'n."

"If the Indian doesn't mind, I do need someone to see to the pack mules. Benton!"

"Sir?"

"Bring up those mules."

"What you have in mind doing with them two mules?" Hook asked as Billy Benton brought their pair of pack animals up and halted beside Lockhart.

"These mules carry what extra ammunition Company C has along," the captain explained. "I'm putting it in charge of the Snake here."

He turned to Two Sleep, whose black-cherry eyes finally veered to touch the captain's face. Lockhart asked, "You understand what's expected of you?"

The Shoshone nodded. "I guard the mules with my life."

Lockhart flashed a grin, motioning Benton forward with the picket ropes strung back to the mules. "I can see I've made a good choice in this matter. Thank you . . . Two Sleep."

It was the first time Jonah could recall any of the Rangers, much less the captain himself, calling the warrior by name. As if until this moment he had been just an Injun. A faceless, nameless red-belly. But in these minutes before the bloodletting, Two Sleep had somehow become one of them. Worthy of no less an honor than standing watch over their supply of cartridges.

No matter that there were biscuits and beans and bacon in those packs. The Shoshone had just been asked to protect what was even more precious, perhaps life sustaining. The bullets.

"For some of you this charge will be the first time you ever rode into something like this," Lockhart continued, reining his horse to the side and easing on down the line of Rangers. "Hell, I gotta admit I never rode into a bunch of Comanche that's been ready for us. No matter is it—your green will be worn off by the time the second shot is fired and you've got a whiff of gunpowder in your nostrils, men."

When the captain reached the end of the line, he sawed his mount about and brought his horse back to the middle, where he stopped to face his thirty. "You'll ride out at my order. I will take the point, and no man will allow his mount to pass mine. Make yourselves clear on that. When we begin, spread out ten feet apart, and keep the same pace as those on either side of you. Our success or failure will depend on us staying together."

Lockhart drew the back of his glove across his lips, chewed the lower lip a moment, then continued. "If one of you becomes separated from the company, do all that is in your power to make it back to us. In the end we may be pressed to dismount and fort up behind the bodies of our horses. If I give that order, we will circle Two Sleep and the mules. Re-form around the pack mules before we start dropping the horses."

"Dropping the horses, Captain?" asked Wig Danville. "Shoot 'em?"

"Yes."

"But, sir—I say ride. And ride hard. We fort up, them Comanche gonna swallow us up for sure."

"Danville, there's a lot of old frontiersmen who can tell you chapter and verse of their own history where the few held out against the many—and held the day."

"You run, Wig," Coffee added, "the Comanche got us separated. Chase us down one at a time."

"What the sergeant says is the gospel according to Lamar Lockhart," the captain added. "We stay together."

"We all live," Deacon Johns bellowed in that brimstone-laced voice of his, "or we all go to the bosom of the Lord our God together."

"Together," Lockhart reminded them. "Likely, it will be fighting these red-bellies to the last ditch and victory to the strongest."

"That ol' sulfur-belly of Satan's son is about to get his due from a jealous God!" Deacon Johns bellowed.

Then they all fell silent again as Lockhart's eyes went up and down the long line. Only when he had done so did the captain gently nudge his horse about. "Let's move out, Sergeant Coffee."

"You heard the captain!" Coffee bawled. "Move out!"

They closed on a mile of the village within a few heartbeats. Was no problem for any man to make out the village by then. A smudge of oily brown haze hung over the lodges. Morning cook fires. In the midst of the lodges there was the flicker of movement. Off to the right and beyond, Jonah could make out what extra animals the tribe could claim. Those that had not been brought into camp and readied. The warriors were already easing out of the village, disappearing for a moment as they led their ponies down the far slope of a wide arroyo, before reappearing on the near side where they halted. Waiting as more, and ever more came up.

Lockhart raised himself in the stirrups and twisted about to the left. Then the right, assuring himself of the readiness of his line spread out from him like great, undulating wings. Jonah sat two away from the end of the right flank. Behind them, riding center on Lockhart's tail root, came the Shoshone with those two pack mules strung out at a walk behind him.

The captain raised his left hand and made a quick circle with it, then brought the arm down.

Not a one of them uttered a word but as a body urged their mounts into a lope behind Lockhart as he settled back to his saddle.

They crossed that first quarter of a mile as the Comanche themselves began to spread out, milling a bit, but spreading left and right as the Rangers had formed. Within a moment the center of that line began to surge forward at a walk, away from the side of the arroyo.

All Jonah had to do was break through the Comanche and get across that arroyo. Into the village and find the boys. Before he figured the Comanche could escape with their prisoners.

There was a lot of dust coming from the north now, hung like a faint smudge against the blue of the midday sky. Far and beyond the pony herd.

Jonah figured some of the Comanche were already skedaddling. Retreating north. Fleeing as soon as the first cry had gone out that white men were coming. Damn, but that dust lay a long way off to the north. Far enough away that Hook prayed his boys were not already among those first to escape. To have that kind of head start.

"Good Lord!" exclaimed the man beside him.

Jonah's attention was yanked back to the warriors ahead of them as they passed the half-mile point. The Comanche horsemen still moved forward at no more than a walk, the heads of their ponies bobbing, a'flutter with scalp locks lashed to hackamores and shields and the muzzles of rifles and just back of the foot-long iron points on their buffalo lances. It seemed the number of riders doubled, then doubled again of a sudden as more and more appeared on the near side of that dusty arroyo. As if sprung from the ground itself.

"Quiet in the ranks!" Coffee snarled as more of the Rangers uttered surprise at getting their first good view of the numbers they were now facing.

But they held, and not one turned back nor slowed his gait. Jonah's heart swelled to be among these men who had helped bring him here to get his boys. These, the cold, cast-iron, double-riveted sort who now showed what they were made of, showed that they possessed the nerve few men are ever pressed to dig deep enough to find within themselves.

Then Lockhart was standing again in his stirrups, twisting about to give his command. "For Texas and our families! *Charge!*"

His words were barely uttered, driven on across that line by the cold breeze when Company C hammered their horses into a gallop behind their captain: the ringing of bit and spur chains, the clinking of stirrup irons, of buckles against cinches, the tinkling of bridle snaps and linkings, the groans of saddle leather and the squeak of fenders and skirts, the rubbing of the tall boots . . . then the air above the thirty blistered with their shouts and yells and profane vows. Hook's own throat ached with his *ki-yi-yi*-ing rebel wolf-cry as they galloped thigh by thigh.

As if that were the very cue for their own action, the Comanche burst into a ragged charge, closing the last quarter of a mile left to that arroyo in the space of a half-dozen heartbeats. Only enough time for Jonah to fire one shot with the Winchester before he booted it and yanked out his first belt gun.

He fired it once, then a second time as they closed on the fluttering line of half-naked horsemen glistening copper and wild-eyed in the midday winter sun. Hook stuffed the two thick latigo reins between his browned teeth and slid the second pistol from its holster.

There was time to fire one shot with it and a third from his right hand before the two lines collided in a crash of dust and stinging, swinging, swirling confusion. To his right he watched one of the Rangers go down, hurled from his saddle at the end of a warrior's lance. Jonah reined up savagely, his tired mount fighting the bit as he sawed about, firing at the warrior who had toppled the Ranger.

For the most part, the Comanche line had charged on through the Ranger flanks without great damage. Two more of Lockhart's men had been spilled, but they had clambered back to their knees, continuing to fire at the backs of the Comanche as the great warrior front came about, screeching and singing out their death songs.

He looked for Two Sleep, found the Shoshone just this side of the arroyo, struggling with the frightened mules near Lockhart. Barking his orders in that loose-shouldered way of his in the dust, noise, and confusion, the captain's mouth was no more than a black O in his shadowy face. No telling what he was ordering. But he was pointing, waving his pistol hand as his horse pranced high-headed, round and round in a tight circle.

Then Jonah saw what Lockhart was hollering about. More warriors were swarming out of the village now, plunging down into the arroyo, catching the Rangers between the two groups of painted horsemen.

Hook really didn't need to hear the captain's voice to sense what order was being given. He saw those who were closest to Lockhart whirl about and retreat, falling back on Two Sleep. Come the time to fort up.

There in some of the brush by the lip of that snow-crusted arroyo smeared darkly with a narrow trickle of runoff against its far side.

"Throw them down!" they were yelling at each other. "Throws 'em down!"

The first of the horses were falling as Hook slid his mount to a halt near Two Sleep and stuffed one of the pistols away. He snugged the animal's muzzle down tight, struggling to shoulder the animal up beside Callicott's horse already down and kicking its last. He fought him, fought the smell of blood and gunpowder strung in thick layers in the air. Stuffing the gun's barrel in front of the ear, he pulled the trigger. The big roan yanked its head away, thrashing as its legs went to water beneath its great weight. He barely had time to leap out of the way as it crashed onto the thin, icy crust of snow and lay there at Hook's feet heaving its head, as if willing itself to stand. Then, as its life seemed to ebb before his eyes, the roan lay almost still in a matter of moments, still except for the last wheezing cries coming from that heaving chest. In a shudder it was done.

"Awright, boys!" Niles Coffee was yelling. "In a matter of minutes there's gonna be lead smacking around here, thicker'n smoked bees!"

Jonah dropped behind it as the new line of warriors came splashing across the narrow creek and flung sand from a couple hundred hooves in great golden cascades like roosters' tails. To his left came one of the men running for the barricade on foot. Slade Rule slid behind the carcass of horse, his chin whiskers and the front of his dirty shirt smeared with blood. The man rolled onto his side, wheezing, trying to speak, his back and chest pocked with uncounted bullet holes.

"You made it," Jonah said, kneeling over him. Gazing into the fear-drenched, teary eyes of that youngster beneath him. "You hang on for now—you're gonna make it rest of the way."

As Jonah tried to inch away, Rule snagged his sleeve, pulling him back, his mouth working mechanically, soundlessly against the great cacophony of battle snarling around them: bullets whining past or thudding into the bodies of their dying horses, the cursing of men, the bellows of Lockhart's and Coffee's and Deacon Johns's orders, the cries of the wounded Rangers, the shrill death songs of the enemy, the wailing of the women across that arroyo . . . in the village where Jonah had intended to go.

"Good and kind, brother Jesus!" the deacon shrieked, half standing, firing with a pistol in each hand. "Heartily smite these heathen sinners!"

As he gazed back down at the Ranger, Rule's eyes widened, then eased half-down the mast. His hand loosened on Jonah's arm as the rest of his body slumped. Hook used two thumbs to ease the eyelids closed.

"What the hell are those bastards up to now?" June Callicott was hollering, half standing at the barricade of carcasses.

Hook found the greater number of warriors breaking off their attack after those first few grinding minutes. The Rangers, what was left of Company C inside that ring of carcasses, lay waiting among the sprawled and leg-flung horses for the next rush by the Comanche.

"Sonsabitches gonna work us down with their goddamned wheel," Coffee reminded them.

Harley Pettis dropped his serious bulk to his knees. "They re-forming, Sarge?"

Coffee and the rest watched the horsemen pulling off. The second wave from the village joined up with the first, swirling about one another, working themselves up into a fighting frenzy, shrieking at one another, waving lances and shaking scalps.

"Looks like they're ready to wear us down, boys!" Lockhart promised them.

But as the Rangers watched, breaking open the actions on their pistols to dump empty cartridges, jamming new ammunition into their heated weapons, the lords of the southern plains surprisingly did not form into that spinning, death-carrying wheel that would work itself around and around its prey, inch by inch, yard by yard, moment by moment grinding away, working ever closer to the white man until the enemy could be overrun in one great sweep of terror.

Instead, the Comanche drew off.

Stunned, slack-jawed in shock, Jonah stood, watching the horsemen drive their ponies into the arroyo, plunging across the sand and up the far side into the remnants of the village where all was of a sudden panic.

Above the screaming and wailing of the women, the barking of the dogs and the war cries of the men, above it all floated the first distant, but no less distinct, notes of a bugle.

43

"HOOK! GET BACK here!"

Most of the Rangers had to be in shock, finding themselves between two overwhelming waves of battle-frenzied warriors in those first few minutes of panic, only to watch utterly dumbfounded as the horsemen drew off their attack.

"Hook! Goddammit—you'll be killed!"

Jonah heard Lockhart's voice behind him as he vaulted the horse carcass and skidded down the loose, giving sand at the icy side of the arroyo. His high-heeled riding boots felt clumsy in sand as he plowed through, heading for the narrow stream, for the far side, for the village suddenly up, screaming and on the run.

Just who the hell was that outfit?

Goddamned soldiers, he grumbled—and they'd go and chase off the Comanche before he could get into the village to find the boys.

If the boys were still alive.

Chances were if the village found itself between the attacking Rangers and some soldier outfit, they'd slaughter any prisoners they still held.

The cold water lashed up against his bare skin, assaulting face and hands—as he ran flat out for the far side of the arroyo, aware for the first time of two dozen or more warriors racing along that north lip, skidding their ponies to a halt and dismounting on the run. In a blood fury.

Jonah turned to find out he was not alone. Behind him came a half dozen, maybe more, of the others. Every one of them firing their pistols and yelling at him, some even snarling at the warriors who had set up their own howl as they fired back and began dropping over the lip to spill into the snow-crusted arroyo, ready for some close, dirty fighting of it.

If he could just break through them, Jonah knew he could claw his way up the side and get into that village before the soldiers overran it. His boys—they might be mistook for Injuns in the dust and confusion by some green-gilled, nervous soldier who would shoot a white youngster by mistake.

A bullet hissed past his ear. He dropped on instinct. Jonah whirled in a crouch to find the warrior lunging for him at the same time the Comanche and Rangers closed ranks in a clattering collision that reverberated across the bottom of that arroyo. Hook rose to meet the screaming, painted demon hurling down on him like the master of hell itself.

The Comanche was young, strong. They grappled, stumbled backward. The warrior threw Jonah to the ground.

For a moment Hook stared up at the Indian's eyes, not startled to find his enemy no more than a youth. The predictable foolishness of these young warriors—come back to cover the retreat of their village in the face of the soldier charge. The distant firing loomed closer still above the rim of the arroyo as he struggled with the warrior, who suddenly gripped a knife.

Glinting in the sun, it sailed overhead, then hung suspended there for a moment at the end of the youth's arm. Jonah mightily lunged for that wrist with one hand, his right leaping to the Comanche's throat, where he locked his fingers into a noose around the windpipe.

In but a moment Jonah sensed the arm weaken slightly, felt the shudder of his enemy as the Comanche fought for breath, clawing at the white man's hand crabbed at his throat. Heaving himself up off his shoulders and hips, Hook desperately threw the strong youth to the side.

All about them men clashed and grappled in the thick of close quarters: grunting, crying out, cursing, yelling, begging for help. The smack of weapons against bone and sinew. The soggy slap of bodies pitched into the shallow, icy creek.

For that critical heartbeat the Comanche warrior lay gasping, his mouth a huge O, wheezing, coughing for breath as he rolled onto his side. Eyes wide with fury, hate, for the white man who had near killed him.

Hook threw himself atop the warrior as a war cry from beyond bit Jonah's ears. All around him the rest of the fight faded as Hook landed on the Comanche trying to rise, wrestling his enemy back down, pinning the warrior by dropping a knee against the youth's throat. Hook dragged the knife from the Indian's hand.

With his left Jonah savagely yanked back on the man's long hair, surprised to find it something other than black. He laid the edge of the blade under one ear as the wild eyes went wider, glaring into Jonah's face.

Hook's hand froze. He studied the hazel eyes, the sharp slash of nose, the crease of cheekbone no longer disguised beneath the war paint smeared in their combat. Hope. Fear. Desperation—

"Jere— . . . Jeremiah?"

As quickly the Comanche's grunt of exertion faded. The warrior's eyes stared back at Jonah's face as the Indian stopped wrenching at the hand locked in his scalp, stopped yanking at the wrist and hand and knife pressed against his jugular. Jonah watched something like wonder, something of disbelief come into those eyes. Something almost familiar. The look he imagined Gritta would have in her eyes when at last he held her in his arms.

"P-pa?"

"Oh, dear Jesus . . . ," Hook whispered, his hands opening, releasing his son's hair, letting the knife tumble into the sand. He could not take his eyes off the eyes of the one beneath him, seeing there the question, as well as the recognition, then the return of question and confusion.

Of a sudden there Jonah also saw the horror of something come to contort the face of his son.

"No-o-o-o-o-o!" Jeremiah shouted, drowning out everything else around them.

At first Jonah only sensed the dull pressure of it. No real pain. Just an instant of burning in his back, a metallic skittering along his ribs . . . then the cold.

A gunshot roared so close, Jonah flinched.

And the icy-hot pressure was gone, gone as quickly as he had realized it was there. For a moment he gazed back at the face of his oldest son, realizing that he was slipping, slowly releasing his grip on everything— losing consciousness.

Oh, God! his mind cried out, not sure if his lips really formed the words or not . . . dear God! To come this close. To hold Jeremiah so close and now to lose it all. Not this way, God. Not this way!

He had some distant recognition that men were shouting all around them now as Jeremiah heaved himself up on his knees, catching Jonah as he crumpled slowly, slowly, his lips moving wordlessly, muttering prayers . . . tears flooding his eyes.

As he closed them for that last time, Jonah recognized the tears in Jeremiah's eyes, saw their tracks streaking down through the shiny, smeared, dust-furred war paint.

Tears.

Antelope had tumbled down the loose, snow-crusted side of the arroyo onto the icy sand without stopping, racing headlong for his brother as the white man spun Tall One onto his back and jammed the knife along his brother's throat.

Shrieking his powerful war song as he closed on the enemy, Antelope hurtled forward through the cascades of ice and stinging sand thrown up by others colliding, grunting, locked together in deadly combat. He had first to save his brother from this enemy ready to cut Tall One's throat.

His own throat filled with the screech of the Kwahadi death song as he pistoned back his powerful right arm. At the end of that arm he brandished the haft of a long war club cruelly studded with three eight-inch iron blades. His father had given him that weapon when Antelope went on his first scalp raid.

Tall One's eyes saw him coming.

Antelope's brother yelled out, screaming something in the confusion and the noise as Antelope's own blood hammered hotly in his ears. No worry—soon enough Antelope would save Tall One's life.

In a white-hot fury he swung the war club downward with all the force he could muster in that arm and shoulder. Tall One pushed against his enemy at that moment: instead of burying the three blades deep in the white man's back, Antelope struck the shoulder blade, slicing down against the collarbone itself. Blood spurted into the air flecked with icy crystals as the weapon slid deeper still through layers of muscle and tendon.

Still not deep enough.

Tall One screamed again, putting up an arm as if to stop him as

Antelope drew the club back for a second swinging blow. The one he hoped would be the killing strike. Finish off the enemy—

His chest burned, like a rope of fire pulled taut to sear through it. Then feeling was gone in him. Not all, but most, as control fled his body on hawk's wings and the club tumbled out of his hand, spilling into the sand. He went to his knees.

He stared at the club, trying to reach out for it, helpless as he saw the blood splattered all over him. Not knowing in that moment if it was the white man's, or his own. Another . . . then a third rope of fire burned through his chest.

Antelope crumpled sideways to the sand. Alone. His eyes staring blindly at his older brother . . . not understanding why Tall One cradled the white man.

The enemy.

He died, blank-eyed, hoping he had killed the *tai-bo*, hoping he had dispatched his enemy's soul to hell.

There was little time for Jeremiah to react, hardly more time than it took him to holler out—throwing his arm up to try to fend off the war club, an instant to try pushing his father to the side when Antelope came careening off the slope of the arroyo, that weapon held high as it sailed downward in its arc of death.

Jeremiah cried out again, watching the first bullet hit Antelope, jerking his body upward, blood splattering as the lead exited the chest in a crimson corona. His young brother wobbled to his knees, crouching there suspended over their father as the blood came coughing from Zeke's mouth, dribbling from his nose as a second, then a third bullet smashed into his chest. Blood flung over Jeremiah as his brother crumpled to the side.

How he yearned to go to gather Zeke into his arms as he cradled his father's limp, bloody body. He could only kneel, clutching his father as in horror he watched his brother's legs convulse, watched the red-stained fingers in that now empty hand twitch. Saw those dark eyes in the midst of that sand-caked war paint staring back at him.

Blank and wide. Without expression.

Jeremiah prayed that meant Zeke had died without pain.

There was, after all, no pain he could see in his young brother's eyes as

Jeremiah rocked and rocked, and rocked his father, calling out for someone to come help him. Then realized he was screaming in Comanche.

That was when Two Sleep had come over to kneel with Sergeant Coffee and June Callicott beside the warrior who had his bloodstained arms locked around Jonah Hook.

Slowly, concentrating on how finally to say it after all these years of hearing the name, the Shoshone had asked, "Jeremiah?"

And the Comanche had nodded. Then finally said in crude, stuttering English, "Jeremiah Hook . . . me."

Coffee and Callicott had gently rolled Jonah over before Two Sleep tore strips from his own cotton shirt to make bandages to lay on the gaping wounds: muscles torn asunder, lying purple and red against the whitish-purple of bone. Jonah's breath whistled through his blood-flecked nose, and at the back of his throat he gurgled slightly.

They had to tell Jonah about all that days later when he had the strength to listen in those rare times he came to and opened his glazed eyes. Two days after the fight, after burning and destroying the village, Colonel Davidson's buffalo soldiers had pulled out for the east. Two more days and Captain Lockhart had started his own men south. Two Sleep helped John Corn and June Callicott craft the half-dozen travois they used to pull their wounded behind captured Comanche ponies.

The Rangers buried their dead there in the middle of that small circle of frozen horseflesh.

Jeremiah cleaned his brother's body, then wrapped Ezekiel Hook in a blanket and buffalo robe he claimed from the lodges before the whole village was put to the torch by the buffalo soldiers.

When at last it came time for the Rangers to go, Jeremiah had knelt over his father, gently awakening him before Lockhart started Company C south.

"You bring Zeke along?" Jonah had asked that cloudy morning that promised an afternoon squall of sleet boiling on the horizon.

Jeremiah had nodded. "Like you asked."

Now his son's English had gotten better for all the practice over the past weeks as they followed Company C south by east toward Jacksboro and Fort Richardson. It was there that Jonah looked up after that awful, bouncing ride he suffered in the travois and beheld Captain Lamar

Lockhart come back on foot, removing his hat. The Ranger chief stood above him a moment, as if that courageous man were of a sudden fiddle-footed and shy.

"Time for you to head on home, I s'pose, Jonah Hook," Lockhart had said.

"S'pose I can. Least I found my boys." His eyes had stung as he stretched the healing flesh to reach into his pocket, the only one he had, a pocket sewn in the greasy shirt over his heart. It was there the Rangers carried their badges.

Jonah pulled out his six-pointed star and offered it to the sad-eyed captain. Lockhart took it reluctantly.

"Won't be needing it now," Hook said, tiring from the talk already.

"You keep it, Private," Lockhart said, backing off a step and putting his hat back on his head while more of the company gathered in a crescent behind him. "Just want you to know, Jonah Hook—the Rangers will always be in need of men like you."

"By damn if that ain't the Lord's honest truth," Deacon Johns added.

When Lockhart saluted the man lashed to the travois, there was a rustle as the others of Company C did the same.

"We wish you God's speed as you take this long trail back home," the deacon said, coming forward to squeeze Hook's hand with his strong, veiny paw.

"Going home only for as long as I can't sit a horse, Deacon. Still got another out there I swore I'd find."

"May the good Lord watch over you and keep you in the palm of His hand," Johns said, squeezing Hook's hand again before he turned away to join Coffee, Callicott, Pettis, and the rest.

"Don't make yourself a stranger you ever come down into Texas again," Lockhart said, his voice cracking, though it filled with cheer. "You ask for me—or Company C. Ain't nothing you'll ever want for in west Texas."

That had been painful, bouncing weeks ago. Watching Lamar Lockhart and his company of Rangers move off quietly. Good men he would remember for the rest of his days.

Two Sleep had done most of the bartering for provisions. Jeremiah's halting English still came hard those two days they hung close by at Richardson and Jacksboro before finally pushing north one dawn as the yellow light stirked up into the blue-gray of a late-winter sky. They were heading east by north for Missouri: two riders and five horses, a wounded man slung on one bouncing travois, along with a long, narrow bundle encased in a buffalo skin and bound by rawhide strips for its journey.

Through those Indian nations granted reservations in the Territories, they finally crossed the Arkansas and into the thickly wooded hills that Jonah began to recognize as winter whimpered its last. He was able to ride that last week, able to stay in the saddle a few hours more every day, his left arm lashed tightly to his chest to keep that broken collarbone from moving, to keep the pain down across the shoulder blade. Doing what he could with the tightness of the muscles and his own damned hide, so tight it didn't feel as if it were really his, more like he had tried on a suit of skin a size or two too small.

But he figured it would fit, eventually—like a pair of tight boots, once he got a chance to work those muscles and that new skin a bit. The wounds hurt, more than anything had hurt him in his life as he put the muscles and tendons, sinew and skin to work at last in early April. Hard, hard work.

The other two had pleaded with Jonah to let them help him as he resolutely drove the shovel into the old mound of dirt beside the first of the graves he swore he would fill.

"She's my sister, pa," Jeremiah said ultimately, struggling until he found the words.

Jonah saw his son's eyes fill with pools, thinking that this must be just how his own young face must have looked of a time when he had asked a childlike Gritta Moser to be his wife and life companion, remembering how her acceptance had brought tears to his eyes.

"All right, son. I'll be pleased to have your help."

Jeremiah had taken their only shovel from Jonah's hands and put his strong back into throwing the sod back into that dark, empty hole. He made short work of it, then straightened.

"Next one . . . my hole?"

"Yes," Jonah answered softly. "Your grave. Fill it. I found you, Jeremiah. Fill it like you filled Hattie's."

Without reply, the young man bent to the work and soon had the second of the graves nearly full as Two Sleep looked on. Without the benefit of body nor coffin, and the effect of years of rain and snow eating away the mounds of dirt Jonah had left beside those empty holes back of a cold January in sixty-seven, the first two graves appeared more to be slight depressions than mounded scars marking a person's final resting place.

Jeremiah came over to stand with his father beside the third hole. "This by mine hole—it for Zeke?"

Jonah could only nod, clearing his throat. He turned to the Shoshone, who stood close, his own eyes glistening, his jaw motionless. "Two Sleep—you help Jeremiah ease his brother down in that hole?"

Between the two of them they got Zeke lowered on ropes, then stood, waiting for Jonah as he stopped at the foot of the grave, when it started to snow. Hook knelt, scooped up some of the years-hardened soil, and tossed it in. Landing on the buffalo hide, the dirt made a dull but distinct noise there in the quiet of that late afternoon near the empty shell of the cabin the man had built for his woman and family years gone the way of time everlasting. Behind them among the hills the heavier snow crept down the slopes, falling softly without a sound but for the frosty breathing of those men and their animals near the private graveyard Jonah Hook had made of his private quest.

"I'll always carry this pain in my heart for you, Zeke. Found your sister. Found your brother. It hurts, goddammit—hurts knowing I was a little late finding you, son. That's a pain I'll end up carrying in my heart for the rest of my days. As much a pain as having to think that you never really knowed me as a father . . . you was so young when I walked off to fight a war."

The snow hit the shoulders of his canvas mackinaw with a soft hiss as Jonah stepped back and motioned with his free arm to the others. "A war I ain't been able to come home from yet."

Without a word between them Jeremiah and Two Sleep took turns hurriedly scooping dirt into Ezekiel's grave. When they were finished, it was the only one of the three holes crowned with a rounded top. Jeremiah's and Hattie's had been filled with dirt only.

Yonder, on the far side of Hattie's and right beneath the bare, skeletal, spreading arms of the elm, remained a single dark, gaping hole that stood out starkly against the new snow thinly blanketing the ground.

Jonah was already kneeling at the side of that last empty grave when Two Sleep came up to stand across from him on the far side of the yawning hole. Jonah heard Jeremiah come up beside him. The young man knelt, laying an arm across his father's wounded shoulder.

Jonah gazed briefly at his son, eyes wet again. "I'm going back out there again, Jeremiah."

The youth nodded, able to keep his own eyes from spilling.

"Me and Two Sleep going after your ma," Jonah said, turning to look across that empty grave at the Shoshone with what his eyes made of an unspoken question.

The warrior nodded, his dark, ropy hands folded in front of him here among the spirits in Jonah Hook's own private burial ground.

"I'm going with you, pa."

The words came so strong, so sure, no faltering as they were spoken, that Jonah took his eyes off the Shoshone to look back at the face of his son. "Don't think I could take you, Jeremiah. Gonna be a dangerous trail I'm taking now."

"Look at you, pa. All stove up."

"I'll heal."

"I know you will. Still, it don't make no matter what you say."

"I'm your pa, Jeremiah."

He shook his head, his eyes brimming. "But I ain't a little boy no more."

That stung him, then as quickly filled Jonah with pride. "I . . . I plainly see you ain't no little boy no more."

Jeremiah reached out and folded his father into his arms. "But that don't mean I ain't your son no more. Nothing ever gonna change that. I know now that nothing ever could change that."

Refusing to believe what his heart told him, Hook started to choke out the words, "I ain't so sure I should—"

"She'll always be my mother," Jeremiah interrupted, turning to look down into the dark hole in the midst of all of that white swathing the ground. A wet, spring snow. "I owe her just as much to try as you do, pa."

His heart leapt, burning with his love for that youngster he hadn't watched grow up. Burning with love for his son who had swiftly crossed all those years they had been apart by bridging that great gulf with his own love. For a moment Jonah wondered where Jeremiah could have ever learned that sort of love . . . then he knew, thinking suddenly on Gritta once more, here beside her empty grave.

His voice cracked as he said, "You always did sort of favor your mother, son."

Jonah realized Jeremiah had gotten the best his mother had to give him. It was always that way with Gritta: giving everything to her man and their children.

"I want to do this for you too, pa." Jeremiah helped his father stand in the cold as the wind shifted, swinging out of the south.

"You sure about this, son?"

He nodded, straightening his strong back. "I ain't really asking you, pa. I'm *telling* you what I'm going to do. With you . . . or without you: I'm going after my mother."

Jonah brought the young man into his arms and hugged him fiercely. Holding him like he had never held Jeremiah before. As a man.

"Son, let's go find your mother."

And as they turned from that open black hole, so like the empty place torn through the middle of Jonah's heart, the snow became a cold rain.

A slow, tearful, winter rain.

Epilogue

NATE DEIDECKER DARED not admit it, but he was relieved to know that Jonah Hook would be getting him back to the cabin tomorrow afternoon.

Still, with all his fears, this horseback ride into the splendid serenity of the Big Horns had been one of the singular events in the life of the young newsman. Something he vowed he would tell his grandchildren about when they gathered at his knee. Funny to think on that now, for there had been times in the past three days Nate had entertained serious doubts of ever living long enough to father any children, much less come to enjoy his grandchildren.

What stories he would regale them with, sons, daughters, grandsons, and granddaughters all—tales to make them cringe, tales that would make their hair stand on end, make their eyes grow wide and their mouths O in surprise. These true tales of Jonah Hook.

The sun was glorious beyond belief falling into the west beyond their camp that night on the western slope of the mountains. Out there beyond, yonder in Teddy Roosevelt's Yellowstone Park, it seemed to be settling, as here the light bled away to magnificent stillness. How the air of these evenings hummed with a radiant alpenglow, cooling quickly as the old frontiersman puttered about the camp he made them that night. Having started the fire and left Deidecker to tend it, Hook had proceeded to erect the newsman's small dog tent, unfurling in it Deidecker's canvas bedroll wrapped around its wool blankets. Then Jonah had unpacked the cast-iron skillet and small kettle, along with that monster of a battered pot capable of making a gallon of coffee. From a nearby freshet running through the meadow Hook had drawn them water, then set the blackened vessel on the flames to boil.

The haunch of a young doe Jonah had shot at midmorning was sliced, and two thick slabs of the bloody meat now covered the bottom of the old man's skillet, ready for frying when the time came. The singular, invigorating smell to the air of these mountain evenings made Nate all the hungrier. If Jonah hadn't protected the loin steaks, Deidecker might well have tried to raise a slice or two and wolf it down raw.

In the past three days of travel through this wilderness he had come to understand why the plainsmen said what they did about eating when a man had the chance to—a man never knew when his next meal would come. Try as he might, though, Nathan Deidecker could not get used to rising early, even before the sun had warmed the air, to eat a big breakfast before they would ride all day without stopping for a midday meal. This pushing his body to its limits was something new to the reporter born and raised in Iowa, gone after six early years of news work to Nebraska when he had the offer of a position with the prestigious *Omaha Bee.*

"So the chromo back at your cabin wasn't you at all, was it, Jonah?"

With that question coming out of the blue after so much silence shared between them, the old man looked up from the prairie onion he was slicing with a belt knife. "You had it figured all wrong, Nate?" He chuckled easily. Then he stared somewhere past the newsman, saying, "No fault of your'n. Jeremiah did favor me in some ways. Near a spitting image of me in my younger days. That boy got the worst of me, Gritta always said. And I always answered by saying Jeremiah got the best of her."

Then Hook's eyes came back to Deidecker's face as he said, "Proud to think you thought Jeremiah was me of a time. That boy was really a handsome lad—more so than I ever was. But, then, I always was proud of my boys . . . both of 'em."

"You still miss Zeke, I can tell."

"Shows that much, does it?" He sighed. "Yes. Proud of my youngest.

He died defending his people. Died fighting for the ones he loved. I have to remind myself of that when I get feeling like there's little else left for an old man like me. And then too I remind myself that I gave my boys a good legacy. There's something real decent about my boy dying defending those he loved."

Nate allowed the old frontiersman some time down in his thoughts. Later, as a breeze came up, Deidecker asked, "So Jeremiah did go with you to find her—Gritta—like you said he wanted to there at the side of the woman's grave?"

Loose-shouldered, Hook shrugged, answering. "We'll talk more about that last hunt when we get back to home tomorrow afternoon. After we see to Gritta."

"She cook when you're gone?"

He wagged his head. "No. Have to leave her food to eat. Can't let her get her hands on matches. It's just that . . . she's got so forgetful, she might hurt herself. I leave her food what I've already cooked if she gets to being hungry. It ain't often that she eats more'n a mouthful at a time. For the life of me don't know how she keeps up her strength way she does."

"At first I thought—well, about that picture at the cabin—thought the woman in the picture was Grass Singing, the Pawnee woman you told me about meeting in Abilene. Then I later had it figured she was Pipe Woman."

"Shad's daughter?" Hook asked, his eyes gone wistful in looking at the sunset, the last rosy rays of Spanish gold streaking through the quaking aspen snatched and teased by the breeze. "That's one woman would've been a handful for any man to tackle, Nate. In or out of the blankets. My, but was she ever a prize, that one."

"Do I detect some old longing there, Jonah?"

He shrugged. "No doubt to it, son. Things been different . . . well, let's just say other men might'n stayed on with her and give up what everyone claimed was a hopeless chase."

"But you didn't give up, Jonah. That's the miracle of all of this to me—and you got Gritta back."

"Me and Jeremiah brung her back, Nate."

"Where is Jeremiah now? Does he live close?"

"No," he answered, an immense sadness in that single word. "Down in the Territories."

"Didn't you know? Last year Congress made the place a state, Jonah."

"They have, have they?" A faint smile crossed his face. "Good for them. The Injuns, that is."

"Call it Oklahoma. Some say it means 'home of the red man.' "

"Home of the red man. Fitting, you know?"

"What's Jeremiah do down there? Farm?"

"Last I heard, he was working for the army—training horses for the cavalry. Buys and trains mounts." Abruptly Jonah beamed as proud as any father could, declaring, "He rode with Roosevelt right up San Juan Hill into the teeth of them Spaniards' guns, you know."

"If that doesn't beat all, Jonah!" Nate exclaimed, sensing at least one story that might come from Jeremiah's remarkable life. Taken by the marauders; sold to comancheros; his years among the Comanche and his life as a warrior on the southern plains. Yes, Nate glowed, knowing he had more stories he could write: front-page, banner-headline stories.

Deidecker said, "So Jeremiah was the handsome young man in the chromo you have back at the cabin."

"Yes, Nate. That was took a few years after we went back to Cassville to fill in those two graves in seventy-five. Time I buried Zeke."

Nathan studied the old man. Jonah was frozen, staring down at his hand held motionless over the onion and knife and the bark slab he was using as a cutting board. Deidecker's heart lurched for the pain that remembrance must have caused the old man.

Quietly Deidecker said, "No one could ever blame himself for what happened to Zeke the way you've been blaming yourself all these years."

For a long, long time Jonah did not answer. When he did, he began by working the knife down through the onion again. "Should've brung him back alive too."

"Three out of four—good Lord . . . after all those years, Jonah—my God! Bringing back three out of the four from the clutches of that madman and all the hell he had caused your family."

Jonah glared at the newsman. "Ought'n been different, Nate. Ain't no one left for me to blame now but myself."

"That's the cruelest blame of all, Jonah."

His eyes came up, hooded and accusing, gazing at the newsman. "It's for me to say who I'm gonna blame. And that's the last we're gonna speak of it."

He understood Hook had just told him something important: declared something off-limits from here on out. Feeling chastised, Deidecker contented himself with watching the old man crack one of the doe's thick leg bones on one of the rocks ringing the fire. Jonah then scraped out the marrow into the small kettle. It began to melt, sizzle, and spit as soon as the old man suspended the kettle over the fire from the iron tripod. Jonah dropped the chopped onions through his fingers into the warming marrow, then sat back and sighed, staring into the flames cradling the bottom of the kettle in yellow-tipped tongues of blue.

"Tell me about that woman in the picture then. She was Jeremiah's wife?"

"Zeke's. And those are my grandchildren. Got fourteen grandchildren now, between Jeremiah and Hattie."

"Where did Hattie end up after going east to get her schooling?"

"Lots of stories there too, Nate."

"I don't want to push too hard again, Jonah."

Hook chuckled softly. "She married her a wealthy man. S'pose nowadays they call that sort of man influential. He's a U.S. senator from Pennsylvania."

"Time comes, you'll tell me his name too?"

Hook wagged his head. "No. But you could go and find out—a fella like you could."

Nate nodded. "I suppose I could, Jonah. Each state has only two senators."

"Sort of narrows it down, don't it, Nate? But you digging around for it won't do the young fella no good—no good to see you write up his name in your paper, saying his father-in-law's this high-plains desperado and his mother-in-law was this . . ." Hook stopped of a sudden, wiping the knife off on the front of his pants leg before he held it pointed at Deidecker across the fire. "Let's just get this straight—I don't wanna hear that Hattie and her husband and their young'uns ever get mentioned in your stories. We agreed on that, Nate?"

Deidecker glanced down at the knife blade glinting in the firelight. "You aren't threatening me to keep it out of the story are you, Jonah?"

"No. I'm not threatening you. Never threatened a man in my life. All I'm doing is promising that if you say anything hurts that man, it'll hurt my daughter. And, well—Nate. You know how I feel about folks what go and hurt my family."

The newsman swallowed, not really sure how to read the look on the old man's seamed face, the cold-banked fires in his eyes. "All right,

Jonah. It isn't really important, is it? This is, after all, really *your* story."

"I see them, my grandchildren from time to time. Hattie brings 'em out here of a summer, occasional. Figure it'll be about time next year for them young'uns to see their grandpappy, go fishing and ride horses back into these hills. You see, Gritta and me don't have all that much time left, you know."

"You must be joking, Jonah. You're . . . you seem as strong as a mule."

"Thanks, Nate. I do get by, and that's probably what is important in the end."

"Do you get to see Jeremiah's family much?"

"When I can. He's brought 'em up here a time or two. Mostly I've took Gritta down there to the Territories."

"Oklahoma."

"Yes, to Oka-lahoma. To the reservation where he lived with his wife for years after Quanah Parker's people come in and surrendered to Mackenzie later on in June that year."

"That was seventy-five?"

Hook nodded. "For a long time they called Jeremiah a squaw man. Got so it didn't bother him none."

"Squaw man, eh? What's the name of the woman Jeremiah married?"

Jonah looked up from stirring the chunks of onion in the kettle, as much a look of surprise on his face as Deidecker had ever seen.

"You didn't understand . . . when we was talking about the picture back at the cabin?"

"Understand what, Jonah?"

"That was Prairie Night."

"Prairie . . . Zeke's squaw? Uh, wife?"

He went back to stirring. "A custom among the uncivilized savages, don't you know. A downright civilized one, I might add. Jeremiah done what any Kwahadi would've done for his brother killed in battle: he took in his brother's wife and children. They became his wife and children. He's raised them two like they was his own. And he took that woman as his own wife."

Nate blinked, thinking on the beauty of sentiment practiced by those he had heretofore regarded as savagely primitive in every way.

"Did she go back to Fort Richardson with you, then back up to Missouri to bury Zeke?"

Hook shook his head. "She run off with the rest of the village that escaped the soldiers that day. Escaped with the two young'uns, one still small enough to nurse at her breast those first cold nights without no lodges, nary a blanket for the three of 'em."

"How'd you . . . how'd Jeremiah—"

"After we left Missouri, heading for the land of the Mormons, I took Jeremiah back to the Fort Sill Agency. I knowed the agent there, Haworth. We found my daughter-in-law there. My grandchildren."

"What became of her while you two went off hunting Jubilee Usher?"

"Jeremiah told her he'd come for her and the children soon as he finished some unfinished business. Told her he intended to marry her when he got back. She told him she figured they was already married—him being Antelope's older brother. The gal waited for him, all right—raising them young'uns while Jeremiah was gone." Jonah looked up from the kettle again, his eyes brimming once more. "I figure Jeremiah was tore apart between his two families: called to go find and put back together the one he was raised with . . . called to return to the bosom of the family he was raising of his own."

"He went back among the Comanche?"

"Yes, Nate. I s'pose it was for the sake of them children that he raised 'em among the Kwahadi. Jeremiah been a close friend of Quanah Parker's all these years. Time or two the chief's even said Tall One is the one friend he can count on. Proud that my boy's doing what he can to help his old friend bring the bones of his mother home to the Comanche reservation."

"Cynthia Ann Parker's remains?"

"Jeremiah does what he can, speaks to those'll listen—writes letters for Quanah, asking the Parker clan down in Texas to let the woman's boy take his mother's bones home to the prairie she'd come to love." He raised his eyes to the treetops. They glistened in the dancing fire glow. "Jeremiah's made his pa so damned p-proud."

The old man's voice cracked as he said it, so Hook turned and rose slowly, unsteady at first, then moved off to fetch up one of the packs that he brought back to the fireside. He untied the thongs from the cowhide case and from it began pulling some utensils they would need for their dinner.

An object tumbled to the ground as Hook pulled free a green bottle of pepper. Curious, Nate leaned over and retrieved it, intending to straighten up the spili. "Here, let me help."

Then he stopped, turning that object over slowly: a small cloth-wrapped bundle he moved into the flickering light of their fire. At one time the cotton fabric had been brightly colored, a fine calico fabric. Now it lay in the newsman's hands a dull, grimy scrap of once-vibrant cloth. It smelled deeply of many camp fires. Bringing it under his nose, Nate felt something hard wrapped within the folded bundle of old cloth.

"Something special, Jonah?" he asked, wanting to open it, but afraid he would never get permission. Thinking maybe it contained the ear of an enemy, perhaps one of those shriveled fingertip necklaces he had seen on display in the Smithsonian Institute.

Hook put his hand out to take it, then shook his head, dropping his hand, empty. "No." His eyes leveled on Deidecker. "I figure it's time you looked at what's inside there."

"This cloth, whatever is the story—"

"Zeke's shirt. The one I come on down there in Texas."

"The shirt the whore's child wore?"

"Same."

Through the folds of cloth Nate of a sudden sensed something strange, wild, and unnamed communicated to his fingers. As if the years were reaching out to touch him.

"Go 'head, Nate. It's time you saw the . . . saw what's there."

Reverently he slowly peeled back the layers of faded, worn calico folded over and around the object. Fold by fold he exposed the object he finally pulled out of his lap and into the firelight that sundown in the Big Horns. A rawhide-wrapped wheel about as wide as his hand. Dividing the wheel into four equal quadrants were two twisted rawhide strands, each quadrant a maze of rawhide netting. At their center was lashed a hard, textured object, almost resembling a blackened peach pit.

"Go ahead, Nate. Take a close look."

"Is this what you call a medicine wheel?"

"I suppose folks back east call 'em that. Out here the Injuns call that a *dream catcher.*"

Over Deidecker's hands spilled the long, black tendrils, some of which were flecked with gray. He figured it had belonged to an old warrior.

Just inside the circumference of the stiff rawhide wheel had been lashed a crude circle of stiffened skin from which dangled that thick patch of long, gleaming hair. No more than four inches across. Just the topknot no doubt, Nate thought as he began to stroke that fine black hair flecked with snow. He felt a sudden, evil chill and figured it was nothing more than the thrill of holding such an artifact against his own skin.

"A scalp? A real honest-to-goodness human scalp?" Nate asked.

"Ain't ever seen one before?"

"In museums. Never held one in my own living hands. And I never did see one of these wheels . . . a dream catcher, with a scalp sewn on it."

"That travels with me, wherever I go, Nate," Hook said as the old man bent over the fire, sliding the skillet with the two loin steaks atop the flames.

The fire's glow in the deepening mountain twilight gave the shining hair reflections like a candle in a mirror. Glittering, gleaming beads of light, like black diamonds dancing up and down the full length of the silky strands. "Never knew many Indians, Jonah. And from what I've seen, I can't say as I ever realized an Injun's hair could be so fine to the touch."

"That ain't a Injun's scalp."

Nate's mouth went dry. His heart thundered at his ears. He swallowed and forced the words around his parched tongue. "A . . . a white man's sc-scalp?"

"Yep."

"Who . . . whose scalp is it, Jonah?"

Hook gazed evenly at the newsman. The fire crackled and popped between them, spitting fireflies of sparks into the deepening dark of that immense, all-consuming land. Tiny, iridescent shooting stars born of their wilderness fire sent spiraling skyward toward the great heavenly bodies.

"The one Gritta took herself."